SPECIAL
DELIVERY

Also by Danielle Steel

★Published outside the UK under the title
Passion's Promise

SPECIAL DELIVERY

Danielle Steel

CORGI BOOKS

SPECIAL DELIVERY
A CORGI BOOK : 0552 14507 6

Originally published in Great Britain by Bantam Press, a division of
Transworld Publishers Ltd

PRINTING HISTORY
Bantam Press edition published 1997
Corgi edition published 1998

Set in Bembo by
Phoenix Typesetting, Ilkley, West Yorkshire.

Corgi Books are published by Transworld Publishers Ltd,
61–63 Uxbridge Road, London W5 5SA,
in Australia by Transworld Publishers (Australia) Pty Ltd,
15–25 Helles Avenue, Moorebank, NSW 2170
and in New Zealand by Transworld Publishers (NZ) Ltd,
3 William Pickering Drive, Albany, Auckland.

Reproduced, printed and bound in Great Britain by
Cox & Wyman Ltd, Reading, Berks.

To Tom,
For all the happy times,
with all my love,
d.s.

Chapter One

The tires of the red Ferrari squealed, as it came around the corner and dove neatly into the space where Jack Watson always parked it. It was in the parking lot of his Beverly Hills store, Julie's. Exactly twenty years before, he had named it after his then nine-year-old daughter. It had been a lark to him then, something he was going to do for fun, after deciding to give up producing movies.

He had produced seven or eight low-budget films, none of them remarkable, and before that he had spent half a dozen years, after college, working on and off as an actor. His film career had been relatively minor, filled with all the usual hope and promises that never turned out quite as he planned, and too often turned out to be disappointing. But his luck changed when he got into retail with the unexpected help of an uncle, who had left him some money. Without even trying, it seemed, he wound up with the store that every woman in Los Angeles would have killed to shop in. His wife helped him with the buying at first, but within two years he figured out that he had a better eye for the merchandise than she did. And much to her chagrin, also for the women who wore it. Every woman in town, actresses and socialites, models and just ordinary housewives with money to spend, wanted to go to Julie's . . . and meet Jack Watson. He was one of those men who didn't even have to try. Women were just drawn to him like bees to honey. And he loved it. And them.

Two years after he opened his store, to no one's surprise but his own, his wife left him. And for the past eighteen years, he had to admit, he had never missed her. He had met her on the set of one of his films, she had come to read for him, and spent the next two weeks lost in passion with him in his Malibu cottage. He had been madly in love with her at first, and they were married six months later, his first and only foray into marriage. It had lasted for fifteen years and two kids, but had ended with all the bitterness and venom that, as far as he was concerned, was inevitable in any marriage. He had only been tempted to try it again once in the years afterward, with a woman who was far too smart to have him. She was the only woman who had ever made him want to be faithful to her, and for once he had been. He had been in his forties then, she had been thirty-nine, French, and a very successful artist. They had lived together for two years, and when she died in an accident on her way to meet him in Palm Springs, he had thought he would never recover from it. For the first time in his life, Jack Watson had known real pain. She was everything he had always dreamed of, and in rare moments of seriousness even now, he still said she was the only woman he had ever loved, and he meant it. Dorianne Matthieu was funny and irreverent, sexy and beautiful, and in her own way, utterly outrageous. She didn't put up with anything from him, and she said that only a fool would marry him, but he had never doubted for a moment that she loved him. And he adored her. She took him to Paris to meet her friends, and they had traveled everywhere together, Europe, Asia, Africa, South America. To him, it had always seemed that the moments he spent with her were tinged with magic. Until she died and left him with the resounding emptiness and overwhelming sense of loss that he actually thought might kill him.

There had been women since, lots of them, to fill the nights and the days. In the dozen years since her death, he had hardly ever been alone, not physically anyway, but he had never loved another woman either, nor did he want to. As far as he was concerned, loving was far too painful. At fifty-nine, Jack Watson had everything he had ever wanted: a business that seemed to do nothing but grow and crank out money.

He had opened a Palm Springs store, before Dori died, and another in New York five years later. And for the past two years, he had been thinking about opening one in

San Francisco. But at his age, he was no longer entirely sure he wanted the headaches of further expansion. Maybe if his son, Paul, would come into the business with him, but so far he hadn't had much luck in seducing Paul away from his own film career. At thirty-two, Paul was already a very successful young producer. He was far more successful at it than his father had been, and he genuinely loved it. But Jack had a profound distrust of the insecurities of the film industry, and its almost inevitable disappointments. And he would have given anything to lure Paul into the business. Maybe one day. But surely not for the moment. Paul didn't want to hear it.

Paul loved his work, and his wife. He had been married for the past two years, and the only thing that seemed to be missing from his life, or so he claimed, was a baby. Jack wasn't even sure how much Paul cared, but it was obvious that Jan did. She worked in an art gallery, and Jack always had the impression that she was just hanging around, waiting to have kids. She was a little bland for him, but she was a nice girl, and she obviously made Paul very happy. She was

11

also beautiful; her mother was the long-retired but spectacular-looking actress Amanda Robbins. She was long, lean, and blonde, still wonderful to look at, at fifty. She had given up an extraordinary movie career twenty-six years before to marry a very staid, respectable, and as far as Jack was concerned, extremely boring banker named Matthew Kingston. They had two beautiful daughters, a huge house in Bel Air, and moved in the most respectable circles.

Amanda was one of the few women in Los Angeles who never shopped at Jack's store, and it always amused him, on the rare occasions when their paths crossed, to realize that she absolutely couldn't stand him. She seemed to hate everything he was, and everything he represented. And it wouldn't have surprised him at all to learn that Amanda had done everything in her power to dissuade her daughter from marrying Paul Watson. She and her husband seemed to take a dim view of show business, and they had been sure that eventually Paul would turn out to be just as promiscuous as his father. But he wasn't. Paul was a serious young man, and he had already proven to them that he was a solid, reliable husband. They had eventually accepted him into the fold of their family, although they had never warmed to his father. Jack's reputation was well known in L.A. He was good-looking, seen everywhere, and famous for cruising in and out of bed with every starlet and model who crossed his path, and he made no apology for it. He was always kind to the women he went out with, too much so, in fact. He was generous, intelligent, nice to be around, and always fun to be with. The women he went out with always adored him, and now and then one of them was even foolish enough to think they might 'catch' him for more than just a brief affair. But Jack Watson was too smart for that. He saw to it that they came and went out of his life before they could settle down, or have time to start leaving their clothes in his closet. And he was always painfully honest with them, he made no promises, created no false impressions. He gave them a good time, took them to all the places they had ever read about or dreamed of, wined and dined them in the best restaurants, and before they knew what had hit them, he had moved on, to the next one. And they were left with a pleasant, albeit brief, memory of an affair with a handsome, sexy man, who left them gasping for more, and wishing they had been able to hang on to him for just a little longer.

It was impossible to be angry at Jack, or even stay that way for long. Everything about him was irresistibly charming, even the way he left them. He dated married women once in a while, but had only the nicest things to say about their husbands. Jack Watson was a fun guy, terrific in bed and an incurable playboy, and never pretended for a millisecond to be anything different. And at fifty-nine, he still looked a dozen years younger. He worked out when he had time, swam in the ocean frequently, still had his house in Malibu, and he loved his women nearly as much as his red Ferrari. The only things he really did care about, and was serious about, were his children. Julie and Paul were the lights of his life, and always would be. Their mother was only a dim memory, and one that still made him grateful whenever he thought of her, that she had had the good sense to leave him. For the past eighteen years, he had done exactly what he wanted, even when he was with Dori. He was spoiled, he had money, his business was a huge success, and he was irresistible to women, and what's more, he knew it. Though oddly, there was nothing arrogant about him. He was sexy, and fun, and almost always happy. He loved to have a good time. 'Adorable' was a word women often used to describe him. They liked him, and he liked them.

"Morning, Jack.' The manager of Julie's smiled at him, as he hurried through the store to the private elevator that would take him up to his office. It was on the fourth floor, and was entirely done in steel and black leather. It had been designed for him by a very famous Italian interior designer, yet another woman he had been involved with. She had wanted to leave her architect husband and three kids for him, and he had assured her that living with him would have driven her completely crazy. And by the time their affair ended, he had actually convinced her. Just watching Jack move around his own little world was both exciting and somewhat alarming.

He knew there would be coffee waiting

for him upstairs, and eventually a light lunch. He glanced at his watch. He was late for once. He had decided to be half an hour late for work in order to swim in the ocean, although it was January, but the weather had been warm, even if the water wasn't. He loved swimming in the ocean, loved his house at the beach, and everything about his business. And despite his playing the field with women, he was relentlessly disciplined about his work. It was no accident that Julie's was one of the most successful small chains in the retail business. Several people had approached him over the years about taking it public, but he still wasn't ready to do it. He liked maintaining control, and being the sole owner. He had no one else to consult about his decisions, no one to answer to, no one to badger him or explain to. Julie's was one hundred percent his baby.

When he got to his office, there was a stack of messages neatly laid out on his desk, a list of appointments he had that afternoon, and some swatches he had been expecting from Paris. They were nothing short of splendid. It was Dori who had introduced him to the miracle of French fabrics . . . and

French food . . . and French wine . . . and French women. He still had a soft spot for them, and a lot of the merchandise he carried at Julie's were imports. The best of everything, that was what they promised, and delivered.

The phone rang almost as soon as he sat down, it was the intercom, and he pressed the button as he continued to glance at the French fabrics.

'Hi.' He spoke into the machine casually, in the voice that made women ache for him, but not his secretary, Gladdie. She knew him too well to be affected by him. She had worked for him for five years, and knew everything there was to know about him. And the one group of women who were sacred to him, that he never messed around with, were the ones who worked for him in his office. It was one of the few rules about women in his life that he had never broken. 'Who is it?'

'Paul's on the line. Do you want to talk to him, or shall I tell him you're busy? Your ten-fifteen should be here any minute.'

'He can wait.' It was an appointment he had made to talk to a handbag manufacturer from Milan who dealt mostly in alligator and lizard. 'You keep track of the guy for a few minutes when he gets here. I want to talk to Paul first.' If possible, he tried not to put off his children, and he was smiling as he picked up the receiver. Paul was a great kid, he always had been, and Jack was crazy about him. 'Hi there, what's doing?'

'I thought I'd call and see if you wanted me to pick you up, or if you'd rather meet us there.' Although he was quiet by nature, unlike Jack, today he sounded unusually somber.

'Meet you where?' Paul's offer to pick him up touched no chord of memory. He had no recollection whatsoever of making an appointment with him and usually, when it concerned his children at least, he remembered, but not this time.

'Come on, Dad.' Paul sounded mildly exasperated and somewhat stressed. He was clearly not amused by what his father was saying. 'This is serious. Don't joke about it.'

'I'm not joking,' Jack said, setting the handful of French fabrics down, and glancing at the papers on his desk for some clue to what his son was saying. 'Where are we going?' And then in a rush of embarrassment, he remembered. 'Oh Christ, I . . .' Paul's father-in-law's funeral. How on earth could he have forgotten? But he hadn't written it down, and he must not have told Gladdie he was going, or she would have reminded him both the evening before and that morning.

'You forgot, didn't you, Dad?' Paul's voice was suddenly full of accusation. It was obvious that he didn't want to be messed around with. 'I can't believe it.'

'I didn't forget, I just wasn't thinking about it.'

'Bullshit. You forgot. The service is at noon, there's a luncheon afterward at the house. You don't have to go to that, but I think it would be nice if you were there.' His sister, Julie, had also promised to be there.

'How many people do you think they're having?' Jack asked, wondering suddenly how to rearrange several of his afternoon appointments. This wasn't going to be easy, but it meant something to Paul, so he would try to do it.

'At the lunch? I don't know . . . they

know an awful lot of people, probably two or three hundred.' Jack had been stunned to see more than five hundred people at his son's wedding. People had come from all over the country, mostly because of the Kingstons.

'Then they'll never miss me at the lunch,' Jack said matter-of-factly, 'and thanks for offering to pick me up. I'll meet you there. You should probably be with Jan and her mother and sister anyway. I'll stay somewhat in the distance.'

'Make sure Amanda knows you were there,' Paul instructed. 'Jan would be very upset if her mom thought you hadn't come to the funeral.'

'She'd probably be a lot happier if I didn't,' Jack laughed, making no bones about the mild animosity between them. He had danced with her a couple of times at the wedding, and Amanda Kingston made it clear without saying a word that she thoroughly disliked him. Like everyone else in town, she read about him constantly in the papers. And since giving up her career, she had adopted her husband's very sober view that one should only be in the newspapers when one was born, died, or got married. Jack was usually in the papers for being seen with some moderately well-known actress, or budding starlet, or for giving a bash of some kind at Julie's. The store was famous, as was he, for its fabulous parties for their designers and clients. People begged for invitations to them, but certainly not the Kingstons. And knowing they wouldn't come, he had never bothered to invite them.

'Anyway, be on time, Dad. You'd be late to your own funeral, if you could.'

'Which, hopefully, won't be for a while, thank you very much,' Jack said, thinking of the heart attack that had killed Matthew Kingston. He had died four days before, on the tennis court, and he was two years younger than Jack. Amanda had just turned fifty. The men who had been playing tennis with him had done everything possible to revive him, but they had been unable to do it. At fifty-seven, he was being mourned by his family, the entire banking community, and all those who knew him. But Jack had never liked him. He thought he was pompous, stuffy, and boring.

'I'll see you there, Dad. I have to pick up Jan at her mom's. She spent the night there.'

'Does she need anything? A hat? A dress? I can have one of the girls pull some things for you to pick up on your way over there if you need it.'

'That's okay, Dad.' Paul smiled at his father's voice. He was a pain in the ass sometimes, but he was basically a decent guy, and Paul loved him. 'I think Amanda got them everything they needed. She's in pretty bad shape over Matt, but she's incredibly organized, even now. She's an amazing woman.'

'The Ice Queen,' Jack said, and then regretted it instantly, but the words slipped out before he could stop them.

'That's a lousy thing to say about a woman who just lost her husband.'

'Sorry. I wasn't thinking.' But he wasn't far off the mark. She always looked and seemed totally in control, and absolutely perfect. Just looking at her always gave Jack an almost irresistible urge to mess her up and take her clothes off. The very thought of it even now somehow struck him funny as he hung up the phone, and thought about her, which was something he did very seldom.

He was sorry about her loss, and he still remembered all too well how he had felt when Dori had died, but there was something so distant and cold about Paul's mother-in-law that it made it hard to really empathize much with her. She was so goddamn unbearably perfect. And she still looked incredibly like the way she had when she was Amanda Robbins, and left the screen at twenty-four to marry Matthew Kingston. It had been a huge Hollywood and society wedding, and for years people had guessed and made bets about whether or not she'd get bored and come back into the business. But she didn't. She kept her looks, and her icy beauty, but her career was over forever. It was also easy to believe that Matthew Kingston would never have let her. He acted as though he owned her.

Jack opened the closet in his dressing room, and was glad to see he had left a dark suit in it. It wasn't one of his best, but at least it was appropriate for the occasion, although all the ties he found in the small collection he kept there for emergencies were either red, bright blue, or yellow. He quickly strode out to his outer office to find Gladdie.

'Why didn't you remind me about the funeral?' He scowled at her, but he wasn't really angry and she knew it. He was one of those rare people who always took responsibility for his own mistakes, which was one of the many reasons why she loved working for him. And despite his reputation for being flip and irresponsible, she actually knew him a great deal better. As an employer, he was caring, generous, reliable, and a real pleasure to work for.

'I just thought you had it worked out. Did you forget?' she asked with a smile, and with a sheepish grin, he nodded.

'Freudian, I guess. I hate going to the funerals of men who are younger than I am. Do me a favor, Glad, run down the street to Hermès and get me a dark tie. Nothing too miserable, but just serious enough so I don't embarrass Paul. Nothing with naked women on it.' She laughed at him, and grabbed her purse just as the handbag manufacturer and his assistant came in. It was going to be a very quick meeting.

Jack had ordered a hundred bags by eleven o'clock, and Gladdie was back from Hermès by then with a slate-gray tie with

24

tiny little white geometric figures on it. It was perfect. 'You do good work,' he said gratefully, as he put it around his neck and tied it impeccably without looking in the mirror. He was wearing a dark gray suit and a white shirt, and handmade French oxfords. And he looked incredibly hand-some with sandy blond hair, warm brown eyes, and chiseled features. 'Do I look respectable?'

'I'm not sure that's a word I'd use for you . . . maybe beautiful is more like it.' She smiled at him, totally inured to his charms, which he always found very pleasing about her. Being with Gladdie was always very soothing. She didn't give a damn about his looks or his reputation, or his womanizing, just about his business. 'You look great, honest. Paul will be proud of you.'

'I hope so. Maybe his charming mother-in-law will even refrain from calling the vice squad when she sees me coming. God, I hate funerals.' He could already feel a pall falling over him, it still reminded him of Dori. Christ, that had been awful . . . the shock, and the unbearable pain of it. The sheer misery of trying to understand that she was gone forever. It had taken him years to get over it, although he had tried to fill the void with a thousand women. But there had never been another woman like her. She was so warm, so beautiful, so sexy and mischievous and appealing. She was sensational, and just thinking about her, as he rode the elevator downstairs in his somber outfit shortly before noon, genuinely depressed him. It had been twelve years since she died, and he still missed her.

Jack didn't even notice the women watching him admiringly as he left the store, and slid behind the wheel of his Ferrari. He peeled it away from the curb with immediate speed, and a roar of the powerful engine, and five minutes later he was on Santa Monica Boulevard, heading toward All Saints Episcopal Church, where they were holding the service. It was ten after noon by then, and traffic was worse than he had expected. It was a warm January afternoon in L.A., and everyone in the world seemed to be in their car and going somewhere. He was twenty minutes late when he got to All Saints and slipped quietly into a pew at the back of the church. He couldn't even imagine how many people were there. From where he was sitting it looked like seven or eight hundred, but he was sure it couldn't be that many.

He tried to catch a glimpse of his daughter, Julie, but she was lost in the crowd somewhere. And he couldn't even see Paul at the front of the church, sitting between his wife and her sister. And his view of the widow was completely obscured. All Jack could see and think about was the inexorable inevitability of the coffin, so stark and severe, a rich mahogany with brass handles, covered by a carpet of moss and tiny white orchids. It was beautiful in its own grim way, as were the rest of the flowers in the church. There were orchids everywhere, and somehow without thinking about it, Jack knew that Amanda had done it. There was the same kind of impeccable attention to detail, even at a time like this, that she had shown during their children's wedding.

But Jack quickly forgot about her, and sat lost in his own thoughts, reminded of his own mortality, during the High Episcopal service. A friend spoke, and both sons-in-law. Paul's words were brief and to the point, but very moving, and in spite of himself there were tears in Jack's eyes when he praised his son for it after the service.

'That was very nice, Son,' he said, sounding hoarse for a moment. 'You can speak at mine, when the time comes.' He tried to make light of it, but Paul shook his head with a look of disgust and put an arm around his father's shoulders.

'Don't flatter yourself. I couldn't say a single decent thing about you, and neither could anyone else, so don't bother.'

'Thanks, I'll keep it in mind. Maybe I should give up tennis.'

'Dad . . .' Paul scolded, with a quick warning look. Amanda was approaching, moving quietly through the crowd to the place where she would stand to greet a few of the mourners. And before Jack could move, he found he was looking right at her. She looked amazingly beautiful, and in spite of the years since, still very much a movie star. She was wearing a huge black hat and veil, and a very distinguished black suit, which he suspected immediately had probably been made by a French designer.

'Hello, Jack,' she said calmly. She seemed very much in control, yet the huge blue eyes held so much pain, that he actually felt sorry for her.

'I'm sorry, Amanda.' Even if he wasn't fond of her, it was easy to see how ravaged she was by the loss of her husband. There wasn't much else he could say to her, as she looked away and bowed her head for a moment, and then an instant later she moved on, and Paul went to find Jan, who was standing with her sister.

Jack stayed for another minute or two, saw no one he knew, and then decided to leave quietly without bothering his son. Paul obviously had his hands full.

And half an hour later, Jack was back in his offfice, but he was quiet all afternoon, thinking about them, the family that had lost the man who held them all together. Even if he hadn't liked him, one had to respect him, and feel sorry for the loved ones he had left so swiftly. And all afternoon, no matter what he did, Jack was haunted by Dori. He even took out a photograph of her, something he rarely did, but he kept one way at the back of his desk, for just such moments. And looking down at her smiling face on the beach at Saint-Tropez made him feel more bereft than ever.

Gladdie checked on him once or twice, and sensed that he wanted to be left alone. He even had her cancel his last two appointments. But even depressed, he looked great in the dark suit and the tie she had bought him. And he had no idea that, at that exact moment, in the house in Bel Air, Amanda Kingston was talking about him.

'It was nice of your father to come,' she said to Paul, as the last of their guests finally left them. It had been an endless afternoon for all of them, and despite her unshakable poise, even Amanda looked exhausted.

'He felt very badly about Matthew,' Paul said, touching her arm sympathetically, as she nodded and looked at her daughters.

Both girls were devastated by the loss of their father, and for once, they had even stopped fighting. Jan and her sister, Louise, were only slightly more than a year apart, but in every possible way they were entirely different. And they had battled with each other, night and day, ever since their childhood. But, at least for now, they had made peace in order to comfort their mother. And Paul left them alone quietly, as he went out to the kitchen to help himself to a cup of coffee. The catering staff was still there, clearing away the dishes and glasses left behind by more than three hundred people who had come to pay their respects to the Kingstons.

'I can't believe he's gone,' Amanda said in a whisper, standing with her back to both girls, looking out over their perfectly manicured garden.

'Neither can I,' Jan said, as tears rolled down her cheeks again, and Louise sighed audibly. She had loved him, but she had never gotten along with her father. She always thought he'd been harder on her than he was on Jan, and expected more of her. He had been furious with her when she had decided not to go to law school and had gotten married right out of college. But the marriage was a solid one, and in the first five years she had borne three children. But he had even had something to say about that. He thought she was having too many children. It didn't bother him at all that Jan had never had a real career, nor even wanted one, and had married a man who worked in show business and had a father who was nothing more than a Rodeo Drive merchant. Louise didn't like Paul, and made no bones about it. Her own husband was a Loeb and Loeb attorney and more suitable for a Kingston to marry.

But as Jan cried on the afternoon of the funeral, all Louise could think of was how much her father had criticized her, how diffficult he had been, and how often she had wondered if he even loved her. She would have liked to say something about it, but she knew that neither her mother nor sister would understand. Her mother always hated it when she said anything critical about her father. And as far as her mother was concerned, he was already a saint now.

'I want you both to remember how wonderful he was,' Amanda said as she turned back to them, her chin quivering and her eyes filled with tears. She wore her blond hair straight back in a bun, and as they were both acutely aware, she was far more beautiful than they were, and always had been. She was an extraordinary beauty, and

Louise always hated that about her. Her mother was almost impossible to live up to, and she had always expected both of them to be so perfect. Louise had never really understood the more human side of her, the vulnerability, the insecurities that had followed her throughout her life and lurked behind the exquisite facade. It was Jan who was much closer to their mother, which spawned the continuing resentment between both sisters. Louise had always accused Jan of being their parents' favorite, and Jan had always felt unfairly accused and couldn't see it.

'I want you both to know how very, very much he loved you,' Amanda continued, and then couldn't go on as she began to sob softly. She couldn't believe he was gone, couldn't believe he would never hold her in his arms again. It was her worst nightmare come true. He had been everything she depended on, and she couldn't even begin to imagine a life without him.

'Oh, Mom.' Jan cradled her mother in her arms like a child as her mother sobbed, and Louise quietly left the room and found Paul in the kitchen. He was sitting at the kitchen table, drinking a cup of coffee.

'How is she?' he asked, looking concerned, and Louise shrugged, her own pain visible, but, as usual, mixed with anger. Her kids had gone home with the baby-sitter, and her husband had gone back to the office. And there was no one else but Paul to talk to, whether or not she liked him.

'She's a mess. She was completely dependent on him. He told her when to get up and when to go to bed, what to do, and not do, and who she could be friends with. I don't know why she let him do that to her. It was disgusting.'

'Maybe that was what she needed,' Paul said, looking at his wife's sister with interest. She was always so filled with anger and resentment, and he secretly wondered how happy she really was with her husband. Like all families, they all had their secret agendas and hidden undercurrents. And it always intrigued him to hear the girls talk about their mother. They each saw her differently, but the woman they knew was so different from the cool facade she presented to the world. They saw someone completely dominated and privately frightened. He wondered if that was the real reason why she had never gone back to making movies. Maybe aside from Matthew not wanting her to, she was just too afraid to do it. 'She'll be all right,' he reassured Louise, not knowing what else to say to her, as she poured a glass of wine for herself. She showed too many of the signs of an unhappy woman.

'Jan'll keep an eye on her,' he said to soothe his sister-in-law, but the remark only enraged her.

'Yeah, I'll bet she will. She's always sucking up to her. She always did, even when we were kids. I'm surprised the two of you don't offer to move in with her, that might really impress her. You know, she'll need a lot of help with settling the estate. I'm sure you and Jan will be only too happy to help her do it.'

'Why don't you relax, Lou?' he said, using Jan's name for her, and she glanced at him with smoldering eyes that were surprisingly like her mother's. But other than that, she looked just like her father, handsome, but no more than that. Between the two, Jan was the better looking. 'No one's trying to hurt you.'

'Too late for that,' she said, pouring another glass of wine as soon as she finished the first one. 'They've been doing it for years. Maybe Mom'll grow up now, without Daddy. Maybe we all will,' she said, set down the glass and walked out into the garden, and Paul made no move to follow.

And from inside the study where they sat, Jan and Amanda saw her through the window. 'She's mad at me again,' Jan said. 'She's always mad at me about something.'

'I wish you two would stop fighting,' Amanda said sadly, looking at her younger daughter. 'I always thought when you grew up it would be different, that you'd be the best of friends, especially once you were both married and had children.' It was all she had ever envisioned for them since they were babies, but there was a look of sorrow in Jan's eyes almost as soon as her mother said it.

'Well, I don't . . . do I . . .'

'What?' Her mother looked confused for a moment, and so sad it broke Jan's heart to see her.

'Have children.' Something about the

way she said it caught her mother's attention.

'Don't you want to have children?' Amanda looked shocked, as though the very idea that her daughter didn't want children would be a betrayal.

'Yes,' Jan nodded, and looked at her sister through the window. Lou had had three kids in five years, as easy as pie, as soon as she wanted. And this time it was Jan who was jealous of her. 'Of course I do. We've been trying for a year, and nothing has happened.'

'That doesn't mean anything,' Amanda smiled at her. 'Sometimes it takes a while. Just be patient.'

'It didn't take you "a while." You and Daddy had us in the first two years you were married.' She sighed then, as Amanda patted her hand, and then she looked up at her mother. And what Amanda saw in her eyes tore her heart out, it was not only grief, but fear and bitter disappointment. 'I want Paul to go to a doctor with me, but he won't do it. He thinks I'm crazy to be worried.'

'Did you talk to the doctor yourself, does he think there's a problem?' Amanda was beginning to look seriously concerned about her.

'He doesn't know, but he thinks it's worth looking into. He gave me the name of a specialist, but Paul was furious when I told him. He said his sister has kids, and so does Lou. There's no reason why we should have a problem. But it's not always that simple.' Amanda wondered suddenly if there was something she didn't know, a terrible disease in her daughter's youth, an indiscretion, an abortion, but she didn't dare ask her. It was better to leave that to her doctor.

'Well then, maybe you should listen to Paul, at least for a while, and try not to worry about it.'

'It's all I think of, Mom,' she confessed, as tears ran down her cheeks and spilled onto her dress as her mother watched her in anguish. 'I want a baby so much . . . and I'm so scared I'll never have one.'

'Of course you will . . .' She couldn't bear the thought of seeing her daughter so unhappy, especially now, with having just lost her father. 'You can always adopt, if it doesn't happen later.'

'Paul says he'll never do that. He wants his own children.' Amanda had to hold her tongue, so as not to tell her that Paul sounded not only difficult, but extremely opinionated and selfish.

'You can cross that bridge later. For right now, why don't you just try to relax, and I'll bet you anything, it'll happen before you know it.' Jan nodded, but it was obvious from the look in her eyes that she was anything but convinced now. She had been worrying about it for an entire year, and concern was rapidly turning to panic. But if nothing else, a door had opened between mother and daughter.

'What about you, Mom? Are you going to be okay without Dad?' It was an agonizing question, and brought tears to Amanda's eyes again as she shook her head and wept.

'I can't even imagine living without him. There will never be anyone else in my life, Jan. Never. I couldn't bear it. We've been married for twenty-six years, more than half my lifetime. I can't even begin to think about what I'll do now . . . how do I wake up every morning . . .' Jan took her mother in her arms and let her cry, wishing she could promise her that she'd feel better, but she couldn't imagine her mother living without him either. He had been the life force of their family, he had shielded Amanda from the world, told her what to do about everything, and although he was only seven years older than she, in some ways he had been like a father to her. 'I just can't live without him,' she said, and Jan knew she meant it. They sat and talked about him for another hour, and then finally Paul came back into the room. Lou had left without saying goodbye, she had been crying when she left, after watching them through the window, and Paul had work to do at home. It was nearly six o'clock by then, and sooner or later, they had to leave Amanda, no matter how hard it was for her. She had to learn to face life alone.

She looked so pathetic as they left, standing on the front steps of the Bel Air house in her black suit, waving at them, that Jan burst into tears again the moment they turned the corner.

'My God, Paul, she's just going to die without Daddy.' She couldn't stop crying at the thought of the father she had lost, the sister who hated her, the mother who was in so much pain, and the baby she feared would never come her way. It was all completely overwhelming, and Paul held her hand as they drove home and tried to reassure her.

'She'll be fine in a while. You'll see. Just look at her, she's still young and beautiful. Hell, in six months, she'll have all of Los Angeles pounding on her door, asking her out. Maybe she'll even go back to the movies. She's certainly young enough to do it.'

'She'd never do that, even if she wanted to, because she knows that Daddy never wanted her to go back to making movies. He wanted her to himself, and she did it because she loved him.' Paul didn't say that if that was true Matthew Kingston was probably the most selfish man who had ever lived, because he knew Jan would have killed him if he said it. 'And how could you suggest my mother would go out with anyone? That's disgusting.'

'It's not disgusting,' he said quietly. 'It's real. She's fifty years old, Jan. And your father died, she didn't. You can't really expect her to stay alone forever.' He said it with a small smile, and Jan looked furious as she glanced at him.

'Of course she's not going to go out with anyone. She's not your father, for God's sake. She had a wonderful marriage, and she loved Daddy.'

'Then she'll probably want to get married again. It would be a crime if she didn't.'

'I can't believe what you just said,' Jan said breathlessly, pulling her hand away from his, and staring at him. 'You actually think my mother is going to go out with *men*? You're sick, and you have no respect for anything. And furthermore, you don't know my mother.'

'I guess not, sweetheart,' he said soothingly. 'But I do know people.' She said not another word to him, and stared out the window away from him, furious at what he'd said, as they drove home in silence. Jan would have willingly sworn on a stack of Bibles that her mother would be faithful to her husband's memory for the rest of her life.

Chapter Two

Amanda Kingston took both her daughters to the Biltmore in Santa Barbara in June. Paul was in New York, working on the last details of a movie deal, and Louise's husband, Jerry, was at a legal conference in Denver. And it seemed an ideal opportunity to spend some time together. But as soon as they got to the hotel, and actually sat down and talked, both younger women realized how badly their mother was doing. She still wore black constantly, her hair was pulled tightly back and looked too severe, and she wore no makeup, and as soon as Jan asked how she was, she burst into tears and couldn't stop crying.

It was one of those rare times when both girls put down their animosity, and were united in concern for their mother. And while Amanda was still asleep, they both went downstairs to the dining room for breakfast together on Sunday morning.

'She should see a doctor. She's just too depressed,' Louise said over blueberry pancakes. 'She scares me. I think she ought to be on Prozac . . . or Valium, or something.'

'That'll just make her worse. She needs to get out and see her friends. I ran into Mrs Auberman last week and she said she hasn't seen Mom since Dad died. It's been five months, she can't just sit in the house and cry forever.'

'Maybe she can,' Louise said, looking her sister in the eye, wondering, as she always did, if they had anything at all in common. 'You know, it's what Dad would have wanted. If he could have left instructions to that effect, he would have had her buried with him.'

'That's *disgusting*.' Jan looked at her older sister with instant fury. 'You know how he hated it when she was unhappy!'

'You know how he hated it when she had any kind of a life other than watching us take ballet, or playing bridge with the wives of his partners. I think that subconsciously she thinks he would have wanted her to be just as miserable as she is. I think she should see a shrink,' Louise said bluntly.

'Why don't we take her on a vacation?' It seemed like a nice idea to Jan, who had an easy time taking time off from the gallery, but Louise didn't see how she could leave her children. 'Maybe in September, when they're back in school. We could take her to Paris.'

'Sounds good to me,' Louise said, but when they suggested it to Amanda at lunch, she immediately shook her head, and said she couldn't.

'I couldn't possibly get away now,' she said firmly, 'I still have too much to do for the estate. I don't want that hanging over my head forever.' But they all knew it was an excuse. She just didn't want to rejoin the world of the living, not without Matthew.

'Let the lawyers take care of it, Mom,' Lou said practically, 'they do anyway. It would do you good to get away.'

She hesitated for a long moment, and then shook her head as tears filled her eyes again, and she was honest with them. 'I don't want to. I'd feel too guilty.'

'For what? Spending a little money? You can certainly afford a trip to Paris.' Or many, many of them, as they all knew. That was not the issue. But the real problem was far deeper.

'It's not that, I just . . . I just feel that I don't have the right to do something like that without Matthew . . . Why should I go out and kick up my heels? Why should I have a good time?' She began to sob, but she had to say it, as both girls watched her. 'Why am I still alive and he isn't? It's so unfair. Why did it have to happen?' She had survivor guilt, and neither of them had ever heard her say it.

'It just happened, Mom,' Jan said gently. 'It just did. It wasn't your fault, or his, or anyone's. It was just horrible rotten luck, but you have to go on living . . . for yourself . . . for us . . . just think about it. If you don't want to go to Paris, we'll go to New York for a few days, or San Francisco. But you have to do something. You can't just give up on life, Mom. Daddy wouldn't have wanted you to do that.' But it was obvious, just talking to her on the drive home, that she wasn't ready to do it. She was still too deep in mourning for her husband to even want to go on living, or think about doing anything constructive or amusing.

'How's she doing?' Paul asked when he flew back from New York on Sunday night, and Jan drove him home from the airport.

'She isn't. She's a total mess. Lou thinks she should be on Prozac. I don't know what I think. It's as if she's tried to bury herself with Daddy.'

'Maybe that was what he would have wanted. Maybe she knows that.'

'You sound just like my sister,' Jan said, looking out the window, and then back at him. 'I want to ask you something.' She said it so solemnly that he smiled at her. He was happy to see her after the trip to New York. He had really missed her.

'Sure. You want me to fix her up with my father? No problem. I'll arrange it. He'd love it.' The idea was so outrageous that even Jan laughed, but an instant later, her eyes were serious again, and whatever it was, he could sense that it was important to her.

'I have something else in mind,' she said nervously, not sure how to broach it to him, but desperate to convince him.

'Spit it out, Jan. I'm waiting.'

'I want both of us to go to the doctor. The specialist. It's been six months since the last time we talked about it, and nothing has happened.' She looked earnest and terrified as she asked, but Paul looked less than sympathetic.

'Christ, that again. You never let up, do you? I've been working on the biggest film deal of my career for the past six months, and all you can think about is a baby. No wonder it hasn't happened, Jan. I've been on airplanes more than I've been home. How can you say we have a problem?' To her, it sounded like denial. There were always excuses, plausible things to blame it on, but the bottom line was she hadn't gotten pregnant and they had tried more than he was admitting.

'I just want to know if something is wrong. Maybe we're both fine, or maybe it's me. I want to know so we can deal with it. That's all, is that so much to ask?' Her eyes filled with tears as she said it, and he sighed, looking at her.

'Why don't you have him check you out? And by the time he does, you'll probably be pregnant.' But she no longer thought so, it had been just over a year and a half since they started trying, and even her gynecologist was concerned now, and had urged her to explore it further, if she was serious about having a baby. She didn't tell Paul she had been to see the specialist alone three weeks before, and so far he had found nothing wrong with her, which meant that Paul had to go now.

'Will you go too, after I do?'

'Maybe' was all he would commit to, and with that, he turned the radio on a little too loud, and Jan stared sadly out the window. It was beginning to seem hopeless to her, especially given Paul's attitude.

By August, the specialist had confirmed to her that there was nothing wrong with her, and that either his sperm and her eggs were incompatible in some way, or perhaps the problem, if there was one, was her husband's. But when she brought it up again, Paul was furious with her, he didn't want to be pressured. It was a bad time for him, his big deal was falling through, and he was sick to death of having sex on schedule, and then having her get hysterical two weeks later when she found she wasn't pregnant.

'Just forget it for a while!' he shouted at her one night when she wanted him to make love to her because the time was right. And then he went out for a drink with his father. Jack was seeing someone new, an actress everyone had heard of, and he was in the papers again, almost daily. He also wanted more than ever for Paul to come into the business with him, which as far as Paul was concerned was out of the question. He felt as though everyone in his life wanted something from him.

And in September, Louise and Jan tried to talk Amanda into a trip again, but got nowhere. She had lost fourteen pounds, and looked too thin, and she was still depressed and going nowhere. And by December, both daughters were panicked.

'We've got to do something,' Jan said frantically on the phone to Louise one afternoon, two weeks after Thanksgiving, which had been ghastly. Their mother had cried all through the meal, and she was in such dismal shape, she had even upset the children. 'I can't stand it anymore.'

'Maybe we should just leave her alone,' Louise said philosophically. 'Maybe this is how she wants to spend the rest of her life without Daddy. Who are we to decide it should be different?'

'We're her children, and we can't just let her live like this. I won't let her.'

'Then you figure out something. She doesn't want to hear it from me. She never does. You're the favorite. You go to her house every day and slip pills into her orange juice. I think she has a right to live any way she wants to.'

'Louise, she's dying, for chrissake,' Jan said miserably. 'Can't you see what's happening to her? She has completely given up on life. She might as well have died with Daddy.'

'I don't have the answers, Jan. She's a grown woman, and I'm not a psychiatrist. And frankly, I'm sick to death of watching her feel sorry for herself. I hate seeing her, I hate listening to her. It's pathetic, but she loves it. She's wallowing in guilt because she's alive, and Daddy isn't. So let her. Maybe in some sick way she's happy.'

'I won't let her do it,' Jan insisted.

'You can't bring her to life again, Jan. She has to *want* to do it, and she doesn't. Face it. For once in her life, she's in control of her own life, and maybe this is how she wants to live it. At least Daddy's not telling her what to do now.'

'You make him sound like a monster,' Jan complained.

'He was sometimes. To me anyway.'

As usual, the sisters couldn't agree on anything.

And the week before Christmas, Paul and Jan got an invitation from Paul's father to come to a Christmas bash at Julie's. Jan wasn't in the mood for it this year. Paul was still refusing to see the specialist, and Jan was depressed about it, and worried about her mother. But Paul said his father's feelings would be hurt if they didn't make an effort to at least drop in at the party.

'Why don't you go without me?' Jan said to Paul when the morning of the party came. She just didn't feel like going. 'I promised my mother I'd come by to see her this afternoon, and I'll probably feel even worse once I see her.' She was sliding steadily downhill from life to death, and watching her do it was driving Jan crazy. She felt entirely helpless to stop her.

'Why don't you bring your mother with you?' he suggested offhandedly as he left for work, and Jan looked at him with total irritation.

'Haven't you listened to anything I've said to you for the past year? She's depressed, she's losing weight, she's not seeing anyone. She's just sitting there waiting to die, for chrissake. Do you really think she'd come to one of your father's jazzy parties? You're dreaming.'

'Maybe it would do her good. Ask her at least.' He said it with a smile, and Jan wanted to throw something at him. He just didn't get it.

'You don't know my mother.'

'Just ask her.'

'I might as well ask her to take all her clothes off and run naked through the streets of Bel Air, for chrissake.'

'At least the neighbors would be happy.' Even depressed, she was still a spectacular-looking woman. He had even had a crazy idea about asking her to be in his next movie, but he was afraid to ask Jan what she thought about it. He already knew what she'd tell him. 'Anyway, tell her my father would be thrilled if she'd come. It would lend the store respectability,' he teased, as he kissed her good-bye, and in spite of herself, she let him. She was deeply upset with him for still not seeing the doctor about their inability to have a baby, and she was beginning to think, and had for a while, that there would never be children in their future. In some ways, she was almost as depressed as her mother, she just didn't show it, but most days she felt as bad as her mother.

But when she saw Amanda that afternoon, it broke Jan's heart to see her. She looked thin and tired and pale and as though she had nothing left to live for. At fifty, Amanda felt as though her life were over. Jan tried everything, suggested everything she could think of, she cajoled, she begged, she threatened, she told her that if she didn't pull herself together soon, she and Louise would come and stay with her and drag her out of the house if they had to.

'You girls have better things to do with your time than worry about me. How is Paul's new movie?' She always changed the subject, and the focus of the conversation, to something else, but by the end of the afternoon, Jan was so upset she was actually angry with her, and she said so.

'You know, you make me mad as hell. You have everything to be grateful for, a good life, a beautiful home, two daughters who love you, and all you can do is sit here and feel sorry for yourself and cry over Daddy. Don't you even love us, Mom? Can't you think of anyone but yourself for once? Don't you see how worried we are? Christ, that's all I ever think about anymore. That and the fact that I'm never going to have children.' And without meaning to, she was suddenly crying and her mother had her arms around her, and was holding her, and apologizing for the pain and concern she'd caused them. They were both crying, but for once, the things Jan had said were cathartic, and her mother actually looked a little better. 'You don't even wear makeup anymore, Mom. You don't dress. Your hair looks awful.' It felt good to be honest with her, and for once Amanda laughed through her tears and looked in the mirror appraisingly. And what she saw there was not pleasant. What they both saw in the mirror was a beautiful woman, sad and pale and neglected. And suddenly Jan decided to try Paul's tactic. She told her mother about Jack's party that night at Julie's.

'Go *there*? To the *store*?' As Jan had predicted she would, Amanda looked horrified at the suggestion. 'That's crazy.'

'So is what you've done to yourself in the past year. Come on, Mommy, do it for me. You won't know anyone. Just put on a dress and some makeup and we'll go together. It would make Paul really happy.'

'I'll go out to dinner with you both one night. He'd like that. I'll take you to Spago's.'

'I want you to come out with me now. You don't have to stay long. Five minutes. Just make the effort. For me . . . for Lou . . . for Daddy. . . he wouldn't want to see you like this, Mom. I really believe that.' She nearly held her breath as she looked at her mother. She was absolutely certain that there was no way her mother would go with her, but Amanda stood very still, watching her for a long moment, uncertain.

'Do you really think your father would want me to do it?' she asked, as Jan nodded slowly. It was amazing how much that still meant to her.

'I do, Mom.' It was a lie, but she wanted her mother to believe it, and then, nodding slowly, Amanda turned on her heel and walked into her bedroom, as Jan followed, in amazement. She didn't dare ask her mother what she was doing. But Amanda had marched into her closet, and Jan could hear rustling and the shifting of dresses. It was a full five minutes before she emerged again, carrying a somber black one.

'What do you think of this?' she asked, as Jan looked at her wide-eyed, unable to believe she'd done it. She had finally gotten through to her, and had somehow managed to dynamite her out of her house and her husband's grave. It was beyond amazing.

'I think it's a little severe, don't you?' She followed her mother back inside, afraid to discourage her completely, but the dress was really depressing. 'How about this one?' She pointed to a purple one she knew her mother loved, but her father had loved it too, and Amanda shook her head the moment Jan showed it to her. Instead she chose a pretty navy blue wool dress that had always been too tight and now molded her figure beautifully, and was much younger-looking than the first one. It was, in its own way, as distinguished as she was, and she looked like the star she had once been as she tried it on in front of the mirror. She put on a pair of navy blue high-heel pumps, and a pair of sapphire earrings, and combed her hair back in the smooth knot that had been her signature in many of her pictures, and she put so little makeup on Jan couldn't even see it. 'Maybe a little more, Mom? What do you think?' Amanda looked at herself appraisingly, into it now, and conceded.

'Maybe just a little. I don't want to look like a hooker.'

'I think that would take some real work actually, more than we have time for.' Jan smiled in pleasure as she looked at her mother. She looked spectacular, and like the woman she had known and loved all her life, not the scarecrow she had become in the past year, as she mourned her husband.

'What do you think?' Amanda asked nervously. 'Do I look like me, or the sad sack I've been?' There were tears glistening in her eyes as she said it.

'You look like you, Mom,' Jan said with tears in her own eyes, grateful to whatever Fates had finally convinced her mother. 'Oh God, I love you,' she said, as she held her. Amanda blew her nose daintily in a hand-kerchief, touched up her lipstick again with a practiced hand, and then put the few things she needed into a navy handbag, and looked admiringly at her daughter. Jan was wearing a red wool dress she loved and wore every Christmas, and standing side by side in red and blue, they looked almost like sisters.

'You're a good girl, Jan, and I love you,' she whispered, as they headed toward the front door. Amanda still couldn't believe she'd let Jan talk her into this, but she was determined now to do it. 'We won't stay long though, will we?' she asked nervously as she grabbed a mink coat from the closet in the front hall. She hadn't worn it since her husband's funeral, but she didn't let herself think of that now. She was doing this for her daughter. 'I don't want to stay more than a few minutes.'

'I'll bring you home whenever you want, Mom. I promise.'

'All right then,' she said, looking surprisingly young and vulnerable as she followed Jan through the front door, and as though to say good-bye to someone who wasn't there, she glanced over her shoulder for just an instant, paused, and then closed the door softly behind her.

Chapter Three

The preparations for the party at the store had gone on since early that morning. There were garlands over the doors, and wreaths in all the windows. They closed at four o'clock exactly, and there was a beautiful Christmas tree, all decorated in silver. Jack was pleased when he saw it.

'I know they're not politically correct anymore. But I love 'em. This one's a beauty.' The store was sparkling as he looked around. There were bars in three locations, and cases of French Champagne chilling in the kitchen. And he had hired four musicians to play music, to liven up the atmosphere, but not for dancing. They were expecting two hundred people. It was one of their more exclusive parties, for only their best customers, and a list of celebrities that Jack knew would be there. Unlike their not showing up at most events, they always came to Jack's parties. Everybody loved him, and coming to parties at Julie's.

'Well, Gladdie, how does it look to you?' he asked, as he looked around for one last time before going to change. He had bought a new Armani suit for the occasion.

'Looks good to me, Jack. Really good,' she said, as she admired all the details. She loved his parties. They were always terrific.

'Keep an eye on things for me. I'm going to go upstairs and change,' he said, and disappeared into the elevator. He was back, looking like the cover on *GQ* twenty minutes later. The suit was dark blue, but there was nothing stuffy about it, and the way he wore it made him look like a male model.

'Very handsome,' Gladdie said in an undertone when he came back downstairs again. 'You look terrific. Do you have a date tonight?' she inquired with interest. The last starlet had passed through his hands several weeks before, and she knew he was currently cultivating a well-known model.

'At least a dozen of them,' he laughed. 'Unfortunately, Starr left for Paris this morning. But she had me invite her sister.'

'Very generous of her . . . or very foolish . . .' Gladdie commented with a grin.

'I think she has a friend in Paris.' He smiled, feeling pleased with life, and pleasantly unencumbered, which was how he liked things.

'Are the kids coming tonight?' Gladdie asked, helping herself to a glass of Champagne as the first guests started to come through the door. Elizabeth Taylor had just walked in with Michael Jackson. And Barbra Streisand and a friend were right behind them.

'They said they'd try,' Jack said absently as he went to greet his guests, and within half an hour the place was jumping. The music added to the festive mood, and celebrities came and went, as outside, photographers snapped their pictures, but Jack wouldn't allow them in the building. He wanted everyone to relax and enjoy the party, without fear of the press or the tabloids or the cameras.

It was nearly seven o'clock when Jan and Amanda drove up to the door, and Jan relinquished her car to the valet, and preceded her mother into Julie's. She had been worried on the way that Amanda would suddenly panic and change her mind, and the photographers who leapt at them instantly almost did it. But Jan pulled her into the store as quickly as she could, and Amanda looked suddenly breathless and a little startled when she got there. It was all so dazzling and so festive and so busy. There were faces she recognized everywhere, and two of the actresses she had worked with years before suddenly rushed up to her and threw their arms around her. They were obviously thrilled to see her and wanted to know everything she'd been doing. She managed to tell them about Matt, and that this was the first time she'd been out since he died. And from a little distance, Jan watched her proudly, as she walked over to say hello to her sister-in-law, Julie.

And from across the room, where he was talking to an old friend, Jack suddenly looked at them in amazement. 'I don't believe it . . .' he muttered under his breath and excused himself to greet Jan. 'Would it be rude to say I'm stunned?' he whispered to her, glancing at Amanda, and Jan laughed as she whispered back to him.

'Not as stunned as I am. I've been trying to get her out of the house all year. This is the first time she's been out since Dad died, and probably the first time she's been to a party like this since she retired from the movies.'

'I'm honored,' he said, and sounded as though he meant it, and he waited patiently nearby for Amanda to finish her conversations, and then he walked up to her and thanked her for coming. 'Julie's will never be the same again after this,' he smiled at her. 'You've finally given us the distinction I've always thought we deserved, but couldn't pull off without you.' He was teasing her, but only a little.

'I doubt that, Jack. It's good to see you. It's a beautiful party. I've already run into lots of old friends here.'

'I'm sure they're happy to see you. You'll have to come back more often. We'll throw a party for you anytime you want to come shopping.' He seemed in good spirits, and

Amanda accepted a glass of Champagne from a passing waiter. And as she did, Jack noticed that her hand shook just a little. But there was no other indication whatsoever that she was nervous. She was a thoroughbred to her core, and unlike some of her old co-stars, she looked both beautiful and distinguished. 'You look incredible, Amanda,' he said, hoping he didn't sound too pushy, but it was hard not to notice her looks anywhere, even in a crowd like this one. And amidst the sequin dresses and holiday satins, her well-cut navy wool dress and sapphire earrings made her look even more spectacular than they did. 'Have you been well?' he asked politely.

She hesitated for only a moment. 'More or less,' she said honestly, with a sad smile. 'It's been a pretty rough year. Looking back, I guess I'm just lucky I survived it.' And she meant it.

'I went through that once,' he said thoughtfully, thinking suddenly of Dori. It was the second time that Amanda had made him think of her, more due to the circumstances than to any physical resemblance, or maybe it was just a feeling.

'I thought you were divorced,' Amanda said, looking confused as people all around the room recognized her and pointed discreetly . . . look . . . over there . . . it's Amanda Robbins . . . is she in a movie? . . . haven't seen her in years . . . she looks fabulous . . . do you think she's had a face-lift? . . . still great-looking . . . The room was buzzing, although she seemed oblivious to it. She had enormous presence and poise.

'I was divorced,' Jack said quietly, explaining his comment to her. In his dark suit, standing next to her, he looked almost like her escort. 'But a close friend of mine died thirteen years ago. It wasn't quite the same as what you went through, but it was pretty rugged. She was a very special person.'

'I'm sorry,' Amanda said gently, with eyes that touched his like matchsticks igniting something that almost frightened him when he felt it. Behind the cool facade, she was a powerful and very magnetic woman. And oddly, after her agonizing year, she looked much more alive to him than when she had been with Matthew. But before he could say anything more to her, he got called away to solve some minor problem with the guest list. Two major stars had just turned up at the door, and had not been invited. He told the security guards at the door to let them in, and then got pulled away for something else by Gladdie. And by then, Jan had come to check on her mother.

'How are you doing, Mom? Are you okay?' She hoped she wasn't ready to leave yet. Jan thought it was good for her to be there, and besides, it was a terrific party.

'I'm fine, sweetheart. Thank you for bringing me. I haven't seen some of these people in years, and Jack has been very pleasant.' It was almost an apology for the things she had said about him for the past three years, but he seemed much more respectable to her than he had before, and very comfortable on his own turf. She would have hated to admit it, but she almost liked him. 'When's Paul coming?'

'Any minute, I hope. He was in a meeting.' And shortly after that, Jan got called to the phone by Gladdie. It was Paul, the meeting was taking forever, but he promised that he'd be there as soon as it was over. 'You'll never guess who's here,' she said, sounding happy and mischievous, and he laughed as he listened. She was in a better mood than she'd been in in weeks and he was happy to hear it. The tension between them had been getting increasingly stressful.

'Knowing my father, it could be anyone. Tom Cruise . . . Madonna . . .'

'Better than that,' she smiled as she held the phone, 'Amanda Robbins.'

'You actually got her to go with you? Good job, kid. I'm proud of you. How's she doing?'

'She knows practically everyone here, and she looks terrific. She combed her hair, put on a little makeup, and presto magic, the movie star returns. I wish I had her looks.'

'You've got her beat hands down, baby. Don't ever forget that.'

'I love you,' she said, touched by what he'd said, whether or not he meant it.

'Just keep my father away from her, if she's looking so great. That's one headache we don't need. She'd never speak to me again, and neither would you.'

'I don't think there's any danger of that,' Jan laughed at what he'd said. 'But he's been very nice to her. The place is mobbed, and he's been pretty busy. They keep getting celebrity crashers.'

'Only women, I'm sure. Poor guy, they'll probably eat him alive and tear his suit off . . . life is tough for some of us. That's my daddy. Anyway, sweetheart, I'll be there as soon as I can. Hang in there. I'll call you when I leave the office.'

'See you soon.' It was the nicest exchange they'd had in weeks, and when she went to look for her mother, she saw that she was talking to Jack again, and decided to leave them alone. It wouldn't be such a bad thing if they could be friends finally, and stop complaining about each other. And from the distance, while they talked, Jan could see that her mother was smiling, and Jack seemed very earnest.

As it turned out, he was telling her about his buying trips in Europe, and how much he disliked Milan and preferred Paris. And they were exchanging experiences at Claridge's in London. The two seemed like old friends as Jan drifted away to chat with someone she knew, and another hour had gone by when Paul called again, but this time he sounded frazzled. The meeting hadn't gone well, and when he'd gone downstairs, he found that his car had been towed, and he had no way to get to the party, other than to call a cab, but he wanted Jan to pick him up, and in exchange, he promised to take her to dinner. It was really too late for him to try to get to the party.

'What about my mom? I can't just leave her here,' she said, sounding worried.

'Why don't you have my dad put her in a cab. He might even have a limo or two standing by. He usually does that for big stars who need a ride somewhere. Just ask him.'

'Okay, I'll try. But if she has a fit, I'll call you. I may have to take her home. Otherwise, I'll be there in ten minutes.'

'Be here,' he said firmly. 'I've had a stinking afternoon and I want to see you.' A nice, quiet dinner somewhere sounded great to her too, and she hoped that her mother would be willing to have Jack put her in a cab or a limo.

When she found them again, still together in a corner of the room, she explained the situation to them, and for an instant her mother looked panicked. But Jack stepped into it before Amanda could say a word to her daughter. 'Paul's right. I have two cars right outside. Whenever your mother wants to go home, I'll have one of them drive her. How does that sound to you?' he asked, turning to Amanda, who still looked startled to be deserted by Jan, but she also didn't want to be a burden to her.

'I . . . that's fine . . . actually, you don't have to do that, Jack. I can take a cab. I'm just a short hop away in Bel Air. I'll call a taxi.'

'No,' he said quietly but firmly, 'you'll take the limo. You shouldn't be riding around at this hour in a taxi.' Amanda laughed at his firmness and the attention, and agreed to take the limo. In fact, she began to make noises about leaving, but he looked so disappointed that she was embarrassed, and agreed to stay a little longer. She was actually having a great time. Matthew had always hated parties, and they hardly ever went to any.

Jan kissed her good-bye and went to retrieve her car, and pick up Paul, and Jack kept a paternal eye on Amanda, making sure she had something to drink, a plate of hors d'oeuvres, met his friends, and felt entirely at ease at the party. She was shocked to realize finally that she was one of the last to leave, and it was already eight-thirty.

'How embarrassing . . . you're going to have to kick me out the door to get rid of me,' she said apologetically, and extended a hand to shake his, but he insisted on taking her home himself in the limo.

'Don't be silly, Amanda. It's no trouble for me. We're family, besides it's nice to have a chance to chat after all these years. I'm happy to do it.' There was no getting him to agree to let her go home alone, and he left Gladdie with all the instructions she needed when he left. The party was over, and the friends he had planned to have dinner with had already left without him. He had told them he might join them later, or not, but not to count on it in case something came up. And he had no other obligations. And once they were in the car, and driving up Rodeo Drive, he asked her casually if she'd like to stop somewhere for a bite to eat, just a hamburger or a salad, it was such a good chance to talk about their children. She hesitated, thinking she really should go home, but she had no one to account to. And she was a little hungry. He made a good point. She had been worried about Jan and Paul lately, and she wondered if he had also noticed something strained between them. Maybe that was why he wanted to have dinner with her. She assumed so, and decided it was a good idea, and gratefully accepted his offer.

He had the driver take them to the Ivy on North Robertson, and knowing him as well as they did, they gave him a quiet corner table. George Christy was there too, with a group of friends, and he waved when he saw Jack, and then his eyes grew wide when he saw that he was with Amanda Robbins.

They ordered pasta and salads, and Jack moved comfortably into the gap in the conversation. As he had at the store, he talked about a wide variety of things, painting, art, travel, literature, the theater. He was amazingly well informed and pleasant to talk to, and she realized very quickly that he was not the masher she had thought him. And then finally, when the food came, he brought up the subject of their children.

'Do you think they're okay?' He looked concerned, but he seemed perfectly at ease with her. They seemed able to talk about any topic.

'I don't know,' she said honestly. 'I've been worried about them for a while, but I guess I haven't been much help to Jan. I've been so wrapped up in myself for the past year, I feel as though I've failed her as a mother.'

'That's nonsense,' he said kindly, 'this was the time you needed for you. You can't always be there for everyone else. I'm sure she understood that. She's a terrific girl . . . I just hope Paul is treating her well. She doesn't look happy.'

Amanda sighed then, not wanting to break a confidence, but anxious to share what information she had with Paul's father. This was a perfect opportunity for them to help their children. 'I don't want to say anything I shouldn't, Jack. But I think she's very upset about not getting pregnant.'

'I thought that might be it,' he said, looking pensively at Amanda. 'Have they been trying that seriously? Paul never tells me.'

'From what I understand, for two years now. That can be very depressing.'

'Or a lot of fun, depending on how you look at it,' he said irreverently, and she laughed in spite of herself, and then they both grew serious again.

'They don't look like they're having fun, although she seemed better tonight than she has in a long time. She looked like a little girl when she left to pick up Paul.'

'Maybe she was just relieved to see you feeling better,' he said gently, and Amanda nodded.

'Maybe. The last I heard of it, she wanted Paul to go to a specialist earlier this year, and he didn't want to.'

'That serious then. That's not good news. Do you think he's gone yet?'

'I don't think so, although I know she has.'

'And?'

'I don't know the details,' Amanda admitted to him. 'But I do know they're not pregnant. Or at least I don't think so.'

'They would have told us if it had worked by now. It really is a worrisome problem. I've teased him about it from time to time, insensitive moron that I am . . . and of course now I realize that I shouldn't have. I wonder if I can broach it with him.' He looked pensive.

'I think he worries a lot about his business,' Amanda said fairly. She had grown very fond of Paul in the past three years, just as Jack had of her daughter. They were both nice people.

'Paul worries about everything,' Jack said with a worried frown. 'He's just that kind of person, that's why he's good at what he does, and he's going to be a major player in the film industry one day. Unlike his father, who produced some of the worst movies you've ever seen. Surpassed only by the ones in which I acted. I'm a lot better at women's dresses.'

'I'm sure you're being modest about the films,' Amanda laughed, and then told him how much she liked the store. 'It's beautiful, Jack. I'll have to come back one afternoon to go shopping.' She liked what she had seen there, and much to her surprise, she liked him too. He was intelligent and interesting and fun to be with. The evening had gone very quickly. And as they left the restaurant, he promised her that he would talk to Paul about going to a specialist with Jan.

'He may not appreciate my talking to him about it, but I'll give it a try.'

'I'd really appreciate that,' she said gratefully as they got back into the limo.

'I'll let you know how it works out,' he promised. 'Just think, if we play our cards right, we might be grandparents again by this time next year. Now, there's a thought. I'm turning sixty right after Christmas. That's bad enough without adding more grandchildren . . . for a man like me, that could absolutely destroy my reputation.' She liked the way he made light of it, and she couldn't help laughing about it with him, and then for a serious moment, he talked to her again about Dori, how much she had meant to him, and the fact that he had never wanted to be seriously involved with anyone again since then. 'It's just too painful,' he said honestly. 'I don't want to care that much again about anyone, but my children. When the women in my life leave, I want to wave good-bye and forget them. Not cry for two years and remember them for the rest of my life with sorrow. I can't bring myself to do that.'

'Maybe the right person hasn't come along again, Jack,' she said quietly, thinking of Matthew. She couldn't imagine loving anyone again either, and she said so.

'It's different for you,' he said sensibly, 'you were married for twenty-six years. You haven't been using up your tickets all over the place the way I have. I've just been having fun, and that's all I want. You should have a life with someone else, if that's what you want, after you've looked around for a while,' he said gently. 'You haven't been out here in a long time. You may find you actually enjoy it.'

'I doubt that,' she said honestly. 'I can't even imagine dating again, Jack. Not after all these years. I think I'm past that.'

'You never know what will happen in life, or who'll come along. Somehow life gives us gifts when we least expect them — or a good kick in the behind. Either one. But it's never what you were expecting.'

She nodded, smiling at what he had said, there was a certain truth to it, and then she looked at Jack with a question. 'What was

Paul's mother like?' She had met her briefly at the wedding, but it had been hard to tell, there had been so much going on, so many guests, so many important details.

'Barbara?' He looked surprised at the question. 'She was a monster. Actually, she was the one who cured me from ever wanting to be married, and I'm sure she would tell you the same thing about me, if you asked her. Except of course that she was foolish enough to remarry. I can hardly remember being married to her anymore, fortunately. She left me nineteen years ago. Next year, I'm planning to celebrate the twentieth anniversary of my independence.' They were both laughing as he said it.

'Jack Watson, you are awful and irreverent. I bet if the right woman came along you'd marry her in a minute. You're just too busy chasing starlets and models to find her.'

'How would you know?' he asked, feigning innocence, but convincing no one, certainly not Amanda.

'I read the papers,' she said smugly, and he had the grace to look embarrassed for an instant.

'Well, however that may be, I can assure

you that if I met Mrs Right or Miss Right, I would head for the tallest building and leap to the street immediately. I've learned my lesson. I'm being honest with you, Amanda. I couldn't do it.'

'That's how I feel now, although for different reasons. Oh well, it's not a problem I have to face for the moment,' she said with a small sigh as they reached her front door and she turned to thank him. 'I had a lovely time, Jack, thank you for taking such good care of me, and taking me to dinner to talk about the children.' He looked a little startled when she said it, and then he smiled and nodded.

'I'll call and tell you what Paul says,' he reiterated, and she thanked him again, unlocked her door, went inside, and closed it behind her. She heard the limo drive away as she turned on the light, and was surprised to realize how wrong she had been about him. He was a womanizer certainly, and he made no secret of it, and yet there was far more to him than that. There was something oddly endearing about him, like a young boy gone wild, but with a look in his eyes that made you want to hug him.

For an instant, it almost made warning bells go off in her head. Men like Jack were dangerous, even for fifty-year-old widows, and yet she knew she had nothing to fear from him. He had his chorus line of women, and all they really had in common was their children. But as Jack rode back to Rodeo Drive to check that the store had been properly put to bed, he sat back against the seat and closed his eyes, and all he could see in his mind's eye was Amanda.

Chapter Four

Amanda didn't hear from Jan for the next few days, and Jack called her a week after the party. He said he had something to tell her, and invited her to come to the store, and have lunch with him in his office. And she accepted without any hesitation. She knew full well that his only motive in calling her was to talk about their children.

He was waiting for her downstairs when she arrived and ushered her upstairs to his private office, where lunch had been set up for them with a starched white tablecloth and napkins on the conference room table. They were left alone, and ate lobster salad and caviar and drank Champagne. It was a very elegant little luncheon.

'Do you do this every day?' she asked, teasing him, and he said only when he wanted to impress someone. 'Then consider me impressed, because I am. I eat yogurt every day out of the container.'

'Well, it seems to work. You have an incredible figure, Amanda.' She blushed at what he said, and then they moved on to talk about their children. He said he had had lunch with Paul, and had brought the subject up casually, as casually as one could bring up a subject like that one. He had inquired about why they hadn't gotten around to having children, and Jack said that Paul had been pretty candid about it, and told him much the same thing as Amanda. He had also admitted that he really didn't want to go to a doctor about it. Paul thought it was embarrassing, and he felt as though his manhood and virility were being questioned. But after a lengthy conversation with his father, he had finally agreed to do something about it, even though he didn't want to. He had promised to go to the doctor with Jan right after Christmas. Apparently, her doctor was on vacation until then.

'So I would say, our mission has been accomplished. The first stage of it anyway. Operation Grandchild is in its early stages.'

Amanda was impressed with how good the results had been, and the fact that he had cared enough to do it, and she sat back in her chair and smiled at him in amazement. 'Jack Watson, you are terrific. I can't believe it. Poor Jan has been begging him to go with her for the last year, and he wouldn't do it.'

'He's probably just afraid of me. I told him I'd disinherit him if he didn't.' He smiled at her, pleased by her reaction. She was so obviously grateful to him.

'Seriously, Jack, thank you. Poor Jan wants a baby so badly.'

'What do you suppose will happen if they can't?' He looked worried as he asked her, and she looked concerned too, since Jan had told her that Paul was not in favor of adoption.

'I guess they'll have to face this thing one step at a time. They can always adopt if they don't conceive, but it's hard to believe that in this day and age, with all the fancy methods they use to resolve infertility, they couldn't help them. I'm sure something good will come from all this, with a little patience.'

'Things are so damn complicated now, aren't they? In my day, if you were really lucky, it took you six months to get some girl in the back of your dad's car at the drive-in movie, and if you so much as shook hands with her, she got pregnant. Now everyone is being treated for infertility and having babies made in a petri dish, it sure takes the fun out of dating.' Amanda couldn't help laughing at what he said. It was true, even in her marriage to Matt, she had frequently worried about getting pregnant. She just hoped that Paul and Jan got lucky now, and managed to have a baby. 'I'll keep you posted if I hear anything further,' Jack promised.

'So will I,' Amanda assured him, and then he offered to walk around the store with her. She couldn't resist trying a few things, and he finally left her with the manager of the store and the best of their sales force, and she showed up in his office to thank him again two hours later.

'Did you have fun?' he asked her, as he stood up at his desk when she walked in the room. She looked happy and relaxed and she had had a great time shopping at Julie's.

'I had a ball, and I bought everything in sight, including half a dozen really great bathing suits for next summer from your cruise line.' She had also bought several beautiful nightgowns, a new dress, and a sensational black alligator handbag. 'I bought everything in sight,' she said again, with a degree of embarrassment. 'I haven't been this extravagant ever in my life, but I have to admit I enjoyed it.' She laughed as she confessed, and he found himself staring at how beautiful she was, and wondering how he could get her to have dinner with him.

'Do you like Thai food?' he suddenly asked her out of nowhere.

'Why, do you sell that too? Is there a department I missed? A deli?' She was laughing at him, and she looked sensual and young and happy.

'Yes, actually, I'll show you where it is,' he said convincingly. 'But it's at our other store, and you have to come in my car to get there.'

'Oh, you're a terrible liar, Jack Watson.

You're trying to kidnap me and hold me for ransom, I just know it.'

'What a good idea,' he said, laughing with her. 'What are my chances?'

'Now? Tonight?' It was already five-thirty, but the store was open till nine so their customers could shop for Christmas. 'You gave me lunch today, you don't have to feed me tonight too. I have another idea. Why don't you come out to the house a little later on, and I'll cook you dinner. Nothing fancy, just whatever I find in the fridge, more or less. I owe you one, a big one, for getting Paul to go to the doctor.'

'I'd love it.' He accepted her invitation instantly, and promised to be there at seven o'clock to help her. And as soon as she left, he picked up the phone and canceled the date that he had set up weeks before for that evening. He claimed to have the flu, and the girl he called just laughed at him. She didn't really care, but she knew him a lot better than he suspected.

'What's her name?' The girl he had called couldn't resist a little teasing.

'What makes you think it's another woman?'

'Because you're not gay, and you probably haven't had the flu since you were two. You sound fine to me, Jack . . . good luck with whoever she is.' She was seeing someone else anyway, and he thanked her for being so understanding.

He arrived at Amanda's door at exactly seven o'clock, and she was wearing a pair of gray slacks with a pale blue sweater set and a string of pearls. She looked like a young heiress, but she was wearing an apron.

'Very domestic picture,' he commented as he came in and set down a bottle of very fancy wine he had bought for her, and she laughed at his comment.

'I hope so, after twenty-six years of marriage.'

'You know, I never thought of you that way before, domestic I mean,' Jack confessed as he followed her into the kitchen and she thanked him for the wine. It was an excellent wine, and an impressive vintage. 'I only thought of you in terms of being a movie star. It's hard to forget who you were before. You even look the same. In fact, in my mind, I always think of you as Amanda Robbins, and not Amanda Kingston.'

'Matt hated that,' she said simply. 'A lot of people used to say that.'

'Is that why you never went back?' He was curious about her.

'Probably. Matt wouldn't have wanted me to anyway. We talked about it a lot before we got married. I hadn't been at it long, but I was ready to give it up . . . for something better . . . a man I loved and a family.'

'And was it better? Were you happy?' he asked, as he watched her.

'I loved being with my kids, and with Matt. It was a good life.' She looked pensive for a moment then, as she thought about it. 'It's hard to believe that it's over. Everything shattered so quickly. One minute he was leaving the house with his tennis racket in his hand, and the next he was gone, just two hours later. It's hard to adjust to.'

Jack nodded. 'It sounds dumb to say it, but at least he didn't suffer.'

'I guess that's true, but we did. I wasn't prepared at all. He seemed so young. We never even talked about what would happen if one of us died. We never had time to think about it, or say good-bye, or . . .' Tears filled her eyes and she turned away, and suddenly Jack was behind her, holding her shoulders.

'It's okay . . . I know . . . that's how it was for me with Dori. She had a car accident on the way to meet me. Head-on. She never knew what hit her. But I did. I felt like that goddamn truck had hit me. For a long time, I wished it would have. I kept wanting it to be me, and not her . . . I felt so damn guilty.'

'So did I,' Amanda said as she turned to look at him. He had kind eyes, they were a warm brown, and his hair was a sandy blonde peppered with gray. He was astonishingly good-looking. 'For the last year, I kept wishing I had died instead of Matt. But for the last week or two, I'm suddenly glad I didn't. I've been enjoying my kids again, and doing little things . . . It's funny how things change just the smallest bit, and it makes a difference.' He nodded, and put on one of her aprons over the slacks and black turtleneck sweater he was wearing.

'Okay, enough of this serious stuff, madam. What's for dinner? Do you want me to chop, grate, or puree, or would you

91

rather just watch me get quietly drunk in your kitchen? I can do either.' She laughed at him as he looked at her with amusement. It was so easy to be with him.

'Why don't you sit and relax. Everything is pretty much done already.' She poured him a glass of wine, did a few things in the kitchen, and half an hour later, they had steak, baked potatoes, and salad. She was a good cook, and they talked for hours, sitting at her kitchen table, and afterward they walked into the living room and he glanced at some of the pictures. They were a handsome family, though Matt always looked stiff to him, but Amanda looked lovely in every picture.

'It's a shame you and your daughters are so ugly.'

'Your kids are just as good-looking as mine,' she complimented him, and he laughed.

'We just happen to be extremely attractive people. Everyone in Los Angeles is. They make the ugly people move to some other state, or town, or ship them over the border at midnight. They just round them up and off they go and no one ever sees them again . . . poof. . . no more ugly people.' He liked to play with her, and tease. It was easy to see why he had so much success with women.

'Don't you get tired of it?' she asked him honestly as they sat down. She felt as though she could ask him anything. They were friends now. 'All the women, I mean. I would think it would be exhausting to be with strangers all the time. I can't even imagine having to deal with it, starting all over again constantly, asking all those tedious questions . . .'

'Stop!' He put up a hand with a groan. 'You're destroying my lifestyle. If you make me question it, I may not be able to do it. It's just one way of never getting involved. That's all. It's what I've needed ever since Dori.'

'I'd rather watch TV, or read a book,' Amanda said honestly, and he laughed.

'Well, actually . . . that could be the essence of the difference between men and women. Up until now, if the choice was book, TV, or women, I would have to pick women. But if you make me think about it with any seriousness, I may have to buy myself a new TV set tomorrow morning.'

'You're hopeless.'

'I am. It used to be part of my charm, but I can see that it's rapidly becoming a liability. Maybe we shouldn't discuss this.'

They talked about other things then, their families when they were young, their dreams, their ambitions, their careers, and once again their children. And the night flew by again. It was after midnight when he finally left her. And not quite nine o'clock when he called her the next morning to thank her for dinner. She was still sleeping.

'Did I wake you?' He seemed surprised. She looked like one of those early-rising people, and normally she was, but she had stayed up late the night before, trying to read, and thinking about him.

'No, not at all. I was up,' she lied, looking at the clock and surprised at what time it was. She had a dentist appointment to have her teeth cleaned, and she was about to miss it.

'You're lying,' he said with a grin at his end. 'You were sound asleep and I woke you. The life of the indolent rich. I've been at my desk since eight-thirty.' He had had a number of calls to make to Europe, where it was nine hours later. But she had been preying on his mind, and he had decided to call her on the spur of the moment. And now, hearing her, he was unexpectedly nervous. 'How about dinner tonight?' he asked without preamble, and her eyes opened wide, wondering if she had heard him correctly.

'Tonight?' She had nothing planned, although the following day she had been invited to a Christmas party. 'I . . . aren't you going to get tired of me?'

'I don't think that's possible, and we have a lot to catch up on, don't we?'

'Like what?' She lay on her back and stretched, remembering exactly what he looked like.

'Both our lives. Between us that covers a hundred and ten years, it could take a while, and I figured we really ought to get started, though we made some good inroads last night.'

'Is this how you do it?' she smiled. 'All that charm? A hundred and ten years . . . what a way to think about it. Well, all right, as long as you put it that way, we'd better do it. What did you have in mind?'

'How about dinner at L'Orangerie? I'll pick you up at seven-thirty.'

'Sounds wonderful. I'll be ready.' But as soon as she hung up, she panicked. She sat up in bed and stared across the bedroom she had shared for twenty-six years with her husband. What in God's name was she doing? Was she playing Girl of the Hour with Jack Watson? How stupid was she? She got out of bed and decided to call him to cancel. But as soon as she called, Gladdie told her he had gone into a meeting, but she could leave him a message. But it seemed so rude to just leave him a message saying she couldn't have dinner with him, so she said that it was nothing important.

He called her back at noon anyway, and when she answered the phone, he sounded worried. 'Anything wrong? Are you okay?' He actually sounded as though it mattered to him, which was even more unnerving.

'I'm fine . . . I just thought . . . oh, I don't know, Jack, I was just feeling stupid. I don't want to be the Flavor of the Month. I'm a married woman, or at least I was . . . or I still am . . . in my own mind, and I don't know what the hell I'm doing with you, or what game I'm playing. I can't even bring myself to take off my wedding band, and now I'm having dinner with you every night, and I have no idea where this is going.' She looked and felt exhausted when she finished talking, and at his end, he sounded calm, although he didn't feel it.

'I don't know where this is going either. And if it'll make you feel any better, I'll buy a wedding band too, and then at least we'll be even. People will think we're both cheating on our spouses. I just know I enjoy your company more than I've enjoyed anyone in years, maybe ever. And I can't tell you more than that. All of a sudden, the life I've led for twenty years looks like a bad joke in the back of *Playboy*. I'm embarrassed by it, I want to get rid of it, and God help me for saying this, but I want to be the kind of person you'd be proud to be seen with, because I'm so damn proud to be with you, I can't stand it.'

'But I'm not ready for a relationship,' she said mournfully. 'I don't want to start dating. It's only been a year since I lost Matt,

and I don't know what I'm doing with you
. . . but I love talking to you too . . . and I
don't want to stop, but maybe we should.
Do you think we should cancel dinner
tonight? Do you think this is wrong?' She
sounded so worried that he just wanted to
put his arms around her and hug her.

'It's going to be all right,' he said gently,
'we're not going to do anything you don't
like. We'll just talk about our kids, and
relax. It doesn't have to be more than that
for now . . . or maybe ever.' It cost him
dearly to say that, but he didn't want to
frighten her, or worse yet, to lose her,
before he even won her over. Suddenly it
all mattered to him greatly. And then he had
another thought. 'Maybe we should go
somewhere a little less public for dinner . . .'
L'Orangerie was one of the best restaurants
in L.A., and they were bound to be seen
there. 'What about some little bistro, or
even a pizza?'

'That sounds terrific, Jack. And I'm sorry
I'm such a lunatic. I just wasn't expecting us
to be friends, or not like this anyway . . .
whatever this is.' She laughed nervously and
he tried to reassure her.

'I'll pick you up. You can wear jeans, if you want.'

'Great.' She took him at his word, and when he arrived, she was wearing faded jeans wallpapered to her spectacular body and a big cozy pink angora sweater. He was dying to tell her how great she looked, but he didn't want to scare her.

They drove to La Cienega, and they stopped at a little restaurant she had never even seen before. They were talking animatedly as they walked in, and suddenly she clutched his arm, and turned away with a look of terror.

'What is it?' If she had been married, he would have guessed that she had just seen her husband in the corner, with another woman. All he could see was a young couple dining there, but Amanda was already out the door, and her heart was pounding. 'Who was that?'

'My daughter Louise and her husband, Jerry.'

'Oh my God. That's all right. Aren't we allowed to be eating dinner? We both have our clothes on.' He tried to make light of it, but she looked as though she wanted to run away, and he didn't want that to happen. They walked back to his car, and talked for a moment once they were safely inside it.

'She'd never understand it.'

'She's a grown woman, for heaven's sake. What do your kids expect? For you to stay home for the rest of your life? I'm Jan's father-in-law, I'm harmless.' He tried to look innocent, but this time Amanda laughed at him.

'You are anything but harmless, and you know it. And my kids think you're a masher.'

'That's nice. I hope Jan doesn't think that . . . well, come to think of it, maybe she does. I guess for quite a while now, I've been one. But there's always the possibility that I might reform. Would that count?'

'No. And certainly not tonight. Maybe I should go home.'

'Tell you what, we'll go to Johnny Rocket.' She smiled at the suggestion. It was where the kids hung out, drinking milkshakes and eating hamburgers, just like they did in the fifties.

And when they got there, they sat at the counter and ate chili dogs and fries, and drank milkshakes, and Amanda even managed to laugh at herself, before they ordered coffee.

'Did I look like a complete fool running out of there?' She looked like a kid who had made a huge faux pas, and couldn't believe she'd done it, but Jack loved everything about her.

'No. You looked like a married woman out on a date, who had just seen her husband.'

'That's what I felt like,' she confessed with a sigh, and then glanced up at him. 'Jack, I'm not up to this. Honestly, I'm not. I think you should go back to the chorus line again, you're a lot better off with them, believe me.'

'I think you should let me decide that.' And then out of nowhere, he asked her what she was doing the following week for Christmas.

'The kids are coming to my house on Christmas Eve, they do every year. And then this year we're going to Louise's on Christmas Day. Why? What do you do?'

'Sleep, usually . . . I mean, as in snoring, nothing more exotic than that. Christmas in the retail business is a nightmare. We're open till midnight on Christmas Eve, to accommodate our customers who can't face their shopping until nine o'clock that night, mostly husbands. It's as if they lose their calendars every year and find them at six o'clock on Christmas Eve . . . Oh my God, it's Christmas! I usually take the last shift and then I go home and sleep for two days. It works for me, but I was just wondering if you wanted to go skiing with me the day after. You know, separate rooms, just good friends and all that.'

'I don't think I should. What if someone sees me? It hasn't been a year yet.'

'When will that be?' He honestly couldn't remember.

'On the fourth of January,' she said solemnly, 'and I'm actually not much of a skier.'

'It was just an idea, I thought it might do you good, to get some fresh air, and get away. We could drive up to Lake Tahoe, or stop in San Francisco.'

'Maybe someday,' she said vaguely, and he nodded. He was pushing it, and he knew it. She really wasn't ready.

'Don't worry about it. Why don't you drop by the store one of these days. I'll be there all week, and we can eat caviar in my offfice.' She smiled at the suggestion. In spite of his reputation, and the fact that she wasn't ready for this, she really liked him. And he seemed to understand everything that she was feeling. There was a warm, caring side to him, that had taken her by surprise and caught her off guard completely. And he seemed so much younger than Matt, so full of life, so happy to be with her, and much as she didn't want to feel that way about him, she found that she loved being with him.

They talked about it that night, in the car, on the way home, and he confessed that she was not at all what he had expected her to be, once he got to know her. She was funny and warm and kind and compassionate, and so vulnerable. Everything she said or did, made him want to protect her.

'Can you stand just being friends for a while,' she asked him honestly, 'or maybe even forever? I don't know that I'll ever want to get involved again. I'm just not sure I could ever do that.'

'No one's asking you to make that decision,' he said sanely, and she calmed down and stopped feeling quite as guilty. He came in for a while, and they drank mint tea in her kitchen, and then eventually he lit a fire in the living room, and they talked for a long time about the things that were important to them.

It was two o'clock when he left, and she didn't know where the night had gone. The hours seemed to fly by when they were together. The next morning he was busy at the store, and she spent the day doing all the last-minute details of getting ready for Christmas. She had already bought the tree, and she was decorating it that night when he called her.

'What are you doing?' he asked, sounding tired. He had been at the store for twelve hours, and he was exhausted.

'Decorating the tree,' she said, but she sounded sad, and she had put carols on the stereo, which suddenly seemed even sadder. It was her first Christmas without Matt, her first as a widow.

'Do you want me to come by? I'm leaving the store in half an hour, and you're on my way home. I'd love to see you.'

'I don't think we should,' she said honestly. She still needed time to mourn, and this was one of those private moments. Instead, they talked for a while, and when they hung up, she felt a little better, and he felt worse, and suddenly desperately lonely. He wondered if she was ever going to let go of Matt, or be ready to let someone in behind her walls. He knew that he had glimpsed into her heart, but she was still afraid to let him approach her, and maybe she always would be.

Jack drove slowly past her house on the way home, and he could see the lights blinking on the tree inside, but he couldn't see her. She was sitting in her bedroom, crying, because she was desperately afraid she was falling in love with Jack and she didn't want to. It wasn't fair to Matt, and more than anything, she didn't want to betray him. After twenty-six years she owed him more than that, more than just falling for the first man who came along, no matter how charming he was. And what would happen if she did turn out to be one of the girls in his chorus line? She would have cheapened herself for nothing. And she knew with absolute certainty that, for Matt's sake, and her own, she couldn't let that happen.

Jack called her when he got home, but she didn't answer the phone. She knew instinctively that it was him, and she didn't want to talk to him. She wanted to end this even before it happened.

She turned out the lights that night, and went to bed, and left the music on, and the strains of 'Silent Night' drifted through the house as she cried, for two men, one she had loved for so long, and the other she would never know. It was hard to tell at that exact moment which pain was greater, and which of them she most longed for.

Chapter Five

Jack only called her once or twice over the next few days. He could sense what was happening to her, and he knew how hard it was for her over the holidays. Dori had died in November, and he had stayed drunk for an entire week between Christmas and New Year's.

He wisely left Amanda alone to cope with her feelings privately, but on the morning of Christmas Eve, he had a Christmas gift dropped off for her. It was a small eighteenth-century sketch of an angel that she had admired in the store, and it was very pretty. He wrote a brief note to go with it, and told her that he hoped an angel would be watching over her, this Christmas and always. He signed it 'Jack,' and she was deeply touched when she saw it, and a little while later she called to thank him. She sounded more distant than before, but a lot calmer. She was obviously coming to terms with whatever it was she was feeling. And although he was happy to hear from her, he was careful not to frighten her by being too intimate with her. But right now he was totally swallowed up by the store anyway. They had had a few problems, a small theft, a nearly fatal heart attack the day before, and a small army of lost children. The usual crises over Christmas. They had also lost the gold sequined dress of a famous star, and then found it miraculously, and had had two famous women slugging it out over one man, in cosmetics. The holidays had not been without excitement.

'I hope you have a good time with your kids tonight, though I know it will be hard for you without Matt.'

'He always carved the turkey,' she said sadly. She sounded so small suddenly, and all he wanted to do was put his arms around her.

'Have Paul do it,' Jack said gently. 'I taught him everything I know. About turkeys, not about women.' She smiled at what he said, and asked him if there was any news about Paul. Jack told her that Paul had an appointment to go to the specialist between Christmas and New Year's. 'I hope everything checks out fine,' Jack said hopefully.

'So do I,' she agreed with him, and she suddenly wished she had invited him to dinner, but the children would have wondered why he was there, and he couldn't have left the store anyway, and what point was there in asking him? She wasn't going to pursue a relationship with him. She had already made that decision, and as he sat listening to her on the phone, from his desk, Jack could hear her decision about him in her tone. She had already taken a definite distance from him. He thought about calling someone to go out with him on New Year's Eve, but for once in his life, he didn't even want to. He had already made reservations to go to Tahoe the day after Christmas, and he was going alone.

'Merry Christmas, Amanda,' he said gently before they hung up, and he sat in his office for a long time, thinking about her. He had never known anyone like her.

And that night, as he walked around the store, helping out wherever he was needed, he thought about them eating turkey at her house, the children, and the tree, his own son, and her two daughters, and he suddenly realized what a wasteland his life was. He had spent the last ten years chasing tits and cute little asses in tight blue jeans, and what had it gotten him? Absolutely nothing.

'You don't look like you're having such a good Christmas,' Gladdie said when she left that night. He had given her a beautiful cashmere coat, and an enormous bonus. 'Something wrong? The kids okay?' She worried about him, and she knew there was no hot mama of the moment. She also knew that he had called Paul's mother-in-law several times, and she was afraid that he might be sick, or something might be wrong with the marriage, but Jack had purposely said nothing about it.

'No, I'm fine,' he lied. Except that I've wasted my life, the only woman I ever loved died thirteen years ago, and the best woman I've ever met before or since wants to bury herself with her husband. No big deal, Gladdie. Merry Christmas. 'Just tired, I guess. Christmas in this business is a killer.'

'Every year I tell myself we'll never get through it, but we do,' she smiled. Financially, it had been their best year ever.

'So what are you doing tonight?' He smiled at her as she put her new coat on. It was a soft lavender-blue and she loved it.

'Sleeping with my husband. Literally. The poor guy hasn't seen me awake in six weeks, and he probably won't for another week.'

'You should take a couple of days off. You deserve it.'

'Maybe when you're in Tahoe.' But he knew she wouldn't. She never did. She was the only human being he knew who worked harder than he did.

As he did every year, he worked until after midnight, and he was with the night watchman when they finally locked up at one o'clock in the morning.

'Merry Christmas, Mr Watson.'

'Thanks, Harry. Same to you.' He waved,

and slid slowly into his red Ferrari. But he was too tired to sleep when he got home. He watched television for a while, and thought about calling someone, but by then it was three o'clock in the morning. And for some odd reason, he felt as though those days were over. He just didn't care anymore. There were no legs long enough, no breasts big enough, no skin soft enough to woo him.

'Christ, maybe I'm dying,' he said out loud, and then laughed to himself as he went to bed. Maybe turning sixty was doing it, and not just Amanda. There was no fool like an old fool, and he had certainly been one.

He slept until noon the next day, and thought about calling her, but when he did, she was already gone. She was at Louise's house with her family, eating yet another turkey. He drove out to north L.A. and picked up some Chinese food instead, and then sat on his unmade bed, eating it, and watching football. He called a couple of girls after that, and wanted to ask them out for dinner that night, but everyone was out, and he was actually relieved not to reach them.

He knew Amanda was home that night, but he didn't call. What could he say to her? Are you over your husband yet? Suddenly he felt like a fool for badgering her, and he tossed and turned all night, and thought of her. And finally, the next morning, he couldn't stand it. He was leaving for Tahoe that afternoon, but when she answered the phone he asked her if he could come by for a cup of coffee.

She sounded surprised, and a little worried, but she invited him over anyway. There was always the possibility that he wanted to talk to her about Paul, or Jan, but she didn't think so. And when she saw his face, when she opened the door to him at one o'clock, she knew that it had nothing to do with their children.

'You look tired,' she said, looking concerned about him.

'I am. I can't sleep anymore. Turning sixty is rougher than I thought,' he said with a wry smile. 'I think I'm finally losing my marbles.'

'How's that?' He followed her inside, and they walked into her comfortable kitchen. She had a pot of coffee on, and offered him a cup, and then they sat down at her kitchen table.

He looked at her over his coffee and asked her bluntly, 'I've made a real nuisance of myself, haven't I? I guess mashers don't clean up all that well. I got a little overexcited. I'm sorry if I made you uncomfortable, that was never my intention.' He looked desperately unhappy as he said it, and a lot less than sixty. He looked and felt like a kid again, visiting the one girl in the class who didn't want to go steady with him. 'I know how hard this time is for you. I'm sorry if I made it any harder for you.'

'You didn't, Jack,' she said gently, her eyes boring into his, she looked as unhappy as he felt, and as though she felt so desperately torn that she didn't know what to do about it. 'I know I shouldn't say this to you, but I've missed you.' While he pretended to look calm, his heart flipped over as she said it.

'You have? When?'

'For the past few days. I've missed talking to you, and seeing you. I honest to God don't know what I'm doing.'

'Neither do I. I've been feeling like an utter fool, and the biggest pain in the ass that ever lived. I've been trying to leave you alone, because I figured that was what you wanted.'

'I did.' But there was a catch in her voice as she said it.

'And now?' He held his breath as he waited.

'I don't know.' She looked up at him with eyes the color of a cameo and all he wanted to do was kiss her, but he knew he couldn't.

'Just take your time. You don't need to make any decisions. Go slow. I'm here. I'm not going anywhere . . .' And then he remembered, with a grin. 'Except Lake Tahoe.'

'Now?' She smiled at him, she really liked being with him.

'Later. I still have to go home and pack my ski clothes. I should have packed yesterday, but I was too beat to do it.' She nodded then, and they talked, and a little while later, they were comfortable again, and she was laughing at him. He was describing the incident in the store when the two women got into a fistfight over their common boyfriend.

'Can you imagine what the tabloids would have done with that? And of course, if they got hold of it, both women would have blamed us for squealing. Actually, they deserved it.' He still hadn't told her who they were, and said he wouldn't. He was surprisingly discreet about his business. 'So what are you going to do this week?'

'Nothing much. Maybe I'll see the kids, if they're not too busy.' But he didn't reiterate his invitation to Lake Tahoe. He knew she just wasn't ready. 'Maybe I'll go to a movie. What about you? Are you taking anyone with you?' She was still trying to convince herself they were just friends, and it wouldn't bother her in the least if he was taking a woman along, but it would have, and she knew it.

'No, I'm going alone. I ski better that way.' And then, tired of playing games with her, he took her hand in his and held it. 'I'm going to miss you.' She nodded and said nothing, and then she looked at him, and she would have melted him to his soul if he'd been wearing asbestos. 'What are you doing on New Year's Eve?' he asked casually, and she laughed at him.

'Same thing I do every year. Matthew hated New Year's Eve. We went to bed at ten o'clock every year, and wished each other a Happy New Year the next morning.'

'Sounds exciting.' He smiled.

'What about you?' she asked with interest.

'Mine will be about like yours this year. I might stay up at Tahoe.' And then as he looked at her, he felt suddenly stupid. 'On the other hand, Amanda . . . we could do something a little different. We could hang around together here. Just as friends, and go to movies and watch television together. I don't have to go to work, and there's no law that says we can't be friends, is there?'

'What about your ski trip?'

'I have a bum knee anyway.' He grinned. 'My orthopedist would thank you.'

'And then what? I mean after that . . . that's the part that scares me.' Oddly enough, she found it easy to be honest with him.

'We don't have to worry about that part

yet. No one's keeping score here. We have a right not to be alone over the holidays. Who are we proving what to? You? Me? Our kids? Matt? It's been a year. You paid your dues. If nothing else, we have a right to a little comfort and friendship. How much trouble can we get into at a movie?' He was very convincing.

'With you? Probably more than I dare to think of.'

'I'll sit alone in the back row. I won't even come near you.'

'You're crazy.' She shook her head as she looked at him, trying to will herself to say no to him, to send him away, she knew she should, but everything about him was so damnably appealing.

'I came to the same conclusion myself yesterday – that I'm crazy. Actually, it almost had me worried.'

'Me too,' she laughed again. 'Everything about you has me worried. If I had any sense, I'd tell you that I don't want to see you again until the christening of Paul and Jan's first baby.'

'That could be a while. Even at best, we're talking nine months. That's a long time to forgo movies. So what do you say?'

'I say go to Lake Tahoe, and have a great time, Jack. Call me when you get back sometime.'

'Okay,' he said. He was old enough and wise enough to know when he wasn't going to win. It killed him to leave her, but he got up, wishing that he could convince her. 'Happy New Year,' he said, as he kissed the top of her head and walked out of her kitchen. He was already at the front door, and had opened it, when he heard her say something, and he turned around and saw her standing in the kitchen doorway. 'What did you just say?' The look in her eyes rooted him to the spot. She looked frightened, but strong, and her eyes never left him.

'I said there's a movie I want to see at the Beverly Center. It starts at four, if you want to join me.'

'Do you mean that?' His voice was a whisper in the chill hallway.

'I think I do . . . I want to . . . but I don't know yet.'

'I'll pick you up at three-thirty. Wear jeans. We'll go to the Thai place for dinner.

Okay?' A slow smile dawned in his eyes as she nodded. And without another word, before she could change her mind again, he drove home to cancel his reservations in Tahoe.

Chapter Six

The next five days were magical. They seemed to hang in space like a time warp. They went to movies, walked in the park, talked about anything that came to mind, or sometimes just sat together, in silence. There seemed to be no pressure on either of them. He called the store, but he didn't go in, and of course Gladdie was there. She hadn't taken time off after all. But for the first time in years, he didn't give a damn about Julie's. He just wanted to be with Amanda. Nothing was said, no questions were asked, no answers were offered, and nothing was promised. They just spent time together. And it was exactly what they both needed and wanted.

It was as though day by day Amanda could feel herself healing. And he felt himself becoming the man he had once been, with Dori, only better. He was older and wiser, and had squandered a lot of time in the last thirteen years. It suddenly seemed to him as though it had been someone else's life, and it no longer mattered.

She talked about Matt sometimes, and once she cried about him, but she seemed to feel more peaceful about him. She was slowly accepting that he had died and she had lived, and she wanted to stop feeling guilty about it. And without saying anything to Jack, she had quietly slipped off her wedding ring, and put it away in her jewel box. She had cried over it, but she no longer felt right wearing it. For the first instant it had slipped off she thought it would tear her heart out. She never mentioned it to Jack. But he saw it immediately the next time they had dinner, and knowing what a big step it must have been for her, he diplomatically made no comment.

They ate some good food, in restaurants all over town, where they saw no one they knew, and they saw some of the worst movies ever made, and then laughed about them. He went back to his own place at night, and they hovered in her doorway for a long time, just talking and saying good night. But it wasn't until the day before New Year's Eve that, without thinking, while she was cooking dinner for him that night, he reached out and pulled her to him and kissed her. He had wanted to do that for so long, and he was suddenly terrified that he would frighten her away again, but she looked anything but afraid as she looked up at him with a slow smile afterward, and he felt relief wash over him. He hadn't lost her. They didn't say anything, but he kissed her again later that night, as they sat in the living room, in the dark, holding hands, and looking at the fire he had lit. She felt completely comfortable with him.

And at midnight he went home, and as soon as he got there, he called her.

'I feel like a kid again, Amanda,' he said, and he sounded irresistibly sexy.

'So do I,' she smiled. 'Thank you for going slow with me. This week has been incredible. It was just what I needed. I just wanted some time with you . . . it's a real gift . . . better than Christmas.'

They laughed over the fact that the phone had rung a couple of times that night. They both assumed that it had been her children, but she hadn't answered. She wanted this time for herself, and for him. The children had had their fair share over the years, and so had Matt, and now it was her turn. It was the first time in years she had a life that no one knew about, and that didn't include her family. This was good for her for a change, and she knew it.

They had already planned to go ice-skating the next day, and maybe to another movie. They had seen just about everything in town by then, and they were going to cook dinner on New Year's Eve, and drink Champagne, and try to stay awake until midnight.

'I'm sorry you didn't get to go skiing,' she said generously on the phone to him.

'I'm not,' he laughed at the idea. 'This is a whole lot better. This is the most romantic thing I've ever done in my whole life, and I wouldn't miss it for anything, sure as hell not a bunch of moguls.'

He said good night to her, and wished he could kiss her again, and the next day they laughed like two kids when they went skating. They had a great time. And that night, on New Year's Eve, she made roast duck for him, and a souffle for dessert. It was a perfect dinner.

It was ten o'clock by the time they were in front of the fire again, and he was kissing her, and she was returning his kisses with passion. He poured them each a glass of Champagne, and they drank it faster than they planned. In the warmth of the fire, and the glow of the Champagne, his kisses seemed headier than ever, and she had no idea what time it was when his deep, sexy voice told her that he loved her, and asked her to go to bed with him. She didn't say anything. She only clung to him and nodded. She wanted him more than anything, and for once he couldn't even make himself stop to wonder if she'd regret it. He wanted her too badly. And he followed her into her bedroom. And what he discovered there filled him with wonder, she had a body almost like a girl's, only somehow better. She was long and lean, with fuller breasts than he had expected. He couldn't get enough of her, and she told him she loved him as he entered her, and she could hardly breathe as they moved slowly together. It was something she had never dreamed of or shared before, not with her husband, or the two men who had come before him. For a young girl in Hollywood at the time, she had been surprisingly chaste, but now they brought no history to each other. All they shared was their passion and the present, and when they came, she felt as though the universe had exploded in her head, and her body lay sated beneath him. She loved the noises he made, and the way he touched her, and the feel of him inside her. She was entirely his now, and she fell asleep in his arms soon afterward, long before midnight. There was no sorrow. No regret. And no reckoning. Until the next morning.

She awoke in his arms, as he caressed her breasts, smiling at her, and the sunlight streamed across the room she had shared with her husband. She lay quiet for a long time, and then she looked at Jack, not sure whether to laugh or cry, or make love to him again, and wanting to do all three at the same time. Instead, she slipped slowly out of bed and walked across the room, and then turned to look at him, like a young doe, in all her glory.

'Are you okay?' He watched her, filled with desire for her again, but suddenly worried. She seemed different.

'I'm not sure,' she said quietly, and then sat down in a chair, still naked, looking at him, trying to decide if she was crazy, or just very happy. 'I can't believe I did that last night.' Neither could he, but he had never been happier in his life, and he didn't want to give her up now. He knew who and what she was, and he wanted her desperately. And she had told him she loved him.

'Just don't tell me I got you drunk . . . that will kill me.'

'You didn't,' she looked at him nervously from underneath cream-colored eyelids, 'but was I?' She seemed frightened.

'I don't see how . . . you only had two glasses . . .'

'It was the fire . . . and you kissing me . . . and . . .'

'Amanda, don't do this. Stop torturing

yourself.' He walked across the room to her, and knelt next to her, his own body as splendid as hers was.

'I made love to you in the bed I shared with my husband.' Tears suddenly filled her eyes as he looked at her, refusing to regret he had done it. 'I can't believe I did that. My God, Jack, what kind of woman am I? I was married to the man for twenty-six years, and I made love with you in his bed.' She stood up and began pacing, as he tried not to let himself get angry.

'Don't make it sound like a crime, Amanda. You made love to me, and I made love to you. Amanda . . . I love you. For God's sake, we're grown-ups. You're still alive . . . my God, are you still alive! . . . and I'm more alive than I've been in twenty or thirty years, maybe in my entire lifetime.' The phone rang as he said it, and she made no move to answer. She didn't give a damn who was calling. All she could think of now was her betrayal of her husband.

'It's *his* bed. *Our* bed.' She was openly crying as he watched her pacing, but he was afraid to touch her.

'Then buy a new one,' he exploded at her

in spite of himself. 'It's *your* bed, for chris-
sakes. We'll do it on the floor next time . . .
or at my place . . .'

'You'd need an exorcist to purify your
bed!' she said in tears, and he laughed at her.

'Sweetheart, calm down . . . please . . . it's
just traumatic. It's the first time. I understand that. For chrissake, it's the best sex I
ever had . . . we love each other . . . we just
spent a week together, and we're crazy
about each other. What do you expect?
Christ, we saw every rotten movie in town.
What more do you want? A two-year
engagement?'

'Maybe. He isn't even dead a year yet.'
She sat down again, and cried like a kid, and
all he dared to do was hand her a tissue.

'The anniversary of his death is in three
days. We'll wait. We'll forget this ever
happened.'

'Good. We'll go back to being friends
again. We'll go to movies, and we won't
have sex again. Ever.' She was trying to
make it sound right with herself, but he was
only willing to go so far. He loved her too
much now to lose any part of her, particularly the parts he had discovered the

previous evening. They were pure legend.

'Let's not get crazy about this, shall we? We'll have a cup of coffee, we'll take a shower, and we'll go for a nice long walk, and you'll feel better.'

'I'm a whore, Jack. Just like all the other girls you sleep with.' The phone rang again, and they both ignored it.

'You are *not* a whore. And I don't sleep with anyone anymore except you. Do you understand that? I haven't looked at another woman since you came to the party at the store. You've ruined it for me, and I'm not going to let you ruin it for us too. We love each other, you have a right to that. Do you get that?'

'I don't have a right to sleep with anyone in my husband's bed.' She was distraught, and he was getting exasperated. But he walked over to her, firmly took her hand, and pulled her to her feet.

'Come on, let's get a cup of coffee.' Neither of them did anything to cover themselves and it never occurred to her that she was completely unembarrassed with him. It was as though they had been together forever.

He made her a cup of coffee standing naked in her kitchen, and handed it to her. She drank it black, and it burned going down, but she was a little calmer when they sat down together at the kitchen table. The kitchen was warm, and they sat there together, naked and drinking the hot coffee.

'Do you want the paper?' she asked matter-of-factly, suddenly feeling utterly schizophrenic. One moment she was completely at home with him, the next riddled with guilt and anguish. But she was feeling better again now, as he nodded.

'Sure. I'd like to see the paper.'

'I'll get it.'

She walked to the front door, coffee cup still in hand, opened the front door, and bent down to get the paper. Her front door was completely shielded from sight, and she knew no one would see her. But just as she bent down, she saw Jan's car drive in, and both Jan and Paul stared open-mouthed at her. She grabbed the paper, ran inside, slammed the door, and darted into the kitchen, dropping the paper and spilling her coffee. Jack looked at her in amazement.

'You have to leave!' She was staring at him in horror.

'*Now?*'

'Yes . . . oh shit . . . no, you can't . . . they're outside . . . go out the back door . . . it's behind the laundry.' She pointed in the general direction, waving frantically at him.

'Do you want me to leave like this? Or can I have a minute to put my clothes on?' But just as he asked the question, the door-bell rang, and Amanda nearly jumped a foot when she heard it.

'Oh my God . . . it's them . . . oh my God . . . Jack, what are we going to do?' She was in tears again, and this time he was laughing.

'Who is it? The Fuller Brush man? It's New Year's Day, for chrissake. Just ignore it.'

'It's our *children*, you moron. They *saw* me . . . when I went to get the paper.'

'Which children?'

'How many children do we have, for chrissake? It's Jan and Paul. They looked at me like they thought I was crazy.'

'Well, at least they got that right. Do you want me to answer the door and let them in?'

'No . . . I want you to leave . . . no . . . go hide in the bedroom.'

'Take it easy, sweetheart. Just tell them you're busy and they can come back later.'

'Okay.' He walked quickly toward her bedroom and closed the door, and with shaking hands, Amanda put the chain on, and pulled open the front door two inches to talk to her daughter. 'Hi.' She smiled brightly at them from behind the door. 'Happy New Year.'

'Mom, are you okay?'

'No, actually . . . yes . . . I'm fine. I'm busy . . . I have a headache . . . I'm hungover. Well, actually, I'm not. I had two glasses of Champagne last night. I think I'm allergic to it.'

'Mom, why were you naked on the doorstep? The neighbors might see you.'

'No one saw me.'

'We did.'

'I'm sorry. Well, thank you for coming by, sweetheart. Why don't you both come back later. Like tonight maybe. Or tomorrow. That would be perfect.' Her words were flying like bullets.

'Why can't we come in now?' Jan was

looking extremely worried, but Paul didn't want to push it. It was obviously a bad time. They tried to call first instead of just dropping by, but she hadn't answered the phone. He didn't even think she would be there.

'You can't come in now because of my . . . my headache . . . I'm sleeping.'

'You're not sleeping. You came out to pick up the paper. Mom, what's going on?'

'Nothing. I love you, call me next time you want to drop by. That's only polite, sweetheart . . . it's rude to just drop by . . . but I'm glad you did . . . I'll talk to you later . . .' She gave a little wave, and slammed the door on them. They stood on the doorstep for a minute and then turned and walked back to their car, looking puzzled. It was only when they got back in the car again that Jan looked at her husband with eyes filled with worry.

'Do you think my mother has a drinking problem?'

'Of course not. She just didn't want visitors at this hour. She has a right to that. Hell, maybe she's having an affair with someone, and the guy was still inside. She's still young enough to do stuff like that, you know . . . and your dad's been gone a year . . .' He looked amused by his own suggestion and Jan looked at him with outrage.

'Are you nuts? *My mother?* Do you actually think she would do that? Don't be ridiculous, just because your father never gets out of bed, at his age, doesn't mean my mother is going to behave that way. Paul, that's disgusting.'

'Stranger things have happened.' They were halfway through Bel Air by then, and Amanda was back in her bedroom. Jack had just turned on the shower, and he was grinning at her when she closed the bedroom door and leaned against it, as though fleeing from Interpol in a foreign country.

'What did you tell them? Did you tell them I said hi?' He was amused by her reaction.

'That is the most embarrassing thing that's ever happened to me in my entire life. My children will never forgive me.'

'What, for not letting them in? They should have called first.'

'They did. We didn't answer.'

'Then they shouldn't have come by.

Simple lesson. Do you want to take a shower?'

'No, I want to die.' She threw herself on her bed, and he sat down on the edge of it, and looked at her with deep affection.

'You put yourself through an awful lot of shit. Do you know that?'

'I deserve it,' she said, with tears in her eyes again. 'I'm a terrible person, and one day my children will know it.' And then she looked up at Jack with utter panic as she lay there. 'You won't tell Paul, will you? Oh my God . . . he'll tell Jan, and she'll tell Louise . . .'

'And the next thing you know, it'll be all over the papers. Hell, sweetheart, Paul and I always talk about the women I sleep with. You cannot take that away from me now. He'll think I'm too old to get it up . . .'

'Oh my God. Just kill me.' She rolled over on her stomach and put her face in the pillow while he grinned at her, and leaned over to kiss her spine in little tiny bits and inches. He kissed her all the way from the top of her neck to her bottom. And then he rubbed her back for a minute, and she rolled over slowly, with eyes that reminded him of the night before, and its effect on him was impressive, and instant. She reached her arms up to him, without saying anything, and he leaned down and kissed her, wanting her more than ever.

'I love you, you crazy thing . . .' It had been quite a morning.

'I love you too,' she whispered hoarsely, and pulled him toward her, but this time he looked down at her with a question.

'Wait a minute, before you walk me into this windmill again, would you like to go to another room, or get off the bed maybe . . . how about the couch or the bathtub?' he asked, as he gently felt her breasts, and then let his hands wander slowly downward.

'Never mind . . . it's okay . . .' She was smiling at him, and he laughed softly.

'You say that now . . . but what about later?' he whispered.

'You may have to make love to me again, just to calm me down . . . I think it has a soothing effect . . . it's very therapeutic . . .' she said, reaching out for him, and touching him with her lips until he moaned softly. 'I love you, Jack,' she said as she touched him again gently.

'I love you too, baby,' he said, and then their passion took over, and the insanity of the morning was instantly forgotten.

Chapter Seven

The rest of the New Year weekend went peacefully. Jan called her mother to check on her once, but Amanda was careful to reassure her. She called Louise too, and Jack called Julie, and then Jan and Paul to wish them a Happy New Year.

They stayed at Amanda's house on New Year's Day, made love again that afternoon, and that night went to Malibu to stay at his place. He had a small, comfortable house he had lived in for years, filled with well-loved, handsomely worn objects. There were deep leather chairs, tables covered with books, and some beautiful artwork. And she was surprised to find how at home she felt there.

They walked on the beach the next day, holding hands, and talked about their children. She was still worried about Jan, and hoped that she would be able to get pregnant.

'It's going to kill her if she doesn't,' Amanda said sadly. Having children had meant a lot to her, and she could easily imagine how traumatic it would be for Jan not to have them.

'What about you?' Jack asked her quietly on the way back to the house that afternoon.

'What about me?' She didn't understand the question.

'I don't want you to get pregnant,' he said honestly. 'I assume that's still an issue.' At fifty she was still on the cusp, but she was still so youthful in so many ways, he didn't think her body had changed yet. They had been careful anyway, and he was always responsible about the risk of AIDS, particularly given his previously somewhat libertine lifestyle. But he had been inactive for a while, mostly due to coincidence and circumstance, and the enormous demands of the Christmas season at Julie's. And ever since Amanda had crossed his path, he had had no interest in other women. But after his next AIDS test in the upcoming few days, he would like to give up condoms. But the last thing he wanted was to get her pregnant.

'I never thought of that,' she said, glancing up at him. She had been faithful to her husband for twenty-seven years, including the past year since he died. 'I can't imagine that at my age that's really a problem.' She hadn't gotten pregnant in over twenty years, not since a miscarriage she'd had when Jan was in kindergarten. She still remembered how disappointed she'd been, and how traumatic it was. But the thought of getting pregnant now seemed just plain silly, and she said so.

'Not half so silly as the sight of me running away to Brazil, or signing up as a merchant seaman,' he said bluntly, and she laughed, but he didn't. He'd been through that often enough over the years, women who claimed they were pregnant by him, or called to say they were late, or had forgotten to take the pill. It was a constant headache.

'Well, wait a while,' she smiled. 'One of

these days, I guess it won't be a problem.' She had thought about the change, but had no sign of it yet. Her doctor had said it might not happen for another year or two, or more. And unlike Jan, she had never had a problem getting pregnant.

'I can hardly wait,' he grinned, but he also agreed with her. Even if technically she still could get pregnant, at fifty it didn't seem very likely.

He cooked dinner for her that night, and they sat in front of the fire and watched the full moon hang over the ocean. It was easier for her here, she didn't have to think of Matt. Suddenly, it seemed like a whole new life with Jack Watson. It was amazing to her how, after the agony of the past year, and feeling as though her life had ended, she suddenly felt new again, and young and alive, and as though they had been meant for each other. She wondered if it was wrong to move on this way, but she knew that even if it was, she could no longer stop it. All she wanted was to be with him.

They felt like orphans when he went back to work. She didn't know what to do with herself, and he called her half a dozen times a day, and came by the house for lunch, to make love to her, or just to be with her. And when he went back to the store, she always thought of a multitude of reasons to call him, or to ask him something.

'Am I being a pest?' she asked one day. It was the second time she had called him in an hour. And he had only left her half an hour before that. They were going to their favorite Thai restaurant that evening. It was the perfect hideaway, and they knew they wouldn't run into anyone they knew there. She still didn't want to bump into their children. For the time being anyway, they had agreed to keep the romance a secret.

'You're never a pest. I love talking to you,' he smiled, putting his feet on his desk, as Gladdie came in with a cup of coffee and he thanked her. And then he had an idea. 'Why don't we go to San Francisco for the weekend? I have another site I want to look at up there, on Post Street.'

'I'd love that,' she said. They decided to go that week, and after he hung up, Jack buzzed for Gladdie. She came in with a worried frown, and her notepad.

'Something wrong?' He looked up at her.

In the past six months, they'd had six shipments held up in customs.

'I probably shouldn't ask,' she said with obvious concern, 'but are the kids okay?'

'Sure. Why?' He seemed surprised. Maybe she knew something he didn't.

'I've just noticed that Mrs Kingston has been calling you. I thought maybe . . . I wondered if Paul and Jan . . .' She was embarrassed to ask him. But they'd been married for three years, had no kids, and the world moved pretty fast in L.A. Maybe they were having problems, and Amanda and Jack were talking about them.

'No, they're fine,' he said cryptically with a smile, and as their eyes met, Gladdie suddenly wondered. No one else had been calling him since Christmas. No one important anyway, and even when they did call, he had Gladdie tell 'the girls' he was busy. It took her a minute, but sharp Gladdie got the picture.

'I see,' she said, suddenly amused. Amanda was quite something. But Gladdie would never have thought . . . life sure was funny.

'Just make sure no one else sees, Glad.

We don't want the kids to know yet.'

'Is it serious?' She was so close to him, and had worked for him for so long, that she dared to ask him questions no one else would. She was privy to a lot of information.

He hesitated for a beat before he answered. 'Could be . . .' And then he decided to be honest with her. He was crazy about Amanda. He had never felt like this for any woman since Dori, and Gladdie never knew her. All she knew were the collection of beautiful women who had filed through his life since she'd been there. 'Yes, it is.' Their eyes met as he nodded, and he looked happier and younger than she had ever seen him.

'Wow! That's pretty impressive. The kids'll be pleased, won't they?'

'I think so, but Amanda doesn't. We're going to wait a while to see how it goes before we tell them.' He asked her to make reservations for them then, in the presidential suite at the Fairmont, and an appointment with the realtor for the space on Post Street.

They flew up to San Francisco on Friday

afternoon, and as she walked through the fabulous suite with the unforgettable view, it felt like a honeymoon to Amanda. They had dinner at Fleur de Lys the first night, and room service on the second. And on Saturday they went to look at the commercial space, and he got excited about it in spite of himself. Despite the inevitable headaches of opening a new store, he was falling in love with the idea of bringing Julie's to San Francisco, and he said as much to Amanda.

'I must be nuts to even contemplate the headaches that go with it, at my age.' But lately he had been feeling about half his age, ever since he'd been with Amanda. And he couldn't stop talking about ideas for the new store, the architecture, the decor, the subtly different merchandise he wanted to sell here. He felt like a kid again, and he had always had a soft spot for San Francisco.

He wouldn't really mind spending some time there, particularly if Amanda joined him. They talked about it as they walked back to the hotel from Union Square. It was a steep walk up the hill, and they were breathless but exhilarated when they got back to the Fairmont. He was in great spirits, and so was she, especially when they went back to bed for the rest of the morning.

She hated to leave on Sunday afternoon. It had been the perfect weekend, and on Monday she had lunch with her daughters at the Bistro. Louise was looking well, but Jan seemed very down, and Amanda was worried that she had had bad news from her doctor. But before she could ask her daughters anything, they both commented on how well she looked.

'You look terrific, Mom,' Jan said, looking relieved. She had been worried about her again ever since New Year's. Maybe it had just been a bad morning, but her mother's behavior had been so odd.

'Thank you, sweetheart. So do you.' But Jan's eyes looked so sad. They were halfway through lunch before she decided to talk about it.

'Well Paul finally went to the doctor,' she said, after a pause, and then tears filled her eyes as she continued. Amanda reached out and touched her hand, and for once even Louise looked worried about her.

'And?' her sister prompted her. 'Is he sterile?'

'No,' she said, wiping away a tear, 'he's fine. And so am I. They have no idea why we haven't gotten pregnant. They just said it might take more time, or maybe it'll never happen. They said that even perfectly healthy people don't get pregnant some-times. No one knows why. I guess it's just not meant to happen.' She started to cry and Amanda reached into her handbag for a tissue. Jan blew her nose and then sighed and went on. 'Maybe we'll just never have kids. I asked Paul about adoption again, and he said he'd rather not have children. He only wants a baby that's part of his biolog-ical family, so that rules out any kind of adoption.' She looked devastated and Amanda's heart felt as though it were breaking.

'He might change his mind, sweetheart. And you might still get pregnant. I'm sure you will. Sometimes it takes people a very long time. And then you'll probably have four in a row and wish you could stop it.' They both tried to cheer her up, but it was obvious from the way she looked at them that Jan didn't believe them. And when Amanda told Jack about it that night, he was sorry for both of them.

'Poor kids. Christ, and when I think of all the times I've teased him. He must be ready to kill me.'

'I don't know if he's as upset about it as she is,' Amanda said pensively, she was deeply worried about her daughter. She had looked so down about it, and so hopeless.

'Maybe if they forget about it for a while, it will just happen.'

'That's what I told her. But I think in circumstances like this, it's all you think about. I have friends who went through it.' He nodded, and they talked of other things. They always seemed to have a thousand things to say to each other. He talked to her a lot about the store, and asked her opinion about lines he was buying, particularly the high-end ones. She had great taste and a good eye, and she had already made some useful suggestions. And now he was particularly interested in her input in the store he was planning to open in San Francisco. The opening probably wouldn't be for another year or more, but he wanted to get started.

She liked going to the store on Rodeo to visit him, and Gladdie was impressed each time she saw her. There was no question that Amanda was very striking, but she was also very human, and the two women chatted sometimes. Gladdie was their only confidante and she loved knowing their secret.

The entire month flew by. They spent a weekend in Palm Springs, and in February he took her skiing in Aspen. They had a fabulous time, and ran into a number of his friends, all of whom recognized her. They were enormously impressed to see him with her, and much to her chagrin, there was a small blurb about them in the Aspen paper.

'I hope no one calls L.A. This is no way to tell the children.'

'Maybe we ought to tell them ourselves one of these days.' They had been inseparable for nearly two months now. And they'd been careful to avoid the L.A. press, by staying away from the kind of events that they covered.

But when she had lunch with Jan and Louise again, Jan was still so depressed that Amanda didn't have the heart to tell them.

It seemed selfish somehow to brag about her own happiness when Jan was so unhappy. The only time she smiled was when she laughed and said something about Paul's father.

'Paul thinks he has a serious girlfriend. He's really settled down. Paul says he looks half his age, and goes around grinning like a Cheshire cat. But he doesn't say anything about her. She's probably some nineteen-year-old bimbo. But whoever she is, she seems to be keeping him happy and out of trouble.'

'Knowing him,' Louise said with a look of disdain, 'it's probably a set of quintuplets.'

'Now, girls, poor man . . . he has a right to his own life,' Amanda said nervously, feeling awkward.

'When did you get so charitable about him?' Louise asked, and then the conversation turned to other things. Amanda felt as though she had swallowed her napkin as she looked at them, wondering how she was ever going to tell them.

Amanda told Jack about it that night, and he laughed at her. 'You act like you expect them to think you're a virgin.'

'Worse. I'm their mother. You know what that means. No sex, no boys, no hanky-panky, except with their father.'

'They're adults. They can take it.'

'Maybe.' But he hadn't convinced her. She knew her daughters.

They were staying in Malibu a lot these days, the weather was warm, the beach was heavenly, and she loved being in his house with him. Even after the initial shock of sleeping with him, she was still a little uncomfortable in her own house. It was easier staying at Jack's place. And she cooked breakfast for him every morning, before he left for work and she went back to her own place.

She was scrambling eggs for him the week before Valentine's Day when he wandered into the kitchen, and was surprised to see her looking unhappy.

'Something wrong?' She was always so sunny in the morning that it surprised him. He had the paper under one arm, and he stopped to kiss her on his way to get coffee.

'I don't know . . . not really . . . I don't feel well.' She'd had a headache the day before, and she was feeling slightly queasy.

But lately, after thinking it would never happen to her, she had begun to think her body was going through changes. The signs had been very slight, but nonetheless she had noticed and wondered about it. 'Louise's kids had the flu last week when I dropped by. I probably caught it from them.' She glanced over her shoulder and smiled at him. 'It's not terminal. I'll survive it.'

'I hope so,' he said, looking happy and relaxed as he handed her a mug of coffee. She set it down, and finished his eggs and toast. She had made a big bowl of fruit for him, and she nibbled on a piece of dry toast as she sat down at the table with him, with her coffee. She took a sip, and suddenly just the smell of it overwhelmed her, and he saw it. 'You okay?'

'I'm fine. But I think there's something wrong with the coffee. Has it been here for a while?'

He shook his head, and then picked up the paper. 'I just bought it. Same brand I always buy. I thought you liked it.' He looked disappointed. He liked pleasing her and doing whatever he could to make her happy.

'I do like it usually. It must be me. I'll be fine in a minute.' But after he left for work, she lay down, and she still felt queasy when she drove home later that morning. He called her there and offered to meet her for lunch somewhere, but she told him she thought she should try to sleep off her headache. And by that evening, when he picked her up, she was feeling better. And the next day she was fine. It obviously had been the flu. The next morning even the coffee tasted fine, and she was her usual bright self. Until Valentine's Day, when he brought her a five-pound box of chocolate.

'Good lord! I'm going to weigh four hundred pounds if I eat this.'

'Good. You need it.' He had sent her two dozen long-stemmed red roses that morning, and he was taking her to L'Orangerie for dinner, and he said he didn't give a damn if their children saw them. He opened the box of chocolates for her, and she picked one of the ones she liked best, but the moment she put it in her mouth, she couldn't eat it. He saw the look on her face, and raised an eyebrow. 'Are you feeling sick again?' She'd been fine all week, but just as the coffee had the week before, the chocolate made her feel queasy.

'I'm fine,' she reassured him, and forced herself to eat the chocolate. But when he ordered caviar for her at L'Orangerie, she got that look again, and no matter how hard she tried, she just couldn't swallow it, although she usually loved it.

'I think you should go to a doctor.' He looked worried. She was normally so healthy, and so exuberant, that her obviously feeling so ill frightened him more than he wanted to tell her.

'Louise's kids had this thing for three weeks. Honestly, it's nothing.' But she looked green, and she scarcely touched her dinner.

But in spite of his concerns about her, it was a nice evening anyway. They were both in good spirits, and that night they stayed at her place. They made love when they got home, and it was the happiest Valentine's Day she could remember.

And the next morning, sitting in her kitchen, she finally agreed to tell their children.

'Why not share our happiness with

them?' he asked. What they had together was such a wondrous thing that he wanted them to know about it.

'Maybe you're right,' she agreed. 'They're old enough to deal with it.'

'They better be. We're grandparents, and if they can't deal with knowing about us, they deserve a spanking.'

That afternoon, Jack called Julie, and Amanda called Louise and Jan and they invited them all to dinner at Amanda's. She was going to cook dinner for them, and then afterward, over Champagne, they would tell them. And at least then, as Jack pointed out, they could come out of hiding and go anywhere they wanted. They just wanted them to know that they were happy and in love. There had never been any talk of marriage between them, and Amanda knew full well how strongly Jack felt against it. His first wife had completely cured him.

They set the date for the next week, which, miraculously, suited everyone. Jack said he'd bring the Champagne, and Amanda was busy planning the dinner. There was something very touching about it, and very poignant. And she couldn't help thinking about Matt that afternoon, and how her life had changed. She had loved him deeply for so many years, but he was gone, and she wasn't. Her life had moved on. And hard as it was to believe after so long, she was very much in love with Jack Watson.

She worked frantically all week organizing the dinner and by the time the day came she was a nervous wreck. But when Jack arrived with the wine, the table was set, dinner was well on its way, and she looked lovely.

'I hate to say it, but you don't look like anyone's mother. Certainly not a bunch of kids the age of ours.'

'Thank you,' she smiled, and kissed him, and she could feel his desire for her as he held her. She laughed as he looked at his watch and then at her, and she shook her head. 'We don't have time, you monster.'

'Well, if you open the door naked again, we won't have to tell them anything. Look at it that way.'

'Later,' she promised, and kissed him again. Just touching her drove him crazy.

Julie and Louise and their husbands

arrived on time, and Jan and Paul came shortly after. Everyone looked nice, and they all commented on how pretty the house looked. Amanda had put flowers everywhere, and there seemed to be an aura of celebration. But both Jan and Louise looked enormously surprised to see Jack there. He came out of the kitchen, opening a bottle of wine, and greeted everyone with ease, and then kissed Jan, and his daughter. Julie had already figured it out by then. She had been wondering all week why he had invited her to come to dinner at Amanda's, and she had been very suspicious. After that, it wasn't hard to deduce, for her at least, what he was going to tell them. All she wanted to know was if they were getting married, but she decided to wait and see what they told them.

Jan was very cool to him, and Louise was downright rude, and openly ignored him. And everyone except Julie looked worried. She had a live-and-let-live attitude about everything that had always made everyone love her. She had a happy marriage, good kids, and she had always loved her father, in spite of his outrageous behavior. Paul had always been far more critical of him, and Julie had always suspected he was jealous. Paul was so much milder, more afraid, and although he was handsome, he had never had their father's startling good looks. And as he sat down in Amanda's living room, Paul already looked angry, and he and his wife were exchanging suspicious glances.

The conversation at dinner was strained, although the dinner was good, and it was obvious that Amanda had gone to a lot of trouble. And Jack did his best to help her, he talked easily with everyone, and tried to draw them out in conversation, but it was like trying to drag a grand piano. And finally at dessert, he poured the Champagne, looked around the room, and said that there was something he and Amanda wanted to tell them.

'Oh God, I can't believe this,' Louise said loudly.

'Why don't you wait until we tell you?' Jack said pleasantly, and she looked daggers at him. She had never liked him. And neither had Amanda – she would have liked to remind her of it at that moment.

'Your mother and I,' he glanced at Jan and

Louise, and then at his own son and daughter, 'Amanda and I have been seeing each other for a while. We enjoy each other's company a great deal, and we're very happy together, and we wanted you to know it. That's all, nothing more than that, but we thought you should know what we were up to, and we were both sure,' he smiled at the woman who had brought him so much happiness in the last two and a half months, 'that you would all be happy for us.'

'Well, don't be,' Louise said tartly, and Amanda looked both crushed and startled. 'This is ridiculous. You brought us here to tell us that? That you're sleeping with each other, and we're supposed to congratulate you for it? That's disgusting.'

'So is your attitude, Louise,' Amanda said firmly. 'That's an extremely rude thing to say.' She glanced apologetically at Jack, and then back at her daughter.

'This is an extremely rude thing to do,' Louise said, with open fury, 'to bring us here, to my father's house, to tell us that you two are having an affair. My God, don't you have any decency left, Mom? What about Daddy?'

'What about Daddy?' Amanda said, looking right at her daughter. 'I loved your father very much, and you know it. But Daddy's gone, Louise. It was a terrible shock for all of us, me more than anyone. There were times last year when I thought I wouldn't survive it, when I even wanted to kill myself because I didn't want to live without him. But I have a right to live my life again, and Jack has been wonderful to me.' She reached out and touched his hand, and glanced at him. He was looking upset and worried. 'He's a kind, decent man, and he makes me very happy, Louise.'

'Why don't you just tell us about your sex life, Mom? And how long has this been going on? Did it start before Daddy died? Were you having an affair with him then? Is that it?'

'Louise! How dare you say that! You know that's not true. I started seeing Jack after Jan took me to a party at Julie's.'

'Oh my God . . . I can't believe this . . .' Jan looked at her mother and started to cry, and Paul was shooting dark, angry looks at his father. Jerry, Louise's husband, was staring at his dinner plate, and wishing he didn't have to be there. This was not his problem.

'Why don't you all just calm down for a minute, and let's all act like grown-ups, why don't we?' Julie's was the voice of reason, and Amanda was suddenly grateful to her, although she scarcely knew her.

'I think that's a good idea,' Jack said in the brief breach when everyone was marshaling their forces. 'Let's have some Champagne.' He poured for everyone, and the entire room sat in stony silence. He picked up his glass, and held it up to Amanda. 'To you, sweetheart, thank you for a beautiful dinner.' There were tears in her eyes, and no one touched their glasses.

'So when are you two getting married?' Louise was looking at them with revulsion and open fury.

'We're not.' Jack spoke for them. 'There's no reason to. We're not your age. We're not going to have kids. We can have a good life together without making it legal.' Julie smiled, she knew him well, and how much he hated even the idea of marriage. 'No one's going to lose any money on this deal, if that's what you're all worried about.' He was more than a little annoyed at them, and Amanda could hear it. 'No one is going to lose anything. But what you've gained is two happy parents. We love you, and we wanted to share our happiness with you. It doesn't seem like a lot to ask, to ask you all to be happy for us, and gracious about it.' He was furious at their collective reaction.

'How could you do this, Mom?' Jan asked with tears streaming down her cheeks. 'You *hate* him!' she said, looking daggers at Jack, and he laughed and took Amanda's hand in his own.

'I don't think so, Jan. And we care a lot about your happiness and Paul's. We talk about you all the time . . . that's why it was important to us to tell you.'

'Well, I think you're both disgusting and pathetic,' Louise said, standing up from the table. 'You would think that people your age could keep your pants on, for chrissake. My father's hardly been dead a year, and I guess Little Old Hot Pants Mom just couldn't wait to get out and party.'

'Louise!' Amanda stood up with a look of fury. 'Do you remember how depressed I

163

was, and how worried you all were about me?'

'Little did we know what you'd do when you recovered. Well,' she said derisively, with a pointed look at her husband, which brought him to his feet beside her, 'it was certainly a great evening, and I hope you two little rabbits will be very happy.' With that, she strode to the door, picked up her jacket on the way out, and slammed the door behind them, as Jan burst into tears again and Paul held her.

'Jan, please,' Amanda said, with a look of sorrow. It had been a terrible evening for all of them, but mostly for Jack, and for her.

'Mom, how could you do this? Why did you tell us? Don't you know how embarrassing this is for us? We don't want to know about it.'

'Why not?' Jack asked without embarrassment. 'Why shouldn't your mother share her life with you? Don't you want her to be happy?' He sounded so reasonable that Jan looked at him and stopped crying.

'Why can't she be happy alone? Why can't she just remember my father?'

'Because she's a young, vital, beautiful

woman, Jan. Why should she be alone? Is that what you would do if something happened to Paul?'

'That's different.'

'Why? Because you're younger than we are? Even people our age have a right not to be alone, to companionship, to happiness, to love . . .'

'This isn't about "love,"' Paul said darkly. 'We all know that about you, Dad, don't we?'

'Maybe you don't know me as well as you think you do, Son.'

'I'm happy for you, Dad,' Julie said quietly, and came around the table to kiss him, and then she went and did the same to Amanda, and there were tears in Amanda's eyes as she thanked her. She was the only one who had been decent to them. The others had been a nightmare.

'I'm sorry this has been so hard for all of you,' Amanda said quietly, dabbing at her eyes with her napkin. She felt as though she were going to start sobbing any minute, and she didn't want to give them that satisfaction, but it was incredibly hard not to. 'We didn't want to upset you, but it seemed more honest to tell you. I didn't want to lie to you.' She looked at Jan, and in the same instant Jan realized that Paul had been right on New Year's Day with his outrageous suggestion. There had been a man in the house. It was Paul's father. She closed her eyes in horror.

'We hope you'll adjust in time,' Jack said quietly, and Paul said something in a whisper to Jan, and they both got up and left the table, and put their coats on.

'We're going,' Jan said, looking like an angry child from the doorway. It was exactly the way she had looked when she was five years old and getting ready to have a tantrum.

'I love you,' Amanda said sadly from the table, too beaten to get up, or try to stop her. And the door closed softly behind them, as Julie and her husband stood up, and she came around again to her father. She was a pretty girl and she looked just like him.

'I'm sorry, Dad. They were awful.'

'They sure were.' He glanced at Amanda with a worried expression. She had predicted that it would be hard for them, but neither of them had expected this onslaught.

'They'll get over it. I think part of it is just the shock of knowing that their dad has been replaced in some ways,' and then she smiled, 'and it's hard to think of your parents having fun . . . and having sex.' She blushed. 'You guys are supposed to be institutions, not people,' she said wisely, and her father smiled proudly at her. She was a terrific young woman, and in their own way, so were the others, but they didn't have the largeness of spirit that she did.

'I guess it was too much for them. You were right,' he glanced at Amanda, 'we shouldn't have told them.'

'I'm glad we did,' she said, and totally surprised him. She left her place at the table and came to stand next to him, with Julie and her husband. 'We did the right thing, and if they can't live with it or even try to deal with it, then that's not our problem. We have a right to more in our lives than just being parents. The only thing that bothers me is that I never realized I had such totally selfish children. But I'm not giving up my life for them. I'm not going to stop being there for them, or loving them, and if they can't be there for me, then that's their loss.' Julie put her arms around her then, and Amanda's chin quivered as she held her. And a few minutes later, Julie and her husband left, and Jack took Amanda in his arms and she sobbed piteously. And he felt desperately sorry for her. The evening had been such a disappointment.

'I'm so sorry, sweetheart. What a bunch of rotten kids we have,' he said, with a smile. But he was angry that they had hurt her.

'Yours are fine, or Julie at least. Mine were the ones who were awful.'

'They want their daddy. And they don't think you have a right to a life with anyone else. It's pretty simple. I didn't take it personally. I understand it. But I hate what they did to you. They'll get over it.'

'Maybe.' She didn't sound convinced, but oddly enough it didn't make her regret anything they had done. It only made her feel closer to Jack, and that night they went to Malibu, after she cleaned up the dining room and put the dishes in the dishwasher.

She didn't want to be in the house where her children had been so unpleasant to them. She wanted to be at Jack's, in his big comfortable bed, in his arms, and she wanted to forget everything that had happened.

She still looked sad when they went to bed that night, and he held her in his arms, and they talked about it for a long time. He wished that there was some way he could make it better.

'Give them time, sweetheart. I guess even at their age, it's a big adjustment.'

'They're happy. Why can't I be?'

'Because you're their mom. You heard what Julie said. Parents, and certainly people our age, aren't supposed to have sex, God forbid. They think it's disgusting.'

'They should only know . . . it's a lot better than it was at their age.'

'Shhh . . . let's keep that a secret!' he said, and kissed her tenderly, and a moment later she could feel how aroused he was and how much he wanted her, and she wanted him just as badly. They made love hungrily, and afterward, he heard a soft chuckle in the darkness. 'What are you laughing at?' But he was pleased that she was obviously feeling better.

'That morning on New Year's Day when Jan saw me naked on the doorstep, and I wouldn't let her in. She must be having a fit over it. I guess I looked pretty silly.'

'You looked pretty good to me . . . "silly" isn't a word I would have used to describe you.' But she had been silly that day, and they both knew it. She had been in a total panic.

'Maybe we should put the children up for adoption,' she said sleepily, turning on her side toward him, as he kissed her.

'That's a great idea. We'll invite them to dinner and tell them.'

'Hmmm . . . great idea . . . you bring . . . the . . . Champagne . . .' But she was already asleep in his arms as she said it, and he looked at her with a slow smile. She was quite a woman, and he wouldn't have given her up for anything in the world, no matter what their kids said, or how angry they were at them. He was going to hang on to her now for dear life.

Chapter Eight

The rest of February disappeared in the blink of an eye, and in March the children were still cool to Amanda. She and Jack talked about it from time to time, and he knew how much it bothered her, but there was nothing they could do about it, except wait for them to come around once they'd adjusted. Jan hardly ever called her mother anymore, and Louise was openly hostile to her whenever Amanda went to visit the children. In her case, her reaction was particularly hard to understand, since she had never gotten along with her father.

But Amanda and Jack were so busy these days that at least most of the time, she was distracted. But there was no denying that her daughters' reaction to them was taking a toll on her. She seemed to have stomach problems all the time, and constant indigestion. And Jack was still urging her to go to see a doctor.

'This has gone on for a while. I think you should check it out. You could be getting an ulcer.'

'I could be.' She hadn't been able to drink coffee in weeks, and she had been exhausted ever since the unhappy meeting with her children, but she also knew that it was very obviously due to her own emotions. She had hated to see them all so angry. And once in a while now, she had nightmares about Matthew. He always accused her of something in her dreams, and any psychiatrist probably would have told her she felt guilty. But not enough so to change her feelings. She was more in love with Jack than ever. And the romance had blossomed.

He invited her to the Academy Awards in March. They were early this year, and he was always invited by his more important clients. Amanda hadn't been to them in years, not since she won one herself, and she was excited about going with him. And he ordered a dress for her from Julie's. It was a fabulous white satin Jean-Louis Scherrer with black-beaded shoulders and a small train that lingered elegantly behind her. And when the big night came, and he picked her up, she took his breath away. She looked every inch a queen, and the big star she had once been. It was as though, with him, she had regained what she had once been, and added to it. In the past few months, she had acquired a patina of happiness over her old glamour.

'Wow!' he said admiringly. The dress hadn't looked half as beautiful when he first saw it. On her, it looked exquisite, and it molded every inch of her fabulous figure. Her long blond hair was piled high on her head in soft curls and a French twist. And she was wearing diamond earrings and a diamond bracelet. She looked truly splendid.

'You look incredible!' he said with a low whistle. Her skin was as creamy pale as the white satin. 'The photographers are going to go crazy.'

'I doubt that,' she said modestly, and took

his arm as they walked out to the waiting limousine. He was carrying her short white mink jacket.

When they stepped out of the car at the Shrine Auditorium, the crowd cheered for her. They recognized her immediately, and shouted her name, and just as he had predicted, a wall of photographers engulfed them. He could feel her hand shake a little as he took it in his own and he smiled down at her. Her husband had kept her away from all this for more than twenty years, and now suddenly she was back, and no longer accustomed to it. There was an elegant, gentle grace about her that made her even more alluring.

'Are you all right?' he asked, looking at her with concern. She looked a little nervous, but she smiled up at him and nodded.

They made their way through the press, and the crowds in the lobby, and then slowly to their seats in the auditorium, among all the stars that the entire country and world adored and longed for. Several people waved at them, and Jack smiled broadly at a number of his clients. He looked proud and at ease, and completely comfortable to be there.

And then the ceremony began, and as usual, it took forever. The TV cameras panned across them constantly, and they all felt as though they'd been there all year by the time it was over. The award for Best Actor had gone to a new face this year, and the Oscar for Best Actress had gone to an old favorite who had held her prize aloft and gave a whoop of glee while everyone got to their feet and cheered her.

'*Finally!*' she said with a huge smile. It had taken her forty years to win it. And Amanda couldn't help remembering how she had felt nearly thirty years before on a night like this. It had been one of the most exciting things that had ever happened to her. And now, it seemed so long ago, and still a warm memory, but so much less important.

'What was it like for you?' he asked with a smile, as they left the auditorium through throngs that barely seemed to move. It was worse than riding the New York subway.

'It was incredible,' she said, smiling at him. 'I thought I was going to explode with excitement. I never even thought I'd get the nomination, let alone win it. I was twenty-two . . . it was terrific.' It was nice to be able to admit how much it had meant to her. Her husband had never liked it when she talked about it.

They barely moved ten feet in the next ten minutes, and people kept coming up to them, to talk and comment on the awards and just to say hello, as they all waited to leave the theater. The press was complicating everything, stopping stars as they left, and interviewing them right in the midst of the crowd, creating bottlenecks that couldn't be passed through.

'Think we'll ever get out of here tonight?' Jack Nicholson asked as they pressed by him, and Amanda shook her head with a smile. She had never met him, but admired him greatly.

'Do you know him?' Jack asked with interest.

'No. But I like his movies.'

'We should rent yours sometime,' he said. He had never thought of it, she spoke so little about her career. Matthew had taught her not to.

'How depressing,' she laughed. 'I can't

176

think of anything worse than seeing what I looked like thirty years ago, and then having to look at myself in the mirror. Besides, I wasn't much of an actress.'

Jack shook his head at her modesty, and they moved a few inches and then were trapped in total gridlock, and the heat and crowd around them was oppressive. She felt as though she were going to melt, and she could just imagine what Jack felt like in his tuxedo. But in spite of the discomforts people were in good spirits, and everyone was laughing and talking and waving at friends they couldn't get to. But just as Jack saw one of his favorite clients about twenty feet away from them, Amanda began to feel dizzy. Jack was mouthing bits of a conversation and pointing to the exits as he rolled his eyes, and Amanda suddenly heard a buzzing in her ears, and her head started pounding. But Jack hadn't noticed. After a while, she tugged at his sleeve, and when he looked back at her, he was startled to see that she had gone deathly pale in just a few minutes.

'I'm not feeling very well,' she whispered to him, 'it's so hot in here . . . I'm sorry . . .'

'Do you want to sit down?' He couldn't blame her. It was giving him a headache too, and the camera lights still focused on them weren't helping, and the heat was very oppressive. It was also impossible to reach the seats again. They were trapped in the aisles, and they would have had to fly to get there. Jack realized that as soon as he'd said it, and he glanced at Amanda's face again. She was suddenly not just pale, she was green, and she was blinking as though she was having trouble seeing. He got a firm grip on her arm, and tried to guide her out of the aisle through the crowd, but it was hopeless.

'Jack . . .' she said weakly, looking at him, and as he looked at her, her eyelids fluttered, her eyes rolled back, and she fainted, and he just managed to catch her as a ripple went through the crowd immediately around her, and a woman gasped as she saw it. Jack was holding Amanda in his arms, and somebody started shouting. People were trying to move for them, everyone was asking what had happened, and Jack was worried sick about her.

'Give us some air, please . . . move back!'

A man next to him was shouting, 'Call the paramedics!' Suddenly it was hysteria all around them, and Amanda was still lifeless in his arms. He swept her off her feet, and her head rested against his chest, just as two ushers appeared out of nowhere with smelling salts and an ice pack, asking what happened. But at the same moment, Amanda began stirring, and glanced up at Jack, with no idea of what had happened to her.

'You fainted, sweetheart . . . it's the heat . . . just take it easy . . .' And like the Red Sea parting, the crush of people moved just enough to let him carry her to a row of seats and he set her down gently. And within seconds, a crew of paramedics arrived and looked down at Amanda, as Jack explained that she had fainted.

'How do you feel now?' one of the paramedics asked her.

'Incredibly foolish,' Amanda said, smiling weakly at Jack with a look of apology. 'I'm really sorry.'

'Don't be silly,' he said, looking worried. She was still light-headed and he could see it. She didn't look as though she could have stood up and walked out of the theater, but she wanted to try it.

'We'll get a wheelchair,' one of the ushers offered, and Amanda looked horrified. 'No, really . . . I'm fine . . . We'll go when the crowd thins out a little.'

But the ushers offered to take her out a back exit instead, and Jack urged them to do that. The paramedics said she was free to go, as long as she felt up to it, but they suggested she see her doctor in the morning, and Jack seconded the motion with a grim expression. He had been telling her that for a month, and she wouldn't listen.

He put a powerful arm around her waist, and half carried her to the exit between the ushers, and a moment later they were out in the air, and she felt better. She took a deep breath and thanked everyone, and apologized profusely for the trouble she'd caused them. She was deeply grateful that they hadn't been spotted by the press. There was no one waiting for them, and Jack left her with the ushers just long enough to find the limo, and then came back and got her into it. Five minutes later, they were driving away, and she was leaning against the backseat with an exhausted expression.

'I'm so sorry,' she said for the ten thou-
sandth time. 'I don't know what happened.'

'That's why you have to see the doctor.'

'I think it was just the heat and the crowd.
I couldn't breathe all of a sudden,' she said,
sipping a glass of water he handed her from
the bar in the limo. 'People always faint at
the Academy Awards, Jack. I'm just sorry I
did it this year.'

'Well, don't do it again!' He leaned over
and kissed her. She still looked beautiful, but
very pale. And he was very worried about
her. 'You scared me to death in there. It's a
good thing it was so damn crowded, so you
couldn't fall when you fainted. At least you
didn't hit your head or anything.'

'Thank you, Jack.' He took such good
care of her, and when they got back to his
house, she took off her dress, and he tucked
her into bed, and she looked like a teenager
with her fancy hairdo and her blond hair and
her makeup and diamond earrings still on,
and then she giggled. 'I can't believe I did
that.'

'It was very dramatic,' he chided, loosen-
ing his tie, and smiling at her. 'Can I get you

anything? Water? Tea?' She puckered her brows as she thought about it and then smiled at him. She was starving.

'How about ice cream?'

'Ice cream?' He looked startled at the question. 'You must be feeling better at least. I'll see what we've got. What flavor?'

'Mmm . . . coffee.'

'Coming right up.' He saluted, and came back with a bowlful two minutes later, and one for him too, and he sat on the bed next to her as they ate it. 'Maybe you were just hungry,' he said hopefully, but he didn't think so. She'd been looking pale lately, and he'd been trying not to see it. She'd been looking great for a while, and now lately, she looked tired. But he knew she was still upset about her children, and they weren't making it any easier for her. They refused to offer any acknowledgment whatsoever, let alone approval, of her relationship with Jack Watson.

But Jack had decided to take the matter in hand himself the next day. As soon as they got up, he asked her for the number and called her doctor. He told the nurse what had happened the night before, and asked for an appointment that morning for Amanda Kingston.

'And you are?' the nurse asked pointedly. She was new there, and she didn't know Amanda.

'Mr Watson,' he said, writing down the time of the appointment.

'Are you Mrs Kingston's husband?'

'No . . . I'm her friend. I'll be there with her.'

'Fine, Mr Watson. We'll see you at eleven.' The appointment was in Beverly Hills, and after he brought Amanda a cup of tea and told her about it, he decided to go for a walk on the beach by himself. She seemed happy to stay in bed that morning, and he suspected correctly that she did not feel as well as she pretended. But he didn't challenge her about it. They would know more, hopefully, when they went to the doctor.

But as he walked down the beach alone, his thoughts seemed to fly in all directions, and he began to run, as though to escape the terror of what he was thinking. Anything was possible . . . she could have a brain tumor . . . bone cancer . . . something that had grown and spread and metastasized without their even knowing it was there. He could only imagine the worst scenarios and when he finally stopped running and sat down, he realized he was crying. But it was happening to him all over again. He had found the one woman in millions he could love, and something terrible was happening to her. He was terrified she was dying. It was going to be just like Dori, he thought as he sobbed, he was going to lose her, and he couldn't bear it. He put his face down on his knees, and huddled there, crying like a child, and he couldn't even turn to her for comfort. He didn't want to frighten her, but more than anything he didn't want to lose her.

He was gone for nearly an hour, and when he came back she was dressed and waiting, and she looked better than she had earlier, but he was still worried. Nothing was going to reassure him now except the word from the doctor that she wasn't suffering from anything terminal, or malignant. He just couldn't stand it. But he spoke to her with forced cheer, as he put his jacket on and looked at his watch. It was time to leave, in case they ran into traffic.

'All set?' he asked nervously. He didn't know why, but he felt as though he were going to the guillotine. It was as though his life was never going to be the same again, and he was never going to come back here to this house again, in the same easy spirit. He was bracing himself for the worst news he could imagine, because he loved her.

'Sweetheart,' she said gently, before they left, looking up at him with eyes that tore his heart out, 'I'm all right. I promise. They'll probably just tell us I have an ulcer. I had one years ago, when the girls were small, and these days that's pretty simple to deal with. A couple of pills, and it'll disappear like magic.'

'You should have gone weeks ago,' he reproached her, as they walked to his Ferrari.

'I was busy,' she said primly, and got in beside him. She loved riding in the car with him usually, but this morning on the way into town, his fast turns and sharp moves made her feel sick, but she didn't dare tell him. She knew he would have been even more frantic.

Her doctor was in the medical building at 435 North Bedford, the waiting room was full when they got there, and it seemed to take forever. Jack glanced at magazines, and Amanda just sat there with her eyes closed, waiting. He looked over at her from time to time and he hated her pallor and the obvious look of discomfort. He knew she wasn't in pain, he had asked her that, but she just didn't feel well. And there was no way she could still sell him the story about catching the flu from Louise's kids, that had been more than a month before. This was something far more scary.

A nurse in the doorway finally called her name, and Jack watched as she went in, and smiled at her encouragingly when she glanced over her shoulder. She was nervous too, but they were trying to put a good face on it for each other. But neither of them were convincing.

And even Amanda had to admit that it was a relief to finally sit there with her doctor. He was kind, and a familiar face, and she had gone to him for nearly twenty years. He had also been Matt's doctor, and he asked her now if she was very lonely. She was embarrassed to tell him about Jack, although he was sitting in the waiting room large as life, so she just nodded, and began telling him her symptoms. She told him about the flu the month before, the occasional queasiness, and her absolute inability to drink coffee or eat chocolate, which she took as a sure sign of an ulcer.

He asked her if she'd seen her gynecologist recently and had a mammogram and a Pap smear, and she admitted that she hadn't. She had been due for both when Matt died so suddenly, and just hadn't bothered since then.

'You should, you know,' he scolded her. 'At your age, you should have both every year.' And she promised that she'd take care of it immediately, and then he asked her if she had any warning signs of menopause, and she explained that lately she was beginning to think that she had some.

He nodded. At fifty-one, that didn't surprise him. 'Hot flashes?'

'No, not yet. I'm just tired a lot, and irregular.' A number of her friends complained of fatigue all the time, although she'd never had that before. But lately, she was constantly exhausted. At first, she had just thought it was a side effect of her new love life. But in the past few weeks, she didn't think so. She could hardly put one foot in front of the other.

He asked her about a lot of other things, and he was inclined to agree with her. Probably the onset of menopause, and possibly an ulcer.

'I'm going to send you to the hospital for a sonogram,' he explained to her. 'Let's see what that shows, we can always do a GI series after that if it's indicated, but let's not rush into anything yet. And I want you to see your gynecologist tomorrow. He can give you some hormone replacement therapy that may pick you up almost immediately. It's worth talking to him about.' She listened and nodded, as he handed her a slip of paper, and told her where to go at Cedars Sinai. And he told her they'd either give her the results there if the radiologist was there, or he'd call her the next day to tell her if she had an ulcer. 'All right?' He smiled at her and stood up, and walked her to the door of his office. And then she went to find Jack, who looked grim as he waited, but he broke into a smile the minute he saw her. He looked like a kid who had lost his mother and finally found her. She had been gone for nearly an hour.

'What did he say?'

'Pretty much what I thought. Some . . . um . . . changes in my body . . . and maybe an ulcer. I have to go to the hospital for a sonogram now. Do you want me to drop you off at the store on the way? I hate to waste your whole day with this nonsense. He took forever.'

'I'm coming with you,' Jack said firmly, but he was relieved that nothing worse had turned up, at least not so far.

'Did he think there was anything to worry about?' Jack asked as they got to the car, but she shook her head, looking a little mournful.

'He thought I might need hormones. That's depressing enough. I feel like an old woman.'

'Oh sweetheart . . . come on . . . You're a baby.' He always made her feel better, and she smiled sheepishly as she slipped into the passenger seat in the Ferrari and he roared down North Bedford to Cedars Sinai.

At the hospital, they had to wait forever again, but they finally called her in, and this time Jack decided to come with her. He didn't like hospitals, and he didn't like them messing with her without some supervision. A technician had already explained to them that there was nothing invasive about the test. They would put gel on her abdomen, and roll a transducer around on it, and an image would appear on a screen to tell them if she had any growths or cysts, or possibly an ulcer. It sounded pretty simple. But he still wanted to be with her.

She undressed in a cubicle, and emerged in a white gown and her shoes, feeling foolish, and he smiled at her as she lay down. They gave him a stool just behind her head, where he could see the screen too, but all it looked like was a weather map of Atlanta. They applied the gel, and the technician began rolling the transducer, much like a microphone, around on her stomach with a little mild pressure. All it felt was cold, and the whole thing was pretty boring. And then they both saw the technician frown, and concentrate on an area low on her stomach. And the pressure of the transducer felt mildly uncomfortable to Amanda while she did it. The technician said she'd be right back, and went to get someone to look at it with her. This time a young resident came, and he introduced himself to both of them, and then glanced at the sonogram with interest.

'Something wrong?' Amanda asked, trying to feign a calm she didn't feel. She was beginning to panic. It was easy to see that they had seen something that either worried or perplexed them. But the resident was nonchalant when he answered.

'Not at all. We just like to be sure of what we see here. Four eyes are better than two sometimes, but I think we have a pretty clear picture. When was your last period, Mrs Kingston?'

'Two months ago,' she said, in a choked voice. She obviously had something wrong with her ovaries . . . or her uterus . . . it wasn't change of life at all . . . it was cancer . . . She couldn't even look at Jack as she said it, but the resident nodded.

'That sounds about right,' he said, nodding, and then zoomed in the sonogram screen for a closer view, pressed a button, and a white asterisk appeared on the screen over something that was throbbing. 'Right here.' He pointed at the asterisk with a finger and smiled at them. 'Can you see that?' She nodded, and Jack stared at it blindly. Clearly, that was the root of the problem. 'Do you know what that is, Mr and Mrs Kingston?' At their age, it was obvious to him that they were married. Why else would they be together?

'A tumor?' she asked hoarsely, as Jack closed his eyes in terror.

'A baby. I'd say you're just about two months pregnant. In fact, if you hold for a minute here, I can computerize your due date.'

'My *what*?' She sat bolt upright and knocked the transducer right off her stomach. 'I'm *what*?' She turned to look at Jack as she heard a noise just behind her, and she turned around just in time to see him slip right off the stool, where he had been sitting, on his way to the floor. He had fainted. 'Oh my God . . . I've killed him . . . somebody help him!' Her bare bottom was sticking out of the gown as she bent over him, and he groaned horribly and touched his head as he stirred, and the resident hit a panic button, and a team of paramedics came running. Jack was awake by then, and Amanda could already feel the lump on the back of his head as she knelt beside him. 'Oh God . . . I'm so sorry . . . are you okay? . . .' The resident sent the paramedics away and the technician went to get some ice, as Jack sat up slowly.

'I'm fine. I just tried to commit suicide, that's all. Why did you stop me?'

'I take it this is a surprise to both of you,' the resident smiled benignly. 'It happens that way sometimes, particularly with late babies.'

'*Late?*' Amanda turned to look at him. 'I thought the show was over.'

'Did you think you were experiencing signs of menopause?' he asked, and she nodded, as Amanda helped Jack onto the table. He lay down and she applied the ice pack that the technician had brought them.

'Do you think he has a concussion?' she asked worriedly, but the doctor shone a light in Jack's eyes, and assured her he didn't.

'You're lucky I didn't have a heart attack,'

Jack said to Amanda. 'How did that happen?' But they both knew. They had given up condoms in January, after the results of his AIDS test. She had been so sure she wouldn't get pregnant. It had never occurred to her that this could happen. 'I can't believe this,' he groaned again and closed his eyes. He had an unbelievable headache.

'Neither can I,' Amanda said softly, staring at the frozen image on the screen that was their baby. And 'October 3' had appeared on the screen, since they last looked at it.

'There's your due date,' the resident told them happily, and Jack felt an over-whelming desire to kill him. 'We'll send a report to your doctor. Congratulations!' And with that, he strode out of the room to the next patient he had to see and the tech-nician handed them a picture that had been spat out of the machine in the last few seconds.

'That's your baby's first picture.' She smiled at them both, and began resetting the machine for the next patient. They needed the room, and Jack got up slowly and looked at Amanda.

'I don't believe it,' he said hoarsely. He looked worse than she did. She was suddenly feeling much better knowing that at least she didn't have cancer, or even an ulcer. Just a baby.

'I don't believe it either.' She glanced at him in embarrassment. 'I'll put my clothes on.' She was back in a minute, and they walked slowly out of the room, still carrying the bag of ice chips. Jack looked like the patient. Neither of them said a word until they got to the car, and then he just stood there and stared at her. He felt as though his whole life was passing before him. It had happened to him before, but not like this, not with a woman he cared about so much, and not so totally out of the blue like that. With thirty-year-olds, you knew you were in trouble when you took chances. But at fifty-one? Jesus. 'I can't believe I'm pregnant.' She was still holding the picture and he saw it.

'Throw that thing away. It scares me.' The little thing that had been throbbing had been the baby's heart, and the doctor had told them that the fetus was healthy. But she clung to the picture now and looked at it as she sat in the Ferrari. 'Do you want to go somewhere and talk? Or just go home and try to absorb it?' He knew this would be a big step for her, and he was sorry for her. It was a shame it had happened to them. But in the end, maybe it would bring them even closer, at least he hoped so. And he planned to be there for her.

'Do you have to go to the office?'

'Probably. But if you want to go talk about it, I'll call Gladdie. You'd better call your doctor.' She nodded as he started the car and called Gladdie from the car phone.

'I don't know what to say,' Amanda said softly, looking at him. This was terrifying and amazing. She couldn't even think yet of all the implications.

'It's my fault,' he said glumly, 'I should have been careful. I was just so happy to be rid of those damn things after all these years, I guess I got carried away . . . and pretty stupid.'

'I never thought this could happen,' she said, still in shock.

'Yeah, teenage pregnancy in your fifties,' he smiled at her then, and leaned over and kissed her. 'I love you. I'm just glad you're

196

okay, and it was nothing worse.' As far as that went, he was relieved, but he was sorry for her. 'At least this we can fix,' he said comfortingly as they stopped at a stoplight, and she looked over at him in confusion.

'What does that mean?' Her voice was very small and tight as she asked him.

'Well, you're not going to keep the pregnancy, at our age. That's ridiculous. And besides, neither of us wants more kids. What would we do with a baby?'

'What does everyone else do?'

'They're usually twenty years younger than we are, and they're married.' And then as he looked at her face, he pulled over. 'Are you telling me you want to keep it?' She didn't answer him, but the look in her eyes filled him with terror. 'Are you crazy? I'm sixty years old, and you're fifty-one. We're not married, and your children already hate me. How do you think this little piece of news would go over?' He couldn't believe it. It had never even dawned on him that she might want to have the baby.

'It's our life, not theirs . . . and the baby's, Jack, you're asking me to kill a live human being.' Her eyes were filled with pain now.

'Bullshit.' He was raising his voice to her for the first time since he'd known her. 'I'm asking you to be reasonable, for chrissake, Amanda. You cannot consider keeping this baby.'

'I will *not* kill it.' She hadn't even thought about it yet, but suddenly she knew clearly, without a moment's doubt, that she didn't want an abortion.

'It's not a baby. It's a blob. It's a nothing on a TV screen. And it's a threat to our sanity, and our life together. Don't you understand that? We can't do this!' He shouted at her, and she glared at him and said nothing. 'I can't do it, then. I *won't* do it, and you can't force me! I've been through this before, and I'm not going to be pushed into having a kid at my age. You *have* to have an abortion.' He wanted to shake her, but he would never have hurt her, even in his total outrage.

'I don't *have* to do anything, Jack. And I'm not some bimbo trying to force you, or trick you, into marriage. I didn't want this either. But I'm not going to be forced into doing something I don't believe in because you're too chickenshit to deal with a little reality here. I *am* pregnant, and it *is* our baby.'

'And you *are* crazy. It must be the hormones. Oh my God, I can't believe this,' he said, shoving the car into gear and heading toward Bel Air, to her house. 'Look,' he said, turning to her as he sped down Rodeo, 'you can do whatever you want, Amanda, but *I'm* not having this baby. I'm not doing night feedings, and earaches, and Little League. I'm not going to make a fool of myself going to his college graduation when I'm ninety.'

'You'd only be eighty. Eighty-two to be exact. And what's more, you're a coward.' And as she said it, she began to cry, and he tried to control himself and reason with her.

'Look, sweetheart . . . I know how you must feel. It's a shock. First we thought there was something terrible wrong with you, and now you're pregnant. You're not thinking clearly. An abortion is a terrible thing. I know that. I understand it. But think what this would do to your life, never mind mine. Do you really want to start all over again? Driving car pool at sixty?'

'You seem to do all right driving at your age. I'm sure I could manage to hold on to my license for the next nine years, if I work at it. And no, this isn't what I'd have chosen. I'm not stupid. But it wasn't my choice, or yours, it was God's. He gave us this incredible gift. We don't have the right to just throw it away . . .' She was crying again as she looked at him, trying to reach him. But she could see it was hopeless, and she bowed her head and just cried then. 'Jack, I can't do it.'

'You never told me you were religious,' he said sadly, feeling betrayed, and sorry for her, but angry anyway. She had no right to do this to him. Dori never would have.

'I feel very strongly about this,' she said, in a small, clear voice as they pulled up in front of her house and he looked at her.

'So do I, Amanda. And nothing you say is going to sway me. I won't be a part of it. I don't want to know anything about it. If you have an abortion, I'll be there for you. I'll hold you. I'll cry with you. I'll love you forever. But I am not going to be

200

forced into having a baby at my age.' And he meant it.

'Other men your age do it all the time. Especially here, in L.A. Half the fathers I see in my gynecologist's office with their thirty-year-old wives out to here,' she showed him and he almost winced, 'are older than you are.'

'Then they're senile. I'm very clear about how I feel about this. I'm out of here, Amanda, if you have this baby.'

'Good-bye then,' she said, looking at him with sudden hatred. 'Do whatever the hell you want, it's your life, but this is mine, and my body, and my baby. And you can't have any of it, so to hell with you, Jack Watson. Go back to all your stupid bimbos, and I hope you knock them all up. You deserve it.'

'Thanks for playing,' he said as she got out of the car, and slammed the door so hard it rattled everything in it. And she never looked back as she ran to her house, unlocked the door, and disappeared inside it.

Five seconds later, she heard the Ferrari

roar away, and sat down in the front hall and sobbed. She had lost him. She had lost everything . . . but she wasn't going to give in. She had no choice now. She was going to have the baby. But what in God's name was she going to tell the children?

Chapter Nine

The next three days were a nightmare for both of them. For the first time in years, he even shouted at Gladdie. She didn't know what was wrong with him, but whatever it was, she knew it was Big Time. And the fact that Amanda wasn't calling hadn't gone unnoticed. He didn't even take Julie's or Paul's calls, when they phoned him. He spoke to no one.

And Amanda locked herself in her house and acted as though she had gone back into mourning. Louise came by with the kids, and she wouldn't let them in. She told them she had a migraine, and she looked it. She looked awful.

'What's wrong with Mom?' Louise finally called Jan to ask her if she knew anything, but all Jan knew was that her father-in-law wasn't talking to Paul either. 'Maybe they broke up, the sex fiends. Please God, tell me it's true. Hallelujah.'

'Oh come on, Lou,' Jan chided her older sister, and Louise was startled.

'What, are you on their team now?'

'No, but you know, they are adults, and Daddy's gone. Maybe they have a right to do what they want, as long as they do it discreetly.'

'Don't give me that. They're disgusting,' Louise said bluntly.

'Whatever happened to all that stuff you said after Daddy died, about Mom having a right to her own life now, and all that? Maybe we don't have a right to interfere, or even to disapprove. What makes us the source of all judgment?'

'Shit, Jan. What did you do? Find religion? She's your mother. She's behaving like a slut. She's having an affair.'

'She's single and she's over fifty. She has a right to do whatever she wants. I'm beginning to think we all behaved like jerks when she told us.'

'Well, I don't. And I just hope he dumped her.'

'Maybe she dumped him.'

'Just so someone did it.'

But by week's end, Amanda still wasn't talking to anyone, and no one had seen her. And both girls were worried. In truth, she was sitting around and crying all the time, from the emotions, and the shock of losing Jack, and the hormones. She felt as though her life was over, and yet at the same time she was overwhelmed at the prospect of a new life just beginning. But she couldn't imagine a life now without Jack. She hadn't heard a word from him since she'd last seen him, and he hadn't even called her.

He was shouting at every employee who crossed him and working till midnight every night. And when he got home, he just sat on the couch, staring into space, trying not to think of her and how she'd betrayed him. He still couldn't believe it. How could she do this to him? It wasn't her fault she'd gotten pregnant, not entirely, but the fact that she wouldn't get rid of it seemed like the ultimate betrayal. And then, just as he'd be thinking how angry he was at her, he would suddenly remember something she had said, or done . . . or the way she looked when he made love to her, or in the morning when she woke up, and he missed her so much he thought it would kill him. But he was determined not to call her.

But all he could think of, all he dreamed or knew or wanted was Amanda. She was driving him crazy. And he walked down the beach at Malibu for hours on Sunday morning. He swam, and then he ran, and then he just sat there, looking out to sea, thinking of her, and he knew he couldn't stand it. He had to call her.

He fought with himself about it all that afternoon, and at eight o'clock that night, he called her. He didn't even know what to say. He just wanted to hear her voice again. Just for a minute. But he wasn't going to see her. There was no point now. He didn't want to get sucked into this insanity she was creating.

But when he got through, her machine was on, and she didn't pick up. She didn't even know he had called until the next morning when she checked it. She hardly ever bothered to check the machine now. For the first few days of their estrangement, she had checked it hourly. But she gave up by the weekend. It had been eight days now. But finally, he had reached out to her. She almost couldn't believe it. She'd begun to think that he had vanished out of her life forever. She listened to the message, and he sounded strained and uncomfortable. He said he just wanted to make sure she was okay, and feeling well. And then he had hung up. She erased the message and went back to bed. All she wanted to do was sleep now. She was exhausted. She remembered that from her earlier pregnancies, only it was worse this time. She was even more tired. She wasn't sure if it was her age, or the fact that Jack had left her. But whatever it was, she slept eighteen hours a day now.

She never returned his call, and by Tuesday, he wondered if she had gotten the message. Maybe her machine wasn't working. This time he dialed her from the office, between meetings. And he said almost the same thing he had said the first time. She heard it late that night, and wondered why he was calling. Why bother? He had made his position clear. She never wanted to see him again, or talk to him. She cried while she listened to it and went back to bed with a bowl of ice cream. That was all she ate now.

The only calls she did return were from her daughters. She didn't want them to drop by, so she figured she'd better call them. She told them she had a terrible virus, and was taking antibiotics and she'd get back to them when she felt better. Neither of them believed her.

'She's lying,' Louise said when she called Jan on Tuesday. 'She sounds fine, physically. Maybe she's having a nervous breakdown.'

'Why don't we just leave her alone?' Jan suggested. But that night she told Paul she thought the romance was over. He thought so too. His father was behaving like Godzilla.

'I ran into him this afternoon. He looks like he hasn't combed his hair in a week, and he acts like he's going to kill someone. I think she dumped him.'

'Maybe he dumped her,' Jan said sadly, wondering if it was their fault, and feeling guilty about it. Her mother didn't deserve what they had done to her, but there was nothing they could do now.

And when the cleaning lady came she found Amanda watching daytime television. She had become addicted to the soap operas and talk shows where women cried about their husbands who were sleeping with the neighbor, a German shepherd, and at least two of their sisters. She watched them, and cried, while eating ice cream.

'I'm going to get fat,' she announced to the television set one afternoon, eating her second bowl of ice cream. 'So what?' she answered. She was going to get very, very fat, and no one decent was ever going to speak to her again. And Jack Watson was a bastard. He was probably back to sleeping with starlets.

But instead, Jack was still shouting at Gladdie and making everyone miserable. It had been nearly two weeks now.

'Look, could you do me a favor,' Gladdie said finally on Friday afternoon after two weeks of his insane behavior. 'Could you at least talk to her? Maybe you two can work something out. If not, you're going to drive the rest of us crazy. This entire office is becoming candidates for Prozac, thanks to you. Just call her.'

'What makes you think I'm not talking to her?' he asked sheepishly, wondering how Gladdie always knew everything. He thought she was psychic.

'Have you looked at yourself lately, Jack? You shave twice a week. God knows when you last combed your hair. You've worn the same suit for three days. You're starting to look like a homeless person. Believe me, this look is not good for business.'

'I'm sorry. I've been upset,' he said, looking as miserable as he felt. This was almost worse than when he lost Dori. Because Amanda was right here, only minutes away, and he still loved her. That was the bitch of it. But he had behaved like a monster to her, and she hadn't returned any of his phone calls. He had called four times now. 'Besides, she doesn't want to talk to me,' he said sadly, and Gladdie patted his shoulder like a mother.

'Believe me, she does. She probably looks

worse than you do. What did you do to her anyway?' She figured it was his fault, or he wouldn't be feeling so guilty.

'You don't want to know,' he said, shamefaced.

'Probably not,' Gladdie admitted. 'Why don't you go over and see her?'

'She won't let me in. Why should she? I walked off on her when she needed me . . . I threatened her, Glad . . . I was a total asshole.'

'She probably loves you anyway. Women are like that. They have a lot of tolerance for assholes. In fact, some women even love them. Go see her.'

'I can't.' He looked like a kid as Gladdie shook her head in exasperation.

'I'll drive you. Just do it.'

'Okay, okay. I'll go tomorrow.'

'Now,' she said, closing his appointment book. 'You don't have any appointments, and no one here can stand you. Do everyone a favor. Go see her. Or I'm starting a petition.'

'You're a pain in the ass.' He grinned at her and stood up. He looked better already. 'But I love you.' He looked down at her fondly. 'Thank you. If she slams the door in my face, or won't let me in, I'll be back in ten minutes.'

'I'm going to start lighting candles,' she said, as he rushed through the door, anxious to get there, to see her, to tell her what he'd been thinking, and praying that she'd see him. He was at her house in less than five minutes in the Ferrari. And he rang the doorbell forever, but she didn't answer. He wasn't sure if she was home. The garage door was locked, so he couldn't see if her car was in it. But he walked around the house and started knocking on her bedroom windows.

And as she lay in bed, watching *Oprah*, she heard it.

She thought it was a bird at first, or a cat, and then she began to panic. She thought it might be a burglar, checking to see if anyone was home. She was going to call 911, and then she decided to go to her bathroom window and see if she could see someone by peeking through the curtains. She tiptoed into the other room, holding her panic button to the security system, and then she saw him. He looked terrible, and he was still tapping on her window.

She opened the bathroom window then, and stuck her head out. 'What are you doing?' She looked as bad as he did. She hadn't bothered to comb her hair in days, it was just pulled back and stuffed into an elastic, and she hadn't worn makeup since she last saw him. 'Stop that!' she shouted at him. 'You're going to break the window.'

'Then let me in,' he said, smiling at her. It was so good to see her, but she only shook her head. She looked miserable, and he thought her face looked a little fuller. She actually looked very pretty.

'I don't want to see you,' she said, slamming the window shut, and he came to stand at the bathroom window then, and they looked at each other through the windowpanes. She couldn't believe how much she still loved him, and how glad she was to see him. She hated herself for it. 'Go away!' she mouthed, making shooing gestures, but he pressed his face against the glass and made terrible faces, and in spite of herself, she laughed at him.

'Come on, Amanda, please.' He begged her, and she thought about it for a minute, and then disappeared. He had no idea what she was doing. But a minute later, she came through the back door, barefoot and wearing a nightgown. His heart leapt when he saw her.

'What time do you go to bed now?' It was four in the afternoon, and he remembered the nightgown, though with him, she hadn't worn them often.

'I went to bed two weeks ago. And I've been there ever since, eating ice cream and watching *Oprah*. I'm going to become fat and disgusting and I don't give a damn,' she said as he followed her into her kitchen. And then she turned to look at him. There was something so vulnerable in her eyes that it touched him to his very soul, and he wondered again how he could have been stupid enough to leave her. 'Why did you come to see me?' she asked, with a ravaged look that tore his heart out.

'Because I love you, and I'm a moron . . . and Gladdie made me.' He smiled sheepishly as he said it. 'She said no one can stand me. I've been pretty awful. Why didn't you return my phone calls?' He looked hurt when he asked her and she shrugged and opened the freezer.

'Do you want some ice cream?' she asked distractedly. It was becoming an obsession, and it amused him. It reminded him of eating ice cream with her in bed. Their favorite flavor was coffee. 'All I have left is vanilla.'

'That's pathetic. Have you eaten anything else for the last two weeks?' he asked with a look of concern, and she shook her head as she dished up two bowls of vanilla. 'That's not good for the baby.'

'What do you care?' She looked him straight in the eye as she said it. 'That's a little hypocritical, isn't it? Since you wanted me to kill it.' She handed him the bowl and they both sat down at the kitchen table.

'I didn't want you to *kill* it. I was just trying to preserve my sanity, and our life . . . at your expense . . .' He finished sadly. 'I was an asshole. I'm sorry, Amanda.' He pushed the bowl of ice cream away, and just sat across the table from her as she watched him. 'I was just so shocked, I didn't expect that.' It was the understatement of all time and she smiled at him.

'Neither did I.' At one blow, she had lost the man and gained the baby, neither of which she either wanted or expected. 'I'm so sorry, Jack.' He reached across the table and took her hand in his.

'It's not your fault . . . not entirely anyway . . .' He knew she hadn't misled him. It had never occurred to either of them, not with any seriousness at least, that she might get pregnant. They had just dismissed it. 'How are you feeling?'

'Fat,' she laughed. 'I must have gained five pounds eating ice cream.'

'You don't look it.' But there was a softness about her face, a different light in her eyes. He remembered that about his ex-wife when she'd been pregnant with their kids. There was a kind of glow about her. 'You look beautiful.'

'It must be the hairdo.' She smiled sadly. Just seeing him like this reminded her of how much she missed him. She still didn't know why he had come to see her, and she assumed it was so they could part without hard feelings. At least it was a cleaner way to do it. And maybe one day, in spite of himself, he'd come to see the baby.

'I don't suppose you'd want to go out to dinner with me . . . maybe to 31 Flavors, or

Ben & Jerry's?' he asked, looking sheepish.

'Why?' What was the point now?

'Because I miss you. I've been completely crazy for the past two weeks. It's a wonder Gladdie didn't leave me.'

'I haven't been so great either. I just sleep all day, and eat ice cream. And cry at daytime television.'

'I wish I'd been here.'

'So do I,' she said softly, and looked away from him. It was almost too painful to see him, as he stood up and walked around the table.

'I love you, Amanda . . . I want to come back, if you'll have me. I promise I won't be a jerk about this. I'll do whatever you want. You can have the baby. I'll buy it shoes. I'll buy you ice cream. I just don't want to lose you.' There were tears in his eyes as he said it, and she looked up at him, unable to believe what she was hearing.

'Do you mean that?'

'About the ice cream? I swear it . . . yes, I mean it. I'm not going to leave you alone to go through this. I think you're crazy, but I love you, and it's my baby too, God help me. Just don't laugh at me when I get confused and push the stroller into the traffic because my Alzheimer's is out of control. Get me a nurse if I need one.'

'I'll get you anything you want,' she said as she stood up and he took her in his arms, and held her. 'I love you so much. I thought I would die without you.'

'Me too,' he said, and pulled her closer. 'God, Amanda . . . I don't want to lose you.' And then, looking worried about it, he asked her if she thought they should get married.

'You don't have to do that,' she said, shaking her head as they walked slowly toward her bedroom. 'I don't expect it.'

'No, but maybe the kid does. Maybe we should ask him.'

'Maybe it's a girl.'

'Let's not talk about it. You're making me nervous. So are we getting married?' He was prepared to do right by her, whatever it took him, but she surprised him.

'Let's not. We don't have to. There's no law that says we have to be married. Maybe later. Let's see how it goes with us.'

'You're very modern, Mrs Kingston.'

'No, I just love you.' They were in her

bedroom by then and he had his arms around her and he was kissing her. He was back, and she was never going to let him go now, and before they knew it, her night-gown was on the floor, with his clothes, and they were in bed where they had first made love, and where they had probably conceived their baby. It was his bed now, theirs, not Matthew's, or anyone else's. And as he made love to her, he knew with utter certainty, how much he loved her.

And as they lay in each other's arms that night, they talked about what they were going to do, and how they were going to tell their children.

'I can hardly wait,' he laughed. 'If you thought the last dinner was bad, wait for this one.' She had to laugh about it too. It was all you could do. And then she turned to him with a smile and asked him how much he loved her. 'More than you'll ever know, more than life itself. Why? What did you have in mind?'

'I was just wondering if you loved me enough to get me a bowl of ice cream.' He looked at her and laughed, and propped himself up on one elbow.

'Maybe we should just move the freezer into the bedroom.'

'That's a great idea.' She laughed at him, and he kissed her again, and it was a while before either of them remembered the ice cream.

Chapter Ten

This time they decided not to delude themselves, and pretend that their children were going to be happy for them. And Amanda decided, when she planned it with Jack, not to make dinner for them. They were going to invite them over for cocktails. It was going to be short and to the point, and probably horrible. But they were going to tell their children collectively that she was pregnant. And then the roof would fall in. But at least this time they both expected it.

Everyone arrived at six-fifteen. Julie was sweet when she came in, both Jan and Louise were tense, and Paul was more pleasant than usual to his father. They had already discussed it amongst themselves, and they were braced for it. They figured that Jack and Amanda were telling them they were getting married. They weren't pleased about it, and Louise had already said she was going to try to talk her out of it. But at least they knew what to expect now.

They all sat down in the living room. Jack served drinks. He poured himself a Scotch, and the others drank wine. Amanda had nothing. And Louise had water. And she decided to take the bull by the horns while the others waited politely.

'Okay,' she said, looking glib, 'when's the wedding?'

'It isn't,' Amanda said calmly. 'We're not getting married. Not for the moment anyway. We've decided to wait. But we wanted you to know, I'm pregnant.' You could have heard a pin drop in the room, and Louise turned the color of chalk as she stared at her mother.

'Tell me you're joking. It's April Fools' and I forgot to look at my calendar. Tell me you didn't say that.'

'I did. It came as a shock to us too. But there it is. There's no point hiding from it.

It's due in October.' She glanced over at Jack and he gave her thumbs-up. She was doing fine, and it took a full five minutes for it to hit them.

'I take it you're not having an abortion.' As usual, Louise was the spokesperson for the two sisters. Jan had been shocked into silence. And this time, even Julie was quiet. Paul was looking daggers at his father.

'No, I'm not having an abortion. We discussed it,' she said, skimming the truth a bit, 'but I don't want to. At my age, this is kind of a gift, and I want to keep it. I know how difficult this will be for all of you, and it stunned me too. But there it is, guys . . . I'm human.' There were tears in her eyes, and Jack walked across the room and sat down next to her and put an arm around her.

'I think your mother has a lot of courage. A lot of women her age wouldn't do this.'

'I think my mother has a screw loose,' Louise said as she stood up and signaled to her husband, who got up absently. 'You're nuts, Mom. I think you're both senile. You'll go to any lengths to embarrass us. I don't even want to think what Daddy would say about this. It's beyond thinking.'

'Well, Louise, he's not here to think anything about it. This is my life,' Amanda said calmly.

'And ours, for all you care about it.' But before she had even finished her sentence, they all heard Jan sobbing, and she was on her feet too, and looking at her mother with hatred.

'I can't believe you'd do this to me, Mom. I can't have a baby, so you show off to everyone that you can still have one. How cruel is that? And how rotten? How could you do this to us?' It was obvious from the look on Paul's face that he agreed with his wife completely. Both of Amanda's children and their spouses started to leave without saying another word, and Jan was distraught and leaning against her husband. Amanda tried to go to her, but Paul stopped her.

'Why don't you leave us alone for once, and just keep all your good news to yourselves for a change? What do you want from us? Blood? Congratulations? Well, screw you both. How do you think Jan is feeling?'

'I can see how she's feeling, Paul,'

Amanda said with tears running down her face. 'The last thing on earth I wanted to do was hurt her. But this happened to us. It's our lives, and our problem, and our baby.'

'Well, good luck with it. And don't invite us to the christening, Dad.' He glanced at Jack with open fury. 'We're not coming.' The door slammed rapidly behind them, and Amanda cried in Jack's arms, as Julie watched them. She was quiet this time, and when Amanda settled down, she spoke to both of them. But it was obvious that she was still startled.

'I'm sorry, Dad. I'm sorry for both of you. This can't be easy. But it's hard for us too. It's kind of a big leap for all of us. But who knows, maybe in the end it will be a blessing. I hope so.'

'So do I,' Jack said softly, looking at Amanda. She had certainly taken a tough route when she made her decision, but she knew that. And they had expected it to be rough when they told the children. Julie and her husband left quietly. And Jack and Amanda sat staring at each other in silence.

'You knew it would be like this,' he said gently.

'I know,' she sniffed. 'But you always hope it won't be. You always think they'll jump up and throw their arms around you, like they did when they were kids, little kids, and tell you how much they love you, and it's okay, and they think you're terrific. Instead, they're always passing judgment, and angry at you, and think that whatever it is you're doing is wrong and you did it to hurt them. It's as if your only function in life, as a parent, is to exist in whatever way they want you. Anything different, or out of the ordinary, or inconvenient, just makes them angry. Why is it that children, however old they are, *never* have compassion for their parents?'

'Maybe we don't deserve it,' he said, looking tired. 'Maybe they just think we're selfish. And we are sometimes. But we have a right to that. We give them so much when they're little, and when we think it's finally our turn, they turn around and tell us it isn't. We don't have a turn. As far as they're concerned, we're on their time. I think you just have to do what you're doing, and make your own life. If they can live with it, fine. If they can't, let them deal with it. We can't give up the rest of our lives for our children. The only thing that depresses me is that we're about to do it all over again. I'm going to slide right into the sunset with some little shit telling me what an asshole I am, and how I ruined his life because I'm still sleeping with his mother. And believe me, I will be. I plan to be making love to you until they put me away with a shovel, and if you ever get pregnant again, next time, I swear I'll never sleep with you again. I want you on birth control pills till you're eighty.' She couldn't help laughing at what he said, some of it was so true. One's children always seem to think that you owe them every-thing, and they owe you nothing. It was an interesting concept.

'I felt so badly for Jan,' she said solemnly. What she had said had been so agonized and so painful.

'So did I. Paul looked as though he wanted to kill me. It's as though we did this so I could prove my virility and make him look bad. Christ, I would do anything to see them have a baby.'

'So would I,' she said, and then to take their minds off all of it, he took her to dinner. But for the moment, they had given up Thai food. Amanda couldn't even think about it without getting heartburn.

And that night, they lay in bed and talked for a long time. Jack fell asleep eventually, but Amanda didn't. She got up and made some hot milk, and drank chamomile tea, but her mind seemed to be whirling. She kept thinking about Jan and what she had said. Amanda slept fitfully all night, and the next day, she looked at Jack mournfully over breakfast.

'I have something to say to you,' she said, and he glanced up at her. She looked tired.

'Are you okay?' He always worried about her, and now he worried about the baby. This was just what he hadn't wanted.

'I'm fine,' she reassured him. But she didn't look it. She looked awful. 'I had an idea last night.'

'In your condition that could be dangerous. You probably want me to buy out Häagen-Dazs, or Ben & Jerry's.'

'I'm serious.'

'So am I. I'm buying stock in the companies. You are the single biggest consumer of ice cream west of the Rockies.' She had already gained eight pounds and was barely three months pregnant. 'Okay, okay, I'll be serious. What is it?'

She started to cry before she even told him, and he realized instantly that it was serious. But she talked about Jan and Paul and what they had said the night before, and how greatly it had pained her.

'Sweetheart, it upset me too. But there's nothing we can do about it. They just have to see what happens, and keep trying.'

'Maybe not. That was my idea. You didn't want this baby anyway, Jack. And maybe we are too old. Maybe this is the greatest gift we can give them. Maybe this is why it happened. I want to give them the baby.' He looked stunned when she said it.

'Are you serious? You want to give them the baby?' She nodded as she cried, and he put his arms around her.

'I don't think you should do that. This is your baby. Our baby. It would be so hard for you to give it up once you had it.'

'I don't care. I want to do this for Jan, and for Paul. Will you let me?'

'You can do anything you want. It's an extraordinary thing to do, and people will talk about it. But who gives a damn? If that's what you want, and what they want, then do it.'

'I wanted to ask you first.'

He nodded. 'I think it's the greatest gift you can give them, and since Paul is so opposed to adoption, it certainly solves the issue of the genes. I just want you to be sure you can do it.'

'I know I can. I want to. If it's all right with you, I want to talk to her this morning. Will you call Paul?'

'All right, I'll take him to lunch. If he'll see me.'

'I'll have Jan call him after I talk to her, and tell him this is important.'

'You're an amazing woman, sweetheart. And full of surprises and rare gifts.' He was still amazed by her when he left for the store that morning. She didn't even bother to call Jan. She drove to her house before she left for the gallery, and Jan was so surprised, in spite of her resistance, she opened the door to her mother. And when Amanda told her what she had in mind, the two women sat and cried. At first Jan was shocked, and didn't want to do it, but after Amanda talked to her for a while, she wanted it very badly.

'Would you really do that for me, Mom?'

'Yes, I would,' Amanda said firmly, drying her eyes, and smiling at her daughter. 'I'd like nothing better.'

'What if you change your mind? Or Jack does?'

'We won't. If we give you our word, we'll do it. This is something we both want to do. Very much. I hope you'll let us.'

'I'll talk to Paul.' Jan looked excited as she ran to the telephone, and was surprised to learn that Jack had already called him, and Paul already had some vague idea as to why his father wanted to see him. Jan explained the rest to him, and there were tears in his eyes as he listened.

'I can't believe they'd do that,' he whispered. 'Why?'

'Because they love us,' Jan said, starting to cry again as her mother stood near her. 'Mom says we can both be there when the baby is born, and it's ours right from that very minute.'

'What if they change their minds?'

'I don't think they will, Paul. She really means it.'

'We'll talk about it,' he said, afraid to get his hopes up. But he saw his father for lunch, and talked to Jan about it that night, and the next morning they called their respective parents, and accepted. Their mood was jubilant, and Amanda felt as though she had done something worthwhile and wonderful, and she knew she'd never regret it.

'I can't believe you,' Jack said, in awe of her. 'I just hope you're not sorry later.'

'I won't be. I'm absolutely sure. I don't care how much I love this baby once it's born, they should have it. You were probably right anyway. Maybe I will be too old to car pool at sixty.'

'You'd be cute at any age. And at least you can see the baby whenever you want to.' That was something. He knew this wouldn't be easy for her. And then he had an idea. 'Why don't we go away somewhere? Just the two of us, for a vacation. What about Paris?'

'Wow! I'd love that.' The girls had suggested it to her the summer before, but she hadn't been in the mood then. But she couldn't think of anything she'd like more than a trip to Paris with Jack Watson.

They went in June when she was five and a half months pregnant. They stayed at the Ritz and had a fabulous time. They went out for dinner every night, shopped, went to the Louvre and the ballet, and walked all over Paris. She had never felt better. In spite of the ice cream, she hadn't gained much weight, and Jack thought she looked terrific. Everything they said about pregnant women being beautiful seemed to hold true for her. The only thing she was sorry about was that she couldn't buy really great clothes while she was pregnant.

'We'll come back in November, I promise.' He was worried that she'd be depressed then. He still thought that giving up the baby would be hard for her, but she had never wavered once in her resolve to give it to their children.

They had a terrific time, and stopped in London for a few days on the way home. And in July he took her to Lake Tahoe. But in August, her doctor told her she couldn't travel. She was seven and a half months pregnant, and she was hardly a young mother. The baby was large, and the doctor was afraid it would come early.

'My others were both late,' she said confidently, and her obstetrician laughed at her openly.

'And how old were you then?'

'All right, all right. I'll be good. I promise.'

They knew that the baby was healthy, and a boy, she had had amniocentesis before they went to Europe. And Jan and Paul were going crazy over names. Louise, on the other hand, was still being silent and had scarcely spoken to her mother.

'She'll get over it,' Jack reassured her. He just wanted her to be happy. And he did everything he could to distract her. But all she thought of now was the baby. She wanted to buy clothes for it, teddy bears, cribs and tiny little underwear, and mountains of diapers. She seemed to go shopping almost daily, and whenever possible, she insisted he come with her.

'What are people going to think, for God's sake? I look like the baby's grandfather.' He was still mortified every time she took him shopping, and whenever someone asked, he said what they were buying was for their grandchild.

'What does that make me? Your daughter?'

'How about my wife? You know, that could be arranged.' They had been going out for eight months by then, but whenever he said it, she ignored him. She didn't want to think about anything at the moment, except the baby. She even made Jack come to the doctor with her.

The first time he had gone had been mortifying, and he had wanted to crawl out the door with a mask on. Instead, he had held the newspaper over his face, and tried to pretend he didn't know her.

'I'm not going in,' he whispered from behind the *Los Angeles Times*. Everyone in the waiting room looked about fourteen to him. It looked like a summer camp for unwed mothers. They were all pretty girls from Beverly Hills with blond hair and short dresses. They looked as though they'd been taking candy from strangers.

'Don't be ridiculous. All they do is listen to the heartbeat. It's exciting,' she whispered back to him, and he peeked around the paper. There was a boy in blue jeans across from him. He looked like a child actor.

'You can tell me about it. I'll wait for you in the car,' he said firmly. But she looked so devastated when he tried to leave, that he sat down again with a mortified expression, and the boy in the blue jeans asked him if it was his first baby. 'My children are older than you are,' Jack said miserably. The boy said he was twenty-three, it was their second child. But his father and stepmother had had one the year before.

'He's sixty-five,' the boy said with a broad smile.

'Did he survive it?'

'Yeah. They had twins. In vitro. They tried for two years. My stepmom is forty.'

'Lucky devils,' Jack said wryly, and then said to Amanda in the examining room that people were crazy. 'Why would a sixty-five-year-old man *want* to have a baby? Imagine doing this "in vitro." At least we had a good time when we did it.'

'Want to try again?' she teased him, and he rolled his eyes. But when the doctor handed the stethoscope to him and he heard the baby's heartbeat, even Jack was excited. It was suddenly so real that it brought tears to his eyes.

'That's my grandchild!' he said, too loud, because the stethoscope in his ears made him think he was speaking softly, which he wasn't.

'Is this your father?' the doctor asked her then, looking confused. 'I thought he was your husband.'

'Actually, my husband died a year and a half ago,' she explained, and the doctor smiled at her benignly. Like all the people in Beverly Hills, these people were clearly more than a little eccentric.

But the baby was fine, and Jack couldn't stop talking about it all the way back to Julie's.

'Next time we should really bring Jan and Paul,' he said, and Amanda agreed with him, pleased that he was excited about the baby. She had to see the doctor nearly every week now. He wanted to keep a close eye on her. He was still concerned that she might deliver early, and to Jack at least, her belly looked enormous. He couldn't remember either of his children being that size in utero, but Amanda was also very slender, so it showed more.

But the very worst experience for him was the Lamaze classes they began on the fifteenth of August. There were twelve couples, mostly in shorts, beards, and Birkenstocks, lying on the floor of a conference room at Cedars Sinai. Jack had come from a meeting at the office in a Brioni suit and shirt and tie, and they looked at him like a visitor from another planet. Amanda was already there, waiting for him, and she looked very relaxed in white shorts and a huge pink T-shirt and sandals. She had just had her nails done, and she looked like a model. The people there were too young to even realize she had ever been an actress. Outside, the temperature was blazing, and Jack looked hot and frazzled when he got there.

'Sorry I'm late, sweetheart. I couldn't get rid of the textile guys from Paris. They wanted to schmooze forever.'

'It's fine,' she whispered with a smile, 'they just started.' There were charts on the wall showing varying stages of a woman's dilated cervix. And Jack glanced over at it with horror.

'What is that?'

'A cervix. Dilated. Don't worry about it.'

'It looks awful.' He had spent the arrival of both his children in a bar, getting drunk with a friend. In those days, fathers didn't have to do anything more exotic than show up afterward, with flowers.

He glanced around the room then, and realized that, as usual, almost everyone there was the age of his children. But he was almost used to that by then. What he was not used to were the photographs they showed, or the diagrams, or the training film they had promised at the end of the session. He was looking grimmer by the second.

The only part he found even remotely bearable, though embarrassing, were the exercises he had to do with Amanda, holding her legs, or helping her breathe. And the woman at the front of the room talked constantly about the miseries of something called 'transition.'

'What is *that*?' he said to his 'wife' after the sixth time she'd said it. But he had said it too loudly, and the instructor had heard him.

'It's the most painful part of labor,' she

said with a sadistic smile, 'when you go from this . . .' she pointed to a chart '. . . to this. It's a little bit like taking your upper lip and pulling it over the top of your head.' She moved on to the next question.

'Doesn't this scare you?' he whispered, a lot more softly this time, to Amanda.

'No, it's fine,' she whispered back. 'I've been through it.'

'Did you do it without drugs?' The woman at the front of the room kept warning them about the evils of anesthesia, and had made it clear that 'real' women didn't ask for medication.

'Of course not.' Amanda grinned at him between puffing breaths and panting. 'They can give me everything they've got. In the parking lot preferably. I'm no hero.'

'I'm glad to hear it. What about me? Will they give me some too?' He was beginning to feel as though he was going to need it. He hated the people in the class, hated the way they looked, the things they said, and the stupid questions they asked. It was a wonder any of them had ever gotten pregnant. Apparently, even morons could do it. But what he hated most was their instructor.

And when she announced that the film today was an actual caesarean, Jack began to glance longingly toward the exits.

'Don't you want something to drink, sweetheart?' he asked casually. 'It's so hot in here.' Actually, the air conditioner was on, and it was freezing.

'Just close your eyes. I won't tell.' The purpose of the film was so that if any of them had an emergency C-section, the husbands would be prepared and present. If they had seen it, and had a certificate from the class to prove it, they could stay in the operating room and watch. If not, they had to wait outside, with the sissies. But Jack knew that there was no way he could have been there anyway, not without general anesthesia.

'I'll be right back,' he whispered, too loud again.

'Where are you going?' Amanda asked.

'To the men's room,' he whispered.

'We'll wait for you, Mr Kingston!' the voice at the front of the room proclaimed loudly. 'You won't want to miss this.' He gave a quelling look at his 'wife,' and was back in under five minutes.

And with that, they started the film that

almost killed him. He had been in the army for two years as a kid, but no training film they had shown him there rivaled this one. Even the one on gonorrhea was a pleasant memory compared to what looked like the sawing in half of some poor woman. She cried through most of it, looked as though she was in terrible pain, there was blood everywhere, and before the lights came up, Jack whispered to Amanda that he was nauseous.

'I told you. Don't look.' She squeezed his hand and leaned over to kiss him.

'Kingstons!' The voice from hell sliced through the room. 'Are you paying attention? There will be a brief quiz on this subject.'

'Shit. Why can't we watch them operating on hemorrhoids?'

'Shhhh . . .' Amanda was laughing at him. He was hopeless. They never went back again. She didn't want natural childbirth anyway. She had tried it for about an hour with Louise, and she knew better.

But the last weeks of her pregnancy seemed very easy to her. On Labor Day weekend, she was eight months pregnant, and bored to death. They had gone to a movie, eaten Chinese food and walked down the beach at Malibu, which was not quite as easy as it had been. She felt fine, but she was slow now and enormous.

They were sitting on his deck, drinking iced tea, when Paul called them. He wanted to know how Amanda was, and asked if they could come by later. And Jack said, when he hung up, that Paul sounded a little nervous.

'Do you think something's wrong?' Amanda asked, looking worried.

'I don't think so. Maybe they're just getting anxious about the baby.'

'So am I,' she said unconvincingly. She had been remarkably calm all through it. 'If this thing gets any bigger I won't fit into the elevator at Cedars Sinai.'

'Boys are like that,' Jack said with a smile. 'Paul was a big baby too. His mother was mad at me for six months. She was such a little darling.'

'She gave you great kids,' Amanda reminded him charitably, and he rolled his eyes at her.

'Don't be such a good guy. She was a witch, trust me.'

Paul and Jan came by late that afternoon, and Jack made drinks while they sat on the deck with Amanda, watching the sunset. It was a gorgeous afternoon, and Amanda was thinking about going swimming.

'Is the baby okay?' Jan asked, looking at her mother with concern. She was so huge it was scary, but Amanda didn't seem to mind it. She looked amazingly peaceful.

'He's fine. Waiting for you, sweetheart,' Amanda said with a smile, and Jack came back and handed the young people sangria. He noticed that both of them took long sips before speaking. And he wondered what was cooking.

'Something wrong?' Jack decided to break the ice, and the young couple shook their heads in unison, looking like guilty teenagers, and then laughed nervously as they looked from her mother to his father.

'No,' Paul spoke for them. Jan was too nervous. 'But there's something we want to tell you . . . or we thought we should anyway. You should really be the first to know . . .'

Jan stepped in then, with tears in her eyes

as she looked at her mother, 'Mom, I'm pregnant.'

'You are? Oh baby, how terrific. When did that happen?'

'About six weeks ago. I wanted to be sure before I told you. But the doctor has confirmed it and said I'm fine. I had a sonogram this week and everything's perfect. They even gave us a picture.'

'I remember that,' Jack said, looking at them. But he wondered what the rest was. There was more to this story, he knew, as he waited.

Jan and Paul both took a deep breath then, and looked from one to the other of their parents. 'I know this will probably screw up your plans, but we just don't know . . . we don't think . . . I'm not sure we should . . .'

Jack said it for them. 'You don't want our baby.' Amanda looked stunned as both their children shook their heads, and then qualified it.

'Unless you two really don't want to keep it. If you don't want it, then of course . . .' Paul was trying to be fair to them, but it was obvious that now that they were having their own child, they didn't want her mother's. 'We're really sorry.'

'That's all right, Son,' Jack said calmly. 'Things work out for the best sometimes. Now, why don't you two run along.' He looked at his daughter-in-law and congratulated her with a kiss and a hug. 'I want to talk to your mother.'

'We understand. I know this must be a little hard on you, Dad.' They sounded young and insensitive and unaware, and yet at the same time, he didn't blame them. And he wasn't sorry either.

'It's fine, Son.'

They were gone within ten minutes, and Amanda looked as though someone had let the air out of her tires. It definitely required a shift in her thinking. She had done everything not to get attached to this child, and now suddenly it was hers again, and she had to rethink it.

'Wow, there's a quick change of pace. I'm happy for them though.' She looked at Jack from where she sat, checking for a negative reaction, but there was none. He seemed fine about it. But the way things were, he had no real obligation either. 'I guess that takes us back to the beginning.'

'Maybe,' he said noncommittally. 'Why don't we just let it sink in for a day or two, and talk about it later,' he suggested, and it seemed like a good idea to her. They both needed time to digest it, although her style was usually to solve problems on the instant. But this was different. This involved major life decisions. Or maybe none at all. The baby was due in four weeks. There was nothing left to decide now. And she had bought everything the baby needed, for her daughter. All she had to do now was have it. 'Come on, let's take a walk down the beach.' She didn't say anything, but they didn't make it far, and in a little while they came back, and she wandered into his bedroom. She had been so happy here. They had spent such good times in each other's company. And their love had grown in countless ways in the nine months they'd been together.

'Want to take a nap?' he offered casually, as he walked into the room behind her.

'I'd like that. I'm exhausted.' The emotional shock of having the baby given back to them had left her feeling drained, elated in some ways, and frightened and worried in others, and more than anything, concerned about Jack's reaction. It had been such a perfect solution for them, and they'd both been comfortable with it. 'Are you going to leave me again?' she asked in a soft voice, trying not to sound as frightened as she was, as the setting sun was framed in the picture window in his bedroom.

'Of course not. I love you . . . and I love him . . . poor little guy, he's getting kicked around like a football.'

'From where I sit, it feels like he's doing all the kicking.' Jack loved feeling him move and kick and dance around. Sometimes when she lay against him as she slept it made him smile just to feel it. And he knew how worried she must be now. She didn't deserve this. And he realized again what a fool he had been from the beginning.

He lay down next to her, and very gently kissed her. 'What are my chances of making love to you at this stage in the game?' They hadn't tried it in two weeks, and already by then it had been quite a challenge. She smiled when he asked her.

248

'The doctor says we can do it on the way to the hospital, if you want to.'

'I want to.' And he looked as though he meant it.

'You're a brave man,' she whispered with a smile, and he peeled off her bathing suit and rubbed a hand across her belly. And at that exact moment, the baby gave a huge kick and they both laughed.

'I think he heard what I asked you, and I'm not so sure he liked it.' They lay together for a while, and he held her, and eventually, their passion took over. It was gentle and slow, and better than either of them would have expected. And when Amanda fell asleep next to him, he put his bathing suit on and walked back out to the beach. There was a lot to think about, a lot to decide. And he smiled, as he glanced at her from the doorway.

Chapter Eleven

Jack cooked dinner for her that night, and he seemed very quiet to Amanda. She was afraid that he was upset about what Jan and Paul had said. But when she asked him, he said that he wasn't. He seemed very comfortable, and at peace with himself, and when they sat on the deck afterward and looked up at the stars, he reached for her hand, and leaned over to kiss her. It was a perfect evening.

'There's something I want to ask you,' he said finally. She couldn't imagine what was coming. She turned to look at him with a mildly worried frown. 'I did a lot of thinking this afternoon. Actually, I've done a lot of thinking lately. It just seemed so easy to let Jan and Paul take the baby. It was easier to let you make that decision.'

'It seemed such a great thing to do for them.' She sounded disappointed. She still wasn't sure what she was feeling.

'It was. You were incredible to do it. But it was never right. Maybe whatever Powers there are knew that, and got her pregnant.' He paused, but only for an instant. 'I want us to keep the baby. He's our son . . . I really want him.' There were tears in his eyes in the darkness, but she couldn't see them.

'You do?' For the second time that day she looked as though someone could have knocked her over with a feather. 'Are you sure?'

'Of course I'm sure. And I'm tired of all this stupid modern bullshit. I want us to get married. Now. Tomorrow. Immediately. I don't want our son to be born out of wedlock.'

'That still gives you four weeks.' Amanda smiled at him, wondering if he really meant it, or was just being noble. 'You don't have to do this. I love you just as much as if we were married.'

'So do I. So why not be? This is such a dumb way to do things. I live in Malibu, and you live in Bel Air, and we sleep together on weekends? I want to be there for night feedings and runny noses, and his first step and first tooth, and your first gray hair, and . . .' He was smiling at her, and she was laughing at him.

'I hate to tell you, you've already missed it. About ten years ago, in fact.'

'Then I don't want to miss the rest. I don't know what I've been thinking. I've been so busy protecting myself for the last twenty years, that I forgot about protecting you. More importantly, I'd forgotten how good this can be. I just don't want part of it, or the easy times. I want all of it. I want to be there if you get sick, or if you're happy, or sad, or need me. And I want you there for me too. Even if I start to drool at the same time he does.' He gently touched her belly and she put his finger to her lips and kissed it.

'I want to be there for you too,' she said softly. 'And you have been there for me.' And then suddenly, she looked worried again. 'You don't think it's too soon?' But this time, he laughed out loud, and their neighbors could have heard him.

'Amanda, I love you. Have you looked at yourself? That's quite a profile. No, it's not a moment too soon. Not a minute. Let's get married next weekend. I'll call the kids, and if one of them has one lousy word to say about it, I'm going to disinherit them, and I'm going to say so. And that includes Louise! It's time those kids gave you a little support for a change, instead of just taking from you, or expecting you to accept them, and let them say anything they damn well please to you. I want to see smiles this time, and hear congratulations! They owe us this one.' And she could see from the fire in his eyes that he wasn't kidding and she loved it.

And the next day, he did exactly what he said he would. He called all their kids and told them he and Amanda were getting married. The wedding was set for the following Saturday. Jack had asked an old friend, a judge, to marry them. He was going to do it at the store, and afterward they were having a reception for two hundred people. And Jack and Gladdie did everything. Much as Amanda would have hated to admit it to him, she was finally too tired to do it. She suddenly felt fourteen months pregnant, and she looked it.

He even found a dress for her, a beautiful cream-colored Gazar that fell over her vast form like petals. It was perfect. She was going to wear flowers in her hair, and carry a bouquet of tube roses, philanopsis orchids, and freesia. Both her daughters had agreed to be there, and Jack had invited them both to come to the store to pick out their dresses. Jan had come willingly, but of course Louise didn't. But she had promised Jack on the phone that on the day of the wedding, she'd be pleasant. And she was furious he'd called her. She thought her mother should have done it. She was always furious about something.

And when the day of the wedding came, Jack and Amanda took a short walk down the beach in Malibu and then she went back to her place to dress with her daughters. Both of them had agreed to help her. And she was as nervous as any bride, as her hands trembled when she slipped her dress on. The hairdresser had come to do her hair, in the smooth chignon that had been her trademark, and she looked spectacular, even eight and a half months pregnant.

'You look nice, Mom.' Louise stood behind her, and spoke to the reflection in the mirror, when Jan went downstairs to check the flowers.

'Thank you,' Amanda said gratefully, and then slowly she turned to face her. 'You're not too angry at me?' But even if she was, Amanda was doing exactly what she wanted.

'I'm not angry. I still miss Dad though. Even if he was a pain in the neck sometimes.' Her eyes filled with tears as she said it. She had not only forgiven her mother finally, but her father.

'I miss him too, Lou.' Amanda took her older daughter in her arms and held her for a moment and then pulled away to look at her. She was difficult, but essentially a decent person. 'But I love Jack too.'

'He's a nice guy,' Louise conceded, and then her eyes clouded again. There was something she had to ask her. 'Would you have done it for me, Mom? I mean give me the baby, if I couldn't have one.' The question had tormented her from the beginning.

'Of course I would. I would do it for either of you.'

'I always thought you loved her more. She was always so special to you.' Louise's voice choked on a sob, and her mother was shocked by what she was saying.

'So were you. You're both special. I love both of you. Of course I'd have done that for you. How could you think I wouldn't?'

'Stupid, I guess. Jerry said you would when I talked to him about it.'

'Then he's smarter than you are.'

And then Louise surprised her even further. 'I'm glad you're keeping it. It'll be good for you. It'll keep you young . . . or drive you crazy.'

'Probably both.' Amanda laughed through her own tears, as Jan walked into the room, and Amanda hugged Louise once more and a secret look passed between them. Nothing like that had ever happened. And then she turned to both of them, and asked them if they'd be with her when she had the baby. 'I don't think Jack's going to make it. He almost threw up in Lamaze class.'

Louise laughed at what she said, and

looked enormously flattered. 'So did Jerry. But he was fine when the time came. Maybe Jack will be too.'

'I don't think his vintage does childbirth.'

'Well, we'll be there.' Jan put an arm through her sister's, and they both smiled at their mother.

'It won't be for another two or three weeks. Just make sure I can reach you when the time comes.'

'Don't worry, Mom,' they said in chorus, and with that the limousine arrived, and the photographer. And they almost forgot her bouquet. She was so nervous she was breathless, but she looked terrific. And they helped her into the car, and they were all laughing at how hard it was to get her in it. She could hardly move now.

And when they arrived at the store, all three of them were dazzled. The flowers were spectacular, and there was literally a solid ceiling of flowers above them. There were orchids and roses and lilies of the valley. It was the most beautiful thing Amanda had ever seen, and when she stood next to Jack with the judge, and her children at her side, she was suddenly overcome with emotion. It meant just as much to her, or perhaps more, as her first wedding. She was wiser now, and knew how lucky she was to have him. And at this time in their lives, they suited each other to perfection.

The judge declared them man and wife, and this time, just as Jack had requested of them, there were smiles and congratulations, and they genuinely meant it. The whole family posed for photographs, and drank Champagne, except for Amanda, who drank ginger ale. And twenty minutes later, the guests arrived. It seemed like an enormous wedding.

Everyone was still there at midnight, and Amanda was so tired that Jack didn't dare keep her there a moment longer. She threw her bouquet from the staircase, and Gladdie caught it, while George Christy wrote down names. He was the only member of the press that Jack had invited. And as they ran to the car, the staff threw petals at them. They weren't going far. They were spending two days at the Bel Air, two blocks from her house, but Amanda could hardly wait to get there and take her clothes off. It had been the happiest day of her life, but she was beyond exhausted, and she looked it. Jack put an arm around her in the car. He had insisted on driving to the Bel Air in his red Ferrari, and it was covered with balloons and white satin ribbons, and someone had written on it in shaving cream 'Just Married.'

'I feel like a kid again,' he beamed at her. He had loved it.

'I feel like a grandmother,' she laughed, 'a very fat one. You and Gladdie did such a great job. It was all so perfect. I can't wait to see the pictures.'

He had ordered Champagne in the room, and more ginger ale for her. There was a stack of videos, and as soon as the bellboy left he helped her take her clothes off. She could hardly move as she lay on the bed in her pantyhose and her bra. She had had a backache for hours, but she didn't want to spoil the moment and tell him. She lay back on the bed with a happy sigh, and let her head fall back in a mountain of down pillows.

'Oh my God . . . I've died and gone to heaven . . .' she said with a smile, and he looked down at her, a happy man. This was everything he wanted. The past was gone now.

'Can I get you anything?' he asked, as he took off his tie.

'A forklift,' she grinned at him. 'I'm never going to be able to get up if I have to go to the bathroom.'

'I'll carry you,' he said gallantly.

'It would kill you.'

He dropped his suit on a chair, and came to lie beside her, drinking Champagne and eating the strawberries and truffles the hotel had left at their bedside. 'Try one of these,' he said, putting a chocolate in her mouth, and she sighed contentedly, as he started to flip through the movies. 'How about a porno?'

'I'm not sure I'm up to it,' she laughed.

'On our wedding night?' He looked disappointed.

'We don't have to do that anymore. We're married.' He grinned at her, and put a movie on, and it was so awful, she laughed at it with him. But when he got amorous, she looked at him with a mournful expression. 'Baby, I'd like to, but I don't think I can even take the rest of my clothes off.'

'I'll help you,' he said hopefully, but she could see that he had had a lot of wine, and she didn't take him seriously, as she lumbered out of bed and went to the bathroom. She had been a thousand times that night, and lying on the bed her backache had gotten worse instead of better.

'I think I'll take a shower,' she said from the bathroom doorway.

'Now?' It was one o'clock in the morning, but somehow she thought it might make her feel better. She was beyond exhausted. She hated to feel so rotten on their wedding night, but it had been a long day and a long night. And she had been on her feet for hours. They felt like footballs.

But the shower made her feel better, and when she came back to the bedroom, they were still going at it on TV, and Jack was snoring softly. She sat down on the bed for a minute and just looked at him, thinking about how odd life was. How life put you together with different people at different times. She couldn't imagine being with anyone but him now.

He stirred slightly as she slipped into bed next to him, and a minute later, she turned the light and the TV off. But as soon as she lay down, the baby started kicking. It was going to be a long night at this rate, she thought to herself. She lay there for what seemed like ages, but she couldn't sleep. She still had the backache, and now along with it, she felt a very odd kind of pressure, as though the baby was pushing his head downward. And then suddenly, a twinge at the very bottom of her belly struck a chord of memory. She was in labor. And the twinges were contractions.

They were mild at first. And she noticed that it was fully ten minutes before she had the next one. They were slow and steady and regular, and at three in the morning, as she still lay in the dark next to him, they were coming every five minutes. She wasn't sure if she should wake him. It seemed silly if it was too early. But he heard her when she went to the bathroom.

'You okay?' he muttered sleepily when she came back to bed and moved closer to him.

'I think I'm having the baby,' she whispered.

He sat bolt upright. '*Now*? *Here*? I'll call

the doctor.' He instantly flipped the light on, and they both squinted.

'I don't think it's time yet.' But as soon as she said it, she had a good hard pain that made her grit her teeth and writhe beside him. But it was over in less than a minute.

'Are you crazy? Do you want to have the baby here?' He jumped out of bed and put his pants on, and she was laughing at him when the next pain came. But suddenly they were coming every two minutes.

'I haven't even unpacked my suitcase,' she said between pains. 'I wanted to spend at least one night here.'

'I'll bring you back here, I swear, after we have the baby. Anytime you want. Now get your ass out of bed so we can get to the doctor before you have this baby.'

'I meant I have nothing to wear.'

'What's wrong with what you were wearing?'

'I can't wear my wedding dress to the hospital. I'll look silly.'

'I won't tell anyone what it is. Just get dressed, Amanda, for God's sake . . . What are you doing? . . .'

'I'm having a contraction,' she said

between clenched teeth again, and almost as soon as she did he clutched his stomach.

'I think the Champagne was poisoned.'

'Maybe you're in labor too,' she said when the pain stopped. 'Call Jan and Louise,' she said, crawling out of bed. But she was having a hard time standing up now.

'I'll call an ambulance.''

'I don't *want* an ambulance.' She was trapped between laughter and tears when the next pain came. 'You drive me.'

'I can't. I'm blind drunk. Can't you see that?'

'No, you look fine to me. Then I'll drive. Just call Jan and Louise.'

'I don't know their numbers, and if you don't put your damn wedding dress on right now, I'm calling the police and having you arrested.'

'That would be nice,' she said in muffled tones as she slipped the wedding dress over her head and clutched her stomach. But when she tried to put her shoes on, she found her feet were too swollen. 'I'll have to go barefoot,' she said practically.

'For God's sake . . . Amanda . . . please . . .' He threw her suitcase on the bed, and started pawing through it. And miraculously, he found a pair of slippers. 'Put these on.'

'What is it about you people in retail? Why couldn't I just go barefoot?'

'You'd look foolish.' They were standing in the doorway of the room by then, and it was just after four o'clock in the morning, but the next pain was so hard that she had to lean against the doorway. Just watching her, Jack started to moan, and she put an arm around him as they left the room and walked slowly to the front of the hotel, where he had parked the car. It felt as if it took forever to get there. In truth, it took more than ten minutes, and she was beginning to worry, that she'd have the baby before they ever reached the Ferrari.

She slipped into the driver's seat, and held her hand out to him, praying that he had remembered to bring the keys. She didn't want to wait a minute longer. But fortunately, they were in his pocket. And he handed them over to her, and slipped into the car beside her. And as they careened out of the parking lot through Bel Air, she gave him Jan's number and told him to call her.

'Tell her to call Louise. Just tell them to meet me there, in labor and delivery. We'll be there in five minutes.'

'They'll probably send me to geriatrics.'

'Just relax, you'll be fine,' she said, smiling at him. It was a hell of a way to spend a honeymoon. Any minute they were going to have a baby. So much so, that she had to pull off the road for the next contraction.

'Oh my God,' he screamed at her, 'what are you doing?'

'I'm trying not to wreck your Ferrari while I have a contraction,' she said, sounding more like the girl in *The Exorcist* than the woman he had just married, and he looked at her in horror.

'Shit! I think you're in transition!'

'Don't tell me what I'm in, just shut up and call my goddamn daughter.'

'That's it . . . that's it . . . that's what the monster at the hospital said . . . she said you'd start behaving like someone I don't even know. *That's* transition!' She wasn't sure if she wanted to laugh or kill him. But at least he called Jan then, and announced that her mother was in transition.

'Is this a joke?' Jan asked, she'd been

sound asleep and she didn't know what he was talking about. It was obvious he had had too much to drink at the wedding.

'Of course this isn't a joke,' he shouted into the phone, sounding hysterical. 'She's having the baby and we're on the way to the hospital, and she's in transition. She sounds like a total stranger.'

'Are you sure it's Mom?' Jan laughed at him. He was an even bigger mess than her mother had predicted.

'Well, she's wearing your mother's wedding dress at least. And she wants you to call Louise. But hurry!'

'We'll be there in ten minutes!' she said, and hung up just as Amanda screeched into the hospital driveway, and threw open the door to the Ferrari, with an exasperated look at her brand-new husband.

'You park it. I'm busy. And don't scratch the car, my husband will kill you.'

'Very funny, lady. Very funny, whoever you are. Looks just like my wife too,' he said to a night guard, who shook his head and pointed to where Jack could park it. He figured they were probably on drugs, everyone in L.A. was.

Amanda was already in the lobby by then, and sitting in a wheelchair. She had given them her doctor's name, and just as they had learned in Lamaze, she was panting and blowing. The contractions were getting ugly.

'What are you doing?' Jack asked as he looked at her, and then he remembered. 'I forgot my stopwatch.' But a nurse was already wheeling her into the elevator, as she clutched the arms of the wheelchair. She was making Jack very nervous. 'Baby, are you okay? . . . I mean really . . .'

'What does it look like?' Her voice was barely audible through the contraction, but she sounded a little more like herself now. Maybe she wasn't in transition.

'It looks miserable,' he said honestly, 'worse than that.'

'It *is* worse than that. It's like having your guts ripped open with a chain saw.'

'What happened to the thing with the upper lip?'

'That comes later.'

'I can hardly wait.'

They wheeled her into a room on the third floor, and she exchanged her clothes for a faded hospital gown, and they handed Jack a shower cap and a pair of green pajamas.

'What's that for?' He looked panicked.

'You, if you want to see your baby born,' the nurse told him without ceremony, and then called for a resident to check Amanda.

He appeared in the labor room two minutes later, while Jack was changing, and announced that Amanda was at eight centimeters and going fast. She was at nine by the time he was finished.

'Get me an epidural,' she said, clutching the bars on the side of the bed through the next contraction . . . 'morphine . . . Demerol . . . anything . . . give me something . . .'

'It's too late, Mrs Kingston,' the nurse said soothingly. 'You should have been here at seven centimeters.'

'I was busy. I was driving to the hospital in my husband's fucking Ferrari.' She was crying then. This wasn't funny. And she turned around to look at the resident and the nurse with fury. 'Are you telling me that if I had been here half an hour ago, I could have had an epidural? This is your fault,' she said to Jack miserably as he emerged from the bathroom looking like a scrub nurse.

'What's my fault? Oh this . . .' he looked at the enormous belly, 'I guess it is. And by the way,' he turned to the doctor imperiously, 'she's not Mrs Kingston.'

'She's not?' He looked startled and picked up the chart. It said it plainly. 'It says here she's Mrs Kingston.'

'She's Mrs Watson,' Jack corrected, still drunk from the unknown quantities of Champagne he had drunk at their wedding.

It was going to be hours, possibly days, before he was sober, and Amanda knew it.

'Never mind who I am. Just get my doctor. Where is he?'

'I'm right here, Amanda,' a voice from the doorway said coolly.

'Good. I want drugs, and they won't give them to me.' He talked to the resident for a minute and then nodded.

'How about a little morphine?'

'Sounds terrific.' They attached her to a monitor, gave her the shot, and started an intravenous on her, all in under five minutes. But just watching them do all of it had made Jack violently nauseous. He was sitting with his eyes closed in a chair in the corner, with the room spinning around him.

'Let's get Mr Watson a cup of coffee, black, shall we?' the doctor said, and the nurse raised an eyebrow.

'IV?'

'Good idea.' The medical team chuckled, and Jack opened one eye and looked at them as Amanda suffered through the next pain, but the morphine had at least taken the edge off.

'Why is everyone so loud here?' Jack complained just as Jan and Louise walked in, and went straight to their mother.

'You shouldn't be here,' she told Jan groggily. The morphine was making her sleepy.

'Why not, Mom?' She touched her cheek gently and stroked her hair, as Louise went to get her ice chips. When she was in labor, it had been all she wanted .

'Because you'll never want to have children. This is awful,' and then she added as an afterthought, having closed her eyes for just a minute, 'but it's worth it. I love you, baby,' she whispered to her and then drifted off again, as Louise came back into the room with the ice chips. 'I love you too, Louise,' she said, and gratefully accepted the ice chips. Jack was still sitting in the corner, drinking coffee.

And at five o'clock, when the doctor checked her again, they decided she was ready to go to the delivery room, but the morphine was wearing off by then, and Amanda was complaining.

'I feel awful . . . why do I feel so awful . . . ?'

'Because you're having a baby,' Louise told her, as Jack walked over to stand beside her. He was looking a lot more sober.

'How are you doing, sweetheart?' he asked, looking sympathetic.

'I feel awful.'

'I'll bet you do.' And then he looked at the nurse with annoyance. 'Can't you give her something? Why don't you put her out, for chrissake?'

'Because she's having a baby, not brain surgery, and she has to push now.'

'I don't want to push. I hate pushing. I hate everything. I hate this.' All the morphine had done was make her feel groggy and out of it, but she still felt every pain.

'It'll be over soon,' he said as he followed the gurney to the delivery room, wondering how he had gotten roped into this. He didn't want to see it, but he didn't want to leave her either. And her two daughters were following right behind him. The equipment in the room alone made him feel dizzy. They offered each of them a stool near her head, and propped her up to a nearly sitting position with her feet in stirrups, and over in the corner was a small plastic bassinet, with a heat light on it, to keep it warm for the baby. It suddenly made it all so real to him. They were here for a reason. Something great was happening. They weren't just there to watch her suffer.

But after a while, it began to feel as though that was why they had come here. She pushed for two hours and got nowhere. The baby was enormous. There were whispers among the medical team, and the doctor glanced at the clock and nodded. 'We'll give her another ten minutes.' But Jack was alert by now, and he had heard them.

'What does that mean?'

'The baby's not moving much, Jack,' the doctor said quietly. 'And Amanda's pretty tired. We may have to give her a hand here.'

'What kind of a hand?' He looked panicked. He knew even before they told him. The training film. The caesarean. The one that looked like they had cut the woman in half with the chain saw. And he looked at the doctor in open terror. 'Do you have to?'

'We'll see. Maybe not, if she helps us.' Amanda was miserable by then, she was crying and clutching his hands, and both her daughters looked worried. But Jack looked worse than she did. And five minutes later, there had been no improvement. They were standing around waiting for the next pain, when an alarm went off, and the entire room seemed to be filled with buzzing and everyone leaped into action around her.

'What is that? What happened?' Jack looked panicked, and totally sober.

'It's the fetal monitor, Jack. The baby's in trouble,' the doctor explained, but he was too busy to say more. There were instructions flying everywhere, and the anesthesiologist was saying something to Amanda and she was crying.

'What kind of trouble?' Jack was desperate to know what was happening and no one would tell him.

'You have to leave the room now, all of you,' the doctor said loudly, and then to the anesthesiologist: 'Do we have time for an epidural?'

'I'll try it,' he answered. More running, more instructions, noise everywhere, and Amanda reaching for Jack's hand like a wounded animal as she lay there. The girls had already left the room by then, but Jack knew he couldn't leave her. He couldn't do this to her.

'I took the class,' he told anyone who would listen. 'I took the Lamaze class with the film on C-sections . . .' But no one was listening, their eyes were glued to the monitor, and they were still trying unsuccessfully to wrest his son from Amanda.

The epidural was in place by then, and the doctor looked at Jack sternly. 'Sit down, and talk to her.' They put a screen in front of her so he couldn't see the surgery, only her face, and the anesthesiologist seemed to be doing a thousand things at once, and there were trays of instruments being moved around as Jack tried not to watch them. But all he could see now were her eyes, her face, and the terror he saw there.

'It's all right, baby, I'm here. It's going to be fine. They'll have the baby out in a minute.' He found himself silently praying that he wasn't lying to her.

'Is he okay? Is the baby okay, Jack?' She was crying and talking all at once, but she felt no pain now, just a lot of tugging and pulling. And Jack kept his eyes on her, telling her how much he loved her.

'The baby's fine,' he kept telling her, willing it to be true, praying that nothing had happened to the baby. He didn't want that to happen to her. She had been through too much now. The baby had to come through it. But the surgery seemed to take forever. There was sweat falling off Jack's face onto the drape next to her, and his tears mixed with hers as they waited. There was an endless ticking in the room, and then a sudden silence as she began to cry harder. It was as though she knew, as though she sensed that something terrible was about to happen, and all he could do was kiss her and tell her how much he loved her. But how would he ever make it up to her if the baby died? He knew that no matter what he did, he couldn't. And as he looked at her, willing their son to live, they suddenly heard a small wailing sound that filled the room, and her eyes opened wide in wonder.

'Is he okay?' She was completely worn out, but it was all she wanted to know now, and the doctor was quick to reassure her.

'He's fine.' They cut the cord, and put him in the scale to weigh him as Jack went to look at his boy, his son. Nine pounds twelve ounces. Almost ten pounds. He had fought hard to get here. He had her big blue eyes, and a look of astonishment on his face as though he had arrived sooner than he meant to. And he had. He was almost three weeks early.

They cleaned him up and wrapped him in a blanket then, and lay him next to his mother, but her arms were still strapped to boards and she couldn't hold him. Jack held him for her, and his eyes filled with tears as he watched Amanda look at her son for the first time, and touch him with her cheek.

Nothing had ever moved him more than this woman he had come to love so much, and the baby neither of them had expected. He was a small dream being born, a large hope for the future, a special delivery from heaven. And suddenly Jack didn't feel old, but young, as he looked down at them. It was a gift of magic for the future. Like opening a window onto sunlight.

'He's so beautiful,' she whispered as she looked up at Jack. 'He looks like you.'

'I hope not,' he said, with tears rolling down his cheeks as he bent to kiss her. 'Thank you,' he said to her '. . . for not giving him up . . . for wanting him when I didn't.'

'I love you,' she said sleepily. It was eight o'clock in the morning, and their baby was ten minutes old now.

'I love you too,' he said, watching her as she drifted off to sleep, and they took the baby away to the nursery, while they finished ministering to his mother. He sat for a long time, watching her, and when they rolled her back to her room finally, after the recovery room, she was still sound asleep, and he was still with her.

The others were waiting for them there, they had already heard the news, Paul was there too, and they were all smiling.

'Congratulations!' Louise was the first to say it, and for once, she meant it.

THE END

THE GIFT
by Danielle Steel

On a June day, a young woman in a summer dress steps off a Chicago-bound bus into a small midwestern town. She doesn't intend to stay. She is just passing through. Yet her stopping here has a reason, and it is part of a story you will never forget.

The time is the 1950s, when life was simpler, people still believed in dreams, and family was, very nearly, everything. On a tree-lined street in the heartland of America an extraordinary set of events begins to unfold. A happy home is shattered by a child's senseless death, a loving marriage starts to unravel, and a stranger arrives — a young woman who will touch many lives before she moves on. She and a young man will meet and fall in love. Their love, so innocent and full of hope, helps to restore a family's dreams. And all of their lives will be changed forever by the precious gift she leaves them.

0 552 14245 X

WINGS
by Danielle Steel

From her family's dusty farmland airstrip near Chicago, the child Cassie O'Malley would look at the planes sitting shimmering in the moonlight. Her First World War veteran father Pat wanted his son to be a pilot, not his reckless red-haired daughter. But ever since she could remember, Cassie had felt the pull of taking to the skies, and her father's partner Nick, fellow air ace and airborne daredevil, was willing to break all the rules to teach her to fly.

When Cassie was invited to California to become a test pilot, her record-breaking flights soon made her a media darling. Risking her life, pushing herself to her limits, in a world preparing for the Second World War, she decided to chart her own course and pursue her own destiny, whatever it cost her.

Wings is set in a time of constant change, when the world was on the brink of war and the skies were filled with adventurers, a time when courage and daring forever changed modern-day aviation.

0 552 13748 0

LIGHTNING
by Danielle Steel

As a partner in one of New York's most prestigious law firms, Alexandra Parker barely manages to juggle husband, career, and the three-year-old child she gave birth to at forty. Then lightning strikes – a routine medical check-up turns her world upside-down when tests reveal shattering news. Her husband Sam, a Wall Street whiz-kid, is as proud of his long-time marriage to Alex as he is of his successful career – until he is caught off guard by Alex's illness. Terrified of losing his wife and family, Sam fails to provide any kind of emotional support for Alex or his daughter.

Almost overnight, Sam takes his distance from Alex, and they become strangers. As lightning strikes them again, Sam's promising career suddenly explodes into disaster, and his very life and identity are challenged. With his future hanging in the balance, Alex must decide what she feels for Sam, if life will ever be the same for them again, or if she must move on without him.

Lightning tells the story of a family thrust into uncertainty. In this significant novel Danielle Steel explores whether the bonds of love and marriage can withstand life's most unexpected bolts of lightning.

0 552 13749 9

FIVE DAYS IN PARIS
by Danielle Steel

Peter Haskell, president of a major pharmaceutical company, has everything: power, position, and a family for which he has sacrificed a great deal. Olivia Thatcher is the wife of a famous senator, who has given to her husband's ambitions and career until her soul is bone-dry. She is trapped in a web of duty and obligation, married to a man she once loved and no longer even knows; when her son died, a piece of Olivia died too.

On the night of a bomb threat, Olivia and Peter meet accidentally in Paris. Their lives converge for one magical moment in the Place Vendôme, and in a cafe in Montmartre their hearts are laid bare. Peter, once so sure of his marriage and success, is faced with the jeopardy of his professional career – Olivia, no longer sure of anything, knows that she cannot go on any more. When Olivia disappears, only Peter suspects that it may not be foul play, and he has to find her again. But where will they go from there? Five days in Paris is all they have.

A novel about honour and commitment, love and integrity, and about finding hope again, *Five Days in Paris* will change your life forever.

0 552 14378 2

MALICE
by Danielle Steel

At seventeen, on the night of her mother's funeral, Grace Adams is attacked. A young woman with secrets too horrible to tell, with hurts so deep they may never heal, Grace will not tell the truth about the attack. She is beautiful enough for men to want her but, after a lifetime of being a victim, now she must pay the price for other people's sins.

From the depths of an Illinois women's prison to a Chicago modelling agency, and from there to a challenging career in New York, Grace carries the past with her wherever she goes. In healing her own pain, she reaches out to battered women and children who live a nightmare she knows only too well. When Grace meets Charles Mackenzie, a New York lawyer, she has found a man who wants nothing from her – except to heal her, to hear her secrets and to give her the family she so desperately wants. But with happiness finally within her grasp, Grace is at her most vulnerable – in danger of losing everything to an enemy from her past, an enemy bent on malice.

Malice tells the story of a woman who transforms a life of pain into a blessing for others. Revealing both the stark reality of domestic abuse and the healing power of love, *Malice* is more than superb fiction. It is a piece of life.

0 552 14131 3

SILENT HONOUR
by Danielle Steel

Set against a vivid backdrop of war and change, *Silent Honour* tells of the triumph of a woman caught between cultures and determined to survive.

In August 1941 Hiroko, eighteen years old and torn between her mother's belief in ancient traditions and her father's passion for modern ideas, leaves Kyoto to come to California for an education. To Hiroko, California is a different world – a world of barbecues, station wagons and college. Her cousins in California have become more American than Japanese – and Hiroko also finds a link between her old and new worlds when she becomes friendly with Peter, her uncle's university assistant. But on December 7 1941 Pearl Harbor is bombed by the Japanese, and within hours, war is declared. Suddenly Hiroko has become an enemy in a foreign land. Terrified, begging to go home, she is ordered by her father to stay. But as the military is empowered to remove the Japanese from their communities, Hiroko and her family end up in the detention centre, where they fight to stay alive amid the drama of life and death in the camp.

This extraordinary novel creates a portrait of human tragedy and strength, divided loyalties and love. Danielle Steel portrays the human cost of that terrible time in history, as well as the remarkable courage of a people whose honour and dignity transcended the chaos that surrounded them.

0 552 14132 1

THE RANCH
by Danielle Steel

Mary Stuart, Tanya and Zoe had been inseparable in college, but had not seen each other for twenty years or more. Marriage, motherhood and careers had kept them apart until one summer, at a sprawling ranch in Wyoming, the three women are reunited and reach out to each other again.

Once they shared everything, but now pretence between them runs high. Mary Stuart, married for twenty-two years to a Manhattan lawyer, masks the guilt and fear that her husband will never forgive her for their son's death. Tanya, a singer and rock star, enjoys all the trappings of fame and success – a mansion in Bel Air, legions of fans, and a broken heart for the children she wanted but never had, and the men who have taken advantage of her, and the tabloids that have rocked her life. Zoe has her hands full as single mother to an adopted two-year-old, and as a doctor at an Aids clinic in San Francisco, until unexpected news forces her to re-evaluate both her future, and her current life.

But their friendship is still a bond they all treasure and share. For each of the women, a few weeks at the ranch bring healing and release, as old hurts are buried, ancient secrets revealed, and hope is renewed.

0 552 14133 X

A LIST OF OTHER DANIELLE STEEL TITLES
AVAILABLE FROM CORGI BOOKS
AND BANTAM PRESS

13523 2	NO GREATER LOVE	£5.99
13525 9	HEARTBEAT	£5.99
13522 4	DADDY	£5.99
13524 0	MESSAGE FROM NAM	£5.99
13745 6	JEWELS	£5.99
13746 4	MIXED BLESSINGS	£5.99
13526 7	VANISHED	£5.99
13747 2	ACCIDENT	£5.99
14245 X	THE GIFT	£4.99
13748 0	WINGS	£5.99
13749 9	LIGHTNING	£5.99
14378 2	FIVE DAYS IN PARIS	£5.99
14131 3	MALICE	£5.99
14132 1	SILENT HONOUR	£5.99
14133 X	THE RANCH	£5.99
14401 0	LIGHTNING AUDIO	£12.99★
14362 6	VANISHED AUDIO	£8.99★
14395 2	FIVE DAYS IN PARIS AUDIO	£12.99★
14374 X	THE GIFT AUDIO	£9.99★
50208 5	THE RANCH	£14.99★
47761 7	SILENT HONOUR AUDIO	£14.99★
04074 0	SPECIAL DELIVERY (Hardback)	£9.99
04071 6	THE GHOST (Hardback)	£16.99
04069 4	THE LONG ROAD HOME (Hardback)	£16.99

Born in Paris in 1947, Chris... ...rst visited Egypt when he was seventeen, w... ...dy Egyptology and archaeology at the Sorbo... ...ow one of the world's leading Egyptologists. H... ...hor of the internationally bestselling RAMSES and ... MYSTERIES OF OSIRIS series, and several other novels on Ancient Egypt. Christian Jacq lives in Switzerland.

About the Translator

Sue Dyson is a prolific author of both fiction and non-fiction,
including over thirty novels both contemporary and historical.
She has also translated a wide variety of French fiction.

Tutankhamun
The Last Secret

Christian Jacq

Translated by Sue Dyson

POCKET
BOOKS

London · New York · Sydney · Toronto
A CBS COMPANY

First published in France by XO Editions under the title
Toutankhamon: L'Ultime Secret, 2008
First published in Great Britain by Simon & Schuster UK Ltd, 2009
This edition first published by Pocket Books, 2009
An imprint of Simon & Schuster UK Ltd
A CBS COMPANY

1 3 5 7 9 10 8 6 4 2

Simon & Schuster UK Ltd
1st Floor
222 Gray's Inn Road
London WC1X 8HB

www.simonandschuster.co.uk

Simon & Schuster Australia
Sydney

A CIP catalogue record for this book is available from the British Library

ISBN: 978-1-84739-392-0

Typeset by Ellipsis Books Limited, Glasgow
Printed and bound in Great Britain by
CPI Cox & Wyman, Reading, Berkshire RG1 8EX

This tale probably belongs in the realms of fiction. Nevertheless, I have had to alter the names of certain characters, as it seems sometimes the truth can be surprising.

Ch. J.

1

*Do you want to know who you really are? Be in Cairo in a
fortnight, on 28 April 1951. Come to Saint Sergio's Church at
8 p.m. You will be contacted. If you do this, you will have a
chance to find out. If not, you will for ever remain a stranger
to yourself. And your whole life will have been nothing but
shadows and illusions.*

As he read this incredible message for the tenth time, Mark
Wilder bumped into a passer-by. Startled, he apologized, raised
his head and saw the obelisk that had been erected in Central
Park in 1881. People called it 'Cleopatra's Needle', but in
reality it was the work of one of the greatest pharaohs of ancient
Egypt, Tuthmosis III. Placed under the protection of Thoth, the
god of wise men, this monarch enjoyed a long reign[*] and wrote
the *Book of the Hidden Room,* which was intended to resurrect
the royal soul at the heart of the light.

Walking along aimlessly, Mark Wilder had not expected this
encounter with the stone column, which soared upwards and
attracted positive forces. The hieroglyphs carved on the obelisk
spoke of Tuthmosis III's festival of regeneration and his ability
to pass on celestial energy magically to the human race. A
universe far removed from the bustle of New York and the
ferocious world of corporate lawyers, of which Mark was one

[*] 1504–1450 BC.

of the most brilliant. So brilliant, in fact, that he was expected to have an outstanding career in politics, culminating at the very least in a senator's post. The influential members of the President's inner circle had already noticed him and were unanimous in their opinion. He was a perfect symbol of the American miracle, with all the qualities required to take up high office and serve his country.

But Mark wanted to get his breath back. At the age of forty-two, he was still at the peak of fitness; he ran marathons and could hold his own against top-notch tennis players. As a confirmed bachelor with a substantial fortune and nothing more to prove in his profession, where he had achieved success after success, he had decided to take a year's sabbatical and travel the world, exploring different countries and cultures in order to clear his mind. His right-hand man, Dusty Malone, was more than capable of running the office and taking care of current cases. In the event of an emergency, he would know how to reach his boss.

Just as he was reading through his itinerary, Mark had received this surprising letter from Cairo. To all outward appearances it was an idiotic joke. A month earlier, when he was battling a stubborn opponent he had eventually overcome, he would have thrown it into the waste-paper basket. Now, on the eve of his departure, he wondered. His hunter's instinct told him to be wary of reacting too rationally.

Mark strode back across Central Park to his luxurious Manhattan office. Walking had always helped him to find solutions to complex problems, and he still avoided cars and lifts as much as possible.

The first three months of this year, 1951, had seen his firm win several resounding victories. Mark's practice was regarded as the foremost in New York, and the finest legal minds vied with each other for a chance to join his team; but first they had to get past Dusty Malone and his infallible nose for trouble.

Dusty was Mark's confidant and his only real friend. He was

not jealous of his boss, since he was perfectly content with his role as second in command, and he enjoyed a happy family life with a buxom wife and two fine daughters.

'Ah, there you are!' exclaimed Dusty, puffing on his Cuban cigar. 'Before you vanish, you must give me your opinion on three thick case files. Then I'll take care of managing them. And seeing as your year's rest won't last longer than three weeks, normal life will recommence shortly. Three weeks – I'm exaggerating . . . After a fortnight of hotels, beaches, pretty but brainless girls and boring guided tours, you'll take the first plane back to New York!'

Sure that his prediction was correct, Dusty snapped his broad, flowery braces and gazed at the man with the wide forehead, brown eyes and athletic build, his whole being dominated by an aura of calm strength; a man he had always wholeheartedly admired.

'What do you think of this letter?' asked Mark, handling it to him.

Dusty snorted with laughter. 'Absolute rubbish! Surely you're not going to attach any importance to the ramblings of some foreigner? And it isn't even signed!'

'I don't know Egypt. A first stop there might be rather appealing.'

'Well, I *do* know Egypt: it's a veritable powder keg! Have you forgotten the 1948 war? The Israelis beat the hell out of the Egyptians, and there were serious disturbances in Cairo. There were countless attacks on Western businessmen, large stores, cinemas, the offices of English and French businesses, and, of course, Jewish ones. Bombs went off in the Jewish quarter and there were dozens of victims.'

'The war is over, Dusty.'

'Don't be so sure! Since the state of Israel was recognized by the Western powers, the situation seems extremely tense. Egypt has never signed the peace treaty, only an armistice that could be broken at any moment.'

'King Farouk doesn't give the impression of being a bloodthirsty conqueror,' objected Mark.

'He's crooked – and patient. During the summer of 1948 he seized numerous assets belonging to Westerners. The lucky ones were out of Egypt at the time; the others were imprisoned. Lots of residents who'd lived in the country for a long time were ruined. And Farouk's soldiers, aided by his political police, had no hesitation in murdering people and killing French soldiers. Only the British can stand up to him. But he wants to drive them out, get back the Suez Canal and confirm himself as the spiritual and temporal leader of the Middle East.'

Mark smiled. 'From what the papers say, he prefers spending his time gambling ridiculous amounts of money in the casinos of Alexandria, Monte Carlo and Deauville.'

Dusty chewed on his cigar. 'OK, the big tub of lard is a great gambler, I'll grant you that. Apparently he can lose more than fifty thousand dollars in a single evening. But he's still a dangerous guy, one who gets rid of all his opponents.'

'I'm not one of them,' the lawyer pointed out. 'An ordinary tourist is no threat to his throne.'

'Don't go there, Mark. You'll be wasting your time. Go and laze about in the Caribbean for a few days and then hurry back.'

'Finding out who I really am . . . It's tempting.'

'Good God! Is a man like you really going to fall for a line like that?'

'Life can be strange, Dusty. Maybe it's offering me the chance to solve a mystery.'

Malone pounded his forehead with his clenched fist. 'So now you're into metaphysics? Go and have fun in Cairo, then, go and see the pyramids and Saint Sergio's Church, say hello to the Sphinx from me and then get back here. We have work to do.'

2

Father Pacomas was living out a peaceful old age in the heart of Old Cairo. Time seemed to have forgotten the old scholar, who possessed an immense library teeming with Egyptian, Coptic, Greek and Aramaic texts. The priest knew how to read hieroglyphs and was happy to receive visits from young researchers and give them his precious advice.

That morning, his visitor was a very agitated woman shopkeeper, who was looking for a different kind of knowledge.

'Father, help me, I beg of you!'

'What ails you, my child?'

'I am possessed by a demon!'

'How can you be so certain?'

'Customers have stopped buying my baskets, my husband has lost interest in me and my children keep attacking me!'

'It's just a bad phase.'

'No, Father, it's a demon! Yesterday, my hands were covered in blood. Every night, my bed moves, the furniture creaks and a black shape passes through the house, laughing. Please, help me.'

'Have you consulted your parish priest?'

'He can't do anything for me. Everyone knows you are the greatest magician in Cairo and that you have already saved hundreds of victims from demons. Have pity. Don't abandon me!'

'Let me see.'

Her eyes filled with hope, the shopkeeper allowed herself to be examined.

Abbot Pacomas felt her hands and feet, listened to her heart and laid his hand on the nape of her neck.

'No doubt about it,' he concluded. 'You have indeed fallen prey to an *afarit*, an aggressive creature that deprives you of breath and corrupts your blood.'

'Can you . . . Can you help me?'

'I shall try. Kneel and pray to the Virgin.'

The possessed woman did so.

The abbot donned a long white robe; white was the only colour that enabled him to communicate with the invisible world.

Then he consulted a grimoire dating from the age of the Ptolemies and intoned a series of extremely ancient incantations addressed to the king of the demons. This forced it to answer him and reveal the identity of the *afarit* that was tormenting the unfortunate woman. It was a virulent, gnawing demon, summoned up by a jealous female relative.

Pacomas fashioned a statuette out of wax, engraved the attacker's name on it and heated it up in a bronze vessel.

Grimacing, the possessed woman fell on to her back, her arms stretched out sideways.

While the flames were consuming the *afarit*, the abbot burned incense and poured holy water on to the victim's forehead, chest, hands and feet.

At peace now, she stood up. 'I feel well, so well!'

'You have been delivered, my child. Paint your bedroom door red and wear this talisman.'

The old man handed the young woman a small square of linen covered in indecipherable signs.

'Father . . . How can I thank you? I shall give you half of everything I possess, I . . .'

'I do not want anything, my child. It is enough to see that you are healed.'

The shopkeeper kissed the exorcist's hands.

'May God keep you alive for many years, Father!'

'May His will be done.'

The shopkeeper left, light-hearted and happy now.

Pacomas locked the door to his library and entered an underground chamber whose existence was known only to himself.

Who could have guessed that the habit of a Coptic monk, venerated by the entire Christian community of Cairo, concealed the last priest of the god Amon? Despite the Christianization of Egypt, followed by the Arab invasion, the Ancients' tradition of initiation had never been interrupted. True, most of the faithful had left this inhospitable land and taken refuge in the West, founding communities and building cathedrals where the message continued to be passed on in a symbolic form. But in spite of everything, a few groups had survived in Egypt itself.

But now, this long lineage was in danger of dying out.

Pacomas's underground chapel was a house of eternity built by his ancestors during the last days of the pharaohs. There was a threshold of pink granite, a silver floor, two lotus-shaped pillars, an acacia-wood plinth for the solar boat, an offertory table and a naos containing a gold statuette of the goddess Maat, the embodiment of righteousness and correctness in the universe.

Each morning, in the name of the initiates who had passed on to the eternal East, Pacomas – whose name meant 'loyal follower of Khnum', the ram-headed potter god who fashioned living beings on his wheel – celebrated the ritual awakening of the divine powers. In this way he preserved a fragment of harmony in a world afflicted by terrible madness, disorder and cruelty.

Soon, his heart would cease to beat and he would join his ancestors. Before that happened, he must pass on the vital information he possessed, though he could not exploit it himself, and fulfil a mission whose importance transcended himself and his era. This course of action might prove futile, but he had promised to carry it out and he would keep his word, even at the risk of being condemned by Osiris's court and seeing his soul fed to the soul-eater.

So the last priest of Amon had written to Mark Wilder, to invite him to a meeting during which he would reveal his true identity.

But would a brilliant American corporate lawyer, with limitless ambitions, pay any heed to such a strange letter?

Pacomas spoke the words of 'leave on command', the 'offering given by pharaoh' and the 'coming in peace' of the reunited soul, composed of Ra, the day sun, and Osiris, the sun of the night. A soft light filled the shrine, and the priest felt himself transported into the presence of his ancestors who, for thousands of years, had maintained the link between the visible and the invisible.

Would Amon, 'the hidden god', the One who begat the multitude while remaining One, consent to answer him?

When the ritual was over, Pacomas looked at the copy of the letter he had sent to Mark Wilder.

At the foot of the document the hieroglyph of the two running legs had appeared. There could be no confusion about its meaning: Mark Wilder would come.

3

Mark fell asleep during takeoff and did not wake up until the plane landed in Cairo. He found aeroplanes the ideal place in which to relax. Up in the air, where nobody could contact him, he could at last get some restorative sleep.

Disembarkation procedures were carried out in a cheerful hubbub, although the policemen and Customs officers did not look particularly friendly. As he retrieved his luggage, the lawyer learned his first word of Arabic, and one of the most important: *bakshish*, or 'tip'. Built in the middle of the desert close to Heliopolis, an ancient site that had become a fashionable suburb of the capital, the airport linked the old land of the pharaohs to the modern world.

As he was looking for the travel agent who was supposed to meet him, a loud voice called out: 'Mark! It's you ... Is it really you?'

'John!'

'I'm so pleased to see you again! Is it business or pleasure?'

'Pleasure.'

'Which hotel?'

'The Mena House.'

'An excellent choice! If you like, I'll take you there.'

Mark spotted a little fellow struggling through the crowd brandishing a placard with his name on it.

'Someone's meeting me and ...'

'Don't worry. I'll sort it out.'

The little fellow seemed particularly pleased with his *bakshish*, and John took charge of the luggage.

'I wouldn't want to mess up your plans,' ventured Mark.

'You've only just set foot in the East, my friend! Here, time is elastic. Don't worry: I brought a client to the airport, and my next meeting isn't until around midnight, at a politician's house. Cairo never sleeps. And in the afternoon all the officials have a long siesta.'

John Hopkins was an international broker with an easy manner. In his forties, he was alert, of average height and deeply tanned. Extremely intelligent and widely travelled, he had a talent for clinching complex contracts with dubious countries. He had turned to Mark's firm for assistance several times and had always been more than happy with the results. Quite apart from their business relationship, the two men had struck up a rapport and had enjoyed several fiercely contested games of tennis before turning their attentions to the joys of gastronomy.

John's Mercedes plunged into Cairo's insane traffic.

'There's only one rule of the road here,' he said, 'and that's to intimidate your opponent. The road signs are purely decorative. Welcome to Cairo, Mark! It's an exhausting city, simple and complicated at the same time. To the east are the old neighbourhoods, with countless mosques and palaces, more or less in ruins; to the west you'll find the modern districts, a little piece of Europe, with hotels, shops and private clubs. They throw some magnificent parties there, packed with elegant women. If you have money, it's a great life.'

The Mercedes overtook a crowded bus. Clusters of people clung to its windows.

'Overpopulation is the main problem,' said John. 'Sixteen million people were living in Cairo in 1930, and there'll soon be twenty-five million. And it's likely to get worse. The peasants stream in from the countryside to set up home in the city, where they hope to find a better life. And government vetoes don't stop them. Buildings are being thrown up just about everywhere, and people are packed into housing that's often unsanitary – all the ingredients for a major explosion. Yet the country is wealthy, and industries are faring rather well. But only a very small minority derive the full benefit. And the other problem is galloping inflation, which is ruining the middle classes. In short, wealth and poverty coexist to a surprising degree. Sometimes, flour, sugar or petrol is rationed. And fewer than two per cent of Egyptians own more than half of the cultivated land. Add to that the people's resentment and disappointment after the recent military defeat of 1948, and you can understand how serious the situation is.'

'So why are you here?' asked Mark.

'Cotton. I've invested a lot of money and I want to get my stake back. Unfortunately, a scandal has just broken out on the Alexandria Stock Exchange. Speculators manipulated the exchange rates and were caught red-handed. As the wife of a minister was apparently involved in the fraud, popular anger is rising. Say, Mark . . . Why don't you give me a hand to clean up the mess?'

'I'm on vacation, John.'

'Knowing you, it won't last more than a week!'

'I need some rest, and there must be lots to see in Egypt.'

'You won't be disappointed! But all the same . . . You'll soon get back your taste for work, and I really could do with your help to stave off a disaster.'

'We'll see, John. Look out!'

As the Mercedes was passing the Opera House, a red sports car blocked its way.

With a violent swing of the wheel, John managed to avoid hitting it and swerved perilously close to a group of pedestrians, who screamed in terror, before bringing the car to a halt a few centimetres from the pavement.

'That madman ought to be locked up. But nobody will dare arrest him.'

'Why?' asked Mark in surprise.

'Because that's King Farouk himself. He drives his Rolls-Royces and his Cadillacs like a lunatic, hitting everything in his path. Did you see the colour of that bomb on wheels? Bright red! It's reserved for his immense stable of cars, so that the traffic police won't stop him. And yet he had a serious accident when he was twenty-four. But you'd swear it only made him want to drive faster. One day, another psychopath tried to overtake him . . . The king shot his tyres out! And the air is filled with the sound of Farouk's wailing car horns, imitating alarm bells, tunes played on a barrel organ, even the yelping of a dog that's been run over.'

'And that's the fellow who rules Egypt?'

'For the time being, Mark, for the time being . . . You have to admit that his policies are effective and, despite its mounting grievances, the army continues to obey him. Anyway, forget all that and have a good time. At the Mena House, that won't be difficult.'

The luxurious hotel, which stood at the foot of the pyramids, had originally been one of Khedive Ismail's hunting lodges. Then, in 1869, during the celebrations for the opening of the Suez Canal, the building had housed illustrious guests before being opened up to tourism. The British loved to take their afternoon tea on the shady terrace. Vast bedrooms, furnished in the Eastern style, were reminiscent of a palace from the Thousand and One Nights. A swimming pool lay like an oasis amid carefully tended gardens; a place made for dreaming and relaxation.

Zealous staff dealt with Mark's luggage, and an attentive maître d'hôtel showed the two Americans to his best table.

'I often come here,' said John. 'It's a quiet place, far from the bustle of Cairo. I recommend the salad with spring onions to start, followed by lamb roasted with grapes. And we can even enjoy a good French wine.'

Mark felt very strange. For the first time in his life he had no familiar landmarks, and he began to wonder if he had really landed. The great pyramid of Khufu loomed close by, an awe-inspiring witness to this unexpected meeting.

He had barely scratched the surface of Egypt, and yet he already knew that it was unlike any other country. Despite the modernity, the magic of the past had not disappeared. And whatever might happen, he would not regret gazing up at this unforgettably blue sky, or breathing this air, whose purity seemed born of its alliance with the desert.

'I've just had a crazy thought, John. Did you write this letter?'

The lawyer handed the document to his friend, who quickly read it.

'No, Mark, I didn't write this surprising summons! If I had, I would have signed it. And besides, I wouldn't have contacted you like that. "Do you want to know who you really are?" . . . What does that mean?'

'Perhaps I'll soon find out.'

'At first glance it looks like a joke.'

'At least it will have given me a chance to explore Egypt.'

'Old Cairo is worth a visit, and Saint Sergio's is a beautiful church. But don't forget the pyramids.'

'Don't worry. They're my first port of call.'

'Don't laze around for too long. As soon as you feel ready, call me at this number and we'll talk about my cotton problems. You won't regret it; I'll pay you well. See you later, Mark.'

The lawyer slipped John's business card into his jacket pocket. Then, intoxicated by the splendour of the landscape, he left the Mena House and walked towards the plateau where the pyramids stood.

4

After an excellent night's sleep and a sumptuous breakfast in the garden of the Mena House, Mark visited the great pyramid of Khufu and took a long walk across the Giza plateau to get a better look at the three pyramids. He had forgotten all about business, New York, America and the modern world. Fascinated by the perfection of the stone giants, he felt both reduced to a kind of nothingness and drawn towards the light of a sun so strong that it drove away many tourists from the site, unable to bear the searing heat. According to the locals, this late-April weather had beaten all records.

At sunset, Mark thought once again about his strange rendezvous. He enjoyed a beer before showering and putting on a lightweight suit.

No sooner had he stepped outside the hotel than a brand-new taxi drew up in front of the hotel steps. A smiling, pot-bellied man of about fifty sprang out.

'At your service, sir! Nobody knows Cairo better than I do. Where do you wish to go?'

'Old Cairo.'

'Climb in. I'll give you a good price.'

'Let's discuss that first.'

But the taxi was sparklingly clean, and the lawyer didn't haggle for long.

'My name is Hosni and I have eight children,' revealed the driver. 'What country do you come from?'

'America.'

'We love the Americans! They had to fight for freedom. The British and the French are colonizers. We won't miss them when they leave. Is this your first visit to Egypt?'

'It is.'

'Welcome to our country! Hospitality is sacred here. Are you staying long?'

'That depends.'

'Well, whatever you do, don't be in a hurry! You have to learn to appreciate every moment and discover Cairo's charm little by little. Are you beginning with the Christian churches?'

'That's right.'

'Christians and Muslims, we live in peace. In the past, Jews were tolerated. But because of the creation of the state of Israel and the 1948 war, they have left. *Inshallah!* Don't forget to visit the mosques; they are splendid.'

'I have no intention of forgetting them.'

'What is your profession?'

'I'm a businessman.'

'Ah, business! I would have liked to dabble in business myself. But God did not wish it. After your stay in Cairo, will you be going to Luxor?'

'I don't know yet.'

'Because of business?'

'That's right.'

All these questions were starting to irritate Mark. Seeing that this was the case, the driver concentrated on his driving, which demanded real dexterity.

As they reached the old quarters of the city, the lawyer entered a garishly coloured world that would have horrified many other Americans: donkeys laden with lucerne, mud underfoot, and pestilential odours mingling with the scent of spices; black-veiled women shoulder to shoulder with girls dressed in the Western style; and men in suits and fezzes alongside others wearing the *galabieh*, the many-coloured traditional robe. There were hens on the balconies, goats on the rooftops, and a frantic bustle mingled with a feeling of slowness . . . Mark soaked up the whole spectacle.

'Cairo is the mother of the world,' the driver reminded him. 'Here, all dreams become reality.'

Old Cairo, which covers part of the ancient city of Fostat, was enclosed within the walls of Egypt's Babylon, where the battle between the forces of light and the forces of darkness took place.

The taxi came to a halt.

'Where exactly would you like to go?' asked the driver.

'I was hoping to stroll around on my own.'

'I wouldn't advise it.'

'Why? Is it dangerous?'

'No, but you are likely to miss the most interesting buildings. Everything is more or less hidden away; the outward appearance of the churches is of no interest. Without a good guide, you will miss the essentials.'

'Drive me to Saint Sergio's Church.'

'An excellent choice! I recommend the crypt, where Christ, the Virgin and Joseph stayed for a long time, sheltered from the sun's heat and the cold of the night. It was there, too, that the cradle containing the infant Moses was placed after he was rescued from the waters. Afterwards, you'll certainly want to visit the museum . . .'

'I prefer to study one place in depth rather than disperse my energies.'

'Whatever you say, sir.'

The two men headed into a maze of narrow streets where children were playing. On the walls, Mark made out pictures of Saint George killing the dragon; some balconies were decorated with strings of electric lights, surrounding pictures of Christ. Here and there were heavy iron-studded wooden doors.

The driver led his customer across the museum garden, then they walked down some steps leading to an alleyway. At its end stood Saint Sergio's Church. Its central door was bricked over.

'You can enter by the door on the right-hand side. Take as much time as you like; I'll wait for you here.'

Mark explored the little basilica. Its nave, flanked by aisles, was lined by two rows of marble columns. To the east were three shrines separated from the nave by a partition decorated with polygonal shapes, stars and crosses.

No one.

The American headed for the entrance to the crypt and went down into it. It had a low ceiling and an oppressive atmosphere . . . The Holy Family must have had a difficult time here.

Mark waited patiently for eight o'clock.

Still no one, well after the appointed time.

So the letter had been a hoax. Unless . . . He went back outside.

The driver was sitting down, smoking a cigarette.

'Did you enjoy your visit?'

'It was superb.'

'Do you want to go back to the Mena House?'

'No, I want to stroll around for a while.'

'I can take you to an excellent restaurant . . .'

'No, that's fine, friend. Here's the price we agreed, plus a nice fat *bakshish*. Good night.'

Before the driver could reply, Mark walked quickly away and mingled with the crowd.

After about ten minutes, he bought some jasmine from a delighted little boy and took the opportunity to glance behind him, to make sure that the driver had not followed him.

Reassured, he asked a dignified old man how to get out of Old Cairo and return to the city centre. Speaking a mixture of French and English, he provided friendly directions.

'Do you need a guide?'

Mark turned around.

The voice came from a young woman aged around thirty, with black hair and sea-green eyes, just like the deities painted on the walls of the pharaohs' houses of eternity. She was not only beautiful; she also had charm and grace.

'Well . . . Why not?'

'Why did you not come to the rendezvous alone, Mr Wilder?'

5

After his initial shock, Mark found himself pleasantly intrigued.

'You speak perfect English, young lady.'

'That is vital when one is a tourist guide. I speak other languages, too. Please follow me. We are going to behave as if we were a guide and her client, who wishes to explore the hidden riches of Old Cairo, from the museum garden to the Coptic cemetery. Then nobody will be surprised to see us talking.'

'Since you know my name, may I know yours?'

'Ateya.'

'So it was you who wrote to me and fixed this rendezvous at Saint Sergio's Church?'

'No, Mr Wilder.'

'Then . . . who?'

'Your suspicious behaviour prevents me from answering that question. You missed the eight o'clock meeting, and I do not think there will be another.'

Irritated, the lawyer halted and looked the young woman straight in the eye.

'"Suspicious behaviour"? What's that supposed to mean? I received a bizarre, anonymous letter, and I took it seriously. I followed the instructions, and now you accuse me of goodness knows what! Admit that it was just a stupid hoax, and let's leave it at that.'

19

The woman's eyes flamed. 'Do you regard the truth as a hoax, Mr Wilder?'

'What truth?'

'The truth concerning you.'

'Oh, yes, I was forgetting! I'm supposed to find out who I really am . . .'

'Indeed.'

'Kindly stop making fun of me and tell me the real motives of whoever wrote that letter.'

'I assume that you don't know Egypt very well?'

'This is my first visit.'

'And yet there was a man waiting for you at the airport.'

'How do you know that?'

'I was watching.'

'You were spying on me!'

'I did not trust you, Mr Wilder, and I was right. Quickly, ask me a question about Christian churches!'

Out of the corner of her eye, Ateya was watching a man with a moustache, dressed in European clothes, who was approaching them.

'So, did the Holy Family really stay in Egypt?'

'Indeed they did. What is more, we should not speak of the "flight to Egypt" but of a return to the sources. Christ did not come here to hide. He gathered information from the Wise Men, passed on to the Coptic Church, which preserves it within its shrines.'

The guide launched into a description of the architecture of the primitive basilicas.

The man with the moustache walked away.

'He is an inspector in charge of overseeing the guides,' she explained. 'He regards me as professional and writes excellent reports about me.'

'Well, so much the better for you! The man who hailed me at the airport is called John Hopkins. He's an old friend who happened to be there by chance.'

'Do you believe in chance?' asked the young woman with a smile.

'You think that John was lying in wait for me?'

'When you see him again, ask him. What is he doing in Egypt?'

'He invested in cotton. John's an international broker who lives wherever there's good business to be done. Tomorrow he'll leave for India or China. My firm helps him when he's drawing up complex contracts.'

'And you were unaware that he was in Cairo?'

'Of course.'

On her right wrist, Ateya was wearing a bracelet made of golden ankhs. The jewellery was a small work of art, fashioned by an exceptionally talented goldsmith.

'Where are you staying?' she asked.

'At the Mena House. I have an immense room and a fabulous view of the pyramids. No photograph can do justice to their power. Even if your letter was a farce, I don't regret coming here.'

'Did you choose your own taxi?'

'No, he turned up out of the blue. He asked me a hundred questions and appointed himself as my guide. I found him too persistent, so I shook him off when I came out of Saint Sergio's.'

'Did he give you his name?'

'Hosni.'

'That man is a member of King Farouk's political police, whose job it is to follow foreigners.'

'But . . . I've only just arrived!'

'A guest at the Mena House is not just anybody and clearly merits special attention. By giving Hosni the slip, you're risking serious trouble.'

Perhaps Dusty was right, thought the lawyer. There were more tranquil destinations than Egypt. 'Listen,' he said. 'I don't want to get mixed up in any trouble! Either you explain or I'm going back to New York.'

'Go ahead, Mr Wilder. But if you do, you will never find out who you really are, and you will spend the rest of your life regretting it.'

The seriousness of her tone struck the lawyer. He had a sort of gift for detecting liars and fantasists, and it seemed that Ateya was neither.

'At least tell me if you know who wrote that letter.'

'I do.'

'And do you trust him?'

'I worship him. Given his position, he must remain out of reach and avoid all danger. The presence of your "friend" at the airport and of one of Farouk's police informants is hardly reassuring. You seem like a dangerous person to me, Mr Wilder.'

'I repeat: John is an old friend. And I've been put under surveillance like any other foreigner staying at the Mena House and setting off on his own to wander the streets of Cairo.'

'That is a very optimistic view of the situation.'

'Why shouldn't it be the correct one?'

'Because chance does not exist.'

Constantly on her guard, Ateya kept a watchful eye on passers-by. 'Should I set up another rendezvous or abandon you to your ignorance? After all, you may prefer not to know anything.'

'You arouse my curiosity, you demand that I cooperate blindly, and now you reject me! Isn't that a little too cruel?'

The young woman smiled again. Quite apart from the prospect of meeting the enigmatic individual whom she worshipped, Mark wanted to see her again.

'Do you sincerely wish to know the truth?'

'I do, Ateya.'

She thought for a long time. 'Tomorrow evening, at eight o'clock, leave the Mena House and walk for ten minutes in the direction of Cairo. A car will draw up next to you. The driver will speak my name, and you will say: "God bless you." He will reply: "May the Holy Family protect you." He will take you to see the writer of this letter, and you will discover who you really are.'

6

Limoun Bridge Station served the eastern suburbs of Cairo. There was an atmosphere of agitation, all the more so since the inaccurate train timetables created confusion, confusion that Mahmoud took advantage of in order to melt into the crowd. He knew all the plain-clothes police officers here. Housed in barracks and poorly trained, they occasionally arrested some poor devil and subjected him to a brutal interrogation.

The midday sun was burning hot. There were no troublemakers in sight. Farouk's roving thugs could enjoy a long siesta after a copious lunch, and Mahmoud could consult his informant without fear.

Aged thirty-two, tall and slender, with bright eyes, Mahmoud possessed the gift of remaining unseen. That is why the underground revolutionary group of Free Officers had chosen him as a liaison agent with the many informants they needed to accumulate information and prepare for profound changes in the regime.

The appalling defeat of 1948 had left the Egyptian army in a state of disarray and resentment. However, many soldiers had fought well. But they had quickly realized that, faced with the aggressive spirit and modern weaponry of the Israelis, they had only defective weapons. Their artillery exploded, tearing their users to pieces; their rifles had holes in them; the troops lacked supplies and medical care; wrong orders were followed by counter-orders, and there was no overall strategy. In short, an entire army had been sent out to be massacred.

Who was responsible for this rout? One hero, wounded three times and respected by all the officers and men, wanted to shed light on this disastrous episode. Born in Sudan in 1901, General Naguib, a small, stubborn, courageous man, had demanded a committee of enquiry.

At first glance the results were disappointing, since only his own comrades, petty fraudsters belonging to the artillery and the quartermaster's service, had been arrested in order to calm this irritating general. Appointed in command of the infantry, he, however, persisted in wishing to 'clean out the stables' and came to a conclusion that many other senior officers shared: the real person responsible for the Egyptian defeat, the man who had condemned his own soldiers to an unworthy, shameful death, was none other than King Farouk himself.

The arms dealers guilty of supplying the defective weapons belonged to Farouk's entourage and enjoyed the benefit of his protection. This clique of bandits and cynics had grown wealthy on the corpses of soldiers who had been trapped and defeated from the start.

General Naguib would never forgive Farouk for this monstrous crime; he was unworthy to rule. But the Egyptian army was still weak, incapable of driving out the occupying British forces with whom the monarch got on rather well. And even the politicians in the main party, the Wafd, the so-called defender of the people against Farouk's tyranny, had been involved in the defective weapons affair and received substantial sums of money.

Responding to an appeal from a few men who were determined to protest, General Naguib had consented to lead a group of opponents who expressed their opinions in a regular publication, *The Free Officers' Voice*, in which Naguib wrote incendiary articles signed 'The Unknown Soldier'.

Curiously, the ruling power did not intervene. This laxity

encouraged the conspirators to continue and to assume that they could gain still more ground. Moreover, *Al-Misri*, the influential daily newspaper of the Wafd party, was beginning to relay their protests and had no hesitation in criticizing their main adversary, General Sirri Amer, who was seen as the man who carried out Farouk's dirty work.

As Mahmoud saw it, they must be extremely cautious, for there might be a violent reaction at any moment. Secrecy was strictly maintained and cells were kept completely separate, and up to now the police had not realized the danger.

The key to success was information. So Mahmoud maintained a veritable army of informants, who enabled him to find out the adversary's intentions, in the hope that they would at least be one step ahead of him.

Hosni, the taxi driver, entered the station.

He was one of the most brilliant members of the team. Officially employed by the police, he played a particularly dangerous double game, misinforming his superiors and supplying first-hand information to the Free Officers, whom he supported unreservedly.

Hosni walked past Mahmoud, made as if to head for one of the platforms, then retraced his steps.

As Mahmoud had not moved, there was no danger. The taxi driver lit a cigarette and offered one to Mahmoud, who accepted it.

They could talk in complete safety.

'What's new, Hosni?'

'A rich American, a corporate lawyer, has just arrived at the Mena House. Our agent at the hotel gave me his name: Mark Wilder.'

'Is he just a tourist?'

'I doubt it.'

'Why?'

'He has not specified how long he is going to stay, as if he has come here to carry out a mission but does not know how

25

long it will take. And there is something even more surprising. For someone who claims to be visiting Egypt for the first time, he starts with Saint Sergio's Church – an odd thing to do.'

'He would seem to be a lover of Christian art.'

'In my opinion, he doesn't give a damn about it. He was supposed to meet someone there. But the church was empty. And, even more significantly, as he emerged from the shrine he dismissed me and disappeared. I tried to follow him, but he threw me off, like a professional who knows Old Cairo well.'

'An American spy . . .'

'Without a doubt. I have a nose for these things, and, believe me, that man is definitely no ordinary tourist.'

'Did he go back to the Mena House?'

'He did. He is relaxing for a few hours between two meetings.'

'Put someone on his tail,' ordered Mahmoud. 'Not you; he knows you.'

'My best men are busy elsewhere, but I'll manage somehow.'

'Anything to worry about as regards the police?'

'The usual routine. Nobody takes good old General Naguib seriously. In fact, his attacks suit Farouk. By allowing a lightweight opponent to speak, he shows how broad-minded he is. The British control the Suez Canal and the entire country, Farouk and his protégés get rich, business is booming and the Egyptian army neither wants nor is able to take power. The Free Officers? They're just good talkers who confine themselves to criticizing the regime and who have no solid support.'

'Are the police planning any large-scale operations?'

'None at all. Farouk is convinced that he can reign without any major difficulties for many years. The poverty of the people doesn't cost him any sleep.'

'Next meeting will be here, in a week's time, at sunset. In an emergency, you know how to get in touch with me.'

Hosni crushed his cigarette on the station floor and walked away.

Mark Wilder ... Mahmoud hoped that he really was an American secret agent, and the man he must meet as soon as possible.

7

It was a magnificent evening. First, the Giza pyramids were bathed in the golden rays of the setting sun, then they were blanketed by night, ready to confront the demon of darkness who would attempt to prevent the sun from being reborn. The soft, sweet air made Mark forget the dust of the street and the din of car engines. Following Ateya's instructions, he left the Mena House at eight o'clock and walked in the direction of Cairo.

Barely two minutes later, a grey Peugeot braked suddenly alongside him. The door opened.

'Get in, quickly! You're being followed.'

The American jumped into the car, whose seats sagged with age. It set off again, swerving around a van whose driver sounded his horn in protest.

'Ateya,' said the driver, a powerfully built, bull-necked fellow.

'God bless you.'

'May the Holy Family protect you. Relax, you're safe now. The man following you certainly had time to note down my registration number, but it's a false number plate. I was afraid there would be lots of them and they would jump us.'

'Where are we going?'

'You'll see.'

Mark sensed that he would get nothing out of the driver. The man had no desire to talk and was content to fulfil his mission.

Edgy, and handicapped by poor brakes and no shock absorbers, he drove much too fast, almost colliding with other vehicles as he overtook them and sounding his horn relentlessly. Mark rather worried that they might not reach their destination.

But the heavens were smiling on them, and the driver halted at the gateway to the famous bazaar quarter, which teemed with a motley crowd. He pushed up his right sleeve, revealing a cross tattooed on his wrist.

'Check that your guide has the same tattoo. If not, don't follow him.'

The Peugeot screeched off into the distance.

Mark found himself lost in a crowd composed of as many women as men, dressed in a host of different styles, from well-cut European suits to brightly coloured cotton robes. Everyone seemed to be on the lookout for a good deal, and a lot of haggling was going on. So as not to attract attention, the American pretended to be interested in a stall covered with baskets filled with spices.

Why had he wandered into this shadow theatre? Suddenly he realized how ridiculous the situation was. He, a brilliant New York lawyer, a member of the establishment and a future politician, was being manipulated by a band of jokers, as if he was becoming the reluctant hero of a spy novel! Someone was following him; he had to shake them off; he was being shunted from one place to another ... It was time to wake up. Mark decided to return to the Mena House, pack his things and take the first plane back to New York. Dusty Malone was right: he had no taste for vacations.

A youth with laughing eyes, dressed in a blue robe, grabbed his arm.

'Do you need a guide, boss? I know all the souks, and I'll show you all the best places.'

The bold youth pushed up his right sleeve and quickly pulled it down again. The lawyer had just enough time to glimpse a cross tattooed on his wrist.

'Listen . . .'

'Come on, boss. You won't be disappointed.'

Although annoyed, Mark agreed, solely because he wanted to see Ateya again. Perhaps she would agree to have dinner with him before he left. He wanted to know more about that young woman.

The youth led him into a maze of narrow streets, crowded with stalls and shops, some of them no more than a hole dug into a wall. Everything was on sale, from foodstuffs to quite acceptable glassware, and fabrics ranging from mediocre to luxurious.

The guide did not slow down until he reached the centre of the famous Khan el-Khalili, the bazaar whose thousands of shops dated from the thirteenth century. Close by the Islamic university of Al-Azhar, it had been established by the Mamelukes, whose militias controlled the country in those days. No tourist with an eye for a bargain ever passed up this obligatory stop.

The youth signalled to the Westerner to go right to the back of a coppersmith's shop, where scores of copper items were for sale. The proprietor, rugged sixty-year-old, immediately offered a glass of black tea to this potential customer.

'Take an interest in the wares, boss, and haggle over the prices,' advised the youth. 'But first you must pay me.'

Ten dollars delighted the young Copt, who did not even think of asking for more and disappeared into the crowd, abandoning the foreigner to the mercy of the shopkeeper.

'You are a very lucky man,' he declared. 'I am the finest coppersmith in Cairo and I supply the wealthiest families. Some call me "the Alchemist", because, according to legend, in the old days the men of my clan knew how to transform copper into gold. But that is only a legend . . . Nevertheless, we still manage to produce marvels. Do please look around.'

They were continuing to play games with him. The kid had taken him for a sucker and led him to a member of his brotherhood, who would attempt to sell him as many useless items as possible at the highest price.

'What do you think of this repoussé copper tray? Does it not resemble a sun, lighting up the darkness of seekers who search for the truth? Doubtless it will not suffice. I have much better things at the back of my shop.'

'I'm sorry; I'm not interested.'

'You are mistaken, Mr Wilder. Do not run away from yourself, or you will be lost for ever.'

Stunned, and almost in spite of himself, the American followed the coppersmith, who drew back a curtain and showed him into a long, narrow room filled with copper trays, cups and cooking pots.

At the back of this storeroom stood Ateya, dressed in a white blouse and a red skirt. Softly lit by candles, her beauty was sublime.

Mark was struck dumb.

'Don't you recognize me?' she asked, intrigued.

'Yes, of course I do. But all these precautions . . .'

'They were necessary. Farouk's police consider you an interesting subject, Mr Wilder, and we had to shake them off. We shall wait here for a few minutes in order to check that they really have lost the scent.'

Spending time with Ateya, in this half-light, seemed like a positive privilege, almost a moment of grace.

'Why would the police take an interest in me?'

'Your social position, no doubt. A man of your stature does not pass unnoticed and merits attention. Farouk wants to know everything about the rich foreigners who stay in his country and might be useful to him.'

'Are you ever going to take me to the person who wrote to me?'

She smiled, and Mark knew that, for the first time in his life, he had just fallen hopelessly in love.

This discovery robbed the confirmed bachelor of all critical sense, swept away his certainties and demolished the defences he had spent years building up.

She was the one; that was all there was to it.

And he would follow her to the ends of the earth to savour her presence, taste her mysteries and share her thoughts.

The curtain lifted again, and the coppersmith reappeared.

'The danger is past. You may leave now.'

Ateya and mark emerged from the shop using the little door at the rear, which opened on to a narrow street filled with passers-by.

She walked swiftly to the exit from the souk, where a small Fiat was waiting, guarded by a young Copt. He gave her the key, and she got behind the wheel.

'Get in, Mr Wilder. I am taking you to the most important meeting of your life. You are finally going to find out who you really are.'

8

Although she was a woman, Ateya did not allow herself to be browbeaten by male drivers and, taking reasonable risks, forced her way through the traffic several times to keep to her chosen route. After setting off up El-Azhar Avenue, she reached Midan el-Tahrir Square, close to the Egyptian Museum, and forked off towards the south of Cairo.

Mark remained strangely calm.

'Don't you want to know where we are going?' asked the young Copt in astonishment.

'Destiny is destiny.'

'So you are Egyptian already!'

'Since I don't understand any of what is happening to me, I shall just have to place my trust in you.'

'We are going back to Old Cairo,' she revealed. 'The episode in the bazaar was simply to mislead anyone who might be curious.'

'Saint Sergio's Church again?'

'No, the Hanging Church.'

'I don't understand.'

'The very ancient church of Al-Moallaqa was named the Hanging Church because the eastern and western extremities of the structure rest on two towers dating from the Roman era. So its nave hangs above the passageway leading from one to the other, and which today leads inside. From the eleventh to

33

the fourteenth century, it was the residence of Alexandria's Coptic patriarchs. That is why it still preserves an episcopal throne and remains an especially venerated site.'

'Surely you're not taking me to a meeting with God?'

'Who knows?'

'Why are you taking so much trouble, Ateya?'

'I am happy to carry out the task entrusted to me.'

She halted beside the ancient entrance to Old Cairo, which was marked off by its Roman wall. Immediately, a broad-shouldered fellow sprang out from nowhere to open the door, take the keys and guard the car.

For a second, Mark hesitated. What if this was not a joke after all? What if he really was about to discover a truth he did not want to know?

'Are you afraid?' asked the young woman.

'Possibly.'

'There is still time to go back. The moment you enter the Hanging Church, it will be too late.'

'Lead on.'

With her perfect knowledge of the labyrinthine alleyways, Ateya showed Mark the way without a moment's hesitation. Lost in thought, Mark did not even notice the passers-by. He was experiencing the sensation of going back in time, of setting off on a quest for a spring whose water had become vital to him.

The Hanging Church stood next to the Coptic museum. It had been built according to a traditional layout, with two rows of marble columns, decorated with Corinthian capitals. Ateya and Mark headed for the thirteenth-century iconostasis, separating the nave, where the faithful gathered, from the sanctuary, where the priest officiated.

An old man was gazing at the ebony panels, inlaid with ivory, which marked the border between two worlds. Seven icons adorned the central chapel, dominated by the image of Christ in glory, seated on His throne.

'His resurrection represents the victory of light over death,' said the old man softly. 'Humans are slaves, unaware of how heavy their chains are. And yet they can free themselves from them, as long as they no longer look at themselves but lift their eyes to heaven. Are you ready to look truth in the face, Mr Wilder?'

The American started. 'Was it you who wrote to me?'

'It was indeed.'

Dressed in a black surplice that made him look like any Coptic priest, the monk had a kind face but his eyes were those of an eagle.

The intensity of his gaze frightened Mark. 'That letter. Was it . . . serious?'

'Do you still doubt it?'

'Put yourself in my place! This is so unexpected, so . . .'

'Either you accompany me into the garden of this church or you go back to your hotel and never know the truth. It is your choice.'

'Do I really have a choice?'

'At least once in his lifetime, every individual finds himself at a crossroads. For you, Mr Wilder, that moment has arrived. And the decision is yours alone.'

Decision-making was Mark's livelihood. And yet, today, he felt desperately alone and vulnerable.

Ateya remained silent, as if this situation did not concern her.

Mark reached his decision: 'A little fresh air will do me good.'

The old man led him into an inner courtyard, enlivened by a few bushes and a small garden. Ateya walked away to keep watch.

'Sit down on my left,' ordered the Copt as he sat down on a bench. 'Here, Mr Wilder, three trees nourished the Holy Family. And the Virgin appeared to the patriarch Ephrem, a tenth-century holy man, after three days of fasting and prayer. He saw her standing beside an ancient column linking heaven and earth and realized that the power of the spirit could move mountains, like Mount Mokattam, to the east of Cairo. There, in antiquity, light destroyed the devil and abandoned him to his own destruction, drowned in his own blood.'

'A pretty legend.'

'*Legenda* means "that which must be read and known", Mr Wilder. Nowadays, we neglect the teachings of the Ancients and stuff ourselves with useless anecdotes which rot the mind and bring humanity back to infantilism. Neglecting the legends is the same as choosing the blind alley of ignorance.'

'May I know who you are?'

'Abbot Pacomas, a simple servant of God and of the Christian community, which is threatened with extinction in a country which is overwhelmingly Muslim. We, the Copts, are, however, the authentic descendants of the ancient Egyptians. In 641, when the Arabs invaded the country and imposed Islam on it, we were unable to resist. Today, we are tolerated, but for how long? My brothers are goldsmiths, pharmacists, accountants, dyers and surveyors, but their numbers are steadily decreasing, and our influence, which grows ever more modest, is withering away. I fear that the world's violence will not spare us.'

'I'm sorry to hear that,' observed Mark, 'but can we get back to your letter?'

'You bear a very fine Christian name. Do you know that the Apostle Mark was the founder of the Coptic Church in the year 40? Venetians stole his body in 828 and took it back to the city of the doges, where it served to protect St Mark's basilica. In a certain sense, are you not returning to the land of your ancestor?'

Mark had just realized! This old priest was seeking funds to maintain his community, which was in great distress. Like everyone else, he simply needed money and had sent out hundreds of enigmatic letters to wealthy and influential individuals to lure them to Egypt and tap them for funds.

'I hate having my hand forced, Abbot, and I make my own choices about good works, taking care to check that I haven't been cheated. Without wishing to offend you, I don't approve of the procedure you've used.'

'You misunderstand me, Mr Wilder. My course of action had no material objective and concerned you, and you alone. That procedure has brought you to me.'

His calm, firm tone surprised the lawyer. This old abbot, with his impressive dignity, did not look like a hoaxer or a crook.

'Then speak, I beg of you!'

'It is not so simple,' observed Pacomas. 'Overturning an individual's existence from top to bottom is a serious act, particularly since the revelation of the truth must be accompanied by a commitment on your part and a pact which you will sign. Are you willing to proceed?'

9

The situation was becoming complicated.

As a man of the law, Mark Wilder was not in the habit of signing a document before he had read and reread it. 'Committing myself lightly is out of the question. I want clear explanations.'

Abbot Pacomas closed his eyes for a few moments, as if he was searching deep inside himself for the words he was about to utter. 'We shall proceed in stages,' he decided. 'You are definitely called Mark Wilder?'

'Without a shadow of a doubt.'

'That is your main mistake.'

The lawyer frowned. 'What do you mean?'

'You understood me perfectly well.'

'I fear I did not!'

'I know the name of your real father and your real mother, two exceptional individuals caught up in a whirlwind which did not allow them to bring you up. I swore that I would keep silent until the day when too many perils threatened the existence of Egypt and, beyond that, the precarious balance of our world. As that day has arrived, I must respect the last wishes of your father and entrust you with the mission he wished you to fulfil.'

Dumbfounded, Mark remained silent for a long time. 'This is completely absurd!'

'Your official father was called Antony, and he was a corporate lawyer from New York?'

'He was.'

'And your official mother was called Maria Fontana del Vecchio, born in Naples?'

'Correct.'

'Antony was abrupt and authoritarian, Maria gentle and considerate. They felt real affection for each other, and she never left him even when he was travelling on business.'

'How do you know that?'

'I met them,' replied Abbot Pacomas.

Mark could not believe his ears. 'Met them? . . . Where?'

'Here, in Cairo.'

'My parents never came to Egypt!'

'They omitted to tell you about their stay, in accordance with the oaths they had taken.'

'Oaths . . . ?'

'Antony and Maria swore to your real parents that they would never reveal to you that you were their son and that you were born in Cairo. They kept their word.'

For a moment the bushes in the garden of the Hanging Church began to spin around.

This was subsiding into pure lunacy!

'With respect, Abbot, you are talking utter nonsense!'

'Why would I make up such a tale? I repeat, the secret was well kept, and you would never have known anything if we were not on the eve of grave events. Because you are the spiritual heir to an extraordinary couple, you may perhaps succeed in altering the course of destiny.'

'I loved my parents and they loved me!' protested Mark. 'Unfortunately, my father was a lover of fast cars and my mother didn't disapprove of his passion. They were killed in a car accident when I was fifteen. Instead of giving in to despair, I decided to follow in my father's footsteps and show him what I was capable of, so as to honour his memory. As for my mother, she hoped I would have a political career, serving my country. I am on the point of honouring that wish as well.'

'Your real mission seems much more important to me, Mr Wilder.'

'I don't want to hear another word!'

'On the contrary, you now wish to hear the whole truth.'

'You've got me all wrong, Abbot. I already know the whole truth about my parents.'

'Your father chose a man and a woman of honour, and his choice was a good one. Your mother also had complete confidence in them. Knowing that you were happy, healthy, well cared for and heading for a promising future consoled her a little for being forced to abandon you. She had no choice, and no one could blame her.'

'Why are you so intent on telling me these stupid lies?'

'You have already travelled part of the journey. Now you must go right to the end, knowing that your entire existence will be altered as a result. Remaining between two worlds will merely cause you anguish and dissatisfaction, and you will never forget this conversation. Do not run away from yourself.'

Mark rose to his feet. 'I'm sorry to be impolite, but I really haven't enjoyed meeting you.'

'What if you take the trouble to check what I have said?'

The lawyer was cut to the quick. 'How?'

'Your adoptive parents were forced to regularize your situation in order to turn you into an authentic American. I memorized a piece of information given by Antony Wilder: New York, office 303, annexe B, the key to his administrative problems. And also the name of a doctor: Dr Jonathan Gatwick. I do not know if he is still alive.'

'Abbot, I have no intention of checking out anything. I had the good fortune to have wonderful parents, a happy childhood and adolescence, and I will not allow anyone to sully those moments of happiness.'

'All we have done is touch on the truth, Mr Wilder, and I am a long way from telling you the important part of it.'

'This has been our first and last conversation, Abbot!'

'I shall meditate here every day at the same time, for a month, and I shall wait for you. After then, my duties will summon me elsewhere. If you do not come, you will not find out who you really are.'

'I think I know quite enough! Farewell.'

Ateya stepped in front of the American. 'We shall leave Old Cairo by another route,' she announced.

'As you wish,' snapped Mark, his nerves on edge.

'You seem annoyed.'

'Not annoyed – furious!'

'Usually, Abbot Pacomas brings peace to the soul.'

'If I still possess one, it resembles an erupting volcano! I hate people playing games with me.'

'I have known the abbot for a very long time, and he has never played games with anyone. Do not doubt his words, or you will regret it.'

'Is that a threat?'

'Simply a piece of advice. Pacomas's only fight is against demons.'

The lawyer shrugged. Magic was all that was needed to put the finishing touches to the fairy tale! Without a doubt, there was a lot to be said for America and business. One ought never to leave New York.

At the main entrance to Old Cairo, between the two Roman towers, a green Peugeot was waiting, its engine running.

'This taxi will take you back to the Mena House,' explained the young woman.

'Aren't you coming with me?'

'My mission is at an end.'

'Before I take the plane back, I was hoping to invite you to dinner.'

'I repeat, Mr Wilder: my mission is at an end.'

10

Mark charged into the bar at the Mena House and ordered a triple whisky. His throat was dry and he would dearly have loved a long session with a punchbag. Still just as irritated, he decided to get some fresh air and stride across the Giza plateau.

At nightfall, families gathered at the foot of the great pyramid to eat cakes and enjoy the warm air. They told each other stories, they laughed, they enjoyed the moment. A few relaxed-looking policemen strolled by, complaining about their meagre salaries.

Mark felt energy rising up from the ground. Driving away fatigue, it refreshed the limbs and made them capable of walking to infinity.

Walking around the stone giants was a strange experience. Mark had the impression that he was passing through a wall separating his era from that of the pyramid builders and that he was communicating, in some small way, with the souls of the master builders.

Each word of the conversation with Abbot Pacomas echoed within him like a thunderclap. That old man, with his undeniable aura, was no joker! Of course, he was wrong to pass on unfounded, meaningless rumours. But how had they reached him?

Mark recalled the high points of his childhood and his adolescence, with a stern father and a mother who indulged his every whim. He had to work hard at school to try to be first in his class, and he had been reprimanded if he failed. But there were basketball games with his friends, gargantuan picnics and holidays at the seaside or in the mountains. When his father scolded him too severely, his mother protected him. And the young man gradually developed as the days passed, mixing hard work with the joys of living.

Who could have dreamed of better parents? And yet Abbot Pacomas had sown the seeds of doubt. And since he had challenged him to check out his unlikely theory, Mark would not hesitate to do so.

Back in his room, where a basket of fruit and a bunch of roses had been placed, he managed to contact Dusty Malone through the efforts of an efficient operator.

'How are the pyramids?'

'Indestructible.'

'When are you coming back?'

'I'm planning to take in a little more of the landscape. But I need some information.'

'I knew it,' declared Dusty. 'You're working on a case!'

'If you like. As quickly as possible, track down a doctor called Jonathan Gatwick for me. If he's still alive, use any and every means to make him confess everything he knows about my parents and my birth.'

'Are you serious?'

'Very serious. Threaten him if need be, but make him talk!'

'What else?'

'Dig up whatever you can on an office 303, annexe B, which apparently existed in New York about forty years ago.'

'In what part of the city?'

'I have no idea.'

'Do you take me for Superman?'

'You're much stronger than he is and that's what you're paid for.'

'What's going on, Mark? Your voice sounds strange.'

'I've drunk a little too much.'

'That's not like you. Have you got problems?'

'That will depend on the information you dig up.'

'Tell me more, for God's sake!'

'It's too soon, Dusty, and I don't want to influence you. Delegate your current cases to your assistants and get digging. I'm in a great hurry.'

'Understood, boss. But please avoid doing anything hasty!'

'That's not my style. Give your wife and kids a hug from me.'

As he hung up, Mark regretted having undertaken this ridiculous course of action, which would probably end in nothing. But at least he would have a clear conscience and would be able to return to New York with his mind at rest.

Despite the lateness of the hour, Limoun Bridge Station was still full of travellers waiting for a train and passers-by who had come to smoke a cigarette, go over the events of the day and complain about Farouk's government, which was incapable of resolving their increasingly unbearable day-to-day problems. The rich got richer and the poor got poorer. And people's patience had its limits. Wasn't there one man honest and courageous enough to change the course of destiny?

Hosni spotted Mahmoud, who was reading the Wafd party newspaper.

In other words, plain-clothes policemen were on the prowl in the area.

Heavy and clumsy of step, Hosni headed for a ticket window, queued up and bought a ticket to the suburbs. Mahmoud had folded up his newspaper and lit a cigarette.

The danger was past.

He could give his report to the emissary from the Free Officers.

'What's happening with Mark Wilder?'

'I was not mistaken,' declared Hosni. 'He is definitely a top-level American agent, accustomed to shaking off a tail. One of my men was watching him and saw him walk out of the Mena House and head towards Cairo, unusual behaviour for a tourist. So he followed him, but a few minutes later a car drew up alongside the American and he jumped inside. It set off at top speed.'

Mahmoud nodded.

Wilder's strategy left no further doubt about his real activities.

'Did you get the number plate?'

'Of course, and I asked the relevant department to identify the driver. Waste of time – it doesn't match anything.'

'So, a false number plate as well ... Did Wilder return to the Mena House?'

'That same evening.'

'Do you know who took him back?'

'Unfortunately not. It was one of the employees in reception who told me that the American had returned, but he didn't see the car that brought him. The guy will not be easy to follow. Do you want me to strengthen my surveillance team?'

'No. He would notice and take measures to slip through our fingers. That type of man knows what to do in a hostile setting, and he won't be short of contacts.'

Mahmoud crushed his cigarette nervously with his heel.

'What am I to do?' asked Hosni anxiously.

'Light, discreet surveillance, and no direct intervention. On the other hand, if he leaves the hotel with his luggage, try not to lose him and inform me immediately.'

Hosni had brought Mahmoud excellent news. For the first time in a long time, Mahmoud had hopes of extricating himself from the net in which he felt entangled. But he must still act with extreme caution.

11

Nursing a hangover, Mark spent the morning dozing in his room and drinking coffee. At times he wished he hadn't called Dusty. But at the end of the day, wasn't it better to know where he stood?

At last the phone rang.

It was only reception. A friend wished to see him.

Mark's headache was beginning to fade, and he felt steady on his feet.

Looking rather elegant in his eggshell-white suit, John wore a mocking smile. 'You're as white as a sheet, friend! These Eastern nights are starting to ruin your health.'

'It's not at all what you're thinking.'

'Problems?'

'Nothing serious.'

'If you're free, I'm taking you out for lunch.'

'I was thinking of going easy on the food and . . .'

'Fine, let's stay here. You can have clear vegetable soup and some rice.'

'As you like.'

Comfortably settled in the shade of a broad parasol, the two friends chatted, watched by the great pyramid of Khufu. In ancient times, its covering of white limestone had reflected the sun's rays, producing a dazzling light.

'I have an invitation for you,' declared John. 'Because of

your reputation, you've been chosen as one of the foreign dignitaries summoned to the social event of the year: King Farouk's second marriage. A spectacle not to be missed, believe me, even if the Egyptians still miss the king's first wife, Safi Naz, the "Pure Rose", who fell in love with him when she was fifteen. He called her Farida, "the perfect one, pure and unique", but even so he was the first Egyptian king to cast off his wife, three years ago. The people adored her, and Farouk's behaviour didn't endear him to them.'

'You know, me and weddings—'

'Missing this one is out of the question,' John interrupted. 'You have to get to know Farouk, his entourage and how his court works in order to understand the crisis Egypt is experiencing. Although he was born in Cairo on 11 February 1920, Farouk isn't regarded as a true child of Egypt but as the representative of a Turkish dynasty. He even has French blood in his veins, which doesn't help matters! Through his mother, Princess Nazli, he's descended from a man called Joseph Sève, a hat-maker's son born in Lyons in 1788, and who became a general serving under Mehemet-Ali. Farouk speaks seven languages, and he's criticized for preferring English and French to Arabic. People's hopes when he mounted the throne, on 28 April 1936, are long gone. His twenty-two million subjects believed that his would be a great reign, with more social justice and the realization of three major projects: the federation of Arab states, the annexation of Sudan and the expulsion of the British from the Suez Canal zone. Total failure. And his conduct during the Second World War wasn't exactly brilliant. Pro-Nazi, like the Grand Mufti of Cairo who collaborated with the Germans, Farouk was brutally brought back to his senses by the British. Last year, when free elections were held, he had to come to terms with seeing the old Wafd party win a large majority in the Chamber of Deputies, where they proclaimed their eternal slogan: "Egypt for the Egyptians!" But the party is as corrupt as Farouk himself, and its members seek only to increase their personal wealth. The king now forgets about governing the country and devotes himself to juicy affairs and the pleasures of sex, food and gambling. When the mood takes him, he changes his ministers and appoints new officers to keep the army at heel. The honorary titles of Bey and Pasha are auctioned off for fabulous sums, and a man's fortune is assured if he becomes part of the king's entourage. But the population is no longer turning a blind eye.'

On the lawn of the Mena House, a large-beaked crow hopped towards its goal, a watering can filled with water. Mark was wondering if he, too, had become a sort of target for his companion.

'Why are you telling me all this, John? I'm just an ordinary tourist.'

'Britain and France, two great colonial powers, are in decline. Asia and the Middle East are slipping from their grasp. The Soviet Union and the USA are moving in to take their place. We Americans must not fail to reconquer Egypt. And that requires a perfect understanding of the situation.'

Mark made no attempt to conceal his astonishment. 'It seems to me we've come a long way from your cotton problems!'

'I'm not going to play cat and mouse any longer,' John said with great seriousness. 'Our meeting at the airport owed nothing to chance. I knew that you were taking the plane to Cairo and I was waiting for you.'

'Explain yourself!'

'I belong to an information-gathering service recently created on the orders of President Truman: the Central Intelligence Agency. For the past year I've been working in Egypt, which is regarded as a strategic zone of major importance. As for you, you're my friend, an influential lawyer and a future high-ranking politician.'

'The CIA . . . So it wasn't just a rumour; it really does exist. Are you trying to recruit me?'

'Of course not! Since you're preparing to serve your country and you're in a hot spot at a crucial moment, all I'm asking is that you open your eyes and your ears. When we meet, you can give me a report and I'll take it from there. Even unknowingly, you may gather a piece of information which is vital for the future of the country and American politics. If you refuse, no one will blame you. But if you agree to help me a little, your political career might receive a boost. There'll be no written record, and I give you my word as a friend that your name will never be mentioned.'

'Aren't you running great risks?'

'That comes with the job. My network is firmly in place and invisible. But you can never gather enough information before making major decisions.'

'Overthrowing Farouk, for example?'

'We've not reached that stage, Mark. But I would very much like to have your opinion of him. The king rejected his first wife because she couldn't give him a male heir. If the new wife succeeds in producing one, perhaps Egypt's destiny will be changed. Unless it's too late.'

John finished his beer and Mark drained his glass of water.

'There you are, friend; I've told you everything. Do as you see fit.'

'Thank you for your honesty.'

'See you soon, I hope.'

John left the invitation to Farouk's wedding on the table.

At the start of his stay, Mark would have exploded with fury at being manipulated like this. But now he was caught up in a whirlwind and he could no longer find his bearings. Added to which, he was beginning to appreciate the country's special charm, doubtless because he had fallen in love with Ateya and he would not leave without seeing her again.

He was behaving like a thoughtless adolescent. But how many times in a lifetime did an encounter like that happen?

By now, water was much too uninteresting, and Mark ordered a Bloody Mary. Then he lay down for a long siesta, in the vain hope that he might awake with a clear head.

12

It was already dark when the telephone rang.

Mark awoke with a start, groped around for the phone and picked up the receiver.

'You have a call from New York,' announced the operator.

The lawyer looked at his watch: 9.45 p.m.

'It's me – Dusty,' said a strangely sombre voice. 'Can you hear me, Mark?'

'Loud and clear, Dusty.'

'I made the enquiries you asked for. I had to pull out all the stops, but I got results.'

'You sound angry!'

'Angry . . . ? Let's say amazed.'

'What did you find out that's so amazing?'

'Extraordinary is the right word for it.'

Mark's throat tightened. He would have liked a cheerful report from a mocking Dusty, proving that Abbot Pacomas's 'information' constituted nothing more than the ramblings of a senile old man.

The reality seemed different.

'Did you track down Dr Gatwick?' Mark asked.

'Without any problems. He spent his whole career in New York and is now peacefully retired in a luxury apartment. One of the best obstetricians of his generation, apparently, and a man with a big heart. He spent his holidays in Egypt, teaching his local colleagues effective techniques to use in difficult births.'

'In Egypt . . .'

'The wealthy families of Cairo often called on him. And he remembers your parents very well: charming people who were staying in a villa in Heliopolis.'

'My parents never came to Egypt!'

'They forgot to tell you, Mark. Your mother spent several weeks there while your father was on business. And they took in a pregnant young woman who had to hide her pregnancy from her family or suffer terrible consequences. She gave birth to a boy, then disappeared.'

Mark began to tremble. 'What was she called?'

'Dr Gatwick never knew her name.'

'And the father?'

'Unknown.'

'What became of the child?'

'Your mother was in seventh heaven. She looked after him as if he was her own baby.'

'After I was born, who did she give the baby to?'

Dusty hesitated before answering. Mark switched on the light.

'Dr Gatwick told me that your mother couldn't have children.'

The lapis-lazuli sky, dotted with thousands of stars, came crashing down on Mark's head. 'Your quack must be senile! He's mixing up the cases of several patients.'

'That's possible.'

'What about office 303, annexe B?'

'My pals at City Hall had no trouble tracing it. It was closed about ten years ago, after an administrative reorganization. At the time you were born, it dealt with the naturalization of children adopted from the Middle East.'

'The Middle East,' repeated Mark, stunned. 'What happened to the records?'

'They were transferred to a new organization, with the exception of those dealing with the year you were born, which were destroyed in a fire.'

A long silence followed these revelations.

'Are you still there, Mark?'

'Of course . . . You've done a fantastic job, Dusty.'

'That depends on where one stands. What's this mystery all about?'

'I don't have all the details yet. Thanks to you, I'm getting a clearer picture.'

'Really? I have the impression that you've headed into one hell of a tunnel. Why don't you get on the first plane for New York?'

'I was intending to do just that, but it's no longer possible. I have to remain in Egypt for a while, Dusty, to clarify the situation.'

'Is that really necessary? You're a great boss, admired and respected. You're going to become a statesman . . . vast possibilities are opening up before you. Forget all this crap, Mark, and come home.'

'You keep things going for me, Dusty. I have to understand what's happening to me.'

'OK, boss. But don't stay there too long.'

Like a caged animal, Mark paced back and forth across his room. Then he took a scalding-hot shower lasting a good quarter of an hour. When he turned the water off, the enigma was still there.

If Dr Gatwick had not lied, his mother was not his mother, but this mysterious woman who had given birth in his adoptive parents' Cairo villa, and whose name Abbot Pacomas claimed to know, not to mention that of his true father.

The Wilders were wealthy enough to adopt him, obtain papers with extreme urgency and make the dossier disappear so that their son could never discover his true origins.

This was all crazy!

And yet . . .

It was too late to head for the Hanging Church and question Abbot Pacomas. But tomorrow Mark was going to question him closely and finally get the truth.

Someone knocked at his door.

'A package from His Majesty's palace,' announced the delivery man proudly.

Mark gave him a generous tip and opened the packet, to discover a dinner jacket worthy of the most exclusive New York gatherings.

It was accompanied by a short note: 'His Majesty King Farouk is happy to number you among his guests at the celebration of his marriage, tomorrow, 6 May, at the Abdin Palace. A car will be sent to collect you.'

The note was handwritten and signed by Antonio Pulli, the monarch's right-hand man.

13

Cairo was bubbling with excitement. People loved glamorous weddings, and Farouk had been extremely extravagant. An immense crowd had gathered to witness the arrival of his fiancée, bedecked with jewels and wearing a gown created in Paris, which had cost a fortune. Four thousand soldiers would form a guard of honour for her, army cadets and massed bands would precede the procession as it headed to the royal palace, where thousands of wedding gifts were piled up. And a hundred-and-one-gun salute would proclaim the union of King Farouk and Narriman Sadek, a pretty woman with chestnut hair, streaked here and there with blonde.

Officially, the monarch and his young bride had met by chance and fallen madly in love. In reality, Farouk had noticed her before his divorce and decided to possess her. There was one small difficulty: Narriman was already engaged to a Harvard-educated Egyptian economist. But the king's wishes could not be denied. Brutally excluded from the game, the former fiancé remained furious. As for Narriman, she felt proud and happy to be marrying the most powerful man in the country.

On the orders of her lord and master, she had spent time in Rome to round off her education, to acquire good manners and learn the four languages Farouk considered essential: English, German, French and Italian. A gymnastics coach had helped her to create a perfect body, and a singer had taught her opera arias. Farouk wanted a well-bred, educated, elegant queen.

Egyptians still missed the king's popular first wife, but a day of festivities was always a happy event. For a few hours, they could forget their everyday difficulties.

The Cadillac carrying Mark passed the Opera House, headed up Ibrahim-Pasha Street and arrived at the Abdin Palace, a ponderous baroque building dating from the nineteenth century. Its impressive façade and its vast drawing rooms dotted with marble columns had been created by an Italian architect, Verucci Bey, known as the 'sinister old man' on account of his personality and the austerity of his buildings.

Policemen in ceremonial uniforms were directing the official cars as they shuttled to and fro delivering the guests. Several chamberlains greeted them.

The American handed his invitation to one of them.

'If you would be so kind as to follow me, Mr Wilder.'

They climbed a monumental staircase, watched by the lancers of the king's guard, and Mark was shown into the Suez Canal salon, decorated with large paintings of ships using the waterway.

An army of servants offered the guests cakes and drinks. People chatted, ate and drank, preening themselves in their dinner jackets and fashionable gowns. It was exactly the kind of reception which Mark detested and always did his utmost to avoid.

A nervous-looking man aged around forty approached him.

'Very happy to meet you, Mr Wilder. My name is Antonio Pulli and I have the honour of serving His Majesty.'

The two men shook hands.

'What a magnificent day, don't you think? This wedding will long be remembered by Egyptians, I am quite sure of that. Come, let us find a quieter spot.'

Dressed in the latest European style, swift-moving and decisive, yet utterly without ostentation, Pulli led the lawyer into a slightly smaller salon, where another army of servants were arranging the mountain of wedding presents sent to the happy couple.

'I am originally from Naples,' Pulli went on, 'and my father was responsible for making sure that the electric wiring in this immense palace worked properly. A job demanding extreme precision, believe me! He taught me the trade, and when I was very young I was lucky enough to be able to repair the toys belonging to the future King Farouk. He honoured me with his trust and then his friendship, awarded me the title of Bey and appointed me his private secretary. It is an extremely demanding job, which does not allow me a moment's rest! But I am proud to serve a great monarch and to relieve him of the weight of day-to-day problems. Are you enjoying your stay in Egypt, Mr Wilder?'

'Very much.'

'This is your first visit, is it not?'

'Indeed.'

'Because of its location at the foot of the pyramids, the Mena House is a peerless hotel. It would take many years to explore all of Egypt's riches! But there are other things besides the past and archaeology, Mr Wilder. This extraordinary country must enter the era of modernity and progress, and that is the king's constant concern. Many Westerners, notably the French and the British, still do not understand our people's desire for independence. For an American, it is different: does he not have an innate feeling for freedom?'

'You could say that.'

'Are you planning to confine yourself to tourism,' asked Antonio Pulli, 'or do you plan to take an interest in the world of business, should the opportunity arise?'

'My first goal is to have a change of air and to rest, but who knows? Life sometimes holds surprises, and I'm keeping an open mind.'

'Egypt is a land rich in opportunity,' said Farouk's private secretary, 'and His Majesty is very eager to promote economic development. He alone can put an end to the poverty that still afflicts our people. Corporate law is becoming very complicated, and a lawyer of your reputation could help us in many ways.'

'Why not?' Mark replied cautiously.

'I would have liked to chat longer with you, but this is a very special day and I still have to take care of a few details to ensure that the ceremonial events go off without a hitch. His Majesty wishes the people to share in his happiness. I hope to see you again soon.'

'So do I.'

Mark remained circumspect. By granting him this private meeting on such an occasion, Antonio Pulli had proved the importance he attached to the American visitor. And his offer of a business relationship had been quite clear. But where was he leading?

Suddenly, the clamour rose to fever pitch: the bride was about to arrive at any moment. Wasn't that the bridal march they could hear? Everyone was going to enjoy the ceremony, the banquets, fireworks and the armada of illuminated feluccas on the Nile. No one would sleep tonight.

This was Mark's cue to slip away.

A distinguished European provided him with a crucial piece of information: the address of a clothes shop where he traded his dinner jacket for a less conspicuous outfit and paid an outrageous supplement into the bargain. But this was a day of celebration, and prices were sky-high.

With the aid of a street plan of Cairo he had brought with him, the lawyer explored the centre of a city which was visibly happy to welcome a new queen.

By not returning to the Mena House and mingling with passers-by, Mark was sure to escape from anyone who was following him and not lead them to Abbot Pacomas, who had so much to tell him. This time, the mystery must be dispelled and he must obtain clear explanations. Would they amount to nothing? No, since Dusty's investigation had produced incredible results.

Abbot Pacomas knew that.

Why had he waited so long to write to Mark and finally reveal the truth? Had the climate of tension invading the country influenced his decision? Doubtless Farouk's marriage and the birth of an heir to the dynasty would improve the situation.

Mark thought of Ateya. He missed her. He wanted to talk to her, look at her, gaze on her smile and her elegance. He could no longer imagine life without her. And yet he wasn't even sure that he would ever see her again.

Yes, he would see her again.

He had always been tenacious and always got what he wanted. Abbot Pacomas must know the young woman's address. Mark would explain to him that he was no Don Juan, succumbing to her Eastern charm, would beg her to listen to him carefully and not to say anything final until they had got to know each other better.

And what if Ateya already had a man in her life? Perhaps it was only a fleeting liaison, easy to break. But she was an Egyptian, and he was an American: surely he was indulging in an impossible dream?

His mind on fire, he headed for Old Cairo. The sun was setting, and the festivities were still going on. On this hot May night, the people of Cairo were going to sing and dance, not forgetting to drink to the king and queen's health. Even pious Muslims would sample a little beer or other alcohol tonight.

Mark paced the narrow streets until the appointed meeting time. Thanks to a good memory, he had no trouble finding his way to the Hanging Church. He entered the garden.

Abbot Pacomas was seated on a bench, meditating.

14

Mark sat down on the abbot's left-hand side.

'You were right,' he said nervously. 'The Wilders were only my adoptive parents, and they hid the truth from me.'

'They kept their word, and God will be grateful to them. Do you wish to know the truth, with all the consequences it implies?'

'My presence here proves that I do.'

'I fear you may be here merely to satisfy your curiosity,' ventured Pacomas. 'Have you thought deeply about the importance of your decision?'

'I've taken all the time I needed. While Cairo was celebrating Farouk's marriage, I went for a walk to weigh up the last few days and I came to a conclusion. I now want to know. Everything.'

'My intention is not to do you harm, Mr Wilder, but my revelations will turn your life upside down and lead you on to dangerous paths. You thought your destiny was all mapped out, but now it will be altered and I do not know if you can bear the burden. That is why, before I tell you the names of your real father and mother, I must demand that you swear an oath, promising fearlessly to fulfil the mission with which they have entrusted you from beyond the gates of death.'

'In other words, commit myself without knowing what I'm committing myself to!'

'The decision is yours. Have I not given you sufficient clues already?'

'Why did you decide to contact me?'

'Heaven is troubled and hell is in ferment, Mr Wilder. And if there still exists one small chance of seeing light triumph over darkness, it is you who embodies that chance. It is an immense responsibility, which you may refuse to shoulder. No one will blame you for it.'

'I'm not in the habit of baulking at obstacles.'

'But this one is far, far greater than any you have confronted before.'

'Are you trying to frighten me?'

'Of course. When we face the forces of destruction, fear is the first step we must take. Without it, we remain ignorant and unaware.'

'And what if, in reality, you know nothing? What if this whole story is just a smokescreen to lead me who knows where?'

'Did your investigations not prove the contrary? But you are wondering about my modest appearance and the authenticity of my message. You should know, Mr Wilder, that I belong to a very special lineage, without much in common with the Christianity and Islam which were born in this region and which wish to dominate the world, if necessary by force. When Coptic writing appeared, in the second century before Jesus' birth, the ancient Egyptians were aware that they would soon disappear and that they should henceforth pass on their wisdom in a coded language. Initiates were forced to dress in Christian clothing and subscribe to the new belief in order to survive after the temples were closed and the last resisters slaughtered. Nurtured by the teachings of the Egyptian priests, the Coptic Church separated from Rome and accomplished a miracle: it succeeded in cohabiting with Islam. But miracles do not last, and our situation worsens each day. For us, Egypt is not "the house of slaves" spoken of in the Old Testament book of Exodus, the dwelling of the devil and the place of ignorance, but on the contrary the celestial dwelling, heaven on earth and the temple of the whole world. In 1945, on the Chenoboskion site near

Nag Hammadi in Upper Egypt, archaeologists unearthed one of my ancestors' libraries, made up of texts that the Roman Church refused to include in the Bible, such as the *Gospel of the Egyptians*, the two *Apocalypses of Saint John* or the *True Word*. Very few people were considered worthy to consult these texts, a good many of which are still secret. And it was the same with their true source, the texts written by the great sages of pharaonic Egypt which remain my daily bread.'

Mark felt as though he was listening to a man from another world.

'This is where your oath will lead you,' continued Pacomas, 'if the forces of destruction do not kill you before you succeed in carrying out your mission: to preserve a treasure without which humanity will lose its head and subside into nothingness.'

The American was dumbfounded. 'I don't have the power to save the planet single-handed! Only the heroes of adventure movies can do that.'

'Do not underestimate yourself,' advised Abbot Pacomas, a small smile appearing on his face. 'Sometimes one man alone is enough to change the future.'

'I'm a corporate lawyer, not a Coptic priest specializing in esoteric writings!'

'You are also the son of an exceptional father who found the means to bring about the triumph of light but did not have the chance to use it. That task falls to you, his son. Do you wish to carry on his work and bring it to fruition?'

'Aren't you better qualified than I am?'

'First, at my age I no longer have the ability to undertake the necessary work. Second, only your personal magic, which is identical to that of your father, has a chance of success. Otherwise, I would have allowed you to slumber on quietly.'

Mark was no longer facing a storm but a veritable tornado.

'Let us go to my house,' suggested Abbot Pacomas. 'Before you make your decision, I must peform a rite of protection.'

The old man had difficulty walking and used a cane. Mark

attempted to collect his thoughts as he reflected on the importance of giving one's word, a process viewed with disdain in a modern world where lies had become an essential weapon.

Never before had he been forced to face up to himself and to responsibilities whose weight he could perceive without knowing what they really were.

Abbot Pacomas's house was in a narrow, deserted street where only Copts lived. It had the look of a vast library, made up of manuscripts, parchments and ancient books.

'Wait here a moment, Mr Wilder.'

When the abbot reappeared, he was wearing a white robe and holding a golden phial.

'This contains a holy oil, the oil of happiness, designed to protect spiritual travellers by driving the demons from their path. Please kneel.'

It was a long time since the American had been on his knees! Clumsily, he knelt.

The abbot recited texts calling up the formidable forces contained in the thousand and one kinds of fire which consumed living beings. One by one, he pacified them before anointing Mark's forehead, eyebrows, heart and hands. Mark felt an extraordinary sensation of well-being flood through him.

The tornado died down, Mark's thoughts arranged themselves in their correct places like building blocks in a child's game and he had the feeling that he was finally mastering the situation and finding the best solution after studying a complex file.

Seated in a high-backed armchair, he accepted a glass of amber liquid from Abbot Pacomas.

'An excellent cognac, your father's favourite. At difficult moments, this drink restored his courage.'

Mark sampled the cognac. It was indeed excellent.

'Have you made your decision?' asked the abbot.

'Tell me the truth, and I will undertake the mission entrusted to me by my father from beyond the grave.'

'For several weeks,' Pacomas told him, 'you will be protected from attacks by forces of evil. After that, I must act again. Your oath has unleashed an irreversible process with an uncertain outcome.'

'Who were my parents?'

'We are not in the right place for you to grasp the full importance of that revelation. I feel the Cairo Museum is more appropriate.'

'The museum? But it's the middle of the night!'

'Several hours elapsed during our ritual, Mr Wilder. The sun has been up for some time.'

15

As soon as he entered the Cairo Museum, which some archaeologists compared with Aladdin's cave, Abbot Pacomas seemed rejuvenated and moved more easily. The sight of the incredible number of masterpieces collected here restored his energy, as if he could commune naturally with the immortal souls of the statues.

Pacomas led Mark to the galleries where the countless treasures from Tutankhamun's tomb were exhibited.

Mark was dazzled.

Breathless and stunned by what he saw, he gazed at golden chapels, beds made from gilded wood, chests, statues, thrones and jewels, and stood dumbstruck before the golden mask which expressed an unbelievable intensity of life.

The abbot allowed a profound connection to establish itself between the American and the pharaoh. Without realizing, Mark had stepped across a threshold and was entering a new universe.

Then Pacomas drew his guest aside.

'Your mother was a very beautiful Egyptian woman called Raifa,' he said. 'And your father was Howard Carter, the greatest archaeologist of all time, the one who discovered the tomb of Tutankhamun after long years of searching and frustration. As you gaze on the marvels which he brought to light, you are participating in his Quest and in the very essence of his existence.'

Very slowly, the two men walked through the galleries, lingering over a statuette, a pair of sandals or a necklace.

'Your father was born on 9 May 1874* in London, and spent his childhood in Swaffham, Norfolk, his parents' birthplace. His father, Samuel John Carter, worked for a famous publication, the *Illustrated London News*, which published his drawings of animals and of scenes from rural life. Little Howard followed in his footsteps and also proved to have great talent in drawing and in painting watercolours. Then destiny changed his path radically. In 1890 Professor Percy E. Newberry took the sixteen-year-old Howard to Egypt and instructed him to draw scenes of Egyptian tombs. Your father thus became the youngest member of the Egypt Exploration Fund, a private scientific body dedicated to undertaking digs "for a better knowledge of the history and arts of ancient Egypt, and the illustration of tales from the Old Testament". Later, you will understand the exact meaning of that declaration. Your father fell in love with the land of the pharaohs and trained himself in the field to become an Egyptologist, notably by becoming assistant to the great patron of the day, Sir William Flinders Petrie, who insisted on rigorous working methods. He was also the deputy to a Swiss archaeologist, Sir Edouard Naville, who excavated the temple of the queen Pharaoh Hatshepsut, on the west bank of Thebes. In 1899 the Frenchman Gaston Maspero, who had great respect for Howard Carter, appointed him inspector of monuments for Upper Egypt and Nubia – a considerable success for a young man of twenty-five, who would always be reproached for not going to university and lacking academic qualifications. But nobody knew the ancient sites or the contemporary population better than he did. It was in Luxor that he met a schoolteacher, Raifa, a modern young woman intent on freeing herself from the shackles of tradition. Their conversations grew increasingly intimate, and a great love was born. Despite all that separated

---

* Not in 1873, as is inscribed on his tomb.

them, they could not resist admitting this to each other. Of course, this liaison must remain absolutely secret, so as not to unleash an enormous scandal. In the autumn of 1904 Howard Carter was appointed chief inspector of Lower Egypt and thus took charge of the immense burial ground at Saqqara. There, on 8 January 1905, some drunken Frenchmen brawled with the site's Egyptian guards. Your father took the side of the guards, and the French lodged a complaint against him. Despite the insistence of Maspero, who was under pressure from the authorities, Howard Carter stubbornly refused to apologize to the group of louts. So he was dismissed, his official career ended abruptly and he found himself on the street. As he was in love with Raifa, he did not leave Egypt and managed to survive by painting pictures and trading in antiquities. Although the British didn't like him much, the same could not be said of the Americans or of certain experts from the Metropolitan Museum in New York.'

'New York,' repeated Mark, seeing a picture beginning to take shape.

'In 1907,' Abbot Pacomas continued, 'Howard Carter settled in Luxor. For a long time he'd had only one thought in his head: to conduct excavations in the Valley of the Kings and to discover the tomb of a pharaoh, Tutankhamun, who was present in the royal lists but had disappeared from history. As not a single object with his name on had ever been in circulation, Carter rightly deduced that his tomb must be intact and must contain marvels. An intact pharaoh's tomb ... castles in the air! However, luck smiled on Carter again when he met Lord Carnarvon, who had come to Egypt for health reasons. Intelligent, curious about everything, he decided to occupy his time by engaging in archaeology and employed an expert recommended to him by Maspero: Howard Carter. His horizons opened up once more, and the goal was fixed: to obtain the excavation concession in the Valley of the Kings, where a wealthy American amateur, Theodore Davis, was operating. In December 1911

Raifa gave birth to a boy in Cairo in the greatest secrecy. Thanks to a friend of your father, who was in league with the Metropolitan Museum, she was taken in by the Wilders and received specialist care. Then an unexpected event occurred. As they could not have a child of their own, the Wilders asked if they could adopt you, promising to give you the best education and ensure that you had a brilliant future. Neither Raifa nor Howard Carter could acknowledge you. She would have had serious problems, risking being quietly murdered by her own family; and the dreams of the Egyptologist, who would have been discredited, would have been utterly destroyed. Even though this solution broke their hearts, they had no choice. I do not believe they can be charged with cowardice. They were thinking of your happiness and your future, not theirs, and they swore never to reveal anything. For their part, the Wilders took care of the formalities and henceforth considered you their real son.'

Mark was astonished. 'And now you are trampling on their oath of silence!'

'Needs must,' replied the abbot sharply. 'In June 1914, when he was seventy years old and ill, Davis abandoned the Valley of the Kings to Carnarvon. Howard Carter launched into titanic excavations which, on 26 November 1922, in the last planned season of digs, culminated in the discovery of the steps leading down to Tutankhamun's tomb. Unfortunately, Raifa had passed away and was not there to witness Howard's triumph – a triumph accompanied by many ordeals and injustices and ten years of sometimes superhuman efforts to empty the tomb of its treasures. In 1933 your father fell ill, and the last years of his life were not happy ones. Britain awarded him neither honours nor decorations, as if he were a pariah, and he did not undertake any more excavations. His life and his soul remained linked to Tutankhamun, and to Tutankhamun alone.'

'Did he return to Egypt?'

'He loved this country so much that he continued to spend time in the house he had built at the entrance to the Valley of the Kings. We spent long hours there, conversing. He also liked to have a drink at the Winter Palace, alone, and watch the birds he could draw so well. Still carefully dressed, in fact rather elegant, he retained an impressive dignity. He relived his extraordinary adventure in his thoughts, and never tired of gazing at the west bank, where the goddess of the afterlife received those of "just voice" into her bosom.'

'Where and when did he die?'

'Your father passed away in London on 2 March 1939 and was buried in Putney Vale Cemetery, in the south of the capital. But this earthly end did not put an end to the search for Tutankhamun's treasures and knowledge of the mysteries which he passed on to us. That is why I was obliged to break my silence.'

16

Abbot Pacomas and Mark Wilder halted before one of Tutankhamun's resurrection beds, carved and decorated like a hippopotamus. It embodied the mysterious goddess Ipet, matrix of the universe, whose task was to count those humans capable of transcending the ordeal of death.

'One of your father's first concerns, when he explored this fabulous tomb, was to bring papyri to light. It was hoped that they would provide large amounts of information on the king himself, but also about Akhenaton and his troubled reign, the Hebrews and their time in Egypt, the Exodus and other biblical episodes. Given the enormous number of items and possible hiding places, it would probably demand a lot of time and patience before the excavators could lay their hands on these priceless documents.'

'Were they found?' asked Mark.

'Officially, no. But during his last stay in Egypt, Howard Carter talked to me about them. "If you believe that Egypt is in grave danger," he said, "reveal my son's true identity to him and ask him to take action. In accordance with the laws of Maat and of blood, he alone can use the papyri in the right way." I asked him to tell me where these priceless documents were hidden. He preferred not to tell me, believing that the right moment had not yet come. Given his personality, it was useless to insist. And it was a grave mistake, for he died before passing on his secret to me. Today, Egypt is indeed in great peril. Tragic upheavals are going to occur, both in the political and spiritual arenas. It is not necessary to have second sight to predict a conflict between Israel and the Arab world, considering the rise in intolerance and fanaticism. These conflicts will overspill Egypt's borders and unleash themselves on the world, and we Copts will be swept away. Unless you can find those papyri and the magic they contain enlightens and pacifies minds.'

'"The laws of Maat and of blood . . ." What does that mean?'

'As the physical and spiritual son of Howard Carter, you alone can be the servant of his *ka*, his indestructible vital power. In reanimating it by your faithfulness to his memory and your quest for the truth, you will help to fashion his immortality. This is the solemn oath you have taken, Mark: to find Tutankhamun's papyri. If you refuse, the darkness will triumph.'

In order to escape from a group of noisy tourists, the two men walked away and chose a less popular spot, facing some statuettes, the 'Answerers', capable of hearing the voice of the reborn king, obeying him and carrying out vital tasks for him in the other world.

'You told me that your revelations would turn my life upside down,' the lawyer reminded him, 'and you didn't lie. As for me, I will not retract the oath I have taken. I will accomplish the mission entrusted to me by my father, beyond death.'

Abbot Pacomas concealed his emotion. If the son was as stubborn as the father, all was not lost.

'Where and how do I search?' asked Mark.

'Howard Carter was a secretive man, and he had few friends. Did he share his discovery of the papyri with one of them, or make a direct confession? Arthur Callender, nicknamed "Pecky", was without doubt his closest associate. A former manager of the Egyptian train service, an architect and engineer, this kind, perpetually placid giant was enjoying a peaceful retirement in Armant, south of Luxor, when Carter asked him to help him search Tutankhamun's tomb. As Callender could do anything and never baulked at a job, whether installing electricity or building a crate, he was your father's most valuable assistant. He must have seen the papyri. Unfortunately, he left as soon as the work was completed, and even the date of his death – probably 1937 – remains uncertain. The chemist Alfred Lucas, who died in 1945, and the Egyptologist Newberry, who died in 1949, knew nothing. They helped Carter, who certainly respected them but did not consider them close confidants. When I learned that he was dying, I left for London but unfortunately I arrived too late. Nevertheless, I attended the funeral at Putney Vale Cemetery. It was poorly attended, and there were few people there who might be able to help me, with the exception of two women who were very important in your father's life. The first, his niece Phyllis Walker, showed admirable devotion to him during the final part of his life. It was she who alerted me to the seriousness of Carter's condition, and she was present at his last breath. She had stayed in Luxor with him, and I met her several times. In London she swore to me that she had never heard of Tutankhamun's papyri, and I do not doubt her word.

'The case of the second woman, Lady Evelyn, is more ambiguous. Daughter of Lord Carnarvon, she admired your father and was the first person to enter the funerary chamber, in the greatest secrecy, before the official opening. This beautiful young woman, intelligent and passionate, experienced extraordinary things at Howard Carter's side. But he was a mere commoner; she was an aristocrat. I talked to her at length in London: she did not remember having seen the papyri, but she did not totally deny their existence. That will be one lead to follow, Mark: try to see her and get more from her. We must not forget that Lord Carnarvon was a collector, and that he would have received part of Tutankhamun's treasure if the Egyptian government had not altered the law on the distribution of antiquities. The prestigious family estate at Highclere must be another of your objectives.'

'Did my father not possess his own collection of Egyptian antiquities?'

'Yes, but it was extremely modest. The two most remarkable items were a faience sphinx from the reign of Amenhotep III and an "Answerer" that certainly came from the tomb of Tutankhamun. All his possessions were dispersed at a public auction, and no papyri were included. However, the British lead should not be neglected, for other reasons. First, some of Carter's personal papers are in a museum in Oxford; second, the Egyptologist Gardiner, a specialist in hieroglyphs who worked with Carter and deciphered inscriptions in the tomb, may have vital information.'

'In other words, I must travel to England.'

'I would indeed advise you to begin there. There are two other leads, which are just as important. The Egyptologist Arthur Mace, who died in 1928, was one of your father's principal collaborators. He worked for the Metropolitan Museum, like the photographer Harry Burton, the executor of Howard Carter's will; moreover, Carter left him two hundred and fifty pounds. He had the privilege of taking photographs of the items in the tomb at each stage of the exploration.'

'Is he still alive?'

'Unfortunately, he left this world in 1940. A third individual, Herbert Winlock, was a friend of your father and one of the leading lights at the Metropolitan Museum. He acquired some magnificent items from the Carnarvon collection, including masterpieces from Tutankhamun's tomb. And Carter even had a temporary office in that museum, which played a crucial part throughout his career as an archaeologist.'

'Don't tell me Winlock is dead too!'

'He died on 25 January 1950. Doubtless the Metropolitan Museum in New York has unpublished documents belonging to Carter, or even . . . the papyri! Let us not forget that he bequeathed his beloved house in Luxor, and all its contents, to the museum. A few rather skimpier clues could lead you in the direction of other American museums. I shall give you a complete file, and you will have to check out each of these possibilities.'

'If I understand you correctly, I'm most likely to find Tutankhamun's papyri either in Britain or the United States?'

'That is my opinion. And I am relying on you to hold to your commitment and bring back these vital documents to me as swiftly as possible. Then we shall talk at greater length about Carter and about Tutankhamun's secret message.'

Mark had been expecting a more difficult task. But would it be as simple as he supposed? 'Tell me, Father ... Will this journey be free of danger?'

'Certainly not, my son.'

17

In Luxor, a small provincial town six hundred and thirty kilometres from Cairo, Farouk's wedding had not had the impact it had had in the capital. Here, after the end of the tourist season, which lasted from November to March, life went on in slow motion under the sun of Upper Egypt. The temples of Karnak and Luxor, on the east bank, had only a few visitors now, and the large sites on the west bank, notably the Valley of the Kings, were returning little by little to silence.

However, the professor had not yet left Egypt. Ordinarily, when the overpowering heat began, he headed for Paris, London, Rome, Berlin or New York to meet his colleagues, give lectures or receive new honours. For the last few nights he had not been sleeping well and was reliving strange memories, as if a distant past was rising back up to the surface. So the professor had decided to postpone his departure for a little while, on the pretext of finishing off some administrative tasks.

That morning he had sent away a large number of supplicants, notably a short French Egyptologist, who was as overexcited as she was ambitious, knew everything about everything, and would have won the gold medal if there was a Vanity Olympics. The professor had lunch with some Egyptian officials, who were flattered by his invitation, then showed them the current digs, where work would not restart until autumn.

Back in his office, he sorted through some files.

Suddenly, and for no reason, the torch burst into flame.

It was an ancient torch, discovered in the village of Deir el-Medineh, inhabited by the craftsmen who had built and decorated the houses of eternity in the Valley of the Kings, notably that of Tutankhamun. The professor ought to have given it to the Cairo Museum, but it had served him for a long time as an alarm signal, enabling him to foresee attacks by his enemies.

This time, the flame was particularly bright and strong.

In other words, he had a hard fight to look forward to.

Now the professor understood his discomfort and congratulated himself on listening to his instinct. But he still had to find out the identity of his adversary. As usual, a messenger would knock on his door to inform him.

The old man stood up with difficulty. Years spent working on archaeological digs had worn out his body, but he did not regret all the hard work, for it had brought him many joys and enabled him to build a house where he lived with his children and grandchildren. It had several bedrooms, a kitchen with an oven in one corner, a magnificent collection of terracotta utensils, a reception room with benches, an enclosure for the livestock and a cellar that was an archaeologist's dream. It was, in fact, a New Kingdom tomb, whose low-relief carvings were partially intact, although blackened by smoke. And the well containing the mummies had not been violated.

The old man thought back to that incredible morning in November 1922, when he had unearthed the first step of an ancient stairway, perhaps leading to a tomb entrance. His boss, Howard Carter, had come running up. For so many years he had searched in vain for the last resting place of a mysterious pharaoh, Tutankhamun!

Could this be it, at last?

The old man liked Howard Carter very much. He spoke Arabic, treated his workmen with respect and was happy to roll up his sleeves and work alongside them. Unlike so many other learned men, who were pretentious and distant, he worked on the site and knew the country and its inhabitants very well.

And it was indeed Tutankhamun!

Howard Carter belonged to that category of exceptional individuals who turned their dreams into reality, surmounting all obstacles and never once deviating from their path.

As the old man was drinking a scalding-hot cup of black tea, one of his daughters, clad in black, burst into the house.

'This is terrible, terrible!'

'What has happened?'

'Your third grandson . . .' Her voice cracked with emotion.

'Speak!'

'He is dead.'

'Was it an accident?'

'Much worse! It is the Salawa.'

'The Salawa has returned? Impossible.'

'The sheikh and the imam have confirmed it. The whole of the west bank knows about it already.'

According to custom, the deceased was buried the same day. Already female mourners, comprising family members and neighbours, were raising their voices in lamentation.

The old man was petrified.

It was so long since the Salawa had appeared in Luxor! Some claimed that it was the reincarnation of the fearsome jackal-headed god Anubis, guardian of burial grounds. It devoured children's souls to punish families guilty of misdeeds.

And it had just struck the family of an old man, a close colleague of Howard Carter who had disturbed the repose of Pharaoh Tutankhamun and unveiled secrets which it would have been better to keep buried for ever.

The terrible punishment inflicted by the Salawa was a warning.

The old man must maintain absolute silence and not pass on Carter's confidences to anyone. From now on, the Salawa would once again impose its reign of terror.

John Hopkins had spent a delicious night in the passionate arms of a pretty secretary who worked at the Abdin Palace. Enamoured of Western-style progress, the young woman was delighted to serve the king, enjoy a good salary, be able to dress according to her taste and walk bare-headed in the street. And in the summer, in Alexandria, she basked on the beaches in a swimsuit. In addition, and with no thought of wrongdoing, she provided her lover with information on the functioning of Farouk's palace and the monarch's habits.

The sound of the telephone awoke the CIA agent, who was at last alone in his house and had been hoping to sleep late.

The person on the other end of the line uttered just one word: 'Darling.'

'The sun is rising over the pyramids,' answered John, using that week's code phrase.

'He has gone.'

'Who are you talking about?'

'Mark Wilder. He has just taken the plane for London.'

'London? Are you sure?'

'Certain.'

'Was anybody with him?'

'He was alone.'

'Any contacts, at the airport?'

'None, or so it seems.'

Of course, John was going to alert his London agent. This was not the time to lose the trail of his friend Mark, especially if he was attempting to clinch some shady deal with their British cousins. But why would he betray America?

Mahmoud was writing a summary for General Naguib when he received some disappointing information: the lawyer Mark Wilder had just left Cairo. In other words, his mission in Egypt was at an end.

His destination surprised the Free Officers' liaison agent: London. What was that American spy going to do in England?

Obviously, pass on to his British counterparts whatever he had discovered in Egypt. To provide them with information ... or was it misinformation?

As regards the Egyptian question, and particularly the burning topic of control of the Suez Canal, Mahmoud was well placed to know that the Americans and the British were not getting on. The British wished to continue to rule as absolute masters.

What game was Wilder playing? Doubtless Mahmoud would never find out. Disappointed, he had hoped to be able to use him to escape from the net imprisoning him.

One slender hope remained: that the lawyer would return to Egypt.

And then Mahmoud would take action.

Throughout almost the entire Mass, Ateya had thought not of God but of Mark Wilder. Reproaching herself for this culpable lack of attention, she took Communion fervently, but had to admit to herself that she was missing the American. She liked his manner, his tone of voice, the energy that emanated from him. The bearer of another world, he would open up new horizons to her.

Fortunately, this separation was not a permanent one. According to Abbot Pacomas, Mark Wilder would soon return.

Someone knocked at the professor's door.

'Come in.'

It was his butler, a plump, kindly family man with an affable disposition. He had brought him some tea.

His hands were trembling, and he looked distraught.

'Are you ill?'

'No, professor, no ...'

'Do you have problems?'

'I dare not say ...'

'Tell me, please.'

'You will not believe me!'

'Tell me anyway.'

'The Salawa ... the Salawa has just reappeared, and it has already killed a child!'

The professor nodded. The situation was even more serious than he had supposed. Now there was no question of leaving Luxor.

18

Before leaving for London, Mark had had a long telephone conversation with Dusty Malone, asking him to organize meetings and obtain information on the people he was going to meet. As Dusty was the very personification of efficiency, the lawyer need have no worries.

One of the newspapers that had appeared in Cairo on the morning of his departure had published a surprising article, entitled: 'Who is he?' It provided the character traits of the accused:

Is he intelligent? Is he an idiot? We do not know, for he sometimes thinks like a genius, but his acts are those of a madman. His face has a veneer of innocence, and then the look of a criminal. Is he good? Is he a coward? He has the furious eyes of a tiger but he flees like a rat. He sees, and yet he appears blind. He lives, and yet sometimes one would believe he was dead. He is in heaven and hell at the same time. He has won everything and then lost it all. What he has no longer interests him. He is only interested in what he does not yet possess. He wants everything. He wants to take everything from people, right down to their last shirt. He takes his pleasure in stealing from others what they have, whether it be precious possessions or junk. He steals for the sake of it, he steals from everyone, even from his friends, even from his family. Such is his pleasure; such is his vice. He thinks that no one will notice, for he believes that he is surrounded only by thieves. If he looks at himself, the mirror swells and distorts the series of images he sees of himself: great nationalist, man of glory, thief, chief bandit. These are, at least, the roles which he gives to himself. He never wavers between virtues and sin, for sin attracts him irresistibly and gives him more pleasure than virtue. His friends are upset about this. In an attempt to excuse him they say: 'He's a sick man.' But the people are not mistaken. They say: 'He is the greatest of all thieves.' What is more, no one can be mistaken about this man, since we have all, in one way or another, been his victims.*

Two Egyptian businessmen sitting behind Mark were reading the same article. They burst out laughing.

'What a fine portrait of Farouk!' exclaimed one of them. 'He's the only person who won't recognize it, and he'll send one of his secretaries to the newspaper office to ask the editor the identity of this monster they have described so perfectly.'

Hardly bodes well for the king's future, thought Mark, who, during the flight, attempted to take in Abbot Pacomas's revelations. When he was on a plane, he always felt perfectly relaxed and his thoughts could develop with complete freedom, as if he himself was a bird soaring above earthly events.

So he was the son of an Egyptian woman called Raifa and Howard Carter, the discoverer of Tutankhamun's tomb . . . Was it a dream or reality? Abbot Pacomas was right: knowing who he really was had turned his life upside down, and now he was obliged to undertake a mission for which he was in no way prepared.

The task did not frighten him. On the contrary, he found it exciting. Perhaps he had mastered the complexities of his

* Text quoted by J. Bernard-Derosne in *Farouk*, Paris, 1953, pp. 147–9.

profession as a lawyer; without doubt, he now wanted to discover different dimensions to life. Basically, Abbot Pacomas had presented him with a fabulous gift! As he entered an unknown world, Mark felt a new energy burn within him, coupled with a desire to succeed. Yes, he would find Tutankhamun's papyri and thus, beyond time and death, would participate in his father's extraordinary adventure.

Mark knew London well. It was a pleasant city to live in, and never boring. Working with his British colleagues was not easy, but people who kept an open mind always ended up coming to an agreement. And how could anyone forget that without Britain, the whole of Europe would have been under Nazi jackboots? With exemplary courage and solidarity, the British had faced up to Hitler's monsters.

An employee from the Connaught, the flower of London hotels, was waiting for him at the airport. He took care of the luggage and led him to a Bentley, where he was served one of those ageless Scotch whiskies capable of dispelling the fatigue of any journey.

The CIA agent posted in Arrivals was caught wrong-footed. In the time it took him to get back to his car, the Bentley had disappeared into the traffic.

He would find the lawyer eventually but was likely to receive a severe dressing-down in the meantime.

A delicate, Victorian-style perfume wafted through the suite at the Connaught, which Mark loved to call home whenever he stayed in London. Antique furniture, Persian carpets, a soft bed, deep armchairs perfect for thinking in, sherry accompanying salmon and cucumber canapés, the permanence of old England's culture, never out of fashion and well away from modernism of all kinds ... Mark savoured a few minutes' rest before telephoning Dusty, whose gruff voice expressed its usual determination.

'Settled in OK, boss?'

The Last Secret

'The Connaught still lives up to its reputation. How are things at the office?'

'We're overworked, as usual. I need your advice on a few delicate points.'

Mark dealt with them swiftly, much to Dusty's relief. Final decisions were not his speciality.

'Did you arrange those meetings for me?'

'I did,' replied Dusty, 'but it wasn't easy. It seems your man Gardiner is no barrel of laughs. You're having lunch with him tomorrow at the Ritz, at 12.30 precisely. Suit and tie a must.'

'What have you found out about him?'

'Alan Henderson Gardiner was born in 1879. He looks good for seventy-two, and Egyptologists regard him as the top expert in reading hieroglyphs. He's the author of *Egyptian Grammar*,* which is regarded as authoritative and is used by all students. The guy was born with a silver spoon in his mouth – his sizeable fortune has given him total independence. He thinks a lot of himself and has good business sense. In fact, it was thanks to one of our London agents that I managed to arrange a meeting with one of the most famous New York lawyers. Gardiner is quite happy to meet top personalities, and he thinks you're going to talk to him about international finance.'

'Excellent, Dusty.'

'His opponents say that he behaves like a politician and that no one can get through his hard outer shell. But tell me . . . Why have you travelled all that way to meet a grumpy old scholar?'

'To try to discover the truth.'

'So you really believe that the Wilders were only your adoptive parents?'

'Didn't you supply me with conclusive evidence? The letter from Cairo was no joke.'

Dusty remained silent for a few seconds. 'Are you really feeling OK, boss?'

* First published in 1927.

'Don't worry, I'm feeling great.'

'What have you got yourself mixed up in?'

'It's not very clear yet, but I'm making progress.'

'Well, don't spend too much time sniffing around! We're working hard here.'

'What about my other meeting?'

'Lady Beauchamp? No problem. She'll see you next Monday, for afternoon tea. By the way ... When you meet Gardiner, don't forget to call him "Sir Alan". Or you'll really offend him.'

19

At the Ritz, good taste and respect for tradition still held sway. The hotel's head waiter led Sir Alan, who was dressed in a blue three-piece made-to-measure suit, to the quiet table where Mark was waiting for him.

'It's a great honour to meet a scholar of your stature.'

'Let's sit down, Mr Wilder. I don't suppose you've come from the United States to discuss a problem in Egyptian philology. Shall we order? Then you can explain the reasons for this meeting.'

The bill of fare was acceptable: feuilleté aux champignons and Dover sole, accompanied by a French white wine.

After talking at length about his business, like a student taking an oral examination in front of a particularly strict professor, Mark decided to abandon his strategy and to tackle the subject head-on.

The problem was that Gardiner might clam up, or even leave the table.

'Sir Alan, I've come to talk to you about Carter.'

'Carter? . . . Howard Carter?'

'The man who discovered Tutankhamun's tomb.'

For a moment the Egyptologist seemed lost in thought, then his usual expression returned.

'You were friends, I believe?'

'That is an exaggeration,' Gardiner corrected him sharply. 'I particularly liked Lord Carnarvon, the patron who enabled him to dig in the Valley of the Kings. Carter said of me: "The more I know him, the less I like him." And that feeling was reciprocal. In the autumn of 1934, we actually broke off relations completely.'

'For what reason, Sir Alan?'

'Carter had put me in an unpleasant, even odious position, and his behaviour was inexcusable. He had entrusted me with a faience amulet representing a bull's hoof, the hieroglyph which is read as *uhem* and means "repeat, renew". Of course, he guaranteed to me that this fragile little object didn't come from Tutankhamun's treasure, which belonged to Egypt. The head curator at the Cairo Museum, Rex Engelbach, who detested Carter, stated the contrary! Therefore it had been stolen, and I could be accused of receiving stolen goods. So I returned the amulet and demonstrated my innocence by proving Carter's guilt. But Carter was stubborn and continued to declare that the amulet didn't belong to Tutankhamun, and he criticized my attitude. Relations between us were already lukewarm, and they now became positively icy. I decided to cease all collaboration with an archaeologist who was so lacking in thoroughness and moreover had no qualifications, and not to give him any help with philology.'

Gardiner swallowed a mouthful of wine.

'Deep down, I no longer feel any resentment towards Carter, a man whose excessively stubborn character cost him dear, and I lament the fact that he published only a work designed for the general public, not a scientific study. In order to honour his memory, I have even been in contact with the Egyptian authorities, with the aim of creating a splendid publication that would do justice to Carter's work, that is to say a six-volume report on the tomb of Tutankhamun.'

'Did he discover any papyri?' asked Mark, trying to sound as detached as possible.

Gardiner did not hesitate. 'Indeed, and they are of great historical importance, since the Hebrews are mentioned in them.'

The lawyer managed to keep his cool. So his first contact was the right one! All he had to do was question an expert, then persuade him to hand over the documents. 'And ... did you read them?'

'Of course, like any Egyptologist worthy of the name. Despite its imperfections, the scientific publication* enabled scholars to gain knowledge of these Aramaic papyri, written in the original language of the Bible. They show that, under the second Persian occupation of Egypt, between 343 and 332 BC, the Hebrews were indeed present in the Aswan region and practising their faith there.'

'That's not the era of Tutankhamun,' said Mark in surprise.

'Indeed not,' replied Sir Alan indignantly. 'But who said anything about Tutankhamun?'

'Didn't these papyri come from his tomb?'

'Of course not! Carter discovered them in 1904, and they were published in 1906.'

Mark's disappointment was immense. But one chance still remained. 'But there were papyri in Tutankhamun's tomb, weren't there?'

This time, Gardiner hesitated. 'Carter was convinced of it, but he was wrong. However, when he opened chest no. 43, he really did think he had found a fine collection of writings. But they turned out to be just rolls of linen.'

'There was a considerable number of boxes and chests, wasn't there?'

'Indeed, but none of them contained any papyri.'

'Were they all opened?' asked Mark.

'Of course! And he found clothing, sandals, jewellery and many other items, some more precious than others. But no papyri, to the great disappointment of the scientific world.'

'Are there any Carter archives in Britain?'

---

* A. H. Sayce and A. E. Cowley, *Aramaic Papyri Discovered at Assuan*, London, 1906.

'They are kept in Oxford. In 1945 his niece, Phyllis Walker, handed over numerous documents to the Griffith Institute. Their drawings show the celebrations depicted on the walls of the temple at Luxor, and were made at my request.'

'Could I consult these archives?'

'Would you like a letter of introduction to the curator of the Ashmolean Museum?'

'That would be most kind, Sir Alan.'

'Nothing could be easier. But forget about Tutankhamun's papyri. They never existed.'

In Oxford, thanks to Gardiner's letter, Mark had all the leisure he required to study the Carter archives, which Egyptologists consulted when studying the treasures found in Tutankhamun's tomb. There were also drawings concerning the temple of Deirel-Bahari and notes relating to Carter's archaeological work in Thebes and in the Delta.

But there was not the slightest trace of Tutankhamun's papyri, and the Egyptologist had not written a single line about them.

However, Mark was not discouraged. The first throw of the dice was not always the winning one.

20

Lady Evelyn Beauchamp, the daughter of Lord Carnarvon and the patron and friend of Howard Carter, received Mark for afternoon tea, in a drawing room hung with landscapes. Once he had served Lady Evelyn and her guest, the butler discreetly vanished.

Lady Evelyn was an extremely pretty woman, uncommonly elegant and with a soft voice. Age had no power over her, as if her passion for the wonders of Tutankhamun had succeeded in halting time.

'May I know the reason for your visit, Mr Wilder?'

'It has nothing to do with business. I'd like you to tell me about the last years of Howard Carter's life.'

'Howard Carter,' she repeated, as if the name conjured up strong memories, too long buried.

Mark allowed the elegant lady to abandon herself to her reverie and was careful not to interrupt the flow of images as they surfaced from the past.

'Howard was ill,' she said, 'and he divided his time between Egypt and England. In the winter he stayed in his beloved house in Luxor, which the local people called "Carter's Castle". He was fascinated by the desert and the western bank of Thebes, and it is said that he struck up a friendship with a jackal, the incarnation of Anubis, which visited him at nightfall. In the summer Howard used to spend a few weeks at the Hotel Kulm, in St Moritz, whose manager had lived in Egypt for sixteen years. In 1932 Howard moved house to live at 49 Albert Court, quite a spacious, comfortable apartment in a fine Victorian building. He led a solitary existence, often ate in restaurants and maintained only superficial relationships with a small number of people. He confided in no one. He didn't spend time with any Egyptologists, and I'm sure he took refuge in the memory of those exciting years when he had searched, found and excavated the tomb of Tutankhamun. He, the self-taught archaeologist with a passion, had encountered so many second-rate jealous men, and the authorities had displayed complete ingratitude towards him. How dare he become the greatest archaeologist of all time without a university degree, and how dare he defy official departments and governments! He had no time for flexibility or compromise, detested scholars with hearts as dry as dust, and crooked politicians. But he brought Tutankhamun back to life, and the brilliance of his treasures has brought a new light to our world.'

Lady Evelyn's emotions were infectious. Mark could have listened to her for hours.

'Forgive me for rambling on like that . . . I ought to have asked you first why you're interested in Howard Carter.'

'Do you wish to know the truth, Lady Evelyn?'

'Is it so terrifying?'

'Let's say . . . surprising.'

'As you wish, Mr Wilder.'

'The truth is the only thing that may perhaps make you want to help me. I assume you know of Abbot Pacomas, a Coptic monk?'

'Indeed. I've met him.'

'Howard Carter confided in the abbot and he told me a secret, which up to now has been well guarded: according to Pacomas, I am the son of Carter and an Egyptian woman.'

Lady Evelyn's gaze did not flicker. 'Do you have proof?'

'Only presumptions and Abbot Pacomas's word.'

'Why would he lie? Are you as indomitable, wild, passionate and stubborn as your father?'

'Quite possibly.'

'Then what do you want of me?'

'I've been given a mission: to find Tutankhamun's papyri. According to Gardiner, an unchallenged authority, they never existed. Did Howard Carter mention these documents to you?'

Lady Evelyn thought for a long time. 'They *do* exist,' she said.

'Do you know where they're hidden?'

'I do not, but I have an idea. In memory of Howard, I shall try to explore it. Give my butler a telephone number where you can be contacted. Thank you for enabling me to relive an exciting past, Mr Wilder . . . or should I say Mr Carter?'

Mark spent many long hours at the British Museum among its Egyptian antiquities. Statues, sarcophagi and stelae were beginning to become familiar to him, as if he had been studying this radiant, serene art for a long time. Were his father's experience and hard work unwittingly sustaining him?

Late in the afternoon, as he was drinking a glass of champagne at the Connaught, he was called to the telephone.

It was Lady Evelyn.

'Be at Highclere Castle tomorrow afternoon at 2.30 precisely. Robert Taylor will be waiting for you there. He has received instructions.'

'How can I thank you? I . . .'

'Good luck, and may Howard Carter protect you.'

Highclere Castle, the home of the Carnarvons, was an impressive neo-Gothic building in the middle of an immense park, where cedars of Lebanon dotted well-manicured lawns. Here lay Carter's patron and his dog, Suzy the fox terrier, which had died at the very same moment when her master closed his eyes in a Cairo hospital. In addition to a remarkable library, Highclere boasted the desk and armchair used by Napoleon when he had been defeated and exiled to Elba.

The visitor was greeted by an austere man of indeterminate age and undeniable distinction.

'Mr Mark Wilder, I presume? Lady Evelyn recommended you to me. I am Robert Taylor, the butler at this honourable dwelling. If you would care to follow me . . .'

The American knew that a real butler was much more than a major-domo or a head waiter. Part of the very soul of the castle and the family lineage, he preserved traditions against all attacks, and he knew how to keep secrets.

'I have been in service with the Carnarvons since 1936,' revealed Robert Taylor, 'and the family have honoured me with their entire trust. Assuring me that you were a man of honour, Lady Evelyn ordered me to show you a treasure hidden in this house, on the understanding that you will continue to be unaware of its existence.'

'You have my word.'

The butler nodded and led his guest to a cupboard concealed in the wall separating the smoking room from the library.

'I am aware of the adventurous life of the late Lord Carnarvon, the sixth of that name, and of his friendship with the archaeologist Howard Carter,' said Robert Taylor. 'At that time, and before the conflict with the Egyptian authorities, successful excavators had the right to keep some of their finds.'

Mark's eyes shone with excitement.

In other words, part of Tutankhamun's treasure was here, at Highclere, preserved for many years! And in this secret hiding place, the papyri . . .

'I am going to open this cupboard,' announced the butler, 'and allow you to gaze on its contents. Then you will leave Highclere and forget what you have seen.'

'Again, you have my promise.'

'The promise of a man of honour is worth more than any signature.'

Very slowly, the butler opened the doors.

Within, there were close to three hundred items, forming a small but breathtaking collection of Egyptian antiquities:[*] statuettes, alabaster vases, bronzes, jewellery and a carved wooden head of Pharaoh Amenhotep III, father of the famous Akhenaton. They came from digs carried out by Carter in Thebes and in the Delta, in the service of Lord Carnarvon.

Mark's examination was long and detailed. The butler showed no sign of impatience.

At last, the lawyer had to accept his disappointment: there was no sign of any papyrus.

'Thank you for your trust, Mr Taylor.'

The butler closed the cupboard doors, hermetically tight.

[*] This would not be officially revealed until 1988. See N. Reeves, 'The Search for Tutankhamun, The Final Chapter', *Aramco World*, Washington DC, 39, no. 6, pp. 6–13, and *Le Figaro Magazine*, 6 December 1988, pp. 90–93.

21

When the CIA agent saw Mark Wilder's plane take off for New York, he felt relieved. At last, he was rid of this bothersome individual, whose trail, rather pathetically, he had not managed to pick up until London airport.

So his report would be extremely short and to the point, since he did not know how the lawyer had occupied his time during his stay, where he had gone or whom he had contacted. John would not be pleased, but he couldn't expect the impossible. This guy Wilder had proved devilishly elusive, and the CIA branch in London lacked the personnel necessary to carry out all its many tasks. And after all, this fellow countryman was surely no threat to the security of the United States.

Since he was going home, someone else could deal with his case.

'At long last!' exclaimed Dusty as Mark stepped through the door of his office. 'We're working on a massive case, which will bring us in a pile of money, and we need our master's eye. You know, boss, you've never taken such a long vacation before!'

'And it's not over yet.'

Dusty lit an enormous Cuban cigar. 'How about enlightening me on this tangled affair before I die of suspense?'

'A Coptic abbot revealed my parents' identity to me. My mother was Egyptian, and my father was an Englishman, Howard

Carter, who discovered the tomb of Tutankhamun.'

'Well, that's a good one! But it's no surprise, coming from you. Did your abbot give you irrefutable proof?'

'All I have is his word and a few disturbing clues, notably the ones you obtained.'

'Even for a lawyer like you, that's a rather lightweight portfolio!'

'Don't forget personal belief.'

Dusty exhaled a large cloud of smoke. 'And . . . that's what you have?'

'I'm beginning to.'

'Why did you go to London?'

'Again according to Abbot Pacomas, my father entrusted me with a mission: to find Tutankhamun's papyri, whose contents are explosive. Nobody knows where they are, and I'm the only person who can find the right path, which seemed to lead to England. Total failure.'

Dusty couldn't believe his ears. 'This is some Eastern legend you're telling me, boss! Am I dreaming, or what?'

'According to a reliable source, these papyri really did exist. And the trail goes by way of the Metropolitan Museum, to which Howard Carter was linked in many ways. So we're going to conduct an in-depth investigation before I meet a senior official.'

'Are . . . are you serious?'

'Very serious.'

'And my file . . . Will you look at it?'

'Of course.'

Dusty was relieved. Mark hadn't completely lost his mind.

While the finishing touches were being put to the building for the United Nations, a new organization doomed to powerlessness, and Senator McCarthy's commission was pursuing Communists, the Metropolitan Museum remained a shrine dedicated to ancient but immutable values.

The man in charge was austere and rather starchy. Aware of the importance of his office, he carried it out with great seriousness, regarding himself as the guardian of the Metropolitan Museum's splendid Egyptian antiquities. So he regarded his time as infinitely precious, and granted meetings only to persons of quality.

The great lawyer Mark Wilder was one of these.

'I've just visited the Egyptian department,' Wilder said. 'It's an absolute marvel.'

The director shrugged.

'Doesn't the provenance of certain items pose serious legal problems?' asked the lawyer.

'Certainly not,' snapped the director.

'Are you quite sure?'

'Completely.'

Mark consulted his notes.

'Two rings in glass paste bearing the name of Tutankhamun and a bronze dog from the antechamber of his tomb, a cup containing an unguent, fragments of fabric and matting, two gold nails and two others made of silver, taken from the Pharaoh's sarcophagus . . . Shall I continue?'

'I know that list as well as you do,' snapped the director.

'Under Egyptian law current at the time when Tutankhamun's tomb was discovered, these items should never have left the country.'

'We purchased them in absolutely correct circumstances.'

'From Howard Carter, Lord Carnarvon and their heirs between 1926 and 1940, I know. Nevertheless, don't you think the behaviour of the museum's authorities was a little . . . shady?'

'The Louvre and the British Museum are full of stolen items,' the director reminded him. 'We, on the contrary, negotiated. And you are an American! You ought to be delighted to see these modest pieces preserved in your homeland, as sparse as they are compared with the hundreds of works of art exhibited in Cairo.'

'There's another list of ten items, including a solid-gold ring, which are not definitively attributed to Tutankhamun, according to the museum's files, but whose provenance is in no doubt. And that ring was given to the museum either by Carnarvon or Carter, in gratitude for its assistance.'

'How do you come to be so well informed?'

'It's my job.'

'What exactly do you want?' demanded the director anxiously.

'Access to the museum's stores, and to all the items purchased from Carter, Carnarvon and their heirs.'

'Are you looking for . . . something specific?'

'I'm in a great hurry. And people of goodwill always come to an understanding in the end. If you grant me this authorization immediately, everything will be fine. And whatever happens, I shall be absolutely discreet. You and I are both concerned for the Metropolitan Museum's unsullied reputation, are we not?'

'One of my assistants will accompany you.'

The doors opened.

When he found a scribe's palette, an ivory writing case and brushes donated by Carter's heirs, Mark thought he was getting close to his goal. His father must have entrusted these writing materials and the papyri to the American museum so that he could be certain that they would be safe.

He gazed at other small works of art that had probably belonged to Tutankhamun, such as pots of unguent or a perfume bottle, drew up a complete list, and scrutinized all the files, notes and reports.

There was no trace of any papyri.

22

A storm broke over New York, and Mark Wilder's plane was tossed around like a toy. Indifferent to the other passengers' cries of fear, the lawyer pondered over his fruitless return to America. After exploring every nook and cranny in the Metropolitan Museum, and consulting the archives, he had gone to the Brooklyn Museum, which, in the early 1940s, had purchased a few items from a London antiquarian, who had obtained them from Carter's heirs. A statuette of a woman, a necklace, a spoon for unguents, a miniature vase, an ivory grasshopper ... small marvels that certainly came from Tutankhamun's treasure, but no papyri.

Using the file of information supplied by Abbot Pacomas and the results of Dusty's enquiries, Mark had turned his attentions to the other museums that might have acquired items taken from the king's tomb.

First, there was the William Rockhill Nelson Art Gallery, in Kansas City, which had gold sections taken from one of Tutankhamun's collars, given by Howard Carter himself to his doctor, who had sold them to a London antiquarian, who in turn supplied the museum. The doctor was a trusted man who might also have received the papyri.

Another disappointment.

Next, the Art Museum in Cincinnati, which owned an exceptional work, a bronze panther. It must have been among the wonders placed in the tomb, but it was not accompanied by any papyri. The curator advised Mark to go to the Museum of Art in Cleveland, which, according to rumour, possessed at least one suspicious amulet.

A waste of time.

Finally, there was the Institute at the University of Chicago, founded by James Henry Breasted, who died in 1935. The American Egyptologist had been invited to work in Tutankhamun's tomb, notably on the inscriptions. Although he was received quite warmly, Mark did not gather any useful information at all.

He returned to New York, where – despite the turbulence – his plane eventually managed to land. The pilot's skills were enthusiastically applauded, and as they disembarked the passengers had never appreciated the driving rain as much as they did that day.

The CIA agent instructed to keep watch on Mark Wilder informed his superiors that the lawyer was back home.

Dusty Malone devoured an enormous steak smothered in tomato ketchup and surrounded by giant French fries, accompanied by his second pint of stout. Mark made do with a salad, a lamb chop and a glass of wine.

'Don't despair, boss! Aren't the best jokes the shortest ones? Forget about this crazy affair and focus on what matters. I have excellent news regarding your political career. According to a recent opinion poll, women really like you and you're regarded favourably by all levels of the population, including politicians. In other words, you're the ideal candidate, and there's no opponent who can match you. But be careful. There'll be no shortage of tricks and shady dealing. Still, since you have nothing to hide, any attempts to damage you will rebound on their instigators. It's up to you to hold firm and not yield an inch of ground. Are you listening to me, boss?'

'Yes, of course . . .'

'You're still thinking about Howard Carter and Tutankhamun's papyri!'

'It would be difficult not to, don't you think?'

'It was a nice legend, and it cleared your mind, but the vacation is over. Forget the past, whatever it was, and think only of the future – your future. On my honour, it's going to be brilliant! All doors are opening to you, and you can't give up because of some Eastern fantasy.'

'This is about my father, Dusty, and a promise I must keep.'

'Don't get things mixed up! First, you'd have to be certain that Howard Carter really was your father, and you'll never obtain that proof. Next, did your Egyptian priest make up this mission? Lastly, it's obvious that these papyri, if they ever existed, have disappeared. Supposing that they contained some important, even embarrassing, information, what better solution would their owner have than to destroy them? Whatever way you look at this affair, you'll get the same result: it's over, and you're wasting your time messing around with ghosts. Your reputation is constantly growing, enormous cases are arriving on your desk, and you mustn't put a foot wrong as you prepare for your electoral campaign. Listen to me, boss: the vacation is over.'

Autumn was coming to New York, and Mark had not even noticed summer pass by. The constant flow of work had forced him to take on several top-level colleagues, with the agreement of Dusty, the formidable captain of the team. Numerous influential politicians were openly backing the lawyer's candidature, and his life seemed to be filled with dinners and meetings.

While he was walking alone in Central Park, he noticed Tuthmosis III's obelisk again.

And the hieroglyphs leaped out at him, like tongues of fire burning away the outer shell of darkness and illusions with which he had covered himself.

Business, politics, ambition, career . . . He detached himself from all these, knowing that he must keep the promise he had given to Abbot Pacomas, honour his father's memory and see Ateya again. It was impossible to forget Ateya, or to live without her. Perhaps that's what love was, the absolute need to unite two destinies and journey together towards the same horizon.

And what if Ateya had forgotten him?

As Mark sat down in his office to sign an unbelievably good contract, Dusty sensed that something was amiss.

'You look tired, boss.'

'You're right. I need some rest. I worked too hard over the summer and it's worn me out.'

'A nice weekend in California will put you right.'

'That's not enough.'

'I hope you're not planning on going back to Egypt?'

'They do say October is one of the best months to visit.'

'Just for a brief stay. Do you promise?'

'Why should it turn into a long one?'

Knowing that it would be impossible to prevent his boss from going, Dusty did not argue and instead sorted out the files Mark needed to deal with before he left.

Deep in thought, Mark had come to a conclusion: Abbot Pacomas knew that Tutankhamun's papyri were neither in England nor the United States.

The abbot's aim, in obliging him to travel to these two countries and carry out fruitless research, was to put him to the test and find out if Howard Carter's son was worthy of his father and his mission.

If he became discouraged following this failure and if he did not understand the reason, Pacomas would have been right not to reveal the whole truth to him. On the other hand, if he overcame his disappointment and went back to Egypt, then the abbot would direct him on to the right road.

23

'Hello, Mark! It's great to see you back in Egypt,' said John warmly. 'Did you have a good trip?'

'Excellent.'

'Shall I take you to the Mena House?'

'Yes, please.'

The CIA agent had changed cars. Two porters loaded the lawyer's luggage into the boot of the Cadillac, which shot off into Cairo's anarchic traffic.

'Were you expecting me or did you just happen to be there?'

'You know the answer, Mark. As soon as your name appeared on a passenger manifest, I was informed. It feels as if you've been away for a long time.'

'Were you certain that I would come back?'

'People always come back to Egypt. One visit is never enough. You must have been really busy this summer.'

'I didn't have a single minute to myself.'

'Business and politics ... It seems to me you're becoming more and more important.'

'Let's not exaggerate, John. I'm sailing my boat, and so far the tide has proved rather favourable. But the wind can change.'

'Don't belittle yourself! You're climbing towards the summit and you're going to play an extremely important role. The thing I can't understand is why you travelled to England.'

'Are you spying on me permanently?'

'Not spying – protecting. As I already told you, highly placed individuals are relying a great deal on you, and we're making sure that you're safe.'

'Even in England and the United States?'

'My agents carry out their orders. In London, you threw them off with the air of a professional.'

Mark burst out laughing. 'That was far from my intention! I didn't even notice your guardian angels.'

'A fault in technique on their part, or just competing circumstances ... It can happen. What did you go to England to do?'

'Do I have to answer you?'

'Of course not! But isn't it better to maintain an atmosphere of trust between us?'

'I wanted to wrap up a delicate matter with the aid of a personal contact and to look up some friends.'

'These friends aren't agents in the British secret service, I hope?'

'Certainly not!'

'You see, Mark, we're not always allies, especially with regard to Egypt and the Suez Canal. A bad choice of acquaintances could cause you serious problems. You have only one card to play: the American one.'

'I'm completely convinced of that.'

'In that case, no problem. Here, on the other hand, things aren't going well. Farouk has been on a flashy honeymoon and spent a fortune every day in palaces where he gorged himself even more than usual. One Italian hotelier even said: "Customers at that price ... it can't go on." The Egyptian people aren't content just to detest their king; they're starting to despise him as well. And he's the only one who can't see it. The political situation is becoming unhealthy. Are you planning to stay long?'

'As long as necessary.'

'If the authorities contact you, tell me without delay. Any information you can provide me with, however minimal, may be useful to me to avert a disaster and to safeguard our country's interests.'

The great pyramid of Khufu appeared in the distance. Listening to John with one ear, Mark had eyes only for the imposing structure.

At last he was back home again.

The proximity of the desert, the purity of the air, the blaze of the setting sun, the gentle warmth of an October evening: all these elements made the soul light, capable of communing with the mystery that imbued this sacred land.

Mark was crossing a new frontier. He was passing from the ordinary, heavy, stifling world into the world of beings capable of building rays of light in order to touch the heavens' summit.

The Cadillac halted in front of the Mena House's front steps. Immediately, two employees wearing the tarboosh came out to greet their guest.

'Have a good evening, Mark. Don't do anything I wouldn't.'

The lawyer nodded.

His vast, high-ceilinged room was worthy of a palace. As he sat down on the edge of the huge bed, the lawyer attempted to regain some kind of stability. He hardly knew this country, and yet he was already madly in love with it, as if he had always lived here.

Someone knocked at his door. He opened it.

Her.

It was Ateya, looking sublime in her red dress. Elegance, charm and magic.

'You look . . . You look magnificent!'

'I'm not disturbing you?'

'Please, come in.'

He closed the door of his room softly, so as not to shatter the miracle of the moment. Although still inaccessible, Ateya was standing very close beside him.

'I was hoping you would come back,' she said in a voice that made him shiver. 'The weeks went by, and I began to doubt. And then one of the clerks on reception, a Copt, informed me that you had just arrived.'

'I had a lot of work on, Ateya, and I had to check every piece of information Abbot Pacomas gave me, both in England and America.'

'Do you still trust him absolutely?'

'More than ever!'

'He wishes to speak to you as soon as possible. A taxi is waiting for you.'

'Are you coming with me?'

'No. My task was simply to deliver the instructions to you.'

'When will I see you again, Ateya?'

'I don't know. Hurry.'

She vanished.

Irritated, Mark washed his face and sprinkled himself with aftershave, then left the hotel.

At the bottom of the steps stood a green taxi. The driver had an honest face.

'You are from New York?'

'Correct.'

'If I say "abbot", what do you say?'

'Pacomas.'

'Let's go, Mr Wilder.'

The fellow was certainly skilful. He managed to overtake heavily laden trucks, avoided suicidal pedestrians and grazed the flanks of donkeys pulling carts filled with bricks.

'We're being followed,' he announced. 'A professional. And I can't shake him off. So we'll implement the prearranged plan. I shall drop you off in front of the Opera House. You retrace your steps and get into a black Peugeot, which will stop next to you.'

The driver promptly carried out the manoeuvre.

Caught unawares, the man following them attempted to react, but the tide of traffic prevented him from making a U-turn, and the black Peugeot escaped from him.

Mark's new driver was a small, nervous man. Without uttering a single word, he dropped Mark off near Old Cairo. A youth showed him the Coptic cross tattooed on his wrist and guided him to the Hanging Church.

The lawyer went immediately to the garden.

A monk in a black cassock was seated on the bench, reading an ancient text written in Coptic.

But it was not Abbot Pacomas.

24

Mark hestitated.

Ought he to speak to the monk or leave this place immediately? Had a trap been set for him after silencing Abbot Pacomas?

The priest stood up and walked towards him. 'Follow me, my son.'

The lawyer did so.

Was he making a fatal mistake by trusting a stranger like this? The priest guided him to a narrow street, which was quieter than the main streets of Old Cairo, and pointed to an ancient door studded with nails.

'Knock three times and the door will be opened.'

Mark obeyed.

The door opened, and Abbot Pacomas appeared.

'Come in, Mark.'

The lawyer found himself in an immense library, each shelf of which was laden with carefully bound ancient books.

'This library stores the memories of the Coptic people,' revealed Pacomas. 'Here, I preserve hieroglyphic, Greek, Aramaic and Coptic texts, many of which have not been translated. Have you brought back Tutankhamun's papyri?'

'You know I haven't. You subjected me to a trial to find out if I wanted to, and was capable of, undertaking this search.'

'Did you not have some interesting meetings?'

'Only Lady Evelyn believes these papyri exist, but she was

mistaken in thinking that they were hidden at Highclere. As for the Egyptologists, they have never seen the documents. The American museums have only a few items belonging to Tutankhamun's treasure, and no papyri. Carter's archives, which are kept in Oxford, make no mention of them. And you knew all this already!'

'Indeed,' conceded Pacomas. 'Nevertheless, you had to follow this path yourself in order to appreciate the difficulties. Are you determined to continue, Mark?'

'Doesn't my presence here signify my answer?'

'Let's go and talk in the sitting room. I have an excellent vintage Armagnac, which will help to calm your emotions.'

The drink, accompanied by pastries, deserved to be famous.

'I have reached a conclusion,' declared Mark. 'If they exist, Tutankhamun's papyri can only be in Egypt.'

'You must cease to doubt their reality, and realize that if you continue this search in the land of the pharaohs, we shall unleash hostile forces, which are determined to destroy us and prevent us from revealing the truth. I am not without weapons to combat them, but victory is far from certain. On the one hand, I promise you dangers and harsh confrontations; on the other, there is your brilliant career.'

'It seems to me that the time for choosing is past, since I have already given you my word.'

'You are indeed the worthy son of Howard Carter,' declared Abbot Pacomas. 'Unlike the majority of Egyptologists, he appreciated the scope of the ancient Egyptians' spirituality, though modern scholars regard them as pagans blinded by superstition. According to Carter, on the contrary, they were models of faith and of fidelity to an ideal, something that is inconceivable today, in our world of cynical materialism. "The shadows of the ancient gods still have complete control over us," he confided in me. A superficial study of the mythology and religion of the ancient Egyptians might conclude that we have made progress compared with them. But once we are capable of perceiving their thoughts, we lose all feelings of superiority. No intelligent, sensitive individual can deny that pharaonic art embodied the essential truth, the gift of life to matter through the spirit and radiance of the first morning's light. Despite our technical progress, we have lost the meaning of this. Your father spent hours gazing at the astrological ceiling in the resurrection chamber of Seti I, in the Valley of the Kings. It depicts the immense body of the sky goddess, Nut, which extends across the cosmos. She gives birth to all celestial bodies, which move within her bosom and influence all the many forms of life. Carter declared: "These are not, as has been suggested by a few imbeciles, the product of unsound minds, but symbols with a hidden meaning and lofty consequences, the key to which can only be supplied by the ancient colleges of priests.""*

'And Tutankhamun's papyri would supply that key?' ventured Mark.

'Without a doubt. And there are certain destructive minds that hope never to see it used.'

'Forgive my saying this, Father: how does your sympathy for the spirituality of the ancient Egyptians accord with your Christian faith? In listening to you reporting Carter's opinions, I had the feeling that you shared them and that you were the heir to these colleges of priests, able to decipher the mysteries.'

'We shall talk of this again later,' decreed Abbot Pacomas, refilling the glasses. 'The moment has come for you to resume your Quest, this time in Egypt itself and by using the clues your father left us. The first of them concerns three messengers whom he met when he was searching for the tomb of Akhenaton and Nefertiti in Middle Egypt, a magnificent region where he experienced some of the happiest moments of his life. These three men belonged to a tribe that was rather inaccessible, and to which Howard Carter could have entrusted the papyri.'

* The words and ideas of Carter reported here are, of course, authentic.

'If their chief has them, how will I persuade him to hand them over to me?'

'You will not set out on your own, Mark. You will be accompanied by someone who is very familiar with the story of the messengers and the tribal chief. All you have to do is prove your personal qualities, and I do not doubt your talents as a lawyer for one moment.'

'Is this a new test or do you really not know where the papyri are?' Mark asked suddenly.

'I truly do not know, and the real trials are beginning. Soon, people will know that you are conducting this Quest, and the dangers will start to appear.'

'I think the fauna of New York are just as fearsome, whether in business or politics!'

'Here, we have the addition of demons, which have risen up from the darkness.'

'Don't you know how to defeat them, Father?'

'I shall try.'

'When do I leave?'

'Early next week. The material preparations will be finished, and you will be regarded as one of those rare tourists who wants to see sites that are not often visited, despite their archaeological richness.'

'And when will my companion contact me?'

'The day before you leave. Officially, you will be on a guided excursion.'

'May I know his name?'

'Your companion is one of the best guides in Egypt, a young Coptic woman whom you have already met: Ateya.'

25

On that sunny morning of 7 October 1951, Mark Wilder was just returning from a long walk in the shade of the pyramids when the manager of the Mena House handed him an envelope which had been sent from the royal palace.

It contained an invitation signed by Antonio Pulli, Farouk's private secretary, inviting Mark to dinner the following evening at 11 p.m. at the Scarab. His Majesty wished to meet this exceptional guest.

Mark immediately called John. 'I have a problem.'

'Don't tell me any more over the telephone. Meet me at 5 p.m. in the Metro Cinema.'

Mark ate lunch alone in the gardens of the Mena House, facing the great pyramid of Khufu. Dinner with Farouk did not appeal to him, and he preferred to think about his forthcoming journey to Middle Egypt, along with Ateya. At last they would have time to talk. And perhaps they would return with Tutankhamun's papyri.

As a precaution, the lawyer went to the Cairo Museum, spent half an hour there, then took taxi which dropped him off at the Metro Cinema, one of Cairo's foremost entertainment hot spots. At the forefront of modernity, the auditorium boasted air conditioning, which was responsible for colds and angina.

John bought a ticket, and Mark did likewise. He followed him and sat down beside him, on the back row. At that time of day there were plenty of empty seats. They were showing an American adventure film, with French subtitles. A small screen at the side displayed subtitles in Arabic and Greek.

'Farouk has invited me to dinner at the Scarab,' Mark revealed in a whisper.

'Well, you can't refuse,' John whispered back. 'I assume the invitation's signed by Pulli?'

'Correct.'

'Then it's a major offensive! They're bound to offer you work, and you'll enter his ungracious Majesty's privileged circle. The place he's chosen is no accident: the Scarab is the most famous private club in Cairo. It comprises a gaming room, a dance floor and a restaurant, where Farouk stuffs himself after losing a fortune at poker. For breakfast, he wolfs down thirty eggs, and the menu for his last dinner even revolted his nearest and dearest: bouchées à la reine, sole meunière, mutton chops, roast chicken, pavé de boeuf, lobster, ris de veau, mashed potato, artichokes, rice, peas and cheese, and not forgetting several desserts. And that's not taking account of the thirty or so litres of sugary drinks he consumes in the course of a day. He weighs so much that they've had to make special chairs for him, capable of supporting his bulk. He can hardly walk, but that doesn't slow him down sexually. Whatever you do, if you have a mistress, don't bring her. Assuming the king likes her, she'll spend that same night in his bed. At the Abdin Palace, everything is organized to satisfy the ogre's fantasies, including the installation of cameras designed to film His Royal Majesty's frolics with his conquests. When Farouk appears in a nightclub, husbands and lovers tremble. Which woman will he choose to reawaken his jaded desires?'

'What about the queen?'

'She knows all about it,' replied John, 'but she has to keep quiet. Officially, the pair are gloriously happy. How can Farouk believe that this pantomime will deceive anybody? What he expects from his wife is a son to carry on the dynasty and silence his opponents. His kilos of fat don't make His Majesty any less dangerous, Mark. There's a persistent rumour that the king shot a military doctor who caught him in bed with his wife. The affair was hushed up, and Farouk now entrusts General Sirri Amer with the job of eliminating anyone who gets in the way. Avoid being classified in that category.'

'My sense of diplomacy has its limits, John.'

'Prime Minister Nahas has just dropped a bombshell, on Farouk's orders,' revealed the CIA agent. 'It's difficult to calculate the consequences, but it's bound to cause disturbances. Yesterday, he made a long declaration to Parliament, recalling the circumstances that led him to sign a treaty with the British in 1936. In particular, it allowed them to continue controlling the Suez Canal zone with an army of around ten thousand men, not counting the pilots of the Royal Air Force. At the end of the speech, Nahas flew into a rage: "Today, on behalf of Egypt, I abrogate that treaty. The British must get out immediately!" And Parliament applauded him.'

'Do you think there's going to be a confrontation between the British and the Egyptians?'

'The Egyptian army isn't capable of facing up to the British. According to my information, the British will calm things down. Nevertheless, the people will demonstrate, particularly since the press has just published the real numbers of occupying soldiers in the country: not ten thousand but sixty thousand, in violation of the treaty. Farouk is attempting a poker trick, in order to receive adulation and be regarded as the champion of Egypt's independence, but it's all just show. Although he detests the British, he can't manage without them. Doubtless the processions of enraged nationalists will demand the final evacuation of British troops, and then everyone will calm down again.'

'What if they don't?'

John thought for a long time. On the screen, the hero dispatched ten sinister-looking attackers and rescued his fiancée before she suffered a fate worse than death.

'The British won't give in, Mark. Even Hitler couldn't break their spirit. If Egypt persists in demanding an independence they regard as intolerable, there'll be a bloodbath.'

'And America will emerge from it the victor?'

John hung his head. 'You're already a formidable politician! All I do is obey orders.'

'Meaning?'

'I watch, I don't do anything stupid and I gather as much information as I can, so our leaders can choose the best path. That's why you're set to play such a vital role. I know that soon you'll be an important person and that you must not run any risks. If Farouk attempts to trap you, jump on the first plane for New York. On the other hand, try to take the measure of the situation. Here, in the Middle East and especially in Egypt, the world of tomorrow is being created. What's more, isn't the destiny of the West often played out in the land of the pharaohs?'

'In the realms of espionage, the words "sincerity" and "honesty" clearly have no meaning. However, I'm still naive enough to believe that truth may exist when two men look each other in the eyes. So, John, tell me the truth: is it your job to prepare for violent action against Farouk and impose a new regime?'

'Absolutely not, Mark. The king holds the reins firmly. His political police control the country, and the army, despite its discontent, isn't making any waves. Nevertheless, the lid could blow off the cooking pot at any moment. That's why we must ensure that we're ready to take action and choose the best solution . . . Don't leave the auditorium until the end of the film. The hero's triumph is always the best bit.'

John stood up; Mark gazed fixedly at the screen.

He could not completely trust this old friend who was so persuasive. To him, people were just pieces he moved at will on a chessboard. Mark must just hope that John wanted freedom to triumph, not the victory of some lunatic faction.

The hero killed the villain and was at last able to kiss the heroine in peace. The adventure had finished well, and the audience seemed delighted.

Mark did not notice the small, insignificant man who had been tailing him since he left the Mena House. Thanks to his reliable moped, he had never lost sight of the American, whose behaviour was typical of a secret agent.

So the little man would write an informative report for his section chief, Mahmoud.

26

Mark was in the habit of being early for his meetings with important people. This gave him time to compose himself, even in the middle of chaos, and to prepare for a confrontation from which he must try to emerge the victor.

Meeting Farouk didn't promise to be a picnic, and the lawyer did not take John's warnings lightly. Some people were thrilled to have been noticed by the king; others regretted it bitterly.

The clientele of the Scarab* was extremely high class. As the establishment had obtained a royal decree authorizing it to sell alcohol and open a gaming room, it attracted dignitaries of the regime bearing the titles of Bey and Pasha, smartly uniformed British officers, rich Copts, landowners, Jewish shopkeepers, Italians, Greeks, Turks, Lebanese and other lovers of strong sensations. Everyone smoked, favouring cigars and luxury cigarettes. An Italian orchestra played slow tunes, enabling suitors in dinner jackets to seduce beautiful women in long dresses, dripping with jewels.

Mark was greeted with great courtesy by a maître d'hôtel in bow tie, white waistcoat and black trousers.

'My name is Wilder. His Majesty King Farouk has invited me to dinner.'

---

* All details regarding the Scarab are given by G. Sinoue, whose father was the manager of the establishment, in *Le Colonel et l'Enfant-roi*.

'His Majesty has not yet arrived. I shall show you to his table.'

Dressed in white kaftans with swaths of red fabric for belts, the elegant Nubian waiters dashed to and fro, eager to satisfy the smallest whims of the Scarab's guests.

As in all the other establishments where Farouk came to gamble, drink, eat and look for women, his table was permanently reserved and covered with fruit juices, surrounded by snacks. The maître d'hôtel showed Mark to his seat and immediately served him a glass of champagne.

The atmosphere was relaxed and cheerful, the customers carefree.

Suddenly, the club ground to a halt, and the diners stopped eating.

'The king has arrived,' an Albanian trader whispered to the woman who was his companion for the evening.

Maurice, the proprietor and manager of the Scarab, welcomed the enormous Farouk, accompanied by Antonio Pulli, and showed him to the large round table, watched with interest and anxiety by the revellers. The most beautiful women suddenly wished they were somewhere else.

Mark was on his feet.

Everyone was staring at the Egyptian king's exceptional guest, wondering if he would soon be one of his close confidants and if he would pay a fortune to obtain an honorary title.

'Majesty,' said Antonio Pulli, 'may I present to you the American lawyer Mark Wilder. He owns one of the largest legal businesses in New York and has clients all over the world. Mr Wilder is expected to have a glittering political career ahead of him.'

'Happy to hear it,' replied Farouk, sitting down. 'I am very fond of America and I am also fond of enjoying myself.'

A waiter immediately placed a bowl on the table. It contained balls of coloured paper. One by one, the obese king threw them at the slightly tipsy dancers. Each time he hit a target, his unpleasant laugh obliged everyone in the club to show their satisfaction.

'That is enough,' he decided. 'Now I'm hungry.'

Warned by John that the bill of fare would be colossal, Mark took care only to nibble, so as to stay the distance and not insult the monarch by refusing one of the dishes.

'His Majesty is fatigued after a long day's work in the service of the country,' said Pulli, 'but even so he still wished to meet you. Egypt is honoured to welcome an individual of your stature, Mr Wilder, and we hope that you will appreciate our country's charms.'

'I'm fascinated.'

'Are you enjoying your stay at the Mena House?'

'Everything is perfect.'

The famished king devoured a plate of meatballs. When he paused to take a breath, he fixed his guest with a hard stare. 'Egypt has just broken the 1936 treaty, signed with the British. I want to give Egypt back to the Egyptians. Are you in agreement?'

'Who would not be, Majesty?'

'The British! They always want everything. They humiliated me in the past and think that I have a short memory. They are wrong.'

'The Americans are not the British. They want all peoples to have freedom and autonomy.'

'So much the better, Mr Wilder, so much the better!'

Farouk attacked a magnificent sole meunière. 'The British understand nothing about my country and my people. How dare they insult me, a king? The Germans were more intelligent.'

'Fortunately,' Mark reminded him, 'the Nazis lost the war.'

The atmosphere grew tense. The orchestra kept on playing soft music regardless, and the diners continued to celebrate.

As the first meat dish was served, Farouk downed a litre of fruit juice and – to Pulli's great relief – resumed the conversation. 'We cannot remake history,' conceded the monarch. 'But you and America should know one thing: I alone rule Egypt, I alone decide, and no one will stand in my way.'

'Don't you ever feel in danger, Majesty?'

Farouk's unpleasant laughter rang out again. 'I, in danger? I control everything, Mr Wilder! Egypt is a safe country, totally safe. The Egyptians fear and venerate me. When I married my second wife, they cheered me. What they are waiting for is my son, who will succeed me. Everyone is convinced, and rightly so, that my dynasty will long reign over this country. Therefore you may invest in it in complete security.'

Farouk glanced towards Pulli, indicating that it was his turn to speak. 'We know your firm's deserved reputation, Mr Wilder,' said the king's private secretary, 'and we are impressed by its successes throughout the world. Egypt is modernizing and growing wealthy, but the legal framework of certain dealings needs to be improved. Would you consent to examine certain files, maintaining total confidentiality?'

'You needn't worry; that is the rule.'

'In addition,' went on Pulli, 'we are hoping to develop certain businesses, and not only in the area of cotton. The experience of the American businessmen you know well could be extremely valuable to us. Would you consent to facilitate contacts with senior officials of our government? Your help will, of course, be remunerated.'

'Nothing is impossible.'

By the third meat dish, Farouk was still eating with gusto and seemed particularly radiant.

He tapped his secretary on the arm. 'The tall brunette, with the maroon dress and the pearl necklace.'

'Majesty,' objected Pulli, 'she is a well-known singer!'

'Perfect, perfect . . . Bring her to me.'

Mark stood up. 'I would not wish to importune Your Majesty and prevent you from taking advantage of his evening.'

Farouk smiled. 'I really do like Americans. They have intuition and always make the right moves. Pulli will be in touch with you again, Mr Wilder, and we shall do excellent business. No one has ever regretted working with me and benefiting from my protection.'

27

On the warm evening of 10 October 1951, Mahmoud had a particularly delicate task: to convene a meeting, in great secrecy, of the leaders of the Free Officers and maintain complete safety so that they could appoint the leader who would bring them to power.

According to the analyses carried out by these officers, who were on the brink of rebellion, the people could no longer tolerate Farouk or the British occupiers. By ridding themselves of these parasites, who believed they were untouchable, Egypt could regain the dignity that had been sullied for too long.

But was this hazardous enterprise feasible? Farouk's political police were efficient, and there was no guarantee that the army, controlled as it was by generals loyal to the king, would take part in a revolution.

However, despite Farouk's arrogance and his entourage's certainty that they held all the keys to the country, the situation was becoming explosive. At the University of Cairo, and even in some schools, radical teachers were urging students and pupils to fight against a regime that was corrupt and indifferent to the people's misery. Numerous imams passed on their message and, inside the mosques, asked believers to rebel against injustice and arbitrary decision-making.

Incidents were snowballing; young people were insulting and jostling uniformed Britons in the streets of the capital. Up to now, repression had been severe; the king would not allow things to get out of hand. But could he succeed in extinguishing the anger of the masses?

Even moderates had to recognize that the British administration took little interest in the dreadful living conditions of the majority of the population. They did not open schools or build social housing; young children were allowed to die; sickness was not combated; but good business was being done with Farouk's admirers.

Everywhere, in town and country, nationalist feeling was taking shape and hatred of British colonialism growing. At the Cotton Exchange, there was scandal after scandal. With the aid of the royal family, speculators were growing rich on the backs of the peasantry.

Farouk . . . the hope of an entire people, the heir to the great kings, the monarch who was going to lead his country on to the path of progress and prosperity! Today he was a spineless, cruel pachyderm, clutching on to his privileges and his fortune. The extent of the disappointment explained that of the rage.

For the tenth time, Mahmoud inspected his surroundings. At least ten lookouts were keeping watch on the modest house where the Free Officers would shortly assemble. If the political police had got wind of this meeting, it would be the end of the revolution.

Two days earlier, on 8 October 1951, the Cairo Parliament had unanimously approved an important decision: from now on, the British soldiers controlling the Suez Canal zone would be regarded as illegal occupiers. A great surge of patriotism would fire supporters of their expulsion.

Already, young revolutionaries were causing disturbances, defying the colonizers, who had immediately strengthened security measures and threatened to react harshly if guerrilla warfare broke out. Coolly and firmly, the British flatly refused the insane demands of the Egyptian government. Farouk and his ministers must give up their dreams of autonomy.

The people did not agree. And they began to take action to make life difficult for the occupiers. For example, Customs officers held back items and foodstuffs that the British brought in from their homeland, and the Egyptian employees of the British army planned whirlwind strikes, beginning with train drivers, a strike that would thus make it difficult for troops to be transported and raw materials to be delivered.

A profound movement of opposition was growing, and as yet the Free Officers played only a minor, even derisory role in it. This time, they must take control, use this rising tide, overthrow the corrupt government and show the British that the supporters of independence would not give in.

At the start of his reign, Farouk had attempted to become the spiritual and temporal leader of a state determined to win back its freedom. Quickly giving up this ideal, he was now playing a double game and was content merely to swagger, deceiving his people without annoying the occupying power too much. Given the weakness of the Egyptian army, what did Britain have to fear?

All the leaders of the Free Officers had arrived.

There was no trace of a police presence, apart from the usual neighbourhood informants, who had been placed under close surveillance. Reassured, Mahmoud stepped inside the little house where the real revolution was at last about to take shape.

The officers discussed the help that must be given to the raiding parties harassing British troops, the choice of secure routes for delivering weapons in good condition, and then they moved on to the appointment of their supreme leader, a man who was sufficiently representative in the eyes of the Egyptian people and capable of leading the revolutionaries to victory.

One name came up again and again: that of General Naguib, the hero of the war against Israel, whose integrity was beyond dispute. Under the pseudonym 'the Unknown Soldier', he penned violent articles stigmatizing the regime's corruption. But it remained to be seen whether the courageous and likeable Mohamed Naguib would accept this heavy burden. It was up to the Free Officers to persuade him.

The conspirators went their separate ways.

The absence of adverse incidents proved the serious nature of their organization, founded on secrecy and keeping each cell separate from the others. In reflective mood, Mahmoud headed for a café in Old Cairo where Farouk's police did not hold sway. Anyone who appeared to be a police informant would have been identified immediately.

The man charged with following Mark Wilder over the past few days was sipping a Turkish coffee and smoking a hookah.

Mahmoud sat down opposite him, and the café owner brought him a cup of black tea and a biscuit. The absence of the biscuit would have signified danger.

'The American is not easy to follow,' admitted the smoker. 'He knows he is being watched and uses a variety of techniques to try to throw me off. But up to now I have outwitted him.'

'What interesting news have you learned?'

'He has had two meetings, one public, the other secret. The first was a dinner with Farouk and Pulli, at the Scarab.'

No surprise there, thought Mahmoud. The king attempts to use all foreigners who might, in one way or another, help him to increase his fortune. 'And the second?' he asked.

'The American went to the Metro Cinema. At the back of the auditorium, he had a long discussion with a man I did not manage to identify and whom I cannot even describe. The guy vanished into thin air. I haven't the slightest doubt he's a professional, and he's the American's superior in Egypt.'

'Excellent work, my friend. Continue as you are. If you think you have been spotted, I will replace you.'

With his bonus, the smoker could afford some hashish and forget the uncertainties of the future. Mahmoud left the café and mingled with the crowd.

This man Mark Wilder was indeed a spy who had come to

Egypt to carry out a mission. But why had he gone to England, and who were his real superiors?

Time was short; nobody knew how and in what way the situation would develop. Grave events could plunge Egypt into a chaotic bloodbath. Perhaps Mark Wilder was the man Mahmoud needed to avert that disaster.

28

In Middle Egypt, the month of November was delightful. Ateya and Mark were travelling in an all-terrain vehicle, equipped with everything they would need in the event of a breakdown and driven by an experienced, careful driver. Fatal accidents were frequent, as people often overtook on both sides of these dangerous roads, and no one would give way to anyone else.

Mark forgot about the risks and took advantage of his guide's knowledge to learn about the history and civilization of pharaonic times. For hours, she answered his stream of questions, happy to see him captivated by a culture that was thousands of years old.

Ateya wore no make-up; she was dressed in a red shirt and white linen trousers. Her black hair shone, and she had a light in her eyes that fascinated Mark. At the Beni-Hassan site, the American experienced an unforgettable moment. Down below the tombs, created for dignitaries of the Middle Kingdom at the summit of a cliff, lay a landscape that was both splendid and serene. Along the Nile, dotted with islets of vegetation populated by birds, little gardens displayed every shade of green, harmonizing with the blue of the river. The air was sweet and pure, and there was no sense of time.

If he had dared, he would have taken the young woman's hand. But he did not want to interrupt her meditation, so deeply absorbed was she in the beauty of the place.

Sitting side by side on a low wall, they shared this moment of grace.

'This was the first ancient site discovered by Howard Carter,' she revealed. 'He wasn't yet eighteen when he began working here, under Newberry. He slept in the chapels of the houses of eternity and drew their most beautiful scenes, especially those showing birds frolicking.'

'Do you know about the mission with which Abbot Pacomas has entrusted me?'

'It is up to you to tell me, if you wish and are allowed to do so.'

'I have to find the papyri that belonged to Tutankhamun's treasure. Perhaps Carter put them somewhere safe; perhaps they were stolen. I carried out long and unsuccessful investigations in England and the United States. In reality, this was a test, as Pacomas knew that the papyri hadn't left Egypt. He believes that three messengers can lead me to the right place. What does that mean, Ateya?'

'Three Bedouins who belong to a tribe of nomads. Carter met them in December 1891, when he was searching for the tomb of Akhenaton and Nefertiti. They told him about a tomb in the desert, which had inscriptions and paintings. Officially, when he followed their instructions, Carter found only an alabaster quarry dating from the Old Kingdom.'

'Why do you say "officially"?'

'Throughout his career, Howard Carter was rather tight-lipped about his many finds. Rarely has anyone had such a sense of secrecy. Since the three messengers belonged to an isolated tribe, perhaps they demanded silence when they led Carter to the last dwelling of the mystical pharaoh.'

'And that clan would know where the papyri are hidden . . . unless they actually possess them, because Howard Carter himself entrusted them to the tribe! That's certainly Abbot Pacomas's hypothesis. But how are we to find these messengers or their descendants?'

'One member of my family originates from this region,' revealed the young woman, 'and he knows the tribe of messengers very well. There he is, walking towards us.'

An old man, dressed in a blue *galabieh* – the traditional tunic without collar or belt – was slowly climbing the slope leading to the tombs.

Ateya joined him and gave him her arm to help him up the last few metres.

A long conversation in Arabic ensued between the old man and the young woman. Then he walked back down to his village.

'The situation does not look too good,' she admitted. 'The police are searching for certain members of the tribe of messengers, who are suspected of theft. Currently, they are constantly on the move and are wary of the authorities. Nevertheless, one of the guardians of the El-Bercheh site, not far from here, may agree to help us.'

El-Bercheh, the burial ground where the High Priests of Thoth, god of knowledge, were laid to rest, had been laid waste by looters. There were few tourists, and the locals were extremely wary.

Ateya and Mark climbed to the top of the hill, where they found the tomb of Djehuty-Hotep,[*] one of the few which had not been entirely ruined. When the guardian consented to open the heavy iron gate, this gave access to a chapel where visitors could gaze on an astonishing scene: a veritable army of sturdily built men were hauling a colossus representing the pharaoh seated in majesty. The enormous statue was sliding along a path of silt, constantly moistened with milk. And magic words enabled it to be brought to the temple.

The guardian agreed to talk in a hushed voice with Ateya, out of sight of the villagers. To Mark, the discussions seemed to go on for ever.

---

[*] 'Thoth [Djehuty is the Egyptian name of the god] is in plenitude.'

At last, Ateya walked back to him.

'He knows where the tribe of messengers is currently camped and is willing to guide us there, in exchange for a large sum of money.'

'No problem.'

'We shall leave immediately.'

The trio left the realm of the priests of Thoth and set off along the bed of a dried-up wadi, which had carved out its path between two hills. As he left the valley for the desert, Mark felt real anxiety. The place was disturbing; dark stones absorbed the light and seemed hostile to any human presence.

During the unrelenting walk, the guide did not utter a single word. Then, as the sun was setting and the temperature falling, he stopped beside a stone-built hut. Inside were mats and a stove.

'We are going to drink some tea and sleep here,' announced Ateya.

While the guide was heating up some water, the Egyptian and the American watched the reddening sun disappear.

'Whatever you do, don't leave the hut,' she advised. 'This place is infested with snakes which hunt at night. The sight is magnificent, isn't it? But I always ask myself if the sun will be reborn after confronting the demons of the empire of the dead.'

'Doesn't your religion imply hope?'

'What about you, Mr Wilder? Are you an unbeliever?'

'Up to now, yes. But since taking my first steps in Egypt, I have the impression that the invisible is no less alive than the visible.'

'And you are certainly not at the end of your discoveries! Try to get some sleep; tomorrow promises to be taxing.'

Mark thought of his father who, aged eighteen, had spent many months in this region. At El-Bercheh, living apart from the famous archaeologist Petrie, he had prepared his own meals and eaten them in the modest dwelling he had built with his own hands. Already passionate about the era of Tutankhamun, he had scoured this desert in search of the tomb where Akhenaton the heretic perhaps rested beside the beautiful Nefertiti. Following the indefatigable Carter in his thoughts, Mark fell asleep.

'Wake up,' whispered Ateya. 'Our guide has disappeared.'

The lawyer sat up. 'Perhaps he's waiting for us outside.'

Scarcely had he opened the door when a mass of rifles threatened him. Despite their age, the weapons seemed in working order.

Around twenty menacing men surrounded the hut.

Ateya appeared and talked to them briskly, not showing the slightest sign of fear. The reaction was aggressive.

'Either we follow them,' she translated, 'or they will kill us and abandon our corpses to the wild beasts. And they don't look as if they're joking. I demanded that they take us to their chief.'

'Then let's go.'

They headed deeper into the desert. Neither Ateya nor Mark consented to ride on a donkey. They preferred to walk, surrounded by the men with rifles, who never took their eyes off them.

They reached a tented encampment guarded by several lookouts. Two of them pushed their prisoners inside the largest tent, where an aged man with a white beard sat surrounded by his lieutenants.

'I am the chief of this tribe,' he declared. 'Do you wish to eat and drink?'

'May your hospitality endure,' replied Ateya. 'I am related to your tribe and I have brought an American friend, who wishes to consult you.'

'May your life endure,' said the chief, staring at his guest.

Two women served the assembly black tea, goats' milk and a dish of rice with grilled onions.

'What information do you need?' asked the tribal chief.

'A very long time ago, an archaeologist named Howard Carter

travelled across this region and met three messengers,' Mark recalled. 'They formed bonds of friendship, and Carter may have entrusted them with confidential information concerning me.'

'Why would he do this?'

'Because I am the son of Howard Carter.'

The chief looked at his guest for a long time. 'And I am the last survivor of the three messengers.'

Mark attempted to remain impassive. 'Did my father give you any documents?'

'I guided him in his solitude and showed him his own riches. He loved this land deeply, and we understood each other well. There was trust between us.'

The lawyer hung on the chief's every word.

'I did receive documents,' he said. 'Would you like to see them?'

'I would be very happy to do so.'

The chief snapped his fingers. One of his lieutenants left the tent and returned a few minutes later carrying a worn leather satchel.

'Give it to our guest,' ordered the chief.

With fevered hands, Mark opened the satchel.

He took out a dozen sheets of paper covered in nervous handwriting. Between the paragraphs, there were drawings depicting architectural features.

Notes written in Howard Carter's hand, describing the discoveries he had made thanks to the messengers.

But not the papyri of Tutankhamun.

29

After a frugal lunch with the elders of the tribe of messengers, who were going to move their camp that very day, Ateya and Mark headed back towards Cairo.

The American was doubly disappointed. First, for a few moments he had thought that the chief would hand him Tutankhamun's papyri; second, the young woman had shown little interest in him, as if she was indifferent to his presence.

'The driver will drop you off at the Mena House,' she said.

'Shouldn't I go and see Abbot Pacomas as soon as possible?'

'He will contact you.'

'When can we have dinner together, Ateya?'

'Sorry, I am very busy. The high season for tourism is beginning, and I have to guide several groups.'

'Thank you for everything you've taught me. I hope to see you again soon.'

'As God wills it.'

When Ateya had gone, Mark felt very alone. How could he arouse some feeling in her; what words could he speak to reveal his feelings to her? At nightfall, he left the hotel and walked towards the plateau where the pyramids stood.

A powerful limousine halted alongside him.

Three hooded men leaped out, armed with pistols.

'Get in, quickly!' ordered one of them, pushing him violently inside with the aid of his accomplices.

Mark didn't even have time to struggle. With no chance of gaining the upper hand, he would simply have been beaten up. In two seconds, he was gagged and bound. A band of cloth covered his eyes.

During the journey, which was quite long and sometimes very fast, with much harsh braking and acceleration, not one word was uttered.

At last, the limousine came to a halt and the American was dragged from his seat and pushed into some kind of building. A door banged shut behind him.

He was forced to sit down on a wooden chair. The gag and the blindfold were removed but not the handcuffs.

Facing him was a man of around thirty, with a slender face and questioning eyes. The little room with green-painted walls was lit only by a single, guttering light bulb.

'You are in a working-class district which is entirely under my control,' he announced calmly. 'It is pointless to cry out or attempt to escape. If you wish to leave this place alive, answer my questions honestly, beginning with this one: who are you really, Mr Wilder?'

Another nightmare was beginning!

'My name really is Mark Wilder, and I am an American lawyer spending a few days' holiday in Egypt.'

'A bad start. You do not seem to appreciate the gravity of the situation. My name is Mahmoud, and I belong to the revolutionary movement which is determined to re-establish justice in this country, which is oppressed by a tyrant. And I want to know if you are one of Farouk's henchmen.'

'Me? Certainly not!'

'And yet he invited you to dinner at the Scarab.'

'He wants my firm to deal with some of his business affairs.'

'Your role seems much more murky to me,' replied Mahmoud. 'Why did you leave Egypt for England; why have you returned; what is your mission?'

'It was just a working visit to London.'

'I have a better explanation, Mr Wilder: you are a spy working for Farouk and for England, and you went to England to obtain orders from your superiors. With the aid of the king's political police, you will identify dissidents and eliminate them.'

'This is completely crazy! I'm just a tourist!'

Mahmoud took out a pistol. 'I am in a hurry and I hate liars. The first bullet will destroy your left knee. It is extremely painful and very difficult to repair. The second will be aimed at your right. You will no longer be able to walk. If you persist in saying nothing, you will no longer be of any use to me. So I shall fire the third bullet into the middle of your forehead, and have the satisfaction of eliminating an enemy of the revolution.'

Mahmoud was terrifyingly calm. He did not look as if he was joking.

Mark must make some concessions, without putting Ateya and Abbot Pacomas in danger. 'All right, I'm not an ordinary tourist. According to Winlock, an archaeologist at the Metropolitan Museum who died recently, I may be the son of an Egyptian woman and Howard Carter, the discoverer of Tutankhamun's tomb. At the time of my birth, it was impossible to tell the truth. I had the good fortune to be adopted by wonderful people. And now I am making a pilgrimage, following the tracks of the man who was perhaps my real father.'

'I assume you have a specific goal?'

Mark hesitated. By telling the truth, he hoped to play a decisive card. 'Of course. I'm looking for proof: documents which are as yet unknown and papyri from Tutankhamun's treasure which apparently disappeared mysteriously. By doing so, I'm carrying on the work of Howard Carter, even if I have little chance of success.'

Mahmoud walked slowly around his prisoner. 'Interesting, Mr Wilder, very interesting. You seem to be a persuasive lawyer, and this truth seems so unfeasible that I am inclined to believe you. But it is certainly concealing another. For example, your extremely discreet contact at the Metro Cinema, with a man I know is a spy. Who is he and what work are you doing for him?'

Mahmoud was facing Mark again, and the pistol was pointing at his left knee.

Mark had no choice. It seemed as if his torturer knew everything anyway.

'That man is a former business acquaintance. His name is John, but his surname varies according to the country where he's working. He's now employed by the CIA, an espionage organization recently created in the United States, and he asked me to supply him with information, however minor, on Farouk and his entourage, according to whatever contact I have with him. Apparently, America disapproves of the king's behaviour and of Britain's as well.'

For the first time Mahmoud's face grew less stern. And he slid the pistol back into its holster. 'You have played the game correctly, Mr Wilder, and had a thousand reasons not to lie. Otherwise . . .'

'May I hope to be freed soon?'

'We haven't reached that point yet. First I must inform you that your father also practised the dangerous art of espionage. In 1915, when he was beginning to dig in the Valley of the Kings, he was recruited by the Intelligence Department of the War Office, which was based in Cairo. Deeply anti-German, with a perfect knowledge of Egypt and able to speak Arabic, Carter was an ideal subject. He was raised to the rank of "King's Messenger", in other words charged with transporting official mail and confidential documents. His missions, which are still a mystery, ended in October 1917. I know at least one of them: to search for and preserve all documents relating to the presence of the Hebrews in Egypt, with relation to the Bible and to the Egyptian religion. The political and religious authorities, whether Western or Eastern, particularly did not want to see any explosive texts come to light, liable to come into conflict with beliefs and put religion to fire and the sword.'

'Tutankhamun's papyri, for example . . . So, are you searching for them too?'

Mahmoud avoided the prisoner's gaze. 'If one gives credit to old superstitions, only a son can bring back to life the memory of his father, and succeed where others fail. So you will fulfil this mission, Mr Wilder, but you will also work for me. I need a contact with the CIA, and therefore with your friend John.'

'That's out of the question! I've been dragged into a whirlwind, and I want to get out of it as quickly as possible! Come to an arrangement with some professional spies.'

Mahmoud smiled. 'You best and principal colleague is called Dusty Malone. He married a delectable wife who has given him two adorable little girls. I am very fond of children, Mr Wilder, and I would be very sad if something bad happened to them. Do I make myself clear?'

'You . . . you wouldn't dare!'

'Like you, I have a mission to fulfil. Either you cooperate, or else . . .'

The lawyer looked his torturer straight in the eyes. 'You win.'

Mahmoud removed the handcuffs.

'Now I know that you will not attempt to run away. I have many more explanations to give you, but Cairo is not the right place. We are leaving for the south.'

30

A high-powered limousine carried Mark from Cairo to Mankabad, a village close to the large city of Assiut. Farms, canals, the desert and a chain of mountains – a landscape both harsh and alluring, where peasants worked with their donkeys and placid buffalo slaked their thirst in the lakes. The ancient Egyptians' immense herds of carefully tended cattle had long since disappeared. Women dressed in black, some veiled, others bare-headed, carried earthenware pots filled with foodstuffs, while children played with rag dolls.

Mahmoud led the American from the car and took him to the small garden of a modest house. They sat down on worn carpets laid on the ground, and a young girl served them *ful medammes*.

'Brown beans simmered on a low heat for hours, with the addition of onions, lemon, garlic and cumin,' explained Mahmoud. 'No Egyptian could do without them.'

Mark did not hate them. At least the dish was nourishing. And the girl brought them some local beer.

'We are in the home of the Copts, who are numerous in this region. More than a third of the peasants are Christians, and relations with the Muslim peasants are worsening each day. It will be a big problem in the future.'

'Why have you brought me here?' asked the lawyer.

'To make you understand the importance of the upheaval

which is looming and risks changing the face of this region and of the world, if we do not do something. Like all of us, Mr Wilder, you are the plaything of destiny. And according to an ancient prophecy, which true believers take seriously, a man from the south will play a determining role in liberating the country from repression. So you had to know this place where, many years ago, a solemn oath was taken.'

Mahmoud was served a cup of black tea.

'The opium of the people and a poisoned gift from the British,' he said. 'It comes from Ceylon and we drink far too much of it, on the pretext that it gives us energy. The peasants spend a large part of their income to procure it, and there is no question of altering their habits. However, a profound change is in the wind, and I fear the consequences. You will be the only Westerner to know what I am about to reveal to you. The group of Free Officers, which is determined to take power, has just appointed the brave and likeable General Naguib – a hero loved by the people – as its leader. But he will be a mere puppet whose strings will be pulled by the real leader of the revolutionaries, Gamal Abdel Nasser. He will remain in the shadows for as long as necessary and will get rid of Naguib at the appropriate moment. Nasser was born in Alexandria, on 15 January 1918, but the family home is at Beni-Morr, very near here. This landscape nourished him with its strength. At the age of eight, he lost his mother, whom he adored, and he has never forgiven his father, a postman, for hiding her death from him for several months and remarrying very quickly. Despite a profound feeling of rebellion against society, he embarked on a military career and read a great deal, particularly about the French Revolution. One individual fascinated him, the Scarlet Pimpernel, who was skilled in disguising his identity and capable of taking action without being spotted. As early as 1935, Nasser came to the conclusion that Egypt was in her death throes and must be independent. During a demonstration against the British, in Cairo, a bullet gashed his forehead. He spent a night in prison and met other young patriots there. And it is here, in Mankabad, in January 1938, that he invited a number of officers to a meal where, like us, they ate *ful* and sugar cane.'

'You were one of the guests, I presume?'

'I can still remember the tone of his voice when he spoke the decisive words: "Let this moment be historic, for we are laying the foundations of a great plan. By swearing to remain faithful to our friendship, we shall overturn obstacles." No doubt some of those there thought this was pure idealistic fantasy. Didn't the Second World War sweep away all of these fine plans? In 1941 Nasser himself sank into despair, convinced that it would take a thousand years to accomplish any reforms. In February 1942, when the British treated Farouk like a servant by forcing him to obey them without conditions, the Egyptian army felt deeply humiliated. Naguib even handed his resignation to the king, who refused it. And Nasser sensed that a new state of mind was appearing among the officers. The Mankabad oath was taking shape again. On 15 May 1948 the Arab armies attacked Israel, whose birth had been proclaimed the previous day. It was a disaster. Because of defective equipment, Nasser saw that the Egyptian soldiers had not been sent into battle but to slaughter. Although wounded, he acquitted himself remarkably well at the battle of Faluja, where he became certain of one thing: the great struggle would take place in Egypt. He had an opportunity to have a discussion with some Israeli officers who, for their part, had succeeded in obtaining independence for their country. Nasser swore that he would do likewise and go further, creating a powerful Arab nation based on one culture, one language and one people. Egypt would be the heart and the centre of this revolution. The armistice signed in February 1949 with Israel is, from his point of view, merely a momentary cessation of combat. Since late summer 1949 he has been increasing the number of secret meetings in order to form a real general staff of Free Officers, to drive out the British and put in place a new government.'

'Does he favour Communist principles?' asked Mark, who felt ill at ease in these closed, almost hostile, surroundings.

'Nasser admires Ataturk and the United States; he is above all a nationalist and believes in God. According to him, the theory of evolution does not explain anything, and especially not the way in which the universe was created. But he wants victory and will use any means to obtain it. And I know he is capable of succeeding.'

'Why are you giving me all this information?' asked the lawyer in surprise.

'Because you are the only man capable of helping me. I am a Copt, not a Muslim. And I have been working for the British secret service since I was twenty, for I hoped that Great Britain would ensure my people's prosperity. Today, the contacts are broken, and no British agent will listen to me any more. Nobody knows Nasser's real role; nobody would want to believe it. And I must not put a step wrong, or I will be killed. You, Mr Wilder, are in contact with the CIA. Warn the United States of the danger, tell them to alert Britain and avert disaster. Otherwise, the revolution will happen and will end in a bloodbath. Nasser will lead Egypt to the abyss, and the shock wave will affect the whole of the West. Will you agree to help me?'

Mahmoud's distress was clear.

'I will speak to John,' promised the lawyer.

'Thanks to you, thousands of lives will be spared. Meeting up again is likely to be difficult. If I have information to pass on to you, I will send you either a shoeshine boy or a man carrying bread. The password will be: "Three mandarins for one dollar."'

'I'm not a professional,' objected Mark, 'and—'

'As regards Tutankhamun's papyri, I have some specific information to give you. King Farouk may know a great deal about this subject. To obtain really useful information, you will have to approach a colourful character called Etienne Drioton. He is, in a way, the regime's official Egyptologist and a friend

139

of Farouk. Of French nationality, he has the peculiarity of being a canon. Meet him and try to make him talk. Now I am going to have to rough you up a little to put an end to this long interrogation. And we will release you near your hotel. As far as my hierarchy is concerned, you were just an ordinary businessman who wanted to wheel and deal with the king, like so many others.'

31

With the aid of an extremely tired-looking broom, the municipal employee moved a small heap of dust, which the wind immediately blew back towards him. Imperturbable, he began the process all over again. Soon, the call to prayer would allow him to stop for a while.

A large black car screeched to a halt not far from him. The right rear door opened, a Westerner was thrown out on to the road and the vehicle sped away.

The sweeper approached.

As the man looked stunned, he helped him to his feet.

He had a lump on his forehead, his shirt was torn and his left elbow was bleeding.

'Are you all right, boss?'

'I've felt better,' admitted Mark.

'Better tell the police.'

'No, it was just an accident.'

The sweeper had his doubts, but it wasn't his job to get mixed up in the affairs of foreigners.

'Is the Mena House far from here?'

'Ten minutes' walk at normal pace, straight ahead of you. Do you want me to come with you, boss?'

'No, I'll be fine.'

Mark found a banknote in his trouser pocket and gave it to

the sweeper, who was delighted to have helped his neighbour. He was clearly not an Englishman.

'American, excellent!'

He patted the lawyer on the shoulder, and Mark almost collapsed.

'Take it easy, boss, and may God protect you!'

The porter at the Mena House had never seen a guest in such a state before. 'Have you been attacked, sir?'

'No, it was just a fall.'

'Do you wish to go to hospital?'

'I'd prefer a hot bath.'

'Reception will send you a doctor immediately.'

The doctor's diagnosis was reassuring: nothing broken, just bruising, which would soon go with the aid of arnica cream. A few aspirins would take away the pain.

A burning-hot bath produced the desired effect. Back on form again, Mark called John. They fixed up a meeting for later that evening in the Ezbekeya garden.

In former times, when the annual flood reached Cairo, the vast Ezbekeya square, close to the souk, was flooded out. It became a lake, a popular place for boating. Nowadays, it contained a thirteen-hectare park, planted with exotic trees and surrounded by railings. To enter and walk along its paths, there was an entrance charge of one piastre.

John waited for his friend near the lake. Many Cairo residents liked the place at nightfall. Soon, the two and a half thousand gas jets installed during the reign of the Khedive Ismail would light up the garden and its pathways.

'I was kidnapped, John.'

'Are you kidding?'

'The guy who organized it is called Mahmoud. Do you know him?'

'There are several thousand Mahmouds in Cairo.'

'This one belongs to the inner circle of the Free Officers.'

'Ah . . . So they really exist, then?'

'Is the CIA really well informed?'

'We're here to learn, Mark. And now you can see that I was right to trust you.'

'You've got a nerve! And I've got a fine collection of bumps and bruises! Fortunately, it was only a pretend kidnapping!'

'Could you be a little clearer?'

'You've heard of General Naguib?'

'An obscure hero of the Second World War and of the recent conflict with Israel. He's a colourless individual, of absolutely no importance.'

'Yet the Free Officers have just appointed him supreme leader of their movement.'

'In that case, they won't get very far! The good old general will continue to protest against Farouk's regime and make the king laugh.'

'That's the reason why the real leader chose him. Naguib will be a perfect decoy.'

'The real leader?' John asked anxiously. 'And . . . you know who this leader is?'

'Nasser, the man who swore an oath at Mankabad, a village in Upper Egypt. There, he swore that he would seize power.'

'I've never heard of him.'

The CIA agent's open, friendly face suddenly became closed.

Mark provided him with the information given by Mahmoud.

'There are countless petty conspirators in Cairo, and this Nasser may be just one crank among countless others,' said John.

'That would surprise me.'

'Why, Mark?'

'Because Mahmoud is a double agent, a member of both the Free Officers and the British secret service. Unfortunately, he had to break off all contact with the British, or he would have been unmasked. In any case, his superiors don't take the Free Officers seriously. But Mahmoud thinks that Nasser has exceptional charisma and that he's capable of overthrowing the established order in Egypt and the Middle East. The power of the shock wave, which wouldn't spare Europe, is not difficult to imagine. Mahmoud is very worried. He wants the CIA to warn the British so that they can take the necessary measures.'

John did not display the slightest enthusiasm. 'The British are complicated people, and America conducts its own policy in the Middle East.'

'All the same, Great Britain is our ally.'

'So is France, or so it appears. Don't worry. I'll send a detailed report to my superiors, and a strategy will be decided on at a higher level. I shall investigate this Nasser to find out if he really exists and if he represents a real danger. I don't want to annoy you, but your Mahmoud may just be a hoaxer or even just a smooth talker.'

'He threatened to harm my right-hand man, Dusty Malone, and his family. And I didn't have the impression that he was joking.'

'Don't worry, Mark. First thing tomorrow, their protection will be ensured. But I don't see how an obscure Egyptian officer could act on American territory! It's a bluff.'

'And yet, Mahmoud knows about Dusty and believes he can manipulate me.'

'Did he arrange another meeting with you?'

'No, he'll send me messengers.' Mark paused. 'Now, John, I think I've done enough and I haven't the slightest desire to get mixed up in the world of espionage.'

'As you wish, my friend. But if Mahmoud is serious, he won't leave you in peace. Either he's a puppet, and all the same he may prove dangerous; or he belongs to a revolutionary movement determined to shake up this country, and the collection of information becomes vital. I need your help, Mark, and I'm appealing to your conscience as a future first-rank leader. Let Egypt fall, and you turn the Middle East into a powder keg. Aren't two world wars since the beginning of the century, and millions of dead, enough for you?'

32

The Mena House had the air of a little paradise on the edge of the desert, protected by the great pyramid of Khufu. Here, one could forget humanity's dark face and dream of a golden age.

But the magic no longer worked, and Mark had to admit to the overall negative effect of his stay in Egypt. The time was coming when he must leave this theatre of shadows.

Who was he really? A brilliant business lawyer from New York, whose success had opened the doors to a political career. Soon, he would sample the games of power.

Was he the son of Howard Carter, the discoverer of Tutan-khamun? There was no proof, only question marks and the skilful explanations of an old Coptic priest, a genius at manipulation. What of the papyri that refused to be found, these vital documents with their explosive contents? Pure invention.

John and Mahmoud were manipulators, too, and Mark could no longer tolerate being their puppet. Doubtless they were both lying, and Farouk's reign would continue corruptly and under the yoke of the British army.

And what about John, who had imputed to him the responsibility for two world wars and their victims! He was hardly the saviour of humanity himself, destined to preach Good News to all the bastards on the planet.

In short, it was time to get back to reason and normality.

Mark emptied his whisky glass and went upstairs to his room, to pack his suitcase. In a few hours he would be in New York. He'd enjoy studying the new case files, and then buy Dusty the biggest dinner in the world.

Someone knocked on his door. He opened it.

Ateya.

Ateya, dressed in a red dress with a slender gold collar worthy of the priestesses of ancient Egypt. Her eyes seemed filled with a strange emotion, and her voice trembled a little. 'Reception told me that you've just had an accident.'

'Nothing serious.'

'Can I . . . can I come in?'

'Of course. Take a seat. Would you like a drink?'

'No, thank you.'

'Let me offer you a glass of champagne by way of saying farewell to Egypt.'

The young woman looked aghast. 'I . . . I don't understand.'

'Yes, you do, Ateya! I lock my suitcase, I take a plane and I go home. They're expecting me.'

'It was no accident; it was an attack,' she said. 'Someone tried to kill you, and you are afraid.'

'Afraid, me? Hardly! I've simply had enough of being manipulated like a puppet, and I want to go back to a normal existence. Can you understand that?'

'No.'

Ateya's blunt response surprised the lawyer.

'I was afraid for you,' she admitted, 'and I understand that the load on your shoulders is very heavy. But that is not sufficient reason to give up the task which has been entrusted to you and which goes beyond the mediocre framework of your petty little existence. Money, power, glory, women . . . That is your horizon, Mr Wilder! How grandiose it is, especially when one has had the opportunity to explore other landscapes!'

Ateya's anger overwhelmed him.

He had attempted to erase her from his memory, to flee as quickly as possible so that he no longer had to think about this impossible love, and she had suddenly appeared, like a devastating storm.

'I have a job and obligations,' he reminded her, 'and . . .'

'Isn't your prime obligation to find Tutankhamun's papyri? Apparently, you gave your word. But the word of a lawyer . . .'

'I won't allow that!'

'Farewell, Mr Wilder.'

'No, stay!'

'Why should I obey you?'

'Because you were afraid for me. I was kidnapped and threatened, but it isn't the danger that's making me give up.'

Ateya's deep gaze defied him. 'Then what is the cause of your cowardice?'

'Will you accept a glass of champagne?'

She continued to stare at him.

'This whirlpool is exhausting me, that's all, and I need to get my bearings again.'

'There is nothing more natural, but it is futile to return to New York. On the contrary, continue your Quest. It is only by going forward that you will rediscover your equilibrium, is it not? Abbot Pacomas is waiting for you.'

'Ateya . . .'

Slowly, she drank the golden, sparkling liquid. Mark emptied his glass in a few gulps.

He had never wanted to leave Egypt. He could never have left without seeing her again, and she was the one who had come to him. She, whose emotion – at least for a few moments – had not been feigned.

'What is your decision, Mr Wilder?'

'I will come with you.'

'Finish packing, pay your bill and book a taxi to the airport. I will be waiting for you there and will take you to your new accommodation. I feel it is vital for you to cover your tracks. Then we shall go and see Abbot Pacomas.'

With no further explanation, the young woman left the room. Mark was no longer in control of anything.

33

The move proceeded without a hitch. Mark left his luggage in a fine apartment in the chic Zamalek quarter, where Europeans mixed with Cairo's wealthy inhabitants.

'The building is owned by a friend,' revealed Ateya. 'I live just above.'

'Thank you for this mark of trust. I'm very touched.'

She smiled with an almost knowing sweetness. 'We mustn't waste time.'

A new taxi, belonging to a Copt, dropped Ateya and the American near the Ben Ezra synagogue. In its rear courtyard they found Abbot Pacomas, meditating beside a well.

'Have you settled in, Mark?'

'I couldn't wish for better.'

'Take a close look at this modest well. It is here that the daughter of a pharaoh rescued the cradle of Moses, saved through the will of the Lord and the waters of the Nile. She brought the child to her illustrious father, Akhenaton, who passed on the wisdom of the Egyptians to him and initiated him into the mysteries of the one God. In the temple, lit up by the beauty of Queen Nefertiti, Moses spent time with young Tutankhamun, who was charged with preserving the vital secrets of Egyptian thought and of their history, which concerns us all. Everything was played out in Egypt, Mark, and everything will be played out here again. Did you know that Ibn Tulun, to whom the most beautiful mosque in Cairo was dedicated, brought back a fragment of Noah's Ark from Mount Ararat? The whole of the Koran was revealed on it.* Here, everything is linked. And Tutankhamun's papyri are both the key to the past and the source of the future. Only the son of Howard Carter, heir to his father's spirit, can find them and dispel the darkness.'

'I'm not so sure,' objected Mark. 'Up to now I've followed your instructions unstintingly and haven't achieved anything. If these papyri did exist, someone must have destroyed them. Chasing after a chimera is pointless.'

'It seems that recent events have shaken you.'

'I hate being blown around like a piece of straw in the wind! You've been very convincing, Abbot, and have manipulated me with consummate artistry. I confess that I almost ended up believing the legend in which I was the hero. And then secret servicemen, if that's what they really are, got mixed up in it, and they want to get me involved in their games! A little indigestible, don't you think? It's all too much.'

'Don't you trust the CIA and your old friend John?'

Mark was struck dumb for a few moments. 'You . . . you know him?'

'Given the importance of what is being acted out, it would be a grave mistake not to know the principal participants.'

'Don't tell me you belong to the CIA, too!'

'My brotherhood is much more ancient, Mark, and uses other weapons. I have never met your friend John but, through you, I know him well. He believes in his mission, which consists of developing American influence in Egypt, whether by controlling Farouk, progressively distancing the British or refusing to allow a destructive, anti-Western movement to emerge, such as that of the Muslim Brothers. It is a complex task and a hazardous strategy, in which you play a significant role. John holds you

* According to the Arab historian Maqrizi Ibn Tulun (835–84), founder of the dynasty of the Tulunides, who ruled Egypt.

in high esteem, but when needs must . . . And if he has to sacrifice you in the higher interests of the United States, he will not hesitate to do so. It is up to you to work out how to use him so that he acts in a positive manner and averts a bloodbath, notably by supplying him with the essential information given to you by Mahmoud, the secret emissary of the Free Officers.'

'Mahmoud . . . So you know him, too!'

'Everyone believes him to be a Muslim and in favour of revolution, but he is a Copt and a secret agent in the service of the British. Unfortunately, his employer no longer trusts him and has no faith in the abilities of the Free Officers, regarding their ambitions as pie in the sky. The British army controls the Suez Canal zone, and Farouk's police impose order. Given that he is present at meetings of the highest-level Free Officers, Mahmoud cannot take the smallest risk. From now on he must avoid all contact with British agents, who have all been identified and who are incapable of understanding the way the situation is evolving. Nasser is neither a hoaxer nor a dreamer, but a stubborn planner and a determined worker. In the shadows, he is weaving a network which grows more powerful with each day that passes. By telling you the truth, Mahmoud has exposed himself to an insane degree. But he loves Egypt and fears there will be carnage. Now, Mark, you have become the key man in a drama that is bigger than you are.'

'Unquestionably!'

Sparrowhawks soared above the synagogue's rear courtyard. Abbot Pacomas raised his eyes and gazed for a long time at the sky, as if he knew the paths of these heirs of Horus. Then he smiled. 'Do you believe that this is still the time for you to rebel?'

'I'm a free man and I can break any chains by taking the plane to New York tomorrow morning!'

'This childish prattle is not worthy of you, Mark. When you came to me, agreed to know who you really were and gave your word to find the papyri of Tutankhamun, which your father chose to conceal, you created indestructible bonds with Egypt, and you know that very well. So why do you get upset instead of doing something?'

The American resembled a groggy boxer.

In a few words, this old abbot had just spelled out a truth that he had refused to admit to himself.

'Do not confuse independence and freedom,' advised Pacomas. 'You are only really free at the privileged moment when you no longer have a choice. And you no longer have this choice. By setting out on the path of truth, the only one which has heart and which puts our human condition in its rightful place, you have decided to participate in the only battle which is worth the effort, that of light versus darkness. I did not expect any less from the son of Howard Carter. Nothing ever made him give up.'

Mark closed his eyes.

The words of this abbot from another time had the power of a devastating bomb. And all his skills as a lawyer could not supply him with contradictory arguments.

'I have the feeling that a few major aspects still escape you,' added the abbot. 'That is why we must return to the Cairo Museum. Tutankhamun has a few more surprises in store for you.'

34

The galleries of the Cairo Museum exhibiting the sarcophagi and other items from the tomb of the dignitary Yuya and his wife Tuya were deserted. So their style had an even greater impact on Mark: what a close resemblance to the treasures of Tutankhamun. The same furniture, the same perfect shapes.

'A tradition proscribed by Egyptologists claims that Yuya is the Egyptian transcription of the name Joseph,' explained Abbot Pacomas. 'Forced into exile in Egypt, this Hebrew became First Minister to Tuthmosis IV and served Amenhotep III, the father of Akhenaton. He lived to over a hundred and developed the Faiyum, around a hundred kilometres to the south of Cairo, getting rid of the wild, unmanaged vegetation and creating a vast area of fertile countryside, by directing water into a canal, the Bahr el-Yusuf, whose name records his deed. According to the Bible,* Joseph's mummy was placed in a sarcophagus and, because of his rank, he had the benefit of exceptional funerary furniture, the very same you now see.'†

'A pharaoh had a Hebrew First Minister?' Mark was astonished.

---

* Genesis 50, 26.
† See A. Osman, *Stranger in the Valley of the Kings. The Indentification of Yuya as the Patriarch Joseph*, London, 1987. The tomb of Yuya and Tuya was discovered in 1905.

'In Egypt there was neither racism nor wars over religion,' Abbot Pacomas reminded him. 'Hebrews and Egyptians lived in peace; all that mattered was what the individual was like. That truth, today, is so revolutionary that it would run counter to many political ambitions, in the West as well as the East. The house of eternity belonging to Joseph and his wife was created in the Valley of the Kings, an honour reserved for a few exceptional people.'

'Do Tutankhamun's papyri by any chance contain the proof of what you are saying?'

'One may assume so, Mark, and that is only one detail. According to an Egyptian priest, Manethon, it was in the era of Tutankhamun, following the "thirteen fatal years" of Akhenaton's reign, that the Hebrew Exodus took place, led by Moses, who had become fanatical and was advocating a destructive monotheism. Expelled by the king, he apparently became the head of a faction which, during its wanderings, regretted having left the land of the pharaohs. Your father read this account. That is why, in 1923, he was summoned by the British vice-consul, who ordered him to hand over Tutankhamun's papyri. Was their very existence not a danger to the balance of the Near East, at the time when a Jewish colony was being created in Palestine? And account must also be taken of Egyptian nationalism. The diplomat gave Howard Carter orders not to publish these documents. When he had years of excavations ahead of him, how could your father react? Ignoring this ban would have led to disaster, but he was not going to destroy such testimonies. That is why he hid them carefully.'

'The real story of Joseph, Moses and the Exodus . . . Is that it, the secret of Tutankhamun's papyri?'

'Not only that,' replied Abbot Pacomas. 'I know where they were before your father brought them to light, and I am going to show you that a treasure may house another treasure.'

The two men left the museum galleries devoted to Yuya and Tuya and headed for the galleries housing the wonders taken from the tomb of Tutankhamun. The majority of visitors could not believe their eyes, and some could not take their eyes off the gold mask, the sarcophagus, the jewellery, and so many other works of art.

Abbot Pacomas directed Mark's attention to the four gilded wooden chapels that had been fitted together in the tomb, so that – to the eye – they formed just one.

'As he opened the doors of these chapels, your father had the impression that he was profaning a sacred place, and he hesitated for a long time before he broke the seals, which were still intact. They protected the pharaoh's sarcophagus, which was itself made up of three parts. This was an affirmation of the all-powerful nature of the number seven, the symbol of the secret of life. As you look at these prodigious shrines, Mark, do you find yourself thinking of another treasure, which is much sought after?'

'Do you mean . . . ?'

'The Ark of the Covenant, indeed. Merton, *The Times* correspondent authorized to enter the tomb of Tutankhamun, identified it immediately. From his point of view, there was no doubt: the pharaoh had acquired the supreme treasure of the Hebrews, and the Valley of the Kings had never housed such wealth. This is why the tomb, which is so different from other royal houses of eternity, had been carefully hidden. And it took all your father's genius and perseverance to find it. Tradition says that the Ark of the Covenant was not a single chest but was made up of several smaller gold chests, fitted into each other. Here they are before you, Mark. Thousands of curious eyes admire them, but nobody sees them. And the message revealed on these golden walls remains inaccessible.'

The abbot drew Mark's attention to certain enigmatic depictions, such as a man standing, his head and feet surrounded by a circle of energy formed by the body of a snake, while a form of soul, a bird with the head of a ram and human arms, came forth.

Then he pointed to a hallucinatory scene depicting mutations of light and of the cosmic powers, enabling the process of resurrection to be accomplished.*

'Beyond the substantial historical aspect,' added Pacomas, 'Tutankhamun's papyri gave us the key to reading these symbols and, consequently, the means of gaining access to the secret of the creative light and of eternal life. Do you now understand just what is at stake, the importance of your task?'

Mark stood there, fascinated.

So everything had been revealed and yet remained mysterious! He thought of his father, who had perhaps had the good fortune to decipher these enigmas. Was that the major reason why, at

---

* See A. Piankoff, *The Shrines of Tut-Ankh-Amon*, New York, 1955, pp. 122 and 128 (second chapel).

the end of all that immense toil, he had walled himself away in silence and never undertaken any more digs?

The lawyer would have loved to spend whole days soaking up the message of these four chapels, which together formed one, but he sensed the urgency and importance of his Quest. Finding the papyri was the equivalent to obtaining the code.

'Mahmoud told me about a French canon, Drioton, who is also an Egyptologist with close links to Farouk. Perhaps he will provide me with precious information, especially if the king is interested in Tutankhamun's papyri in one way or another.'

Abbot Pacomas looked worried. 'That is a dangerous lead, but you must follow it. I shall arrange a meeting with him for you.'

157

35

Mark had completely lost his bearings. It was impossible to play the lawyer, sure of himself and his future, while he was so haunted by the vision of Tutankhamun's chapels, which dictated a new form of existence for which nothing had prepared him.

He very much liked his apartment in Zamalek, which was filled with light and was quiet. And when Ateya came to visit him, he forgot all his worries. Barefoot, her lips softly pink, she resembled one of those sublime offering-bearers depicted on the walls of houses of eternity.

'I've brought some French wine, some Egyptian cakes and some English jam,' she announced with a smile. 'There is no lack of good restaurants, but if you don't feel like going out, you mustn't die of hunger and thirst. Here, you will be safe. The building's guard is a Nubian Christian and a faithful friend.'

The young woman placed the provisions on a table.

'Did you enjoy your latest visit to the Cairo Museum?' she asked slyly.

'Ateya . . . You knew that Abbot Pacomas was going to show me the Ark of the Covenant, didn't you?'

'In all honesty, yes.'

'Your role is much more important than you make out. I would like . . .'

'Well, *I* would like to go for a walk. It's a lovely evening, and the sunlight is so gentle that it's almost unreal. Will you come with me?'

In the chic districts of Cairo, the wearing of the veil had almost completely disappeared. Women and young girls strolled around bare-headed, taking advantage of European-style freedom. Even practising Muslims were abandoning this custom.

Ateya had chosen to show Mark the island of Rodah, south of Zamalek. They headed along a path which bordered the Nile, lined with acacias and bougainvillea. Here, the incessant din of the big city faded into the distance, and one could think of the fabulous gardens of the ancient Egyptians where, when evening came, they sat beneath a pergola and enjoyed the gentle north wind.

The air was filled with scents. Ateya seemed happy, almost relaxed. Mark did not want to shatter this magical moment, but he needed to know the truth.

'You're Abbot Pacomas's lieutenant, aren't you?'

'Let's say he grants me his trust.'

'So you know everything about what he does, and everything concerning me.'

'I help the abbot as best I can. He is an extraordinary man, and his sole preoccupation is the good of others.'

'You take too many risks, Ateya. By playing such an active role, you'll eventually attract attention and you'll be in danger.'

'I am aware of that, but what does it matter? The Copts are threatened with extinction; I must fight in my own way to save them. If the whirlwind lays waste to Egypt, they will be the first to be struck down and my ancestors' culture will be destroyed.'

'I can't bear seeing you exposed like this.'

'Why do you care so much, Mr Wilder?'

'Because . . . because I love you.'

The young woman halted, and so did Mark. Not far away, an old gardener was tending a clump of hibiscus. The sun was on the point of setting, and already the Nile was tinged with gold.

'There are words that should not be spoken lightly,' she whispered.

'I didn't know how to say it, but I've stayed here because of you. I have loved you ever since I first met you.'

Ateya gazed at the river. 'Why should I believe you, Mr Wilder?'

'Didn't my real father, Howard Carter, fall in love with an Egyptian woman? Until now, the only passion I've felt has been for my case files and my career. Meeting you has changed everything, and I could never have thought it would.'

'Do you really want to find the papyri of Tutankhamun?'

'As long as I know that you are safe.'

'Who could be, if the storm breaks? And you need my help. Let's go back. We'll have dinner at my place.'

She had not rejected him; she had not been angry with him; she had even agreed to spend the evening with him!

Delighted, Mark savoured this moment, where happiness was still possible. True, it was nothing but a dream, but Ateya was very real and had agreed to hear him out. He did not hide anything of his past from her, all his doubts and his mistakes.

And they entered the Zamalek apartment, bathed in the last rays of the setting sun.

Ateya did not switch the light on. She turned towards Mark.

They remained face to face, gazing into each other's eyes, for what seemed an eternity.

He did not dare to understand.

'Ateya . . .'

When he laid his hand on her cheek, she did not flinch. Slowly, she came closer. When their bodies touched, he stopped breathing for a moment.

Clumsily and tenderly, he put his arms about her.

'I love you too,' she whispered.

Flooded with emotion and desire, he kissed her like a young lover discovering a paradise he had thought was out of reach.

That night, they forgot to have dinner.

36

As he opened his eyes, Mark attempted to reassemble the tattered strips of his marvellous dream so as not to forget a single one.

Of course, that night of love had never existed.

And yet Ateya was there, naked, standing in front of the window, gazing at the sunrise.

The dream did not shatter.

He got up and took her in his arms.

'I think this is serious, Mark. You will be my only love. According to the ancient Egyptians, when a man and a woman live under the same roof, they are married.'

'Since you're a Christian, shouldn't we ask Abbot Pacomas to regularize the situation?'

'Become your wife . . . You're not thinking of that?'

'You will be my only love, Ateya.'

Both knew that their words were not spoken lightly. Beyond the union of their bodies and the celebration of desire, an eternal, unchangeable bond had just been created.

'We are no longer adolescents,' she objected. 'Your life is in New York; mine is here.'

'My life, no: only my business activities. And you are much more important than any career.'

They embraced passionately.

'How I would love to believe you,' she whispered.

'I'm speaking the truth. To prove it to you, I shall fulfil the mission entrusted to me. And then we shall build *our* life together.'

Ateya and Mark were heading for a restaurant in the city centre when a flat-cake seller stopped the American.

'Three mandarins for one dollar.'

In Arabic, 'mandarin' was *Yussef Efendi*, 'Mr Joseph', who was considered responsible for introducing the fruit to Egypt. Mark thought of the biblical Joseph, who was perhaps buried in the Valley of the Kings, and in particular of Mahmoud, who had just used this messenger to contact him.

'Follow me to the black limousine at the corner of the street,' instructed the trader.

The lawyer looked at Ateya. 'I cannot refuse.'

Hands tightly clasped, they gazed into each other's eyes.

Then Mark climbed into the back of the car.

Mahmoud wore a grim expression. 'Head for Jimmy's place,' he ordered the driver, who set off immediately.

The car weaved its way through a bottleneck caused by a head-on collision between a packed bus and a lorry carrying sacks of cement.

'Our driver doesn't speak a word of English,' said Mahmoud, using that language. 'I'm taking you to Nasser; he wants to see you.'

'Why?'

'One of my informants told him about one of our conversations, and Nasser questioned me. I told him who you were and how I was manipulating you. Since he is searching for contacts everywhere, particularly with Americans, he wants to be sure you are reliable and capable of understanding his cause.'

'This meeting isn't without its risks, I assume?'

'Everything that involves Nasser has an element of danger,' conceded Mahmoud. 'But you don't have a choice.'

Mark did not protest. Ateya's love made him invincible. He

wanted to meet the man who was determined to make Farouk tremble.

'Have you contacted Canon Drioton?' Mahmoud asked.

'Not yet. You seem very interested in this business about the papyri.'

'If their contents can cause a disaster, it's better to prevent them from reappearing.'

'And what if, on the contrary, they can enable us to avert one?'

'Then find them as fast as you can.'

'How should I behave in front of Nasser?'

'Doesn't a lawyer know how to adapt to every situation? Be suspicious; he is wily and perspicacious. Above all, don't underestimate him and don't think that you can deceive him with verbal gymnastics. Appear precise and determined. Have you passed the information to the CIA?'

'My friend John is beginning to study it.[*]

The limousine halted some distance from the home of Jimmy, Nasser's code name. Guarded by several armed men, Mahmoud and Mark walked towards a house in Manchiet el-Bakri, a district of Cairo. Protected night and day by lookouts, it had become the revolution's HQ. Here, Nasser stored weapons and had meetings with his colleagues to refine his battle plans.

Modestly furnished, the house was nonetheless acceptably comfortable for a lieutenant-colonel attracted by the West but forcing a life of austerity on himself, with a sofa, bedecked with cushions, in the reception room. Officially, the house's owner was happily welcoming old friends, exercising the sense of hospitality characteristic of Egyptians, and they claimed to be taking part in spiritualist séances.

Farouk's police had noticed nothing suspicious, and Nasser remained completely unknown.

---

[*] On the contacts between the Free Officers and the CIA, see Miles Copeland, *The Game of Nations*, New York, 1969.

As soon as Mark saw him, he became aware of the mental and physical power of this giant of a man. He had the eyes and nose of an eagle about to swoop on its prey, not allowing it the slightest chance of escape.

'I am happy to receive you in my home,' said Nasser with a disturbing half-smile. 'Sit down. Some tea?'

'Thank you.'

The lawyer wondered if he was going to emerge alive from this lair, a sort of hive where supporters of the revolution's secret leader worked without respite.

'Are you a friend of Farouk, Mr Wilder?'

'I was invited to his wedding and I met him at the Scarab, along with Pulli. He wishes me to handle some cases.'

'Accept,' advised Nasser. 'Or he will be suspicious of you and cause you problems. What does America think of the Egyptian situation?'

'It lacks information and is content with what it sees: a king who controls the country, and the Suez Canal, a vital element of the economy, in the hands of the British.'

'Has the humiliation of the army escaped you?'

'Can it really oppose the British forces? America believes in democracy and the emancipation of peoples. Any development in that direction will be supported.'

'Do not count on exporting your democratic model into Egypt,' snapped Nasser. 'Giving freedoms to my people would be the equivalent of leaving little children in the street, and they would swiftly be run over. What we need is an end to tyranny, the return to nationalism and traditional Islam, while distancing ourselves from violence. We can succeed, as long as we are heard and understood. Given your position as a lawyer and politician, will you consent to pass on my plan to the American authorities and ask them, as a minimum, for strict neutrality?'

'I accept.'

'Are the Americans and the British not loyal allies? And yet the British occupy us and oppress us. This injustice is becoming intolerable. If America admits this, I will be extremely grateful.'

'I shall also make that known.'

'Be an effective messenger, Mr Wilder, and we shall avert a tragedy. Above all, be quite sure that, whatever happens, I shall achieve my aims.'

37

'Stay, Mahmoud,' ordered Nasser. 'We must talk.'

The liaison officer of the Free Officers tried to stay calm. Mark had left the revolutionary headquarters unharmed, but would he be as lucky? If Nasser had got wind of his true role, he had only a few minutes left to live.

His leader consulted the Wilder file. In accordance with his method, it comprised mainly photographs, taken from multiple angles. Nasser believed that there was no better way of knowing an individual and how to use him.

'What do you think of that American, Mahmoud?'

'He plays at being a tourist while carrying out the mission given to him by the CIA. But his behaviour revealed what he was up to and I succeeded in identifying him. Thanks to him, we are in direct contact with the American spy network which has recently been established in Europe.'

'What are the real intentions of the United States?'

'I don't know. Perhaps Wilder doesn't know either. He has just uncovered an explosive situation and must await the decision of his superiors.'

'You and your men are not to leave him for a moment. From his photos, the fellow seemed interesting, and he hasn't disappointed me. He will swiftly realize that Farouk is nothing but a water-bag filled with vanity and a worn-out tyrant incapable of action, since corruption and luxury have obscured his vision.

So he will turn to us, the Free Officers, and help us to take power.'

'We must, however, remain wary,' advised Mahmoud. 'As you yourself recalled, the Americans are the allies of the British.'

'America will play its own game, I am certain of that. And she will supply us with weapons to rid ourselves of the occupier. You did good work, Mahmoud, unearthing that man Wilder.'

Relaxed, Nasser lit a cigarette and started reading an English newspaper. Each day, he tried to scan the national and international press, retaining anything that would be useful to him in the future.

The interview was at an end.

His shirt soaked with sweat, Mahmoud left the house in Manchiet el-Bakri and headed for the centre of Cairo.

So the leader of the revolution still trusted him. Relieved, Mahmoud enjoyed a few glasses of whisky before going to bed.

The high-risk meeting between Nasser and Mark had ended well. On account of the strong personality displayed by the man known as the *bikbachi*, 'the postman's son', the American would give a decisive report to John. And the CIA would never lend its aid to such a dangerous character.

The revolution would be nipped in the bud, and the West would force Farouk to reform Egypt peacefully, turning it into a model for the Middle East and a guarantor of peace. Together, economic development and social progress would be encouraged by the European example, distancing the extremists.

Ateya opened the door and flung her arms around Mark's neck.

'I haven't stopped shaking,' she confessed. 'And I've drunk rather too much as well.'

'To be honest, I almost died of fear.'

They undressed each other, hungry for pleasure.

Lying on their backs, side by side, hand in hand, they savoured the miracle of their union. Intense moments of happiness helped them forget everything that was not their love.

'Who did you meet?' asked the young woman.

'Nasser, one of the Free Officers. He's apparently the secret head of a group of revolutionaries.'

'There are dozens like him, almost all manipulated by Farouk's secret police. Israel destroyed the Egyptian army, and Britain is careful not to give it the means to rebuild itself. Many factions dream of independence, but most of the herd won't follow them. The generals appointed by the king control them with an iron fist.'

'All the same, this guy Nasser impressed me . . . He seems determined to take action.'

'He's a braggart, like so many others! His revolution will stop at discussions in cafés and jokes about Cairo. Now I must tell you about a really important person: Canon Drioton.'

'Has Abbot Pacomas managed to fix up a meeting?'

'You and he are having dinner at his house this evening.'

'Do you know him?'

'Pacomas asked me to tell you about him so that you won't be too surprised. Come on, I've prepared a little meal.'

Dressed in light blue djellabas, they ate *kochari*, a dish composed of rice, lentils and grilled onions, and a delicious cream flavoured with vanilla and orange flower.

'Etienne Drioton was born in Nancy, in France, on 21 April 1889,' said Ateya. 'His father published religious books, and young Etienne took advantage of this to publish a grammar of Egyptian hieroglyphs. Despite his Christian commitment, the old civilization of the pharaohs attracted him irresistibly. Georges Benedite, a Jew and the curator of the Louvre museum, succeeded in employing Drioton, a Catholic priest, within his administration, despite the fact that it was very closed. Both an honorary canon of Nancy Cathedral and an Egyptologist, he carried out his first mission in Egypt as early as 1924 and was appointed Head of Antiquities in 1936, succeeding Pierre Lacau.'

'Lacau, the resolute enemy of my father, Howard Carter!'

'Nobody missed Drioton's predecessor, but the government made one demand of Drioton: he must give up his priest's cassock. He could be head of Egyptian archaeology, that was fine, but not while dressed as a priest. Given his love of Egyptology and his sense of humour, he agreed. And from 1936 onwards, he conducted a career as researcher and administrator, at the same time as training young scholars. But that is not the important part. Drioton became a friend of King Farouk, who regards him as his official archaeologist because he dissuaded him from buying fakes and prevented him from looking ridiculous. What's more, he taught the monarch to discover the marvels of pharaonic art by showing him around the great sites. Won over, Farouk grants him the funds necessary for the proper functioning of the Department of Antiquities. And the king has no hesitation in reaching into his own pocket to finance certain excavations. On the other hand, Drioton's frequent visits to the palace have made him deeply unpopular. He is regarded as one of the tyrant's vassals, and people have no hesitation in setting traps for him to bring his morality into question. Up to now, the canon's caution and perspicacity have triumphed. Anyway, Drioton possesses a remarkable speciality: he is the only Egyptologist capable of deciphering the hieroglyphic inscriptions written in cryptographic code, whether a few lines on the flat surface of scarabs or long texts. He has perfected a method of reading this secret writing which attracts the wrath of his colleagues but which he stubbornly defends.'

'So he would be able to translate the enigmatic inscriptions on Tutankhamun's chapels and those on the papyri, which are probably encrypted.'

'Without a doubt. The canon has been certain about one thing for a long time: according to incontestable writings, unknown to the public, the sages of Egypt were monotheistic. But can the priest really accept all the consequences of the Egyptologist's discoveries?'

'The man must be torn,' agreed Mark.

'He doesn't look that way. This meeting could be decisive. If Farouk has procured Tutankhamun's papyri, Drioton must know their hiding place.'

38

A little tipsy, Canon Drioton was a jovial man with a firm handshake. He had abandoned the official tarboosh for a beret and was smoking a pipe. His classic colonial outfit was adorned with a bright red tie, and there was no doubt that this senior official of a Muslim state had received permission from the hierarchy of the Roman Church to wear secular clothes.

Drioton welcomed his old friend Pacomas and Wilder warmly. He introduced them to the two women who looked after his house, his mother and one of his sisters, a secularized nun. Originally from Burgundy, the canon's mother was an exceptional cook, and anyone who had the good fortune to be invited to his table remembered the event fondly. The Drioton family loved food and had a tendency to put on weight.

'How are you, my dear Pacomas?'

'Extremely well, my dear Canon.'

'I think you and your friend are going to enjoy yourselves. After a few entrées, my mother is serving duck with olives and a sauce of her own confection. To what do I owe the honour of meeting this new dinner guest?'

'Mark Wilder is a great American lawyer and politician who has developed a passion for Egypt and really wished to meet you.'

'You flatter me, Mr Wilder. I am merely a modest seeker in the service of Egyptology, that magnificent, complex science which enables us to decode a prodigious civilization. What would you say to a drop of Meursault as an aperitif? We shall then continue with a red Burgundy.'

'You have a very nice place here,' observed Mark.

'Ah, I have even cohabited with some illustrious guests! Shortly before I arrived, the sarcophagi of kings and queens were stored here. Each morning, I said Mass in their presence, in the hope that I wasn't inconveniencing them too much. I almost missed them when they left; those silent, faithful listeners seemed so close to me.'

Mme Drioton senior's reputation was well deserved. Even an ascetic from the depths of the desert could not have resisted her marvellous culinary talents.

'Do you have a particular centre of interest, Mr Wilder?' asked the canon.

'The treasures of Tutankhamun.'

'Gracious, I can quite understand you! Howard Carter's discovery dazzled the entire world. Unfortunately, so many years later the detailed study of those marvels is a long way from being completed.'

'I met Sir Alan Gardiner, in London, and he lamented the fact that Carter did not succeed in publishing a large scientific study on his titanic work.'

'Six volumes were indeed planned. Gardiner is in contact with the Egyptian authorities to bring this project to fruition, but we are in the East, where the art of patience has reached its apogee.'

'I am particularly curious about the papyri,' said Mark.

For a few moments the canon's fork remained suspended in mid-air.

'What papyri?'

'The ones preserved in Tutankhamun's tomb.'

'You are on the wrong track, Mr Wilder. Carter hoped to find some, but he was cruelly disappointed. Not a single leaf of papyrus.'

'Could Howard Carter read hieroglyphs?'

'He was self-taught, the supreme crime in the eyes of university-trained archaeologists! He was constantly slandered and accused of being ignorant, whereas he read hieroglyphs perfectly and wrote them equally well. In the album of a director of irrigation* he even wrote, in May 1919, a dedication inspired by an ancient text to the "powers [*kau*] of his house"! Poor Carter . . . His entire personality and his rejection of concessions served him very badly.'

'So you have no doubts as regards any papyri from Tutankhamun's tomb?'

'None,' Drioton confirmed. 'Forget this chimera and interest yourself in works of art that are real. At least, I hope you do not believe in the pharaoh's curse? What an absurd story! Evidently, when the press printed terrifying words about the profaners, everyone trembled! I can still remember: "May those who sully my name and my tomb be destroyed; I shall destroy anyone who steps across the threshold of my sacred dwelling, I who live eternally! The wings of death will strike down looters." Impressive, isn't it? There's just one awkward detail: the words were entirely made up by journalists and occultists in need of something sensational. Not a single one of these phrases features in the tomb or on the objects it contained. This fraud caused Carter a great deal of trouble. He was accused of exploiting human credulity in order to become a star in the news.'

'Didn't some members of Carter's team die in strange circumstances?' asked Mark.

'Absolutely not!' thundered Drioton. 'Gardiner, who studied the inscriptions in the tomb, is still alive and well, as you saw for yourself. And Dr Derry, who carried out the autopsy on the mummy, is also alive! The photographer Harry Burton, who was very close to Carter, didn't die until 1940, at the age of

* This was Gino Antonio Lucovich. The text was published by T.G.H. James, *The Path to Tutankhamun*, London, 1922, p. 206.

sixty-one. And I could list all the other cases for you. Don't pay any attention to that balderdash; it was just designed to sell papers and it harmed Carter's reputation.'

'Do archaeologists sometimes conceal their finds?'

Drioton choked. A glass of Burgundy washed down the mouthful of duck and enabled him to get his breath back. 'I don't understand your question.'

'Let's suppose that a discovery is a little too . . . explosive. If the scientist feels responsible for future disorder, won't he impose a duty of secrecy on himself?'

'Material circumstances often cause delays in publication,' conceded Drioton, 'but nothing more. What specific example are you thinking of?'

'Tutankhamun's papyri. If they contain revelations that could endanger the balance of this region, or worse, wouldn't the best solution be to put them somewhere safe, far from indiscreet eyes?'

'Unlikely,' said the canon, 'particularly since they never existed! Now, we shall sample two desserts prepared by my mother, a crème brûlée and a lemon mousse. And I have been keeping an old Armagnac for my special guests.'

Strangely silent, Abbot Pacomas was enjoying his food.

'I've undertaken a study of Carter's archives,' revealed Mark. 'After America and Britain, I'm now moving on to Egypt. I assume the Cairo Museum in particular possesses many documents?'

'Indeed,' agreed Drioton.

'Could I gain access to them?'

'In theory, why not . . . But the museum is a veritable Aladdin's cave where it is sometimes difficult to get one's bearings.'

'I can quite imagine the scope of your many tasks, Canon, and I wouldn't wish to get in the way. In one way or another, and without wasting your time, would you consent to help me?'

'Of course, of course . . . I shall ask for an authorization. But don't be in too much of a hurry! One must obtain the agreement of various officials and, above all, track down the archives in question. With tact and patience, we have a good chance of success.'

'I should like to ask another favour.'

Drioton frowned.

'Your reputation as a specialist in Egyptian cryptography has spread all over the world. Could you show me how you read a text in enigmatic writing?'

A broad smile spread across the canon's face. 'One moment.'

He left the table and headed swiftly to his office, returning with a scarab made of faience.

As he sipped his Armagnac, he decoded the text engraved on the flat surface of the scarab, wishing happiness and long life to the pharaoh.

39

There was a strange atmosphere in Abbot Pacomas's library; one that Mark had felt nowhere else. His thousands of ancient books were not inert objects, but rather watchful guardians, whose task was to protect a kind of wisdom that had nothing to do with secular events.

'Is Tutankhamun's curse really nothing more than a fraud?' Mark asked anxiously.

Pacomas reached up to a shelf and took down a thick volume devoted to hieroglyphic inscriptions of the eighteenth dynasty, that of Tutankhamun, and showed his guest the warning of Ursu, a senior dignitary: *He who violates my tomb in the cemetery will be a man hated by the light; he cannot receive water on the altar of Osiris, will die of thirst in the other world and cannot pass on his wealth to his children.*

'Drioton was careful not to quote real texts such as this one, for he is wary of the magic power of the ancient Egyptians, which he prefers to deny. In the case of Tutankhamun, everything began on 6 November 1922, in Luxor, shortly before the discovery of the tomb, when a cobra swallowed Carter's canary, inside his own house. The inhabitants of the west bank were in no doubt: the spirit of the king, in the form of the fearsome uraeus, was giving the archaeologist a serious warning. The golden bird, it was true, heralded the discovery of a tomb filled with gold, but also a tragedy. I was present when Carter and

Lord Carnarvon carried out the official opening of the funerary chamber. One of their enemies, an inspector from the Department of Antiquities called Arthur Weigall, had not been authorized to accompany them and had to be content with observing their triumph, seated on the parapet overlooking Tutankhamun's last dwelling. When he saw Carnarvon walking down the stairway, Weigall said to a reporter: "If he goes down in that state of mind, I don't give him more than six weeks to live." And six weeks later Carnarvon was dead. There was talk of a mosquito bite that had become infected, but also of a pointed object, like a royal arrow, that had apparently wounded him. Whatever the case, at the time he died, at 1.55 a.m. on 5 April 1923, all the lights in Cairo went out, and nobody could explain the cause of the power cut. At the same moment, Suzy, Carnarvon's fox terrier bitch, which had remained at Highclere, howled in despair and accompanied her master into the afterlife. Following the autopsy of Tutankhamun's mummy, in 1925, people were led to believe that the pharaoh and the lord had been afflicted with the same head wound. The creator of the famous detective Sherlock Holmes, Conan Doyle, had no hesitation in expressing a diagnosis, declaring that Tutankhamun had ended the profaner's days. And sudden deaths of visitors to the tomb came one after another, notably those of Lord Carnarvon's half-brother and of Arthur Mace, one of Carter's principal colleagues. A sort of panic spread through Britain, where individuals sent back the Egyptian items they possessed to the British Museum, for fear of falling victim to the curse. American politicians, men who were serious and respected, demanded that mummies kept in museums should be studied to find out if they presented any danger to visitors. As for the prophet of misfortune, Arthur Weigall, he succumbed to an "unknown fever" and was regarded as the twenty-first victim of Tutankhamun.'

'But the individual responsible for the discovery, Howard Carter, survived!'

'In a funny kind of way,' Abbot Pacomas reminded him. 'Ten

years of exhausting toil, during which he was constantly attacked and even expelled from the tomb, not the slightest official recognition, solitude, a long illness, and no more excavations, as if Carter had never proved anything.'

Mark was troubled. 'This curse . . . Do you believe in it?'

'If it existed, would you give up your search for the papyri?'

The gravity of the question impressed the American. 'Fear has never prevented me from moving forward.'

'A particularly fearsome demon exists, the Salawa, endowed with the power of the god Set, who can unleash storms and cataclysms. It sowed terror in Luxor while your father was excavating Tutankhamun's tomb, then slumbered for many years. Now it has reawakened and will attempt to prevent you from succeeding.'

'What does it look like?'

'It looks like the worst of all predators: a man. As long as it remains in the state of a jackal, it is content to guard burial grounds and drive away outsiders. But if it transforms itself into a human, it is preparing to kill or to destroy.'

'Do you have the means to fight it?'

'I hope so,' replied Abbot Pacomas. 'To begin with I shall manufacture a talisman, which you must wear all the time. It will protect you from the worst.'

Despite his certainties as a modern, rational man, Mark was not in good spirits.

With the aid of a finely whittled reed, Pacomas drew several hieroglyphs on a piece of high-quality papyrus: the mirror meant 'life'; the pillar 'stability'; the little column with the floral capital meant 'flourishing'; and the folded fabric 'unity'. He added the image of the twofold lion, 'yesterday and tomorrow', and completed the whole with a prayer to Isis, protector of the child Horus who searched for Set, wishing to destroy him.

The special ink was composed of rose water, saffron and coriander. The abbot rolled up the papyrus and wafted incense over it for a long time. Then he handed it to Mark.

'Whatever you do, make sure you are never parted from this; and may the hidden god, father of fathers and mother of mothers, protect you. The demon of the darkness will detect the presence of the talisman and will not dare approach you, for fear of being destroyed by flames.'

Although sceptical, the American agreed to take this precaution.

'And what if this Salawa is an entirely human killer, working for people who won't allow Tutankhamun's papyri to surface?'

'Be assured that he will behave as one. Thanks to magic, you will detect his approach. After that, you will have to fight. And no one can predict the outcome of the combat.'

'Who is manipulating it?'

'I shall know soon.'

'Has Drioton made up his mind to help me?'

'He will obtain permission to consult the Carter archives, and you may find precious clues in them. But our dear canon is still on the defensive, and he still has much to tell you. You will see each other again, and you must encourage him to confide in you. Beneath the mask of bonhomie, he is a determined and courageous man. And he will defend his friend Farouk because the king, in his own way, is advancing the cause of Egyptology.'

'In other words, I must arm myself with patience.'

'Did you meet Nasser?' Pacomas asked, his tone detached.

'He, too, is a determined guy, but without a trace of bonhomie! That officer is a war leader. In my opinion, it would be a serious mistake not to take him seriously.'

'So Mahmoud was right . . . Nasser really is the secret leader of the revolution. What does he expect of you?'

'He wants me to request aid from the CIA or, at the very least, its neutrality.'

'I don't see how the Free Officers could win over the army and overthrow Farouk. That lumpish tyrant is still formidable and seems to have a firm grip on the country.'

'I shall fulfil my mission by talking to my friend John,' promised Mark, 'and my role will be at an end.'

'Let us hope so.'

'Do you think that Farouk has the Tutankhamun papyri?'

'I don't know. A friend will take you back home.'

The American looked embarrassed.

'You have nothing to hide from Ateya,' said the abbot. 'She is a woman to be trusted, and she still has many more wonders to show you.'

40

It was December, sunny and pleasantly warm. In Luxor, the season of excavations was in full swing. So the professor inspected each site to check on how the work was progressing and make sure that research was being conducted properly. Everyone feared his judgement, for at any moment he could put a spoke in the wheels, or on the other hand make life a lot easier for the teams. Fortunately, he had just got rid of the small, overexcited French Egypytologist who knew everything about everything; she would continue to seethe in Paris, but would no longer disturb the serenity of the west bank of ancient Thebes.

At the entrance to the Valley of the Kings, a foreman of works hailed the professor. A tall man, with a weather-beaten face, he appeared shocked.

'May I speak to you, Professor?'

'I am listening.'

'The Salawa has returned.'

'It is just a legend, my friend.'

'You know very well that it is not! It took another child, last night, and we found its corpse on the path leading to the western peak, where the goddess of silence reigns. We have consulted several sheikhs, and they are unanimous. The crime was committed by the Salawa!'

'Have you alerted the police?'

'Pointless. They are too afraid that they will attract the demon's wrath. During the exploration of the tomb of Tutankhamun, the Salawa constantly terrorized the region, and then it returned to the darkness. Many think that you caused it to be reborn by using the magic incantations of the Ancients.'

'People attribute too many powers to me.'

'You must do something, Professor! Many workmen are ill and no longer wish to work on the digs.'

'Is the Salawa attacking any family in particular?'

'That of Howard Carter's foreman.'

'Above all, the members of this family must speak to no one and keep their children in the house. The Salawa hates those with loose tongues.'

'You . . . you will prevent it from doing harm?'

'Let us pray to God to protect us, my friend.'

The professor lunched with provincial officials, whom he brought up to date with the excavation programmes. He made sure to offer the sums necessary for their good works, so as to preserve a necessary climate of goodwill.

One of them whispered in his ear. 'The people of the west bank seem troubled by an ancient story of ghosts, and they are also talking again about Tutankhamun's curse . . . You have refuted it, naturally?'

'Naturally. I advise you to deploy a few police officers to calm their fears.'

'An excellent idea. We don't want to drive the tourists away. Luxor needs their currency.'

'Have no fear. This incident will not lead to any consequences.'

At sunset, the professor returned to his comfortable house. After filing some reports, he sent away his servants, lit a cigarette and reread the pages of the *Book of Coming Out by Day* devoted to Anubis, the god who had the body of a man and the head of a jackal. Anubis knew the secrets of the world beyond and the paths leading from the visible world to the invisible.

Suddenly, all the lights in the house went out.

And the cigarette burned out.

The professor did not even try to light a candle, for its wick would have been destroyed instantly. Attempting to accustom his eyes to the gloom, he resigned himself to waiting.

And someone knocked at his door.

Muffled knocking, as if made by something metallic.

It was pointless to go and open the door, for his visitor knew how to cross every threshold.

The Salawa moved soundlessly, as if it weighed nothing. And yet it had taken on the appearance of a giant, with a massive torso but a slender, elongated head, reminiscent of a jackal's. Despite the half-light, it gave off an impression of savagery.

'So you have returned! Why have you awoken?'

The Salawa's hands were particularly impressive, its fingers far bigger than normal. It seized a chair and, without any apparent effort, broke it into several pieces.

'So the situation is really serious . . . Is the soul of Howard Carter demanding justice?'

The Salawa nodded.

'So terrorizing the west bank and killing children is not enough to remove the danger,' concluded the professor.

The Salawa nodded again.

'We will not identify the person or persons responsible in Luxor,' he said. 'Must we go to Cairo?'

The Salawa's head nodded a third time.

'Understood. I shall deal with everything. Return to your lair and come to the railway station the day after tomorrow. We will take the same train.'

The Salawa withdrew, and the lights came on again.

The professor was worried. In Cairo, the killer which had emerged from the darkness would be on unknown terrain and its efficiency might be diminished. It must face unfavourable living conditions, very different from those on the bank of the dead. Nevertheless, with the aid of incantations taken from grimoires of sorcery, the professor hoped to get the best from this formidable weapon.

What would its target be? Who was bringing Howard Carter back to life? Why was someone attempting to dig up a truth that had been buried so deep?

The professor opened the wall chest in which he kept, sealed, the most precious of all his files, those devoted to the Tutankhamun affair and the discovery of the papyri whose contents must remain secret for ever.

The red wax seals were intact.

Someone wanted to break them and finish the work of Carter, fortunately imprisoned by the curse that had prevented him from publishing the papyri and revealing to the world the full extent of Tutankhamun's message.

Humanity was degrading day by day, the Middle East would soon catch fire, and fanaticism and stupidity would rule as absolute masters. Nothing must hinder the progress of the darkness. With the aid of the Salawa, the professor would eliminate his adversaries, and nobody would ever break the seals.

41

Garden City was one of the most pleasant places in Cairo. Foreigners and wealthy Egyptians loved to meet in this Victorian enclave, far from the pollution of the capital. Here, the comfort of old Europe and the charm of the East were mingled. There were no dilapidated houses or broken pavements, but high-quality luxury. Who knew that this place had seen, in the time of the gods, the terrifying combat between Horus and Set, on which the fate of the universe depended? Horus had to dominate Set, not kill him. Control of Set's power led to the birth of a dynamic equilibrium, vital for life to flourish.

John sat down opposite Mark.

A waiter hurried to bring them two whiskies and some snacks. The mahogany bar was the match of any in London, and the scene was bathed in comforting sunshine.

'A dream of a place . . . When I sip my aperitif here, I never tire of looking at the island of Rodah. There's something monstrous and fascinating about this city at the same time. It mustn't be allowed to catch fire.'

'I met Nasser, at his headquarters, out of reach of Farouk's police.'

'What are your impressions?'

'He's a powerful man, formidable and determined. He doesn't fear anything or anyone, and he'll fight to the end. In your place, I would take him very seriously.'

'Did he give you a mission?'

'To ask for the support of the CIA or, at least, for its neutrality.'

'Any details about his plans?'

'None. I'm convinced that Mahmoud regards him as the man of the moment, capable of fomenting a real revolution.'

'I've obtained some interesting information about Nasser,' revealed John. 'After studying law, he entered the Cairo Military Academy in 1937 and became firm friends with those who would later form the circle of Free Officers. They talked about their sick country, about the French Revolution and the fall of the monarchy, and of the great popular movement towards freedom. Nasser read a great deal, particularly works on great warriors like Napoleon, Foch and Churchill. Of course, he gave himself a good grounding in the writings of the defenders of Islam and of Arab nationalism, wishing to restore their former power. And he even took the role of Caesar in Shakespeare's *Julius Caesar*! The guy has no lack of ambition, but does he have the abilities to bring it to reality? His family life is completely happy. His wife Tahia, an Iranian, has given him four children. Self-effacing, she respects him and doesn't interfere in his affairs. She knows nothing and therefore cannot be manipulated. In addition, Nasser is the kind of man who is incorruptible. Money doesn't interest him; he's content with his house in Manchiet el-Bakri, likes eating lunch and dinner with his family, and has a fondness for *fromage blanc*. His favourite form of entertainment is the cinema. Not really the portrait of an overexcited revolutionary, but rather of a dreamer, the sort of which there are so many in the Egyptian army. The real head of the Free Officers is good old General Naguib, who's equally incapable of breathing fire into his troops and leading them in an assault on Farouk's palace.'

'If you'd met Nasser, John, you might change your mind.'

'In this country, friend, it's impossible to keep a piece of information confidential for more than a few hours. If Nasser really did have a network, that would mean that he has an almost supernatural sense of secrecy. And his men would be divided up into cells, which would be kept apart so carefully that Farouk's police would never manage to find them. It's fiction!'

'If Nasser has read a lot, perhaps he's inspired by the great strategists.'

'We're in the East; everyone talks.'

'If he's identified that weak point, Nasser may have been able to make progress in the shadows.'

John lit a cigarette. 'He wouldn't have invited you to his house. Nasser acts as the mouthpiece of the Free Officers and simply wants to know if the United States could help him to fight against the British occupiers.'

'And . . . is that our country's intention?'

'I don't know, Mark. I pass on reports to my superiors, and the President decides on how to direct our international policies.'

'Don't we want peace and independence for all peoples?'

'That's not always compatible.'

'In any event, my mission is at an end. Now it's up to the CIA.'

Mark got to his feet.

'Please, sit down and have another whisky.'

'Sorry, I have a meeting.'

'I must insist, Mark. We still have some talking to do.'

'All right, but make it quick.'

The lawyer sat down again. John pulled on his cigarette.

'You're a formidable guy, Mark, and you must understand that you have a vital role to play. Since Nasser welcomed you into his house, he must have a certain amount of trust in you. So you're still a vital element.'

'I'll say it again, John: for me, it's over.'

'Come on, Mark, don't get on your high horse! The CIA is protecting Dusty and his family – don't forget that.'

'Blackmail?'

'One good deed deserves another. You help us, we help you.'

'I'll tell Dusty. He'll alert the authorities and he won't need the CIA any more. Forget him and forget me. Goodbye, John.'

'And what about you? Can you forget Ateya?'

The lawyer turned pale.

'Sorry, friend, but I still need your services and I'll use any means to get them. Either you cooperate or something bad will happen to that young woman to whom you seem so attached.'

'You slimeball!'

'Don't get worked up – it's unworthy of you. Vital events are being played out here, and you're one of the most important players. Either Nasser is a dreamer, and your role will be brief, or he's the man of the future, and your contacts with him will enable us to see clearly and facilitate our influence in this region. Then you'll become a sort of hero, which will help your political career.'

'If you lay a finger on Ateya, I'll—'

'Calm down. I'm just doing my job. And if I die, someone else will replace me. Someone who isn't your friend and who'll manipulate you like a pawn.'

'You dare talk about friendship!'

'I like you, Mark. And there's nothing terrifying about what I'm asking of you: to act as a liaison agent between Nasser and the CIA. By doing so, you'll serve the interests of the United States and of Egypt. As soon as we've adopted a policy, you'll be out of the game and professionals will replace you. And you can continue making love to your beautiful Egyptian girlfriend.

42

After making love with the ardour of teenagers, Ateya and Mark lay in silence for a long time, gazing up at the sun as it set over Cairo.

Then he showed her the talisman made for him by Abbot Pacomas.

'He has cured many people who were threatened by demons,' she told him. 'Pacomas is one of the last people to possess the knowledge of incantations of protection. This talisman will protect you.'

'Even he isn't sure of that,' objected Mark. 'He fears there's going to be a particularly ferocious fight.'

'By continuing the work of your father and searching for the Tutankhamun papyri, you will come into conflict with many enemies, visible and invisible. But today we are together.'

'I have the feeling that we've always known each other, Ateya, and that we've had to walk a very long path in order to come together. I owe this immense happiness to Egypt and to Abbot Pacomas's letter.'

He stroked her hair tenderly, and she pressed herself against him.

'I confess that I'm lost,' Mark went on. 'Nasser is attempting to manipulate me, John has me caught in a net and I'm wondering if Mahmoud is sincere.'

Christian Jacq

'Don't lose sight of your essential goal: finding Tutankhamun's papyri.'

'In order to do so, I'm undoubtedly going to have to get close to Farouk ... and that guy seems dangerous.'

The telephone rang. Ateya answered it, listened without saying a word and hung up.

'That was our Coptic agent at the Mena House, where you're staying officially. You have received a message from Antonio Pulli, inviting you to drinks at the Shepheard Bar tomorrow evening at 6 p.m. If he asks for your new address, give it to him, telling him that it seems more practical for work and meeting business contacts.'

Built in 1841 by an Englishman who was in love with Cairo and rebuilt fifty years later to install modern comforts, the Shepheard Hotel, on the west bank of the Nile, occupied the site of a palace built by Napoleon, the conqueror of an Egypt which could have become French if the general had not taken flight, leaving his subordinates unfortunately bogged down in defeat. A surviving sycamore tree had provided a hiding place for the fanatic who, by killing Kleber, had put an end to the dreams of all the scholars and soldiers who took part in the French expedition to Egypt.

Peace had returned long ago, but the Shepheard's famous terrace remained a place where all Egyptians and foreigners loved to meet. Wealthy tourists came there to slake their thirsts after their excursions, and members of high society chattered as they gazed at the permanent spectacle of the street, filled with barouches and souvenir-merchants. The prestigious hotel had accommodated famous guests like Winston Churchill, and it remained one of the jewels of triumphant Britain. Taking tea at the Shepheard was one of the most important moments in discovering the country.

Although affable and smiling, Antonio Pulli seemed nervous. 'Very pleased to see you again, Mr Wilder. It is a little late for tea ... What would you say to a whisky and soda?'

A waiter dressed in a white *galabieh,* with a long red belt, hurried to please King Farouk's right-hand man.

'It seems you are no longer staying at the Mena House?'

'I'm keeping a room there,' replied the lawyer, 'but I'm renting an apartment in Zamalek. I can arrange my meetings more easily from there.'

'A very pleasant district indeed. So have you given His Majesty's proposal some thought?'

'I'm very fond of Egypt, and I should like to know it better. American investors should not be disappointed.'

'Excellent, excellent . . . I hope you are not paying too much attention to the unfounded criticisms levelled at His Majesty. The king is entirely aware of the poverty that afflicts a section of his population and has undertaken numerous initiatives, founding hospitals and schools, not to mention a university. Thanks to him, we have social security, and the state comes to the aid of the poorest. Farouk has no hesitation in using his own fortune, for example in fighting the flies responsible for trachoma, that fearsome eye disease. Do you know that he flew over the countryside in a plane and threw out thousands of ping-pong balls, which children exchanged for sweets? Sometimes, I concede, the king can be a little flippant. Once, after having quails released over the palace, he shot at the birds and broke many windows. And the gardeners were afraid that he would spray them with the hosepipe! Simple pranks, which are entirely excusable when one knows the weight of responsibilities a monarch faces.'

Mark wondered why Pulli was confiding in him. Doubtless he wished to ask a favour of him.

'His Majesty,' he went on, 'is afflicted with a small failing which is a little more . . . embarrassing. Although the king can have anything he desires, he experiences an unfortunate tendency to steal items, even those of little value, wherever he stays. It could be a simple plate or a bathrobe.'

'His Majesty is a kleptomaniac,' commented Mark.

'In a way . . . Most of the time, I take note of these modest thefts and compensate the owners so they do not make these incidents known. Unfortunately, I am locked in a battle with a stubborn man who wishes to lodge a complaint and inform the press. In the current circumstances, that would be regrettable, very regrettable. Anything that would weaken the king's reputation would be bad for Egypt. So it occurs to me that your skills as a negotiator might be most useful in extricating us from this unfortunate situation.'

Slowly, Mark swallowed a mouthful of whisky. 'Why not, Mr Pulli? But on one condition.'

'What condition?'

'I assume you've heard of the British archaeologist Howard Carter?'

'The most famous of all archaeologists! The discovery of Tutankhamun's tomb thrilled the whole world.'

'Did King Farouk meet Carter?'

Antonio seemed to be searching his memory. 'Yes, he did meet him.'

'His Majesty was interested in Egyptian antiquities. To your knowledge, might he have procured items that came from Tutankhamun's tomb?'

'That is completely impossible,' replied Pulli.

'What is impossible for King Farouk?'

'Only one man could give you a decisive answer, and he is the one you should consult: Canon Etienne Drioton.'

'I shall meet him again, but I would like him to be a little more talkative. Discreet intervention on your part would help me to establish the truth.'

'Drioton is his own man, a faithful friend of His Majesty, and—'

'You have faith in my skills, Mr Pulli, and I in yours.'

'Will you consent to sort out the small matter I have just mentioned?'

'On condition that you coax Drioton out of his silence.'

'Done.'

'Have the file sent to my address in Zamalek – you know it, don't you?'

Antonio Pulli just smiled.

43

Ateya took Mark to see Abbot Pacomas, who wished to speak to him urgently. The scholar was studying a papyrus from the Ptolemaic era, whose magical incantations drove away snakes, scorpions and demons of the night. The ancient Egyptians attached great importance to the protection of sleep, a dangerous period during which the sleeper travelled across the subterranean world before being reborn with the morning sun.

'Canon Drioton has sent me a letter addressed to you,' declared the abbot. 'The administrators of the Cairo Museum authorize you to consult Howard Carter's archives. Here are two letters of recommendation, one in French, the other in Arabic. An assistant curator will expect you tomorrow morning, at six o'clock. Make sure you are not late.'

So Drioton was playing the game. Carter had probably talked about the papyri. All he had to do was consult papers that had long been forgotten.

'There's a price to pay,' revealed Mark, 'preventing a plaintiff from accusing King Farouk of theft.'

'Child's play for a lawyer of your stature! The king will be indebted to you, and Pulli will be eternally grateful – providing you with firm support in these difficult times.'

'Did you know of the existence of these archives?'

'Until our dinner with the canon, I believed they had vanished for ever. The Cairo Museum is sometimes an abyss into which precious finds disappear.'

'Are you sure of Mahmoud's sincerity?'

'Who can completely trust a double agent? And yet he loves his country and wishes to protect it from a bloody revolution. As the British refuse to listen to him and any direct action would condemn him to death, he is obliged to resort to you. If America can prevent Egypt from subsiding into chaos, you and he will have done useful work.'

Ateya and Mark spent an enchanting night, but waking up at 5 a.m. was difficult. It was early January and the wind was brisk, and Mark would have preferred to spend more time enjoying the warmth of a loving woman's body.

She served him some strong coffee, showered with him and then urged him not to be late.

In the East, time did not exist, except for a pernickety bureaucrat full of his own superiority, especially when he was meeting someone with a request to make, and a foreigner to boot.

At 5.55 a.m., Mark arrived at the entrance to the administrative department. At 6 a.m. precisely, he was shown into the office of a man with a moustache and a low forehead, who was apparently busy working on a pile of files. With a brusque gesture, he invited his guest to sit down. Members of staff constantly came and went.

Around twenty minutes later, he looked up. 'What do you want?' asked the man with the moustache.

'Thank you for seeing me. Canon Drioton gave me these two letters of recommendation.'

The lawyer handed them to the man with the moustache, who read them carefully. 'It will be difficult, very difficult, even impossible.'

'I'm in no hurry.'

'There are insurmountable technical difficulties. It would be better not to waste your time.'

'Would you be kind enough to return the canon's letters of recommendation to me?'

Delighted to have won the battle, the official did so.

Mark got to his feet. 'I'm going straight to the palace,' he announced. 'As I have the privilege of working for His Majesty, I shall inform him of the manner in which I've just been treated.'

The man with the moustache gripped the arms of his chair. 'Please, sit down!'

'Sorry. I'm in a hurry now.'

'No, no, don't go! I will take you to the official responsible for the archives, and he will attempt to resolve the problems. Follow me, Mr Wilder.'

The archivist occupied an office cluttered with paperwork and files. The man with the moustache talked to him in Arabic and, judging from the tone he used, was obviously instructing him on what to do.

'I hope your research will be fruitful, Mr Wilder,' he concluded with a friendly smile. 'Forgive me; other meetings await me.'

The archivist had a square head, deep-set eyes and thin lips, and he did not look at all pleased. 'May I see your letters of recommendation?'

'Here they are.'

The expert read slowly.

Coffee was brought, and he ordered that it should be served to his guest. Then a subordinate entered, asking for instructions, followed by a friend who was just passing by, a cousin asking for financial help and another bureaucrat in search of glue and pencils. They all started up discussions with each other, and many cups of coffee were emptied.

Without losing his cool, Mark waited for the archivist to agree to deal with his request.

'Why do you wish to see the Howard Carter archives?' he asked at last.

'For personal research.'

'They are old papers, devoid of all interest.'

'Can anyone ever know that for sure?'

'You may rely on my experience, Mr Wilder.'

'I don't doubt it, but I would still like to examine them myself.'

Irritated, the archivist summoned his second in command and ordered him to take his guest to a room where boxes were stacked up, some of them threatening to topple over. In the centre were a table and some chairs. Mark was invited to sit down, and more coffee was brought.

After an unhurried investigation, the second in command placed some documents in a sorry state on the table. They consisted of an excavation notebook belonging to Howard Carter, plus various notes. These relics deserved a better fate, but the lawyer's uppermost thoughts were of scanning the pages, which might just put him on the trail of Tutankhamun's papyri.

Mark did not notice the hours passing, and nobody dared to disturb him.

Alas, the documents produced no results and not the smallest clue.

It was clear that Drioton knew these archives, and also knew that they contained no mention of any papyri. So he had allowed the American to consult them.

According to Antonio Pulli, the situation was evolving. Drioton must possess an important piece of information, and Mark was determined to obtain it.

44

Mark had a long telephone conversation with his friend and right-hand man, Dusty Malone, to bring himself up to date on current cases and ask him to delegate an expert to sort out King Farouk's little problems. Dusty was managing rather well, and his boss's decisions enabled him to move forward. But he was not pleased about this prolonged stay in Egypt, and he hoped that Mark would soon be back in New York. Evasively, the lawyer promised him that he would do whatever seemed best.

And then he spent some wonderful hours with Ateya before seeing Abbot Pacomas again. The abbot was busy translating a magical papyrus dating from the twenty-sixth dynasty and which had come from the city of Sais, the seat of a famous medical school.

'Do you still have your talisman on you?'

'It never leaves me,' replied Mark.

'Danger is closing in, and I do not know what form it will take. That is why I must take new precautions.'

'Drioton was playing games with me. The Howard Carter archives don't contain a single mention of Tutankhamun's papyri, and he must have known that. But he's going to share his secret with me.'

'At the weekend,' Pacomas revealed, 'the canon goes to his little house in Saqqara, usually alone, to meditate and get his breath back after a stressful week. There you can talk calmly, and he may perhaps tell you the truth. Have you dealt with Farouk?'

'I shall soon have a reassuring answer for him.'

'Our king has just experienced a major setback, which has plunged him into a foul mood. He asked a team of genealogists to establish that he is a descendant of Muhammad so as to present himself in the eyes of his people and of the Arab world as a sort of Islamic Pope. But the Muslim Brothers thwarted the manoeuvre. In their eyes, Farouk is still a corrupt oppressor who cannot pose as a spiritual master. And there is worse: more and more incidents are occurring in the canal zone, and they are increasing in severity. Some British soldiers fired on a procession heading for a cemetery, thinking that it was a terrorist demonstration. The response from the guerrillas was swift: a raiding party blew up an arms depot, killing ten guards. The nerves of the British are on edge. By constantly harassing them, the supporters of independence risk provoking a violent reaction.'

'So is Nasser rejoicing about this?'

'His name is still never spoken,' observed Pacomas, 'and I am not certain that the disturbances are under the Free Officers' control. I won't hide it from you, Mark: the situation is becoming explosive.'

'Then I must see Drioton as a matter of urgency.'

Thanks to Dusty Malone's brilliant results, Mark was able to go to the Abdin Palace before attempting to search the canon's soul. A master of ceremonies took him to Antonio Pulli's office, and Pulli sent away several visitors in order to have a tête-à-tête with the lawyer.

'I have some good news,' announced Mark.

'Wonderful! Have you managed to sort out that little matter?'

'There will be no court case and no scandal. Of course, the former plaintiff will have to be compensated.'

'Of course! Would you be kind enough to let me have the amounts?'

Mark handed Pulli a single sheet of paper. Names were listed, followed by figures.

'That is very reasonable,' said Farouk's trusted man. 'I shall deal with it immediately. His Majesty will be delighted and will undoubtedly ask you to deal with future important cases. Your expertise will help us to make the right decisions.'

'Rumour has it that there's trouble in the Suez Canal zone.'

'Overexcited youths are defying the British soldiers,' conceded Pulli. 'It's a suicidal attitude! Those idiots will fail miserably and provoke disturbances from which no good can come. But have no fear: the king has the situation well in hand, and public order will continue to be firmly maintained. You may recommend the Egyptian market to American investors; they will be delighted.'

Someone knocked repeatedly at the office door.

'Enter,' said Pulli, astonished at this brusque approach.

The senior steward appeared, in a state of high anxiety. He stammered. 'Pulli Bey, Pulli Bey ... You must come immediately, immediately! It is ... I ... How can I tell you ... Come, I beg of you!'

'Forgive me,' Pulli said to Mark. 'Please wait. I shall return.'

Servants were running in all directions, up and down the palace corridors. Some were shouting, some calling to each other, others weeping.

Mark forced himself to remain calm.

Why all this fuss? A mob, an attack on the royal palace ... No, that was highly unlikely. What event could disturb the quiet orderliness of this place, entirely devoted to the cult of Farouk?

Antonio Pulli reappeared.

'The king's son has just been born,' he shouted, 'a month prematurely! Mother and child are in perfect health. His Majesty has a successor, named Ahmed Fouad, and the continuance of the dynasty is assured. Now all challengers will be silenced. The future sovereign weighs more than three kilos, and already seems very strong and lively! You cannot imagine the joy that is going to overwhelm Cairo.'

Antonio Pulli was not mistaken. On 16 January 1952 an official communiqué announced that Queen Narriman had given birth to the Prince of the Upper Nile, Ahmed Fouad, heir to a dynasty that had lasted a hundred and fifty years. A hundred gunshots saluted the beginning of a new era, which would see Farouk's power confirmed, the unification of Egypt and Sudan, and the flourishing of a nation faithful to the monarch and his successor.

Already, hundreds of Cairo's citizens were assembling beneath the windows of the Abdin Palace, which was surrounded by the royal guard wearing ceremonial uniform. Their tarbooshes glistened in the sun, their weapons threatening no one.

The delighted populace filled the capital's main streets with flowers and sang for hours, celebrating the king, the queen and the new heir. Beside himself with happiness, Farouk had a mattress placed at the foot of the cradle, so as not to miss a single instant of the first hours of his son's life – a son he had waited for for so long.

This fabulous event must surely put an end to all tensions. Even those who doubted Farouk believed in the future, in the Prince of the Upper Nile and in Egypt's future prosperity.

Mark emerged from the palace.

The return of calm put an end to his relations with John, the CIA man, and with Mahmoud, the double agent. From now on, he could dedicate himself solely to searching for the Tutankhamun papyri. And the decisive step would be Canon Drioton's confession.

45

Saqqara was a world apart. Far from the bustle of Cairo, the vast burial ground of ancient Memphis, dominated by the step pyramid of Pharaoh Djoser, was dedicated to the desert, to silence and to eternity.

On the orders of Antonio Pulli, a car from the palace took Mark to Canon Drioton's weekend house.

The canon's expression was less jovial than usual as he greeted the American.

'You are a man of considerable influence, Mr Wilder.'

'After my disappointing exploration of the Carter archives, I wish to know the truth. The whole truth.'

'His Majesty wishes to satisfy your request. Please, come in.'

The house was extremely modest, but its atmosphere was calm, well suited to confidential conversations. The canon filled two glasses with a fruity Burgundy and sat down in a sturdy antique armchair. Mark chose to remain standing.

'It is a long story, which implicates the supreme leaders of this country,' began Drioton. 'So it must remain secret. Do you promise me that you will hold your tongue?'

'I promise.'

'In January 1925 Howard Carter met Fouad I, father of Farouk. The meeting was cordial, and this contact at the highest level of state was not fruitless. On 31 December 1927 King Fouad went to Luxor, visited Tutankhamun's tomb and admired Carter's finds. He was visibly delighted at the results. By way of homage, and violating the law governing antiquities, the monarch received an admirable jewel taken from Tutankhamun's treasure. It was decorated with a picture of the pharaoh in his chariot.'

'Who gave it to him?' asked Mark.

'Probably Lord Carnarvon, but I am not certain of that. On the death of Fouad I, on 28 April 1936, Farouk became the illegitimate owner of this little work of art. And in that same year, 1936, he met Howard Carter in the Valley of the Kings.* The archaeologist's career was coming to an end; nevertheless, he made the new master of Egypt aware of the importance of the wonders he had brought back to light.'

'Are you also thinking of Tutankhamun's spiritual message?'

'I am not a believer in esotericism,' Drioton reminded him.

'But you're convinced that the ancient Egyptians believed in one god, and that the sages concealed their teaching beneath symbols. No one who has studied the gold chapels of Tutankhamun could deny it. And I'm not talking about the papyri.'

'After the death of Howard Carter, his niece, Phyllis Walker, made an inventory of his possessions. She discovered some small items in faience and gold, depicting animals, and was able to identify the royal cartouche indicating their provenance: the tomb of Tutankhamun. Carter wanted to leave them to his niece, who had taken such good care of him during his last months. But Phyllis Walker was terrified by the idea of becoming the owner of such treasures. She was adamant that they should return to Egypt. So she asked the executor of her uncle's will to undertake this extremely delicate task. This had to be done with the maximum discretion so that Howard Carter was not

---

* For all the details given in this chapter, see T.G.H. James, *The Path to Tutankhamun*, pp. 407–408, and photo 36.

accused of theft and his memory tarnished. It was impossible to send the items to the Cairo Museum. Carter had too many enemies there, who would have caused a scandal. The diplomatic bag was considered, but the Foreign Office refused, fearing indiscretions. And Carter's great friend, Harry Burton, who attempted to find the right solution, died in 1940. At a loss, Phyllis Walker decided, in March of that year, to write to me. She quite simply offered me all the items from Tutankhamun's tomb that were still in her possession.'

This time, thought Mark, the canon is no longer hiding anything from me, and we're really getting somewhere.

Drioton drank a mouthful of Burgundy. Clearly, he found it disturbing to recall the facts.

'So I found myself in possession of a secret that was rather heavy to bear,' he confessed. 'I replied to Phyllis Walker at the end of April, thanking her for her generosity and assuring her that this gift should neither sully Carter's reputation nor provoke a press campaign. And I had only one solution to avert a disaster: to ask King Farouk himself to receive this treasure. Once His Majesty had consented, no protests could be raised. Placed under seal, the items were handed to the Egyptian consul in London, who sent them by plane. And the king himself made a gift of them to the Cairo Museum.'

'Did Farouk give *all* the treasures of Tutankhamun that were in his possession?' asked Mark.

Drioton appeared embarrassed. 'That will soon be the case.'

'Including the papyri?'

The canon's expression hardened. 'There were no papyri.'

'Do I have your word?'

'You have it! However . . .'

'However?'

'There is another chapter to this story,' admitted the canon, 'and it is even darker. The doctor in charge of studying Tutankhamun's mummy, Dr Derry, behaved like a veritable butcher. The Egyptologists were careful not to reveal this massacre.* And the sufferings of this unfortunate corpse had not ended. During the Second World War, taking advantage of the lack of surveillance in the Valley of the Kings, looters moved it and caused it grave damage. No doubt they were hoping to find jewels.'

'Jewels . . . or the famous papyri?'

'I do not know, Mr Wilder. One of the members of that sinister expedition may perhaps be able to tell you. All his possessions were sequestered by Farouk in 1948, but the individual has succeeded in surviving, and has made himself another small fortune.'

'Does he still live in Cairo?'

'Indeed.'

'What is his name, and where can I find him?'

'We call him "Durand". I shall attempt to contact him and arrange a meeting with you, but I cannot promise anything. If he possesses items that belonged to Tutankhamun, he will keep silent.'

'I'm convinced of the contrary, as long as I offer sufficient money. And I will.'

---

* Not until the investigations by Dr M. Bucaille was the dreadful truth revealed.

46

It was 18 January 1952, and the Copts were celebrating the rites of Epiphany. After the purifications of the previous evening, when the men bathed in the Nile and were anointed with holy water, the faithful recited prayers. Ateya used an ancient rosary with forty-one beads. Mark, although he shared in this ritual moment, had eyes only for her.

When the priest sprinkled the congregation with holy water, the American thought of the sumptuous wedding he would give his future wife. Dusty Malone would organize a celebration everyone there would remember. In the meantime, he was impatient to meet the mysterious Durand. According to Abbot Pacomas, duly informed of Drioton's revelations, there was a chance that this tomb raider was in possession of the Tutankhamun papyri. But he was clearly a greedy man and would demand a fortune for them.

The abbot had not yet identified the enemy which had emerged from the darkness, but he knew that it was coming ever nearer, and he was performing numerous magic rituals every day in order to create a protective barrier around Mark. Given what was at stake and the adversary's ferocity, would that be sufficient?

At the end of the ceremony, Ateya squeezed Mark's hand hard. 'We're allowed to be greedy today,' she decided. 'I shall take you to Groppi's.'

Groppi's was the best tea room and patisserie in Cairo, and

one of the city's highlights. Achille had taken over the business from his father Giacomo, who had come originally from Lugano in Switzerland and who had become chocolatier to the elite. Opened in 1925, the famous shop on the Soliman-Pasha roundabout sold matchless ice creams and cakes. From the Morocco to the Countess Marie and the Neapolitan Surprise, Groppi's ice cream sundaes attracted everybody in Cairo. And the shopkeeper exercised strict control over his products from his vast agricultural estate near the capital. He even offered visits to his dairy and his ultra-modern laboratory.

As they ate, Ateya and Mark talked of love with their eyes. They savoured every moment of this miraculous communion, as if so much happiness might vanish a moment later.

When they emerged from the tea room, a little shoeshine boy approached the couple. 'Three mandarins for one dollar.'

Mark froze. 'Do I wait here or do I follow you?'

'You follow me.'

Ateya held him back. 'Mark . . .'

'I'll see you this evening, my love.'

The child led the American to a little grey Peugeot. He got in the back and sat next to Mahmoud.

The driver set off.

The lawyer felt reassured by the feel of the talisman against his skin. Mahmoud's expression was closed, almost hostile. And what if he had decided to eliminate a contact who had become too visible? Nothing would be easier than to take his prisoner to a place controlled by the revolutionaries and get rid of him.

'You are spinning out love's sweet dream, Mr Wilder. Good for you. It is a chance that must be taken, and that young woman really is magnificent.'

'This is no adventure for me. It's much more serious than you suppose.'

'In that case, good luck. Have you found any trace of the Tutankhamun papyri?'

'Not yet, but I'm progressing step by step.'

'Be suspicious of anything that brings you closer to Farouk. In the event of a conflict of interests, you will count for nothing.'

The car was moving quite slowly and had not left the city centre.

Edgily, Mahmoud lit a cigarette.

'You don't smoke, do you?'

'I've stopped.'

'Me, I've started again. Given the circumstances, I need something to calm me down. Nasser has studied your file and thinks you are interesting. I have been ordered to watch you as much as possible and to provide him with oral reports on your behaviour. No compromising documents must go astray, especially after recent events.'

'What happened?'

'The Free Officers decided to defy the king openly in order to test his abilities to react. A golden opportunity presented itself: the election of the President of the Officers' Club. Nothing important, true, but Nasser persuaded good old General Naguib to put himself at the head of a list featuring several of their companions. Farouk was furious, and let it be known to the electorate that the only man who must win was his henchman, General Sirri Amer, who has been implicated in many scandals and is loathed by all those soldiers who believe in the honour of the army. And the result was a sizeable surprise: Naguib was elected in a landslide victory! It was a terrible snub for the king. Of course, he annulled the vote and installed Sirri Amer as President of the Officers' Club. Nevertheless, Nasser now knows that he has support among his peers. War has been declared between the Free Officers and King Farouk. There has already been one victim, for His Majesty gave his opponents a violent warning. Sirri Amer's gang has just machine-gunned to death a young lieutenant* who was close to General Naguib.

* Abdel Kader Tahar.

They set a trap for him in the Roda district, when he was visiting a group of Muslim Brothers. Just before he died, the victim had time to tell a military doctor: "It was Farouk who had me executed." The underground impact of this incident is considerable. Now Nasser feels in a position of strength. He is too sly to show himself in broad daylight and continues to push Naguib to the forefront. In my opinion, the revolutionary process is going to speed up. And Egypt will suffer chaos. What have the Americans decided, and whom will they support?'

'I don't know, Mahmoud. I've left the game.'

'You will re-enter it, Mr Wilder. Perhaps you will succeed in protecting your friends in New York. But here, in Cairo, the woman you love is at my mercy.'

'You wouldn't dare . . .'

'I don't have a choice. For years I have been risking my life to prevent a bloodbath. If Nasser's revolution is not nipped in the bud, it will happen. So persuade the CIA to intervene, to help Farouk and to muzzle him. By taking economic control of the country in place of the British, the Americans will assure prosperity, and the spectre of murderous confrontations will fade away. Now you alone can help me attain this goal. So I will have no hesitation in using the worst means to force you to act.'

The car halted not far from the Opera House.

Mahmoud opened the door.

'See you soon, Mr Wilder.'

47

General Sir George Erskine, nicknamed 'Strong George', commander-in-chief of British troops in Egypt, was dressing for dinner when his batman brought him an urgent message.

A band of madmen had just attacked a camp at Tell el-Kebir, the most important arms depot in the region.

The general maintained a veneer of calm, finished dressing and immediately summoned his general staff.

'Gentlemen, this insane act is an unacceptable defiance of our authority. I knew that young revolutionaries from Cairo were planning to instigate disturbances in the canal zone. So I sent a warning to the Egyptian government, informing them that I would be forced to use appropriate means to crush the rebels if they attacked one of our bases. Since these ill-mannered individuals did not understand the message, we are going to intervene. After which, these ruffians will learn how to behave.'

At the tenth ring, someone answered.

'I'd like to speak to John,' said Mark.

'Who's calling?'

'His friend, the American lawyer.'

'John's travelling.'

'When will he be back?'

'Call again on the twenty-seventh.'

The person on the other end of the line hung up.

'You seem worried,' commented Ateya.

'According to Mahmoud, Nasser is thinking of speeding up the revolutionary process. He hopes that the Americans will interrupt it to avert a disaster.'

The young woman put her arms around him. 'Are you so worried about the destiny of Egypt?'

'Isn't Egypt the mother of the world? And I know that it's becoming my motherland. This is where I'll marry you.'

'Cairo is where all the most beautiful weddings are held. We have a taste for happiness.'

'You can rely on my friend Dusty to organize an unforgettable reception.'

'Such pretty dreams . . .'

'In my profession,' Mark reminded her, 'dreaming is forbidden. I shall lock you up in a marriage contract you can never escape from. The two of us will be united for all eternity.'

And their kiss went on for ever.

At dawn on 25 January 1952 General Erskine's tanks encircled two barracks in the town of Ismailia, where three hundred and fifty Egyptian police were billeted. Their task was to maintain order in the district. According to Strong George, they had not fulfilled their task at all and, even worse, had given aid to the young attackers from Cairo. So he intended to treat them as rebels and take them prisoner, to show the government where its responsibilities lay.

Inside the main barracks, panic reigned. The chief of police, a captain, managed to contact the Minister of the Interior, whose instructions were specific: do not surrender, resist! Otherwise, the authorities would lose face once and for all and Britain would demonstrate her incontestable supremacy.

But how were they to resist? With old rifles against tanks?

The captain, who had spent time in England and even taken a training course at Scotland Yard, talked to General Erskine.

The general gave him a quarter of an hour to think. The Egyptians refused to lay down their arms.

Strong George saw that he would have to use his firepower, and a rain of shells landed on the barracks. In the face of the enemy's obstinacy, the operation would have to be achieved with the use of mortar fire.

These people are brave but completely mad, thought the British general. By noon, the battle was over. There were three dead and thirteen wounded among the British, with forty-six dead and almost eighty wounded among the Egyptian policemen.

This time, the government would understand who possessed the force and would stop encouraging young madmen to disturb public order.

'What do you think of this sautéed veal with baby vegetables?' Canon Drioton asked his guest.

'It's absolutely wonderful,' replied Mark. 'Please congratulate your mother.'

'That holy woman is a true cordon bleu cook, and the Church ought to list the enjoyment of food as one of the deadly sins.'

The Burgundy proved to be just as good as the food.

'Durand has agreed to meet you,' announced the canon. 'Noon tomorrow, 26 January, at the Turf Club.'

'Did you tell him what I wish to question him about?'

'He has consented to talk to you about a surprising discovery made by Howard Carter.'

'The Tutankhamun papyri?'

'Durand did not speak those words. He will demand a large sum of money and an American passport so he can leave Egypt immediately.'

Abbot Pacomas listened attentively to Mark.

'Whatever you do, do not forget your talisman when you go to the meeting. The danger is growing every day, for the creature of evil is in Cairo and is attempting to track you down. Coptic friends will be dining at the Turf Club and will be sure to act if they think you are in danger.'

'At first sight, this man Durand is in need of money and wants to escape from Farouk. With John's connections, I can obtain a passport for him, as long as the information merits it. Father, I feel as if I am close to a goal.'

'It is indeed possible. May God hear us.'

The taxi that took Mark to Zamalek had great difficulty threading its way through the worse-than-normal traffic jams.

'Has there been an accident?' the American asked the driver.

'No. Young people are demonstrating against a massacre perpetrated by the British in Ismailia. Apparently, they killed hundreds of Egyptian police officers, accusing them of rebellion. As long as our country remains under occupation, we can expect this kind of incident.'

Ateya had prepared a delicious meal: tahini, puréed aubergines, stuffed vine leaves, tomato salad, meatballs on a bed of parsley, and grilled fish.

'This evening, you're the one who seems worried,' commented Mark.

'The British have gone too far. The ministers have met and have talked of breaking off diplomatic relations with Great Britain. The Muslim Brothers have proclaimed a holy war, and a good number of young people will listen to them.'

'This isn't the first incident in the Suez Canal zone. Don't you think that the fever will soon dissipate?'

'I hope so!'

'Tomorrow will be a decisive day. I'm convinced that Durand will reveal the place where Tutankhamun's papyri are hidden.'

'I must get up early,' announced Ateya. 'I'm guiding a group of tourists who want to explore the Coptic churches in Old Cairo. Let's meet up around five o'clock at Groppi's.'

'Gladly, my love. You'll be the first to hear the good news.'

48

At dawn on Saturday 26 January 1952 Ateya kissed Mark on the forehead.

'I have to go to work,' she whispered. 'At one o'clock I'm taking my tourists to lunch at the Shepheard.'

'I'm going to be lazy and sleep late.'

'I'll see you this afternoon, darling, at Groppi's.'

The lawyer went back to sleep, dreaming of the wonderful night he had just spent in the young woman's arms. The more they made love, the more they wanted to.

Relaxed and rested, the lawyer got up very late. The sun was blazing down over the magnificent Zamalek district, populated by rich British people who loved to make the most of the swimming pools, cricket and polo pitches and tennis courts owned by the Sporting Club of Guezira, to which only a few hand-picked Egyptians were admitted. Pretty gardens and detached houses made this little piece of Europe a paradise, where Ateya and he would spend happy days.

Suddenly, he thought about his meeting at noon.

How would this man Durand behave? It was pointless to worry about it in advance. The lawyer knew how to negotiate; he would take all the time necessary to reassure Durand and obtain the best result.

Mark took a long shower, made himself some coffee and

dressed in the distinguished British fashion required of guests at the Turf Club.

He was drinking his first mouthful when a strange spectacle captured his attention.

Columns of black smoke were rising into the Cairo sky.

As soon as dawn broke, thousands of striking students had occupied the university courtyard. Protesting against the massacre in Ismailia, they followed their leaders' instructions and joined up with other demonstrators from the suburbs. Hadn't a minister shouted 'This day will be your day; you will be avenged'? All of them wanted to obtain weapons, fight the British and liberate the Suez Canal zone. This time, as the radio promised, Egypt would not hang its head. And they cheered Soviet Russia, which would provide the people at war with the rifles they needed.

Soon, hundreds of thousands of rebels would occupy the Opera area, paralysing the business quarter.

An intolerable scene greeted the eyes of one of the leaders, a broad-chested giant with a slender head, elongated like that of a jackal.

In front of the famous Badia bar, which featured the best belly dancers in the capital, a policeman was having a drink with one of the establishment's employees.

'Aren't you ashamed to behave like this when your brothers are being murdered by the British?' demanded the Salawa.

The police officer made the mistake of laughing.

With a single punch, he fractured his skull.

'Destroy this place of debauchery!' he ordered the demonstrators.

The Badia was the first to burn. And the violence was unleashed, propagated by young people on mopeds and agitators who brought cans of petrol. For fear of being massacred, the police helped the rioters, and the firemen were afraid to intervene.

When the demonstrators broke down the door of the large Avierino store with iron bars, the Salawa gave a shout of victory.

They also attacked the Cicurel, another shop, selling, in particular, Western fashions; the iron shutters were raised and they burned all the goods with which the West was flooding Cairo. Looters took advantage of this to steal luxury goods, and the mob decided to set fire to the houses of Jews, to Barclays bank and to the Rivoli and Metro Cinemas.

Gigantic flames rose up. Cairo was ablaze.

Mark hurtled down the staircase and bumped into the caretaker.

'Don't go out. It's too dangerous.'

'Do you know what's happening?'

'A band of madmen is running around the city. The forces of order will soon intervene, and calm will be re-established. Here, you are safe.'

'I have an important meeting.'

'Don't take any risks, Mr Wilder. Miss Ateya would be most angry with me if . . .'

'That's the point. I must find her. Do you have a motorbike?'

'I can get you one, but . . .'

'Quickly, please!'

Helmet on his head, his face hidden by a scarf, Mark rode off.

He soon encountered other bikers, throwing Molotov cocktails into gutted shops. The main bars and restaurants of the city centre were ablaze.

When he reached the Turf Club, he had to brake suddenly. Around ten people were attempting to flee, but the Salawa, at the head of a howling mob, pushed them towards the inferno. The demon was careful to break Durand's neck before watching his body burn away, alongside the other victims.

There was now only one command: to destroy everything that symbolized the foreign presence in Cairo.

Mark realized that he would never meet Durand. Now he must snatch Ateya away from this bloodbath.

It would soon be two o'clock . . . Mad with worry, Mark

headed for the Shepheard Hotel, where the young woman was due to have lunch with the tourists.

He arrived too late. The hotel was burning, and the firemen, whose hoses had been sabotaged, had to watch helplessly as the famous hotel was destroyed. Delighted, the crowd scrawled anti-British slogans and laughed as terrified guests ran in all directions.

Mark managed to reach the garden, where the foreigners had taken refuge. There was no trace of Ateya.

There was still Groppi's, the final refuge. Alas, the establishment on Soliman-Pasha Square was now nothing but ashes.

A middle-class man in European clothes was weeping.

'Did everyone get out?' Mark asked him.

'I think so, yes.'

'Why aren't the army and the police doing anything?'

'King Farouk invited their leaders to a banquet in honour of the birth of his heir. There aren't any officers left to give orders until the festivities end.'

And what if the Abdin Palace was the arsonists' next objective? The American had to make many detours to avoid groups of overexcited demonstrators. A new mob was assembling in the direction of the palace, yelling: 'Let's overthrow Farouk!'

A few hundred metres from the palace, the army took action and managed to control the crowd. Mark turned back and headed for Old Cairo. If Ateya had realized the gravity of the situation in time, she had undoubtedly taken refuge with Abbot Pacomas.

Close to his house, two Coptic soldiers intercepted the American. 'Where are you going?'

'I want to see Abbot Pacomas.'

'Impossible.'

'Tell him it's urgent.'

'Your name?'

'Mark Wilder.'

'Wait here.'

Other Copts surrounded the American. In the city centre, the army was putting out the fires, dispersing the rioters and re-establishing order. But would the madness spread to other districts?

A bearded priest came to fetch the lawyer and took him to Pacomas, who was sitting in an armchair, wearing a grave expression.

'Do you know where Ateya is?'

'No, Mark.'

'I'm leaving to search for her.'

'Pointless. Friends are already doing so. Rest and wait.'

'I can't!'

'Rushing off in no particular direction won't help.'

'How can you be so calm?'

'Trust in the Lord and in the magic of His servants.'

Unable to stay still, Mark strode back and forth across the library.

A little after 8 p.m., the short, bearded priest knocked on the door.

Behind him stood Ateya.

49

Alerted by the first columns of smoke, Ateya had taken refuge with her group of tourists in Saint Sergio's Church, waiting for a Copt to announce that the danger was at an end. According to Pacomas, the fire was caused by a malevolent force that had taken possession of people's minds. Coming from Luxor, the Salawa had lit a destructive fire in the hearts of many rebels, intoxicated with violence. So the abbot spent the night chanting magic texts and strengthening the protection around Mark. Without any doubt, the curse linked to the persecution of Tutankhamun's mummy had just taken a devastating turn.

And the only man able to provide a worthwhile clue to the whereabouts of the papyri lay dead and burned in the Turf Club.

'We must not yield to despair,' declared Abbot Pacomas. 'Heaven's voice has not yet been silenced.'

'And yet,' said Mark, 'we've explored every avenue! This time, we really seem to have come to a dead end.'

'This very day, you will receive a sign.'

In the middle of the afternoon of 27 January, Ateya and Mark returned to their apartments in Zamalek. This chic quarter had been spared by the mob, which had concentrated on the centre of Cairo, its hotels and shops. The exact number of victims would never be known, and the city was still in a state of shock, awaiting the reactions of the king and of Great Britain.

Outside the apartment building was a shoeshine boy.

'Three mandarins for one dollar.'

Mark embraced Ateya for a long time, watched goggle-eyed by the boy, then followed his guide to a black Peugeot where Mahmoud was waiting for him. The car drove slowly around the area.

'Is this warning enough for you?' demanded the double agent.

'Did Nasser organize the riots?'

'They had nothing to do with him.'

'Will he not take advantage of the situation to take power?' Mark ventured.

'An attempted coup d'état would be a fatal mistake. We have analysed the events and come to a conclusion: the person responsible for this terrifying day is no other than Farouk himself, in full agreement with the British.'

'Unthinkable!'

'The facts are clear: the king invited all the leaders of the army and the police to lunch, and the forces of order did not intervene until 5 p.m., except to protect the palace. I myself saw policemen watching people light fires, and their only comment was: "Let's let them enjoy themselves a little." Farouk was fully informed and, as soon as he decided, calm was re-established.'

'What were his intentions?'

'First, to get rid of his Prime Minister, Nahas, an old political adversary. That has been achieved. Accusing him of negligence and incompetence, Farouk has replaced him with Maher, who is coming up to seventy, detests his predecessor and will oppose neither the king nor the British. Next, he wants a good reason to re-establish security in the canal zone and thus demonstrate his authority by reassuring the British army, which has just proved its determination and its firepower. That has also been done. This very day, the leaders of the nationalist movement demanding the departure of the British have all been arrested and deported to the desert. The drive for liberation has been halted, and the British secret service and

Farouk have come to an agreement and demonstrated their efficacy. Of course, there is no longer any question of breaking off relations with Great Britain and demanding that the soldiers leave.'

'You should be pleased!'

'On the contrary, Mr Wilder, for this is only an apparent victory. Already, rumours are all over Cairo, and people are accusing Farouk of being a criminal and a sell-out, solely responsible for the two hundred and seventy-seven fires that flared up and caused numerous casualties, both Egyptian and foreign. This strategy makes him even more hateful. And like Britain, he has no awareness of the real danger: Nasser. The lieutenant-colonel summoned all his entourage to a meeting to tell them that he felt ready to seize the capital. Since the army can provide covering fire, shouldn't they take advantage of this opportunity? They would occupy strategic sites and arrest the king and members of his government. No one has approved this plan, which is doomed to failure. The reaction of the British army would be bound to be extremely violent; there would be thousands of dead and Cairo would be occupied again. The thought of carnage had an impact on Nasser, and he stepped back. But he will continue to conspire and maintains his objectives. It is now that he must be broken; your friend John and the United States must stop wasting time. If you can convince them to take action, I will tell you about Durand.'

'Durand? But . . .'

'We shall see each other again soon, Mr Wilder.'

The lawyer had two urgent telephone calls to make, the first to Dusty Malone, the second to John.

Dusty's voice rumbled down the receiver. 'My God, you're alive! Those Egyptians are a bunch of crazies. I warned you.'

'It was just a riot that got out of control.'

'According to the media, the whole of Cairo burned, and there are hundreds of dead!'

'Only the centre was affected,' Mark corrected him, 'and Farouk has re-established order.'

'That city is a powder keg! Tomorrow, it will begin again. You must get out of there, and get out of there now.'

'That's impossible, Dusty.'

'Don't tell me that you have a sacred mission that you have to see through to the end!'

'As usual, you've hit on the truth.'

'Don't rely too much on luck, Mark. Your place is here; you know that. Only bad things happen to you there.'

'I'm being protected effectively, and I have no right to give up. If all my leads come to nothing, I'll come home.'

'Well, there's no lack of work, and several senators want to invite you to dinner!'

'Get them to be patient, and tell them I'm working for the United States. Isn't the Near East one of the keys to the future?'

'What I'm interested in is the pile of new cases!'

'Hack away at the undergrowth, and I'll deal with the rest.'

'Don't stay too long in that dangerous place, Mark.'

'Talk to you soon, Dusty. Love to the wife and kids.'

'We're all expecting you for dinner.'

The second call would be less friendly.

This time, John answered and arranged to meet the lawyer on a felucca, where you could drink tea as you gazed at the Nile, which people from Cairo liked to call 'the sea'. Painted blue, fitted out like a sitting room to meet the demands of British comfort, this particular boat no longer left the quay. Customers could buy alcohol and even drugs. When night fell, certain feluccas became places of pleasure.

John was smoking a cigar.

'This is a bad time, Mark. It's not just the enormous damage and the number of victims, it's the fact that a page is turning. Cairo and the British era have just burned away in front of our eyes, and Egypt is becoming a dubious country in the eyes of the great powers. As for Britain, she's decided to send several warships, including an aircraft carrier, to lie off Alexandria. Suez must not fall into the hands of the revolutionaries.'

'I saw Mahmoud. According to him, Farouk is responsible for the capital burning down.'

'That's possible, but we could also accuse the Communists and the Muslim Brothers, who can no longer tolerate the existence of bars, nightclubs, cinemas and big stores. Plus, poverty feeds rebellion in the masses, who are becoming increasingly hostile to wealthy foreigners.'

'Mahmoud told me that Nasser had temporarily given up the idea of taking power by force. America must exploit this period to stop the revolutionary process and prevent a cataclysm.'

'A choice between Farouk and Nasser . . . That's the problem, and I'm just a guy who obeys orders. Those two men are as dangerous as each other. By getting closer to the British, Farouk distances himself from the United States, which would very much like to see them leave Egypt and the Middle East so that we can succeed them.'

'Would we drop Farouk in favour of Nasser?'

'Mahmoud possibly overestimates his leader. Didn't he take a step back by deciding against a coup d'état? Nasser is probably just an agitator, who freezes at decisive moments. At present, we can control the situation. America advocates general appeasement, both as regards Farouk and the British. Martial law will be in place for at least two months, and I don't see the Egyptian army launching itself into a suicidal rebellion. Good old General Naguib will be able to calm down the Free Officers and make any hotheads see reason.'

'Mahmoud is going to give me some vital information regarding the Tutankhamun papyri,' revealed Mark. 'I've promised to find them and I'll keep my word. In exchange, he wants to know if America has finally decided to take Nasser seriously and prevent him from doing harm.'

Eyes fixed on the Nile, John blew out a cloud of cigar smoke. 'Tell him that we don't take his information lightly, and that the United States has decided to get involved in the Egyptian affair. Several secret agents will soon join my team, and we'll establish contacts with the different protagonists. Since revolutions produce nothing but misfortune, we'll attempt to avert chaos.'

'I want to believe you, John.'

'Well, I want you to find those papyri. Once we've seen their contents, we'll act accordingly.'

50

The café was in a pedestrianized alleyway. Its walls were covered with ceramic tiles, and it was full of old men. They chatted, read the papers, played dice, dominoes or cards, and drank strong, sweet tea or coffee, or a hot infusion with aniseed. Many were smoking the shisha, the water-pipe, as they watched the hot coals slowly burn away. Whether they smoked strong tobacco of good quality or a mixture of molasses and tobacco powder, the result was catastrophic for their lungs. But it was a deeply rooted habit, and the favourite occupation of male citizens of Cairo.

Mark sat down opposite Mahmoud.

'We are safe here. No police informant would dare venture into this café. On the other hand, several who are faithful to the Free Officers are mounting guard. Did you meet John?'

'We had a long discussion.'

'What is his position?'

'He's not convinced that Farouk is the only person responsible for the fires, but he doesn't rule out the possibility. While still wondering about Nasser's ability to foment a revolution, he's studying the problem closely and says that the United States is determined to deal with the Egyptian question properly. Several CIA agents will be strengthening John's team and will establish contacts with the principal players on the political scene.'

Mahmoud let out a long sigh of relief. 'Have the Americans made up their minds to break Nasser?'

'They want to get rid of the British without provoking murderous chaos.'

Mahmoud called for the café owner and ordered a banned drink, a green alcoholic beverage, quite thick and served in a small glass. 'We shall celebrate this, Mr Wilder!'

The lawyer was obliged to toss the whole drink down his throat in one go. The alcohol burned his gullet. Apart from a smell vaguely resembling mint, he could not identify the ingredients.

'At least I shall not have worked in vain,' said Mahmoud. 'If the Americans re-enter the game, Nasser has no chance of success and the revolution will not take place. As for Farouk, he will be forced to bend to the demands of the country's new masters and at last favour the happiness of his people.'

'I've fulfilled my part of the contract, now fulfil yours.'

Mahmoud swallowed his second glass in a single gulp. 'Your man "Durand" was working for the British secret service. He was married to an Englishwoman and kept files on foreigners who frequented the chic places in the capital. In exchange, he received a decent salary and an apartment in Zamalek. His dearest wish was to return to France.'

'Was he involved in Egyptology?'

'He was suspected of participating in small-scale trafficking of antiquities to bulk out his wages, but the police were asked to overlook that detail.'

'So he could have acquired Tutankhamun's papyri.'

'If that is the case, his wife must know where they are hidden. She is called Linda, and here is her address.'

Mahmoud scrawled it on a piece of paper. Mark learned it by heart and tore it up.

'An excellent reaction,' commented the double agent. 'You are becoming a perfect professional.'

'That was my last act. Now I am withdrawing from the game and I wish you good luck. As you suspect, I have an urgent task to perform.'

Once the American had gone, Mahmoud had another drink. On the verge of tipsiness, he felt euphoric.

Linda, Durand's widow, lived in a modern apartment block, near the Catholic convent of Saint Joseph. A *baouab* was mounting guard, seated on a bench. He acted as a concierge, watching who came and went, and kept out anyone who looked suspicious or undesirable. At well over six feet tall and impressively muscular, the Nubian was the ideal man for the job.

'I'm a lawyer and I have a meeting with a friend, Linda, the wife of a French businessman,' Mark told him.

The porter seemed annoyed. 'I'm sorry, you can't see her.'

'Why not?'

'Because she left, yesterday evening.'

'Have you any idea when she's coming back?'

'Never. She's left Egypt for good.'

Although the *baouab* spoke good English, he seemed ill at ease. It was obvious that he was lying. And Mark could not force him to tell the truth.

'Thank you for telling me.'

The lawyer pretended to leave, then hid behind a tree, some distance from the building but close enough to have a good view of the entrance.

A little after sunset, a little man with a moustache, dressed in European clothes, greeted the porter and crossed the threshold.

A light came on in a third-floor apartment: Linda's apartment.

A good hour went by, then the light went out.

When the man with the moustache emerged from the building, Mark followed him and approached him.

'I'm a friend of Linda's and I'd like to know how she's getting on.'

'I don't know her.'

'In that case, what were you doing in her apartment?'

The lawyer kept his right hand in his pocket, as if he was

holding a weapon. And the look on his face told the other man that he wasn't joking.

'I was one of her servants,' he admitted, 'and I had to clean the place before the new tenant arrives.'

'Where is she?'

'She's gone back home to England.'

'That's a lie,' declared Mark. 'I want the truth, or else . . .'

Hatred suddenly flamed in the little man's eyes.

'That bitch was English, and we, the people, detest the British and all other Westerners who have invaded our country and are getting rich on our backs! Thousands of fellahin have become their slaves. Greeks, Italians, Jews and all the others can get right out! Your Linda won't be oppressing us any more.'

'What happened to her?'

'Do you really want to know, foreigner? Well, I'll tell you so that you'll warn your compatriots and then take the first plane out of here! That slut was strangled by the Salawa, a demon which has risen up from the darkness to punish the impious. Your weapons are powerless against it. May it continue to destroy you!'

The little man with the moustache ran for his life.

Mark did not follow him.

51

Shattered, Mark informed Ateya of the latest events, not omitting a single detail.

'The adventure is over,' he said. 'I'll never find the Tutankhamun papyri.'

'Don't be so pessimistic, and don't underestimate Abbot Pacomas. If he entrusted you with such an important mission, it is because he believes you are capable of succeeding.'

'The last lead has been cut off once and for all.'

'Appearances are often deceptive.'

'Where are you taking me?'

'To Matarieh, north of Cairo. The abbot is waiting for us there.'

The very presence of Ateya gave mark some hope. Destiny's blows did not seem to weaken her, as if darkness could not obscure the light that radiated from her.

The young woman was a skilful driver and easily overtook the processions of donkeys pulling carts. Sometimes, one of the beasts would collapse, its heart giving out under the strain.

The suburb of Matarieh was made up of rather dilapidated detached houses. Ateya parked the car not far from a garden, in the shade of a sycamore tree.

Pacomas was sitting on a bench, meditating.

Mark walked slowly towards him.

'This is the place where the Holy Family took refuge,' declared the abbot. According to the Gospel of Saint Matthew,* an angel appeared to Joseph and ordered him to take his wife Mary and his son Jesus to Egypt, because Herod was planning to put the child to death. The Copts commemorate Christ's entrance into Egypt on 19 May with a fine celebration. In reality, it was not a flight, but a return to their origins. Christ came from an Egyptian initiatory brotherhood and attempted to pass on to the world a portion of the pharaonic teachings. A god-king, he succeeded the monarchs of the thirty dynasties which had re-created heaven on earth. And it is here, in Matarieh, after a long journey across the desert, that Jesus brought forth a spring of pure water where travellers slaked their thirst. From the sweat that flowed down the infant's limbs, Mary made a balm designed to cure those who were possessed. It entered into the composition of the oil used during baptism and drove away negative forces.'

'I have failed,' declared Mark.

'Look at that sycamore. It is the symbol and the dwelling of the sky goddess, Nut, who protected the Holy Family. On the border of death and eternal life, she greets those who are "of just voice" and procures the foods of the afterlife for them. In this century of violence and stupidity, whose eyes can still gaze on her mystery?'

'Durand's wife was strangled by the Salawa.'

Pacomas was silent for a long time. 'Sit down, Mark.'

At the feet of the American, Pacomas placed a saucer, in which he burned some alum. From it came a series of bubbles, then the alum was reduced to a carbonized mass.

'The eyes of the darkness have appeared,' said the abbot, 'and they are masculine in nature. Several times the Salawa has got close to you, but it has not identified you. Its prime targets were Durand and his wife, for they possessed vital information.'

'Since they're dead, we've failed completely!'

* 2, 13–14.

'Do not deceive yourself, Mark. The Salawa's intervention is in itself a rich source of teaching. It belongs to a category of demons nourished by a destructive fire, which are used by a very experienced mage. These malevolent spirits pollute wells and springs and control roads and tracks, where they cause fatal accidents. As the sheikhs can no longer combat them, they have asked for the help of the last Coptic priests in possession of effective incantations. I feared that the Salawa had successfully attacked the spring at Matarieh, but fortunately it is intact. If not, the circulation of celestial energy would have been interrupted, and no earthly power could have succeeded in killing the monster. Our struggle continues.'

'How?'

'Every Egyptian knows that, according to legend, the Salawa originates from Luxor. It is there, close to the tomb of Tutankhamun, that a manipulator awakened it. He has brought it to Cairo, made it play the role of arsonist and kill the Durands, who knew what had happened to the papyri. So you must go to Luxor, knowing that your mission is becoming increasingly perilous. You must attempt to contact your father's friends, who may possess vital information. By showing itself, the Salawa made a grave mistake: it showed us where to search. The Tutankhamun papyri probably never left the west bank of Thebes.'

'Who awakened the Salawa?' asked Mark.

'Only a learned and completely unscrupulous person could have committed such a terrifying act. I am thinking of a man of considerable stature who is known as "the professor", a man whose skills are universally admired.'

'Why would he have committed this crime?'

'Because he knows the papyri's content and considers it sufficiently effective to drive away the lies on which modern-day humanity feeds. If it is indeed the professor, the control he exercises over the Salawa proves his determination to strengthen the rule of evil. Do you wish to confront him, Mark?'

'Haven't I passed the point of no return?'

'From now on, you must wear only blue shirts. This is the colour of the god Amon, who holds the secret of life and is the guardian of the creative breath. I must again increase the strength of the protective circle which has prevented the Salawa from identifying you. That is why Ateya is going to drive us to Heliopolis, the most ancient holy city of Egypt, near the tree of the Virgin.'

Heliopolis was the place where the Great Seer had created the *Pyramid Texts*, a collection of incantations for the resurrection of the royal soul. Now all that was left of the prestigious city was an obelisk, around twenty metres tall and dating from the era of Sesostris I.

'Everything was born here,' revealed Pacomas, contemplating the stone needle that pierced the sky and dispelled negative forces. 'In this "city of the Pillar",* the ancient Egyptians perceived the omnipotence of the creative light, which they incorporated in their works. And the Tutankhamun papyri contain the recipe for this inexhaustible energy, the only thing capable of vanquishing death. Look at the magic signs engraved into that stone, Mark. Those are the words of the gods, and you must imbue yourself with them before confronting the demon of the dark and the malevolent brain that manipulates it.'

Mark concentrated on the hieroglyphs and had the feeling that they had a kind of never-changing life, fed by a secret fire. In Central Park he had been merely a spectator; here he was beginning to *see*.

Abbot Pacomas laid the seven seals of Solomon on the neck of Howard Carter's son, as he had once done for his father, and, in ancient Egyptian, spoke the words of the highest magic: 'May knowledge of the light parry the blows of destiny.'

At sunset, Mark emerged from his meditation. He felt as though there was a strange force within him, at once a kind of serenity and a desire for action.

---

* *Iunu* in hieroglyphs; 'On' in the Bible.

Ateya took his hand, her sea-green eyes shining with a strange light. Mark saw her as a different woman, whose magic was almost disturbing.

'We are leaving for Luxor tomorrow,' she told him.

'*We?* I refuse to involve you in such a perilous adventure!'

'Providence is watching over us: in the coming weeks I have to guide some small groups of enthusiasts around that part of the country. And how are you going to contact Carter's Egyptian friends without me?'

Mark had to face facts: without her, it was impossible to make progress.

'Abbot Pacomas has disappeared!' he observed.

'It happens to him from time to time,' said Ateya with a smile. 'Don't worry. He will reappear.'

52

The professor owned several apartments in Cairo. He often lived in an old building close to the museum, where a small army of servants saw to his comfort and well-being. There, he received discreet visits from scientific and administrative authorities. Playing on vanities and ambitions, he continued to pull strings.

It was now February 1952, and the political situation was not improving, despite the government's attempts. Maher, the new Prime Minister, was a skilful, cunning man whose team seemed capable of calming tensions. Rather pro-American, he had the ear of the business community and benefited from the population's trust.

But Farouk was increasingly loathed. Farouk and his clique of courtiers, Farouk and his band of drunkards, ready to eliminate anyone who opposed the tyrant's pleasure.

Following the Cairo fire, the official justifications had convinced no one. And the press had even dared to publish some semblance of an enquiry that tended to implicate the king. Accused of laxity, the Minister of the Interior,* had robustly defended himself. Before 1 p.m. he had given the order to shoot on the rioters, but this order had not been carried out, on the one hand because the police were helping the arsonists, on the other because the supreme authority was opposed to it. Despite

---

* Fouad Sarag el-Dine.

234

an emotive appeal to Farouk, the soldiers had not begun to deploy until late afternoon. Clearly, according to the Minister of the Interior, chance had played no part in these tragic events, which had been carefully organized.

Who benefited from this chaos, except the king? The army obeyed him implicitly, he manipulated the crowd as he wished and he made it known to foreigners and Egyptians alike that he was still the sole master of the country.

Fires, destruction, deaths, massive damage to the city centre, hatred among the communities ... This was what Farouk's brilliant plan had brought, while he hid in his palace, far from his people!

The professor listened to his visitors' recriminations and attached only minor importance to them. In the East, people liked to argue and protest. Actually taking action was a different matter.

The giant with the massive chest and the slender head, elongated like a jackal's, entered his office at midnight.

The Salawa was hungry.

'You have worked well,' conceded the professor. 'The Durands will no longer cause us problems. Come and receive your due.'

With his lighter, the professor fired up some hot coals, mixed with bones.

The Salawa downed them greedily.

'Do you think Durand or his wife had the time to confide in anyone?'

The Salawa shook its head.

'Is there still any adversary who wishes to find the Tutankhamun papyri?'

This time the answer was affirmative.

'Stay here and sleep,' ordered the professor.

The Salawa stretched out and closed its eyes.

Early in the morning the professor paid a visit to the administrative officers of the Cairo Museum. He asked them all how their families were and congratulated them on their excellent work in conserving antiquities. A favourable word from him was translatable into promotion and gifts, so the museum's staff proved affable and cooperative.

Taking account of the Salawa's opinion, the professor set out to find a curious individual who must have visited the museum and who had perhaps spoken to one of the officials to find out more about Tutankhamun.

The professor's best informant, a man with a moustache and a low forehead who was constantly in debt, was absent. He was taking time off after the birth of his eighth child, and his assistant did not have authorization to explore his files. Nevertheless, he did recall that his boss had recently received a visit from a foreigner and had got rid of him by sending him to the archivist. Unusually, no report had been written.

Intrigued, the professor went immediately to see the archivist, whom he found old and ill-tempered. Square-headed, with bags under his deep-set eyes, the official appeared depressed.

'You do not seem happy, my friend.'

'I've been refused a pay rise, my wife wants a divorce and my eldest son refuses to obey me! How do you expect me to be?'

'As regards the pay rise, I could help you.'

'Really? But I suppose it wouldn't come free?'

'You suppose wrong. I admire your work, and good work deserves a good salary.'

'Then you may consider me in your debt.'

'Did you recently receive a visit from a foreigner interested in Tutankhamun?'

'Indeed, Professor.'

'An Egyptologist?'

'I don't think so.'

'What did he want?'

'To consult the Howard Carter archives.'

'For what reason?'

'Personal research. He was persistent and I had to bow to his demands on the orders of my boss. In addition, the man had a letter of recommendation signed by the head of the Antiquities Department, Canon Drioton. I was a little embarrassed, for the Carter papers have suffered a good deal from the passage of time. But the researcher still spent long hours studying them.'

'Did he tell you if he had found what he was looking for?'

'No, Professor.'

'Did you take his name?'

'Of course.'

The archivist consulted his records. 'That lover of old papers is called Mark Wilder.'

'What is his address in Cairo?'

'I don't know.'

'Thank you for your help, dear friend. Next month, you will receive a pay rise.'

The archivist bowed.

The professor was not displeased. He knew the name of the final adversary whom the Salawa must kill. Now he must discover his profession, his intentions and his whereabouts.

Drioton's recommendation tended to prove that Mark Wilder had been admitted to Farouk's entourage. One man could therefore give him all the information he needed: Antonio Pulli, the man behind the king.

53

Ateya and Mark were waiting at Cairo Airport. The plane for Luxor was only two hours late, and this delay did not weigh heavily on them. Before confronting new ordeals, they were savouring their loving complicity, as if the future belonged to them.

A man stepped in front of them. 'We need to talk in private, Mark.'

'John! Are you leaving for Luxor too?'

'I'm sorry, but you're staying in Cairo.'

'Out of the question.'

'Let's go somewhere quiet.'

Ateya nodded her assent and the CIA agent led Mark into a quiet corner.

'As I told Mahmoud,' declared Mark, 'my involvement in your espionage matters is at an end. I have another mission to carry out and I'll not bend to your wishes.'

'You will go to Luxor after doing me one last favour.'

'You didn't understand me properly, John.'

'Friend, don't force me to repeat my threats. If you really love that woman, don't put her in danger.'

Mark's throat tightened. He felt like punching his compatriot in the head.

'What exactly do you want?'

'I want you to take this sealed envelope to Farouk.'

238

John handed Mark the document.

'What's in it?'

'That's top secret.'

'Not to me!'

'The less you know, the better.'

'I demand the truth.'

'As you wish! The CIA is promising Farouk that it will deliver him armoured vehicles and machine guns so that he can put a swift end to any new riots. So the king will understand that he has the support of America and that he is indebted to us.'

'Why am I being forced to act as mailman?'

'Because you don't belong to the secret services and Farouk trusts you. He regards you as a firm ally and will not doubt the veracity of the information. Antonio Pulli will be waiting for you at the Koubbeh Palace at 6 p.m. You will hand this letter to the king in person. If there's any trouble, retain the document and call me. But everything should go OK. Then you can leave for Luxor. So that's where the Tutankhamun papyri are, is it ... ? Don't forget, I'm really interested to hear what they say. Bon voyage, Mark.'

The Koubbeh Palace had no fewer than four hundred rooms and housed an impressive quantity of treasures, among them medals, chests filled with jewels, Fabergé eggs, paperweights decorated with precious stones and a fabulous collection of rare stamps, worthy of that belonging to the Queen of England. Farouk's wardrobe numbered around a hundred suits, ten thousand silk shirts and ten thousand ties.

Only a few people close to the king knew of the existence of more dubious items, such as a signed photograph of Adolf Hitler or a collection of erotic postcards. Obsessed with sex, Farouk also collected arousing marble statues, watches and musical boxes decorated with young nudes, suggestive calendars and even corkscrews designed to arouse the senses.

Antonio Pulli greeted Mark in a large office hung with numerous paintings.

'I received your request for an audience, but His Majesty is a little unwell. Can I help you?'

'Unfortunately not. I have to give him a confidential letter.'

'Be assured, Mr Wilder, that I will carry out this task scrupulously.'

'I don't doubt that, but circumstances force me to place this document in his own hands.'

Irritated, Pulli got to his feet. 'I shall see what I can do.'

Mark waited for over half an hour before Pulli reappeared.

'Follow me. His Majesty has agreed to see you.'

Farouk was in a dressing gown, seated in an armchair capable of supporting his weight, swallowing cakes and drinking orange juice.

'Leave us, Antonio.'

The éminence grise did so.

Mark presented the letter to Farouk, who broke the seal, read it and tore it into a thousand pieces.

'Excellent news, Mr Wilder. I am pleased, very pleased, and I greatly appreciate the attitude of my American friends. You can tell them that they will have cause to congratulate themselves in the future. Now leave me. I need a little rest before an official dinner.'

Mark found Antonio Pulli in the corridor.

'Is all well?'

'Couldn't be better. His Majesty is delighted.'

'Bravo, Mr Wilder! Our collaboration is proving fruitful, and the king likes your effectiveness and your discretion. In these troubled times, the aid of our American friends is like a gift from God. I shall soon have some new cases for you.'

The king's right-hand man really is very well informed, thought the lawyer. 'I'm leaving for Luxor for a few days' rest,' he said.

'A charming place! The temples and tombs alone are worth a visit, and the Valley of the Kings is an unforgettable place.

Ah . . . I almost forgot. An important man asked me how you were enjoying your stay among us. While praising your skills as a lawyer and your stature as a statesman, I reassured him that Egypt has charmed you.'

'May I know who asked about me?'

'We call him "the professor". He knows all the excavation sites, makes and destroys archaeologists' careers and enjoys general esteem. Doubtless you will meet him in Luxor. He will be very happy to chat to you. Have a good trip, Mr Wilder.'

On the way to the airport, Mark was overwhelmed with anxiety.

Now that he had carried out this final mission, he was no use either to Mahmoud or to John and was nothing more than an inconvenient witness to their secret activities. As for Farouk's friendship, there was nothing protective about that.

This was just the moment to get rid of him . . .

No, there were still the Tutankhamun papyri. But did Mahmoud and John really want to see them come to light?

Yes, so that they could seize them and use them as they wished.

At the very moment he found them, Mark would become as inconvenient as he was useless.

There was a crowd of police around and inside the airport. The lawyer was afraid there had been a murder and rushed to find Ateya.

An officer intercepted him and demanded his papers.

'Has anything happened?'

'Nothing serious. Do not worry. Just routine checks.'

Farouk wanted to show that he had a firm grip on the country.

At last he saw her. Sitting next to the departure lounge, Ateya was reading a book on the Valley of the Kings.

The next flight to Luxor was announced.

'Did everything go well?' she asked.

'Yes and no. I handed a confidential letter to Farouk and I hope I'm rid of the CIA. But the professor has discovered my identity.'

54

Mark loved Luxor. Far from the bustle, noise and crowds of Cairo, the little southern city's economy depended mainly on tourism. On the east bank was Karnak, an assemblage of several shrines, and the admirable temple of Luxor; on the west bank were other temples and numerous tombs, across several sites, the Valley of the Kings, Valley of the Queens, Valley of the Nobles and Valley of the Craftsmen. The extent and the richness of this realm of eternity made him dizzy. How many years would it take to explore it? And even then he would not be certain that he had understood all its secrets.

Howard Carter had devoted most of his life to searching for the hidden tomb of an almost-unknown pharaoh, certain that it was somewhere in the Valley of the Kings, carefully hidden. And when he stepped over the threshold for the first time, along with Ateya, Mark suddenly felt in communion with his father's soul. He heard the words he had spoken: 'The mystery of life continues to escape us. The shadows move but are never completely dispelled.'

An access corridor ending in an antechamber flanked by an annexe; a chamber of resurrection complemented by one room: Tutankhamun's modest tomb was a reliquary containing around three thousand five hundred items destined for the transfigured life of the pharaoh once he had become light. All the other tombs in the valley had been looted, their contents destroyed or dispersed. The magic of Tutankhamun, whom only the ignorant classed as a second-rate, unimportant pharaoh, had crossed the centuries until his encounter with Howard Carter.

Mark contemplated the ritual and symbolic scenes of the resurrection chamber, devoted to the opening of the reborn pharaoh's mouth and the sanctification of time, illustrated by baboons, the sacred animals of Thoth. Then his gaze fixed on the gold sarcophagus, which was still in place.

'The ancient Egyptians called the sarcophagus "the master of life",' said Ateya. 'For them it was not a place of death but of transmutation. There, the initiate to the mysteries became an Osiris and, living, passed through the gates of the afterlife.'

Now, facing this human being transformed into divine god, Mark understood the meaning and the scope of Howard Carter's Quest.

This was not just a mere archaeological find, even if it was the most exceptional find in history, but the unearthing of a mystery that touched the very essence of life.

And chance had played no part. The determination of a searcher who was tireless and cheerful; the will of the gods, who were still present despite humanity's blindness; the need to possess the message of Tutankhamun in order to combat the materialism and violence of a world turned head over heels.

Ateya and Mark strolled slowly, and for a long time, through the Valley of the Kings. They drank in the power of this alchemical crucible where Carter, in his own words, had participated in the plenitude and serenity of Isis, the great magician able to reassemble the scattered pieces of the murdered Osiris's body and drag him back from the sleep of death so that she could give birth to the saviour, Horus.

The eternal silence of the valley was not that of nothingness, but the condition vital to the process of resurrection. Here,

* *Neb ankh.*

between these arid cliffs, burned by the sun, nature revealed the mystery.

Was Tutankhamun's sarcophagus not an energy-centre, from which forces emanated that were capable of freeing human beings' hearts and so transforming them into creatures of spirit?

Howard Carter had reached what was vital, essential, and Mark must find the papyri taken from the tomb of Tutankhamun.

Mark and Ateya were far too lost in thought to notice that a fifty-year-old with a square head and greying hair was observing them. Since their arrival in Luxor, he had not taken his eyes off them for a moment.

Drinking a beer in the garden of the Winter Palace, under the blue sky of Luxor, was a moment of grace. Howard had often frequented this legendary hotel, where any Briton worthy of the name drank tea while gazing at the Nile. Here, crucial episodes of the 'Tutankhamun affair' had unfolded, especially when the Egyptologist had opposed the authorities in order to keep the upper hand regarding *his* tomb. Attacked, slandered, barred from the excavation site, Howard Carter had never bowed his head. And when he had returned to Egypt after the end of the works, anonymous and alone, he had appreciated the elegance and the charm of the Winter Palace.

Ateya waited until Mark's thoughts returned from the Valley of the Kings. 'You seem overwhelmed,' she commented.

'"Do you want to know who you *really* are?" . . . Now I know. It's so overwhelming and yet so exciting to be the son of such a father! I only hope I can prove worthy of him by carrying out the mission he entrusted me with from beyond the grave.'

'It seems you have no lack of determination or perseverance.'

'And then you came along, Ateya. Without you, I would have no chance.'

At sunset they walked along the Nile, like two carefree lovers. The gentle north wind provided a delicious coolness, and the river was bedecked in orange, red and gold. In a few minutes the sun would disappear into the western mountain, both to awaken slumbering souls and to undertake a harsh battle against the demons of the dark. Only the skill of the crew on its ship, including particularly the Word and the intuition of causes[*] would enable it to pass through the gates of the underworld one by one, pacify their guardians and kill the monstrous serpent, which was determined to prevent its journey. Knowing the right words of transformation into light was vital. Words that were contained in the Tutankhamun papyri.

'Just for a moment,' admitted Mark, 'I hoped that they would be in the king's tomb. But there's nothing left but empty rooms, with the exception of that fabulous sarcophagus.'

'We shall contact the last witnesses of Carter's adventure,' said Ateya. 'He had some loyal friends among his workmen, and some are sure to provide us with precious information. Abbot Pacomas has drawn up a list of names to help us. Two of Carter's Egyptian assistants even wrote to his niece after their boss's death, to offer their condolences. And your father bequeathed a small sum of money to one of them[†] in recognition of services rendered.'

They dined beside the swimming pool, reliving the dramatic time when Tutankhamun's tomb was discovered. November 1922: the last excavation campaign. Discouraged, no longer believing in the existence of an intact royal tomb containing treasures, Lord Carnarvon stopped financing the onerous, unproductive searches. But Carter succeeded in persuading him to grant him one more chance.

And on the morning of 4 November, the first step on the staircase leading to the sealed door of Tutankhamun's tomb had appeared. Ateya recounted the events in detail, and Mark felt as if he was at his father's side, as fantastic success crowned so many years of toil.

---

[*] *Hou* and *Sia*.
[†] Abd el-Aal Ahmed Sayed.

Then the two lovers returned to Mark's room. The rays of the setting sun lit up the bed on which Ateya and Mark lay, entwined. Facing the Nile and the western peak, they made love.

55

'Is it you, Mark, is it really you?'

'Of course it is, Dusty!'

'Where are you calling from?'

'Luxor, in Upper Egypt.'

'My God! What are you doing down there?'

'I'm exploring. Is everything OK at the office?'

'We're getting by, but I need some urgent decisions!'

'Send a summary of the cases and your opinion to me at the Winter Palace, using the diplomatic bag. I have to go now, but I'll call you back.'

'How long are you going to be away?'

'I don't know, Dusty. That will depend on how my investigation progresses.'

'Answer me honestly: have you got yourself involved with a woman down there?'

'Honestly, yes.'

'Is it . . . serious?'

'Very serious.'

'That's all I need! I hope you're not planning on getting married or anything?'

'I'm absolutely determined to. And you're going to organize the celebrations.'

'I can't wait to meet the happy bride! Why don't you bring her to New York right now? After the Cairo fire, Egypt has become a high-risk country. You're not safe there any more.'

'The CIA is controlling the situation.'

Mark heard a series of groans.

'Don't be too optimistic,' advised Dusty. 'In your place, I'd pack my bags.'

'I have to find the Tutankhamun papyri.'

'Clearly it's impossible to make you change your mind. Be careful, Mark. The rioters in Cairo killed some foreigners, and they'll start all over again. I'll send you the files.'

Four days of work, meeting people and talking.

Four days of disappointment.

Carter's friends and their descendants had vanished; some were dead, while the rest had left without leaving an address. And the few people left in Luxor who had known the archaeologist had nothing to say, other than expressing their respect for this hard-working Englishman who had never looked down on the workmen.

Through sheer stubbornness, Ateya managed to arrange a meeting with a sick old man who lived at Gurnah, on the west bank of Luxor. Before dying, he wanted to talk about the past and the excavations he had taken part in under Carter's direction.

Ateya introduced him to Mark, and they all shared in the ritual black tea, served by the extremely old sister of the centenarian, whose voice shook.

'I can scarcely walk now, and my days are numbered,' he confessed. 'That is why I am not afraid of the Salawa. It is different for the others . . . Since the demon reappeared, everyone knows that the curse of Tutankhamun will strike again. Even the most learned sheikhs are incapable of fighting it. The Salawa has already kidnapped and devoured several children, and it will punish the families of those who talk. Apart from me, nobody will dare to meet you. And I have nothing to tell you but happy memories. Carter was a tough, brave and generous man. He treated his workers well and knew how to fight adversity.'

'Did he find papyri in Tutankhamun's tomb?' Mark asked.

'So it was said, then the opposite was claimed. There were so many rumours and anxiety surrounding every item that was brought to light. I just concentrated on doing my work. And Carter always paid me well. The job wasn't an easy one, though, especially at Deir el-Bahari. His first big discovery, the discovery of the black-skinned pharaoh with the legs of a giant, that's one thing. But his second, the tomb of Queen Hatshepsut, could have cost him his life.'

'What happened?'

'As Carter had good relations with the locals, he was told of the existence of a tomb which was particularly difficult to reach, at the bottom of a wadi in the western cliffs. That was in 1916, when the absence of police and security men made it easy for thieves. And in fact some elders warned Carter that a band of looters had just entered this mysterious tomb. With no concern for the danger, he assembled a few workmen, including myself, and we headed for the site, arriving around midnight, after a long and arduous climb. And there we saw a rope disappearing into a hole. Sounds were coming up from below: the looters were at work. These men were violent, and we ought to have left. But Carter descended into the tomb alone and came face to face with eight bandits. He ordered them to leave the tomb immediately. Otherwise he would abandon them there and go and fetch the police. One against eight . . . They could have killed him. But they were utterly subdued, and chose to run away. And Carter explored the tomb.'

'What did he find there?' asked Mark.

'A magnificent sarcophagus made from quartzite, which is today preserved in the Cairo Museum. The lid depicts Nut, the sky goddess, stretched over the queen with her arm among the deathless stars. It was she who had protected Carter against the looters. And his two exploits at Deir el-Bahari earned him a reputation as a magician, immune to the blows of fate.'

'Your memories are exciting!'

'I have no more. Forgive me, I am tired and I need to sleep.'

'Will you see us again?' Ateya asked.

'That would be futile and dangerous.'

The old man, exhausted, was already dozing off.

Ateya and Mark left his house and walked through the village of Gurnah, built on tombs the inhabitants had looted. It was whispered that some still contained wonderful things.

The pair did not notice the man with the square head and the greying hair, who was following them at a distance. He saw them get into a taxi hired for the day and head for the ferry. With enough information not to lose track of them, he went back to his own car.

At the front of the ferry, overloaded with vehicles, donkeys, poultry and people engaged in intense discussions, Ateya and Mark savoured the refreshing breeze.

'Do you know any more about Carter's discoveries in Deir el-Bahari?' Mark asked Ateya.

'As early as 1893, when he was only nineteen, he worked on the site. In December 1901 he was riding on horseback when, suddenly, his mount's front hooves sank into the sand, and Carter was thrown off. It was a happy accident, since the miraculous hole enabled him to reach the tomb of a Middle Kingdom pharaoh, Montu-Hotep II.* His name means "the warlike power – Montu – is pacified – Hotep". His tomb was immediately named Bab el-Hosan, the "tomb of the horse".'

'Did it contain any treasure?'

'An extraordinary statue, now in the Cairo Museum, depicting the pharaoh seated, wearing the red crown and the white tunic that were worn during the festival of regeneration. The black colour of his flesh symbolized the process of regeneration. Montu-Hotep built the first great temple at Deir el-Bahari, a shrine to Osiris, beside which, much later, Hatshepsut created her terraced temple, "Sacred among the Sacred".† And it fell to

---

* Circa 2061–2010 BC.

† *Djeser djeseru.*

Howard Carter to explore the tomb intended for the Great Royal Wife Hatshepsut before she became pharaoh.'

'What perfect hiding places for Tutankhamun's papyri!'

'It will not be easy to gain access to them,' said Ateya. 'These tombs are closed, visitors are forbidden and very few Egyptologists know them.'

'Who can open them for us?'

'The West Bank Department of Antiquities.'

'I shall just have to use my talents as a lawyer.'

56

Mark's first visit to the West Bank Department of Antiquities was fruitless, for the officials responsible were absent. He was given an appointment for the next day, at 7 a.m.

While Ateya was guiding a small group of enthusiasts in Karnak, Mark went once again to Tutankhamun's tomb, to soak up as much atmosphere as possible in a place where incredible treasures had survived for many centuries, in the silence and darkness. Looters, archaeologists and tourists had trampled the floor of the valley without suspecting that they were walking over this reliquary, containing the secrets of eternity.

The second encounter with the sarcophagus was just as overwhelming as the first. As the *Pyramid Texts* declared, when the pharaoh departed he was not dead, but alive. Freed from his fleshly covering, transformed into gold by the rites, he joined his brothers the gods and reigned among the stars.

As he left the Valley of the Kings for the Winter Palace, Mark underwent a sudden transition. He left a supernatural universe, where time no longer existed, and came up against the world of human turpitude.

The news from Cairo was not good. True, Farouk had appointed a new Prime Minister, Hilaly, nicknamed 'the Don Quixote of the Nile' because he wanted to attack the corruption and unjustifiable privileges of the wealthy. To everyone's surprise, the king had even signed a decree obliging every

Egyptian to write a declaration of absolute honesty regarding the real origins of his wealth! Facing the hostility of the political staff, threatening to reveal the financial speculations of Farouk's entourage, the Prime Minister had abandoned his moralizing plans. Once virtue was dead and buried, people could return to their usual little games, under the paternal gaze of the king, who was indifferent to the people's anger and the disappointment of the army and the middle classes.

It was futile to deceive oneself: the status quo could not continue. Nasser was secretly advancing, as were the CIA. What option would America choose? What kind of Egypt did it want? How would it resolve the thorny problem of the Suez Canal and the British occupation? In Luxor, Mark remained apart from this turmoil, hoping that new disturbances would not break out before he found Tutankhamun's papyri.

Tired after answering countless questions from her tourists, Ateya was glad of a peaceful dinner in the gardens of the Winter Palace. And the words of love Mark spoke wiped away all her tiredness.

A few minutes before 7 a.m. Ateya and Mark entered the office of one of the inspectors of the Department of Antiquities of the west bank of Luxor. Aged around fifty, square-headed with greying hair, the official was drinking coffee as he listened to the grievances of one of his staff.

The visitors were invited to take a seat. First, they must prove patient, above all not interrupt the official, and await the moment when he would deign to take an interest in his guests.

A member of staff brought a tray laden with little cups of Turkish coffee, and the time passed slowly.

The inspector opened a large notebook, leafed through it attentively, wrote a few lines, then looked at the two visitors.

'How may I help you?'

'My name is Mark Wilder, and I'm a lawyer. As I have the good fortune to be able to spend a few days in Luxor and be guided by Miss Ateya, I would like to have access to some of the places forbidden to tourists.'

The inspector toyed with a pencil. 'I have heard of Miss Ateya. Apparently she is an excellent guide. She will show you the wonders of this ancient city. What do you wish to see in particular?'

'The tomb of Montu-Hotep II at Deir el-Bahari and the tomb of Queen Hatshepsut.'

'Those places are difficult to reach and have been closed up for a long time. Why do you want to see them?'

'I'm interested in the life of the archaeologist Howard Carter. After studying his notebooks in the Cairo Museum, I would like to see these two tombs, which he explored.'

'You are behaving like a real archaeologist, Mr Wilder! Are you thinking of changing professions?'

'Don't worry. I'm still an amateur.'

The inspector tapped the tabletop with the point of his pencil. 'I would be very happy to agree to your request, but it will be very difficult. Given the particular nature of these sites, I must submit a written request to my superiors in Cairo. And it is impossible for me to predict when I will receive a response. Nevertheless, you can be sure that for my part I shall do what is necessary. Unfortunately, I cannot promise you a positive outcome.'

'I really appreciate your efforts, Inspector. And I'm certain that you will be successful.'

'*Inshallah*, Mr Wilder. The mysteries of our government are sometimes unfathomable. But there are so many treasures to discover in Luxor! ... your days here will certainly be busy ones.'

Mark sensed that it was time to go.

'Where can I contact you?' asked the inspector.

'I'm staying at the Winter Palace.'

'A legendary hotel, one of Carter's fiefs! You are liable to encounter his ghost there.'

'How many wonderful memories it must have to tell!'

'I hope that your stay among us is an extremely pleasant one.'

New supplicants entered the office.

'I don't like that man,' said Ateya.

'Had you met him before?'

'We ran into each other in Karnak. He doesn't have a good reputation, and his attitude doesn't seem very promising.'

'Do you think he's playing games with us?'

'Not necessarily, but by following all the proper procedures he'll waste a lot of time. It's as if he wants to prevent you seeing those tombs.'

'Perhaps because one of them contains Tutankhamun's papyri ... Does he know that?'

'If he does, the doors will remain locked.'

'Could we force our way in?'

'Unlikely.'

'Let's be a little patient ... If that fails, we'll have to take some risks.'

At 10 a.m. the inspector got rid of a whingeing employee who was demanding a pay rise. Then he turned his attentions to a most important task: phoning the professor on the antiquated internal phone. Fortunately it decided to work.

'I have just seen Mark Wilder and his Egyptian girlfriend. They want to see the tombs in Deir el-Bahari that Carter discovered. I took refuge behind the administrative regulations. What am I to do?'

'Follow procedures. Write a formal letter to your superior.'

'Should we examine the tombs before we receive an answer from Cairo?'

'Absolutely not. Behave entirely normally and merely watch what Wilder does. Each evening, phone me with your report.'

57

Each day Mark went to gaze at Tutankhamun's sarcophagus and bathe in the mysterious aura of his tomb, emptied of its treasures. He had also visited the house of eternity of Pharaoh Seti II several times; Carter had used it as a laboratory and storehouse. But Mark found no trace of any papyrus. Late in the afternoon, before he went to meet Ateya, who was still working as a guide, the lawyer studied the documents sent by Dusty and called him to give him his instructions. The office was so busy that Dusty had had to take on two new colleagues. And New York was buzzing with rumours concerning the political destiny of Mark Wilder, who was on a study visit to the Near East in the interests of the United States.

He had never imagined that destiny would allow him to experience such intense love. In Ateya he knew that he had found his true soulmate.

Her soft, sinuous body stretched out on top of him.

'It's time to wake up,' she whispered.

'I'd rather go on dreaming ... I have my arms around a naked, loving woman, and ...'

'It's the spring festival today! Get ready, we're having a picnic lunch in the country!'

Sham en Nessim, 'the perfume of the breeze', was the Egyptians' favourite festival. Celebrated on Coptic Easter Monday, it brought together Muslims and Christians, the majority of whom had no idea that they were carrying on a tradition dating from the age of the pharaohs. The towns emptied of people, as everyone was eager to find a patch of greenery where they could share the traditional family meal of onions, coloured hard-boiled eggs, puréed beans and fish marinated in brine.* During this banquet, the Ancients paid homage to the fertility of water and earth. Their marriage ensured abundance, beneath the light of the spring sun.

Dressed in brightly coloured dresses and suits, little girls and boys had a wonderful time. Going from house to house, they received fruit or other gifts in exchange for decorated eggs.

Mark bought a garland of jasmine blossom and placed it around his fiancée's neck. They ate lunch in the middle of a field close to a village, sitting on a white tablecloth.

'I shall never forget this spring,' he told her as he kissed her.

'We are not here by chance. One of Abbot Pacomas's disciples lives in this village, a Copt who will tell us the truth about events in Luxor and will, I hope, enable us to meet people who were close to Carter.'

In accordance with the abbot's instructions, the lawyer wore only blue shirts and kept the talisman with him at all times. Even if these precautions seemed derisory to a rational mind, he could feel many strange forces around him.

After lunch the pair walked through a palm grove to a settlement made up of adobe houses with roofs made of plaited palm leaves.

Ateya stopped Mark from setting off along one of the paths.

'That path belongs to an *afarit*,' she explained. 'No one walks along it, because it causes serious leg injuries. We must go around it.'

Like so many other villages, this one had two main meeting places: the insalubrious-looking pond where crockery and

---

* *Fessikh.*

children were washed, and the beaten-earth platform where the villagers laid out those products of the harvest that were controlled by the tax inspectors.

On the walls of one house were scenes relating a pious villager's pilgrimage to Mecca. On the lintels of many doors there were horseshoes and terracotta hands, painted blue.

The Copt's house had one particular feature: its magical protection came in the form of four little diamond shapes. It had a small garden, in which cucumbers, basil, parsley and lettuces were grown.

Ateya opened a wooden door leading to two rooms, one serving both as a bedroom and a kitchen, the other reserved for the donkey and the chickens.

The owner of the house emerged from his siesta.

'Abbot Pacomas sent me,' declared Ateya.

'May God bless him! That man with you . . .'

'He is one of the abbot's disciples. You may speak freely.'

The peasant remained seated. 'A sad festival,' he murmured. 'A very sad festival. A bad wind is blowing on the village and the whole region.'

'What is happening?'

'The Salawa has returned. The curse of Tutankhamun is once again striking down those who have dared to disturb his sleep.'

'Have those who worked closely with Howard Carter been affected?'

'Two of his most loyal workmen have lost grandsons; everyone has gone to ground or is keeping silent. To talk of Carter and his discovery is the equivalent of a death sentence.'

'Have the police carried out an investigation?' Mark asked.

'They swiftly realized who the guilty party was and knew that they could do nothing. No weapon can destroy the Salawa.'

'Is there no way to fight it?'

'Our magic incantations have become powerless, for the kingdom of darkness is steadily growing. We must wait until the Salawa's anger abates and he returns to the fire at the centre of the earth.'

'You knew Carter's best workmen well,' Ateya recalled. 'If we meet one of them in the greatest secrecy, will he agree to speak to us?'

'Don't count on it!'

'It really is of the utmost importance.'

'You cannot imagine what terror is spread by the Salawa! Nobody wants to unleash its fury.'

'I think that I can make it return to its lair,' said the young woman, 'but only if I can obtain certain information.'

The peasant looked Ateya straight in the eyes. 'You speak the truth.'

'Help us, I beg of you. Our God will be grateful to you.'

'There may be one person who is sufficiently brave or crazy ... If he refuses, I will understand why. And if you have no news within three days, leave Luxor without delay. The Salawa would turn on you. Now leave. And head south and skirt around the village ... Evil spirits control the other paths and spread sickness.'

Ateya and Mark respected his warning.

They encountered a group of little girls, proud of their brand-new dresses, and walked swiftly in the direction of their taxi, which took them back to the Winter Palace.

At reception, there was a message from the inspector at the Department of Antiquities.

It authorized Mark Wilder to visit the two tombs in Deir el-Bahari.

58

In the bar at the Winter Palace, Ateya and Mark tried to forget their failure. Despite the official authorization, it had taken them three full days to obtain two separate, skilled teams capable of opening up the tombs of Montu-Hotep II and Queen Hatshepsut, which were difficult to access.

Long and patient exploration had produced nothing. Not the slightest trace of any papyrus, and no possible hiding place. These forgotten tombs were desperately empty.

Of course, the lawyer had enthusiastically thanked the inspector, without showing his disappointment.

'Don't lose hope,' urged the young woman.

'We have no leads. Where do we search next?'

'Pacomas won't abandon us. His prayers will produce a sign from heaven.'

'His disciple hasn't succeeded in persuading his friend to talk to us. All we can do now is return to Cairo and speak to the abbot.'

After one last whisky, they returned to the comfort of Mark's vast bedroom.

On the bed lay a sealed envelope.

Mark tore it open.

'Tomorrow evening we have a meeting with a Copt who lives in a street close to the centre of Luxor. He has agreed to talk

about Howard Carter's digs. But we must be exceptionally
vigilant, for the Salawa is getting closer to us.'

For the first time since he had embarked on the difficult life of
a double agent, Mahmoud was on the point of losing his cool
and yielding to terror. Lieutenant-Colonel Nasser's plans were
so serious that he must inform the Americans as quickly as
possible, via Mark Wilder.

But the American was impossible to find.

His and Ateya's apartments were locked, and nobody had
seen them in Luxor since they left the Winter Palace. According
to a police officer at the airport, a supporter of the Free Officers,
they had not taken the plane.

Were they hiding in Upper Egypt following a grave incident
or had they hired a car to get back to Cairo?

And what if they had been kidnapped or even murdered?

Who would commit such a crime, and why?

Knowing nothing exasperated Mahmoud. He could not contact
the British either; they had long since stopped believing him.
And if he tried to contact the CIA he was liable to be identified
and killed.

So Nasser had free rein to commit an act of insanity. It would
provoke a terrible reaction from Farouk and cause a bloodbath
in Egypt.

However, some of his entourage had advised him against
resorting to violence. But the lieutenant-colonel could no longer
bear the soft approach of General Naguib, who was incapable
of leading a revolution; and he wanted to do something really
big.

Long debates had failed to dissuade him. And then the question
of trust fell like an axe.

Nasser turned his gaze on Mahmoud, his eyes like those of
a bird of prey.

'You, Mahmoud, do you approve of my plan or not?' demanded
Nasser.

'I think it is perilous, but I agree with it. You are our leader; you set our goals, and we must obey you.'

Satisfied, the lieutenant-colonel could not doubt his subordinate's commitment.

'We should take precautions,' Mahmoud continued. 'Since we have succeeded in infiltrating Farouk's information services, let's persuade them that, whatever happens, the army will remain loyal to the king and protect him from any attack.'

Nasser had encouraged this course of action.

Now he was on his way to assassinate General Sirri Amer, Farouk's enforcer, who carried out the dirty work hated by almost all Egyptian soldiers.

This was an act of absolute madness, which would arouse the fury both of the government and of the British. As for the Americans, would they leave the game altogether, terrified by this violence?

Mahmoud smoked one cigarette after another. The death of General Sirri Amer would not remain unpunished. Naguib would be arrested, Nasser and the Free Officers would attempt to cause an army uprising, extremists of every kind would set fire to Cairo again, and the British would massacre anyone who attempted to seize the Suez Canal.

Chaos . . . The chaos he was trying to prevent would destroy Egypt in the coming hours.

At Nasser's HQ, nobody spoke. Everyone was awaiting the results of the commando operation devised by the lieutenant-colonel, whose last words haunted everyone's minds: 'Destiny is inexorable; there are no chance events.'

They drank orange juice, smoked hashish, recalled the leader's observations on the French Revolution, Robespierre, Saint-Just, and how to heal the sick motherland.

And Nasser returned.

White-faced, groggy, his eyes unfocused, he refused the chair that was offered.

'Is General Sirri Amer dead?' Mahmoud asked.

'We fired,' replied Nasser flatly. 'The sound of our weapons was immediately followed by the heart-rending cries of a woman and the terror of a child, which will pursue me to my bed and prevent me from sleeping. A sort of remorse gripped my heart, and I stammered: "Please don't let General Sirri Amer die!"'

Nasser fell silent and retired to his room.

'The general's driver was killed,' revealed one of the members of the raiding party. 'As for him, we don't know if he'll get over it.'

The night was endless.

At dawn, afflicted by a fit of coughing, Mahmoud left the HQ. He would not have been surprised to see armoured cars and hundreds of soldiers.

But the street was quiet, and the bakers were beginning to sell their flat-cakes stuffed with hot broad beans.

As soon as he'd bought the morning paper, Mahmoud took it to Nasser.

The lieutenant-colonel flicked through it anxiously.

'The general did not die!' he exclaimed. 'I haven't slept a wink, and I came to the point where I wanted life for the man I had wanted to kill. That type of action leads nowhere, and from now on I will not resort to terrorism. Without giving up our goals, we will take power in a different way.'

The day was endless.

Mahmoud expected the forces of order to react at any moment. But the district remained sunk in lethargy under the hot spring sun.

Late in the evening, a revolutionary who had infiltrated the palace procured some reliable information: having been skilfully misinformed, Farouk believed in the absolute fidelity of the army and regarded the attempt to assassinate General Sirri Amer as the act of a criminal madman.

The investigation would never lead to Nasser.

59

After the warning of an imminent attack by the Salawa, which Ateya took very seriously, she decided to leave the Winter Palace and take refuge at the house of the priest attached to the largest Coptic church in Luxor. A great admirer of Abbot Pacomas, he offered them a vast room filled with icons of the Virgin, which were endowed with enough magic to repel any demon.

At nightfall they headed for the meeting point. The centre of the little town was filled with passers-by and tourists, haggling over the price of garish souvenirs.

Ateya found the street easily.

Above their host's door were the protective diamond shapes. She asked Mark to knock loudly, three times.

The door opened, and a stooped man of around seventy appeared. 'Come in quickly.'

The dwelling was modest. A number of chairs, wooden chests and wardrobes were crammed into it.

'Take a seat.'

They took their places around a rectangular copper table, and the Copt served them black tea.

Ateya handed him the letter they had found in their room at the Winter Palace.

'I do not fear the Salawa,' he explained. 'For one thing, I have no family; for another, I am sick and must soon go into hospital. I will not come out alive. As I have already entrusted my soul to the all-powerful Lord, I have nothing further to fear in this world. That is why I have agreed to talk to you about Howard Carter, for whom I worked. He often gave me the task of sharing the wages among the workmen. As he spoke Arabic and had lived in Egypt for a long time, he had developed excellent relationships with many of them. He respected them, and they respected him. Yet Carter was not an easy man! Taciturn, bad at small talk, authoritarian, he demanded a great deal from his subordinates, but he led by example. Unlike other archaeologists, he did not simply watch his team working while he did nothing. With him, there was no question of lazing around. He sometimes got angry with idiots who didn't carry out his orders correctly.'

'Did that lead to bad feeling against him?'

'No, for he was a true leader and knew how to act as such. His outbursts woke people up, and nobody could accuse him of being unjust. Thanks to him, a great many peasants took part in long, well-paid excavations and improved their standard of living. On the west bank of Luxor, we have excellent memories of Howard Carter and wish there were many more like him.'

'Were you close to him?' asked Mark.

'No, but I knew them all, and particularly his right-hand man, Ahmed Girigar, to whom Carter dictated his instructions every day. According to him, extreme thoroughness was necessary. He considered himself a privileged intermediary between past and present. If through a lack of care, laziness or ignorance, he said, a researcher reduces the amount of information that could have been extracted from his discoveries, he commits an unforgivable archaeological crime. Nothing is easier than the destruction of testimonies to the past; nothing is more irreversible. Neither fatigue nor rain is a valid excuse. Doesn't an incompetent digger risk, in a few seconds, ruining a unique chance to enrich humanity's knowledge? According to Carter, if all digs had been carried out correctly and methodically, Egyptian archaeology would be twice as rich, for work on-site is of prime importance. He raged at the idea that countless items are abandoned in museum cellars and storerooms with no indication of provenance, without any written report on the place and circumstances of the find.* And the thing he feared most was theft. As soon as the location of Tutankhamun's tomb was discovered, he took infinite precautions, notably by placing a wooden grille at the entrance to the passageway and another, made of iron, in front of the antechamber. Members of the Antiquities Department, soldiers and the best workmen of the time took shifts to keep watch on the tomb day and night. As you can easily imagine, the whole region was buzzing with rumours about a fabulous treasure.'

'So nobody could have stolen anything?' ventured the lawyer.

'Not until 31 October 1929. After that date, because of serious conflicts with the authorities, Carter was no longer in possession of the keys. They were passed from hand to hand. He, who regarded himself as the owner and guardian of the tomb, was no longer allowed to work there, and he left Egypt to make his protests heard, notably in the United States. As his successors proved incapable of continuing the dig by resolving technical difficulties, and as the political situation had changed, Carter was called back and saw his adventure through to the end. During his absence, his enemies were able to enter the tomb.'

'Have you heard about any papyri being discovered?'

'That was one of Carter's great hopes. Such a find was indeed announced, then denied. Then Carter refused to talk about the subject, as if there was some kind of taboo. His solitary nature and sense of secrecy can never be overstated. Even in his writings, he is a long way from saying everything. In particular, he was very careful not to admit that he had explored the whole of the tomb along with Lord Carnarvon and his daughter, Evelyn, before the official opening. But who could reproach him for that?'

'Do you believe that these papyri exist?'

---

* These words of Howard Carter are quoted from his own writings.

The Copt hesitated. 'When I asked Ahmed, Carter's trusted man, he led me to believe that certain mysteries must not be revealed and that his lips would remain sealed. Nevertheless, I am convinced that he confided in the man who introduced him to Carter and who still oversees the villagers' well-being.'

'Who is that?'

'The eldest of the Luxor ferrymen. He owns his own ferry and only transports important people. If anyone knows anything about papyri, he does.'

'First thing tomorrow,' declared Mark, 'we shall meet him.'

'Impossible. He has left town to go to his granddaughter's marriage to a Nubian.'

'When will he be back?'

'Around 20 May. But don't get too excited! This ferryman is an austere, suspicious man.'

'Does he trust you?'

'He respects me, and I respect him.'

'When he returns to Luxor,' said Ateya, 'contact him and tell him about our visit.'

'I don't even know if he will agree to see you!'

'The will of God alone is done. And Abbot Pacomas will ask for His help.'

The old man nodded. 'You must leave by the back door, which opens on to a different street. Do not forget that the Salawa can strike at any moment. Nourished by the blood of its victims, it has considerable strength.'

'What is its preferred appearance?'

'It looks like a tall, broad-chested man. This enables it to loom over human beings and freeze its victim to the spot before killing it. Never return here. If the ferryman consents to talk to you, I will inform you.'

60

Ateya was guiding a new group, while Mark explored the Valley of the Kings. No house of eternity resembled another; each had its own spirit and passed on a specific message, forming the pages of a large book, which the seeker must put back together.

Each evening, the pilgrim ended his day with a visit to the tomb of Tutankhamun and an encounter with the sarcophagus.

Emptied of tourists, the valley returned to silence. The shadows lengthened, and the cliffs turned to gold in the setting sun. As he faced the pharaoh's golden mask, Mark thought of his father, that extraordinary man who had devoted his life to an improbable, even crazy discovery. And yet, through perseverance and courage, he had succeeded.

The ferryman must agree to talk and finally provide the right trail leading to the papyri. At the end of the day, didn't that depend on the will of Tutankhamun himself?

'I'm sorry to interrupt your train of thought,' said a steady voice, 'but I should like to introduce myself. I am known as "the professor", and the guards told me that you come here every day. Such an interest in this tomb intrigues me. Forgive my curiosity; it is a simple scientific reflex and I don't wish to importune you.'

The professor was a man of average height and no distinguishing features. Very elegant, he wore an immaculate white suit. Glasses with tinted lenses concealed his eyes.

Mark asked himself if he had fallen into a trap and if Tutankhamun's tomb was going to be his last dwelling, too. After all, the professor ruled over all the people employed in the Valley of the Kings and could unleash the ferocity of the Salawa at any moment.

It was impossible to take the measure of this adversary, at once invasive and impossible to grasp. Although accustomed to sizing up formidable opponents and finding ways of confronting them, Mark had never met such a fearsome individual, whose calm exterior masked a devastating power, like that of a cobra.

'Are you preparing a study on Tutankhamun?' asked the professor.

'My name is Mark Wilder and I'm a corporate lawyer in New York. Chance caused me to take an interest in the life and work of Howard Carter, the greatest of all Egyptologists. So my path inevitably brought me to this tomb.'

'A very modest place compared with the treasures it contained . . . This tomb was conceived as a reliquary, hidden for ever, whose radiance would enable the pharaohs' souls to endure for ever. Here, in the golden room, the secret of eternity is revealed. Even the king's name is a programme: Tut-ankh-Amon means "living symbol of the mystery". And that life, which comes forth from the mystery and is destined to return to it, can be felt by any attentive visitor. You see, Mr Wilder, this fabulous pharaoh had succeeded in controlling light and incorporating it in the alchemical gold of his sarcophagus. One text tells us that the man "of just voice" became a being of light at the heart of the sun and remained powerful on this earth, without dying a second time. This sarcophagus is not inert; it travels the heavens like a boat, under the protection of the stars, which bring it back to life night after night, day after day. Do the hieroglyphs engraved on the gold mask not proclaim "Living is your face, your right eye is the boat of day, your left eye the boat of night"? Come, let's go into the room that Carter called the "annexe". Very few visitors suspect how important it is.'

Mark was stunned. Why was the professor giving him the benefit of his knowledge, passing on all this vital information?

Obediently, he followed.

'This modest place symbolizes the final stage in resurrection,' revealed the professor. 'My honoured colleagues, the late lamented American Egyptologist Breasted and the English scholar Gardiner, succeeded in deciphering these texts, telling us that Tutankhamun constantly fashioned the symbols of the divinities and had established this house of eternity as if it were at the first moment of creation. Here you are, therefore, at both the origin and the end of all things, Mr Wilder; on the edge of illusory existence and real life.'

The two men remained for some time in the annexe, both silent.

'The time has come to close the tomb,' announced the professor, 'and to return to the world of human beings.'

They emerged slowly. Soon, the sun would set at the heart of the western mountain.

'I hope I have not bored you too much with these Egyptological considerations.'

'On the contrary, you have reinforced my research.'

'Would you mind telling me precisely what topic you are researching?'

'I was convinced that Howard Carter's discovery was of vital importance, and your words confirm that. Who would not be interested in the means of attaining eternal life by perceiving the great mysteries which the monotheistic religions have concealed?'

'In your opinion, Mr Wilder, what would those means be?'

'Aren't they revealed in the Tutankhamun papyri?'

'Those papyri do not exist,' declared the professor. 'The scientific community is unanimous on that point.'

'It has often been mistaken!'

'This time, it is right. Don't waste your time chasing a chimera.'

'Didn't almost all Egyptologists despise Howard Carter and regard his research as demented?'

'Do not persist, Mr Wilder. Egypt is a magnificent country, and you still have many completely real marvels to discover. In New York, you will retain excellent memories of your trip. Do not spoil it by undertaking actions that are doomed to failure. Listen to my advice, and you will spare yourself a great many problems. Enjoy the remainder of your stay.'

'You seem exhausted,' said Ateya worriedly, walking beside Mark on the path along the Nile.

'I met the professor.'

He had remembered every word of their conversation and related it faithfully.

'The threat was barely veiled,' said the young woman. 'Either you leave Egypt and forget about the papyri, and your life is safe, or else . . .'

'I will not give up. But that man seems very dangerous to me.'

The streets of Luxor were unusually busy.

'It is the first night of Ramadan,' explained Ateya. 'Despite the burning heat of May, Muslims may not eat or drink between sunrise and sunset. So when the fast ends, and before dawn, they must eat a substantial meal.'

Housewives prepared celebratory dishes, and believers enjoyed these nights of Ramadan, when the atmosphere was convivial.

A cyclist halted beside the couple.

He pushed up his shirtsleeve, revealing the Coptic cross tattooed on his wrist, and handed a letter to Ateya.

The ferryman had agreed to see them the following day, at dusk, on board his ferry.

61

As the end of the day's fast approached, the streets of Luxor emptied. Hungry and thirsty, Muslims hurried home, dreaming of cool fruit juice and the delicious dishes that were prepared only during Ramadan, such as pastries stuffed with pistachios and almonds, or cakes with angelica and cream. They would spend long hours at the table, telling each other a thousand and one anecdotes.

The minarets of the mosques lit up, and coloured lanterns were hung up everywhere. The sheikhs recited the Koran and reminded believers that man must submit to God and help the poor, secular cares coming second to religious preoccupations. Was it not said that a single wrong look or one lie destroyed the sacred nature of the fast?

Several sections of the population were exempt from fasting, notably some sick people, unclean women and participants in holy war.

Ateya and Mark walked to the quay where the ferry was moored. Although very old and frequently repaired, the boat still sailed from one bank to the other, dozens of times each day.

The ferryman was alone on board.

Seated in an old ebony armchair, he was wearing an ankle-length blue *galabieh* and a white turban. His stern face was deeply lined.

272

In front of him was a low marquetry table, on which stood a teapot and three porcelain cups.

'May your hospitality endure,' said Ateya.

'May your life endure,' replied the ferryman, his voice hoarse. 'I can offer you only a little tea.'

'I have brought flat-cakes and apricot compote,' answered the young woman. 'Allow me to offer them to you.'

The ferryman stared fixedly at Mark. 'You are the son of Howard Carter, are you not?'

Mark was dumbstruck.

'You were hewn from the same stone and you are as stubborn as your father. When he discovered the tomb of Tutankhamun, I had a violent argument with him, accusing him of profaning the tomb, thus unleashing an anger that the cliffs in the Valley of the Kings remember. The principal goal of an archaeologist, he said, was to save works from destruction and thieves. Without the work of Egyptologists, what would remain of the works of art dating from the age of the pharaohs? And he justified himself, with respect to Tutankhamun, by concluding: "This was not an exhumation but a resurrection." He cared more about that resurrection than about his own life.'

'Did he find any papyri?' Mark asked.

The ferryman hesitated. 'That is possible. Much was said of it, but Carter never consented to give any details, as if that treasure ought not to be revealed.'

'And you know nothing more about it?'

'Personally, no. But there is one person who must be aware of the details.'

Ateya and Mark held their breath. Would the ferryman agree to give them a name?

'Security was Howard Carter's obsession,' he continued. 'He needed a man he could trust, a professional who was absolutely honest and capable of preventing anyone from entering the tomb, even if they used force. No one spoke of that exceptional person. Carter himself promised never to mention his name.'

'Why?' Mark asked in astonishment.

'Because the real guardian of the tomb feared the pharaoh's curse. By remaining anonymous, he felt that he was safe from all evil. So he remained with Carter until the excavation site was closed, in 1932, and carried out his mission right to the end.'

'What is that man's name?'

'Why do you want to solve fearsome mysteries? Forget Tutankhamun and return to your ordinary life, far from this tomb and its dangers.'

'I've taken an oath and I shall keep it.'

'If I give you his name,' said the ferryman, 'you risk finding the papyri and unleashing events whose consequences you cannot control.'

'I am aware of that.'

'Are you ready to confront the invisible?'

'I shall not shy away from it.'

'Then so much the worse for you! Tutankhamun's guardian was called Richard Adamson. Born in 1901, he joined the British military police and occupied posts in Palestine and Cairo. In December 1922, at the request of Lord Carnarvon, who had the ear of the authorities, Adamson was engaged to maintain security at the recently discovered tomb, which had become much coveted. In plain clothes, with a revolver hidden in his pocket and an umbrella on his shoulder, he patrolled the site constantly. Invisible and unknown, he was instructed to take action against any suspect. From 5 January 1923 Howard Carter ordered Adamson to actually sleep inside the tomb. He had a camp bed with three blankets, a few books and some candles, as he had refused electric light. Can you imagine the incredible hours he spent in that magic place, right next to the pharaoh with the golden mask? Adamson had a unique experience; that place in the beyond became his home. During the period when Carter no longer had access to the tomb, Richard Adamson returned to England and married. Then, when his boss regained control, he returned to the Valley of the Kings and began to guard Tutankhamun's tomb once more. From 1925 onwards he was a civilian again, and the Metropolitan Museum in New York paid his wages. He remained as a security agent up to the moment when the last item had been transferred to Cairo and Howard Carter left the site. So he was your father's most loyal colleague and he must have been the only person your father entrusted with the secret of where the papyri are hidden.'

There was one question Mark was almost afraid to ask. 'Do you know if Richard Adamson is still alive?'

'No, Mr Wilder. He went back home twenty years ago.'

'Do you have an address, even an old one?'

The ferryman shook his head. 'I have nothing more to tell you, Mr Wilder. It is up to you to manipulate the past and the invisible. And remember that one false move will lead you to the abyss.'

62

At 3 a.m. all the inhabitants of Luxor – including Ateya and Mark – were awakened by a man playing a drum and singing to arouse Muslims from their slumbers so that they might eat before the sun rose.

The night was so hot that it was impossible to get back to sleep. Better to finish packing and drive back to Cairo.

An old Coptic servingwoman gave them some breakfast, and the priest who had taken them in gave them an important piece of information.

'A rumour is circulating: in a small village, about ten kilometres south of Luxor, an extraordinary discovery has been made concerning Tutankhamun. There was an attempted theft, but apparently the treasure is intact.'

'Do you know what it is?' Mark asked.

'People are saying there are papyri.'

'Show us the precise location.'

The priest sketched a map for them.

'I will find it,' said Ateya.

The pair, who had completely lost their appetite, left the city immediately, heading for the countryside.

Twice she stopped their Peugeot to ask the way. Peasants helped her and, when the sun rose after vanquishing the darkness, she set off along an earthen track bordered by small gardens.

A policeman ordered her to stop.

The young woman got out of the car. 'I need to get to the village.'

'Impossible.'

'Why?'

'There is a problem concerning antiquities.'

'Yes, and I am driving an official who needs to get to the site. He is an American expert who is here to assess the situation.'

'Ah ... Go and see my boss. He's at the entrance to the village.'

The senior officer was questioning some fellahin.

Ateya strode up to him determinedly. 'May I introduce Professor Wilder? He has come to evaluate the extent of the damage so that he can report back to the scientific authorities.'

'That's nothing to do with me. Go and see the Inspector of Antiquities. One of the villagers will take you to him.'

Ateya and Mark followed a peasant with a grim expression and a leisurely gait. He left the cultivated area and entered the desert. The path ended in a concrete hut roofed with corrugated iron. Several people were standing by the door, deep in discussion.

Among them was the inspector from Luxor who had authorized them to visit the tombs in Deir el-Bahari discovered by Carter.

'Mr Wilder! What a surprise ... You knew about this site?'

'I was told about recent excavations concerning Tutankhamun.'

'Mere rumours! But we have just had a small incident. On each site, we now maintain very strict surveillance. Each find is carefully registered and numbered and, at the end of the excavation, the items are kept in a building like this one, guarded by police. The entrance is blocked with stones and sealed up; hence, any attempt at theft becomes impossible. And when work begins again, checks are carried out in the presence of officials to verify that everything is intact. This time, something went amiss. The day before yesterday, a woman and a guard quarrelled. The basket she was carrying was overturned, and someone spotted rolls of papyrus hidden among the courgettes.

My superiors entrusted me with the task of inspecting this storehouse of antiquities, to find out if anything has disappeared.'

'Have this woman and her treasure been found?'

'The police are looking for her. If you want more details, go and see the village mayor. He is a very welcoming man, who is very concerned not to have any problems. In my opinion, this business of the papyri is not serious.'

The fellah took the pair back to the village.

As they approached the area where donkeys were unloading sacks of grain, one detail intrigued Ateya. A dozen or so of the beasts, although heavily laden, had halted some distance away, as if they did not wish to cross the space separating them from their destination. Ordinarily, they had need of no one to spur them on, happily trotting forward of their own accord.

There was only one explanation: a demon controlled the path. The donkeys feared it and were waiting for help.

'It is a trap, Mark. We must leave.'

Suddenly, villagers moved in from all directions, surrounding them.

They were armed with sticks tipped with iron blades, and flat-bladed hatchets. Although rudimentary, these weapons were no less fearsome and were quite enough to eliminate adversaries when scores were settled between clans. The police did not get involved, and there were no enquiries.

The papyri had been used as a lure.

Now the pair were encircled.

'Why are you so hostile?' asked the young woman.

'Because that foreigner has unleashed the anger of the Salawa!' roared a toothless man who had been smoking hashish. 'If we kill him, we will be delivered from evil.'

'You are wrong! This man is fighting the Salawa. He will find it and destroy it.'

There was a moment of indecision among the ranks of the aggressors.

'You lie, because you are his accomplice! You will die, too!'

The weapons were brandished menacingly.

Mark had only one card left to play.

Slowly, he showed Abbot Pacomas's papyrus.

When he placed his finger on the *ankh* sign, he spoke the word 'life' and the hieroglyph lit up. Believing that they were seeing flames emerge from the talisman, the fellahin froze and dropped their weapons. The terrified donkeys began to bray, deafeningly loud.

About fifty metres away, hidden behind the trunk of a palm tree, the Salawa was blinded. Overcome by pain, it did not see Ateya and Mark pass through the circle of attackers and run for their lives to the car, watched passively by the police.

This incident had nothing to do with them.

'We're off,' said Ateya with relief, flooring the accelerator.

'The modern world is wrong to deny the existence of magic,' murmured the lawyer.

'Pacomas's magic is particularly effective,' Ateya reminded him.

'I have no doubts about that. Next stop, Cairo.'

63

Three of Luxor's most important citizens came to the ferry as dawn was breaking. During the last hour of a short night, they had consumed a considerable number of spicy dishes and cakes, each more delicious than the previous one. There were good things about Ramadan, but now they had to face a burning-hot day without a drop of water to drink.

There was a crowd on the quay.

The most important citizen approached.

'What is happening?'

The onlookers parted.

The dignitary saw the corpse of the old ferryman, slumped beside some rope.

'He drowned,' explained a boy.

'Assuredly not,' disagreed the owner of a felucca. 'It was the Salawa that killed him. We must never talk when that demon emerges from the darkness. Never.'

The return to Cairo was uneventful. Ateya, an excellent driver, refused to let Mark take the wheel, as she thought he was incapable of adapting to the Egyptian rules of the road. Her vigilance enabled her to avoid at least ten accidents.

Abbot Pacomas laid his hands on their shoulders, magnetizing them.

'You barely escaped death,' he said. 'The Salawa set an

almost perfect trap for you by perverting the souls of the villagers. It was caught off guard when you used the talisman. Now it knows that it must destroy the talisman to fulfil the mission given to it by the professor.'

'Can it do so?' Mark asked worriedly.

'I have followed you constantly and strengthened your protection. But our adversaries' power is so considerable that the outcome remains uncertain.

Ateya looked rested and relaxed. The abbot's magnetism had removed all traces of tiredness.

'We may have the right lead,' announced the American. 'The guard at the tomb of Tutankhamun, whom Carter engaged, was a British soldier named Adamson. Although he doesn't feature in any official documents, he played a determining role. And if anyone knows where the papyri are hidden, that person is Adamson.'

Pacomas served his guests some superb vintage Armagnac.

'That is indeed an extremely important lead. That is why the journey to Luxor was vital. Providing you with the information cost the ferryman his life. The Salawa could not spare him. Now not a single inhabitant of ancient Thebes will dare speak. Only absolute silence may perhaps enable them to escape the monster's jaws.'

Mark appreciated the stimulant effects of his drink. 'I must leave Egypt and track down this man Adamson . . . If he's still alive!'

The abbot closed his eyes for a few moments. 'He is, and your journey will not be futile. Remain constantly on your guard, for the professor will be right behind you. Doubtless your actions caught him unawares. But if you return to Egypt, he will know.'

'I will return,' promised Mark.

'If you find yourself facing him, in a vast office lit by a French window, and if he says to you "I prefer the dusk; the light must be extinguished", do not hesitate for an instant. Run towards that opening and throw yourself into the emptiness. You will have only a fraction of a second to save your life.'

'Can't you prevent this meeting?'

'The hour has come to put an end to your illusions, Mark. The professor will not allow you to discover the papyri without intervening. And he always acts in the same way: he destroys his adversary.'

'Why does he reject the truth?'

Pacomas turned his glass slowly round in his hands.

'Because he is the embodiment of this world, and this world rejects him. Let your vigilance slip for just a moment, and you will fail.'

After recharging Mark's talisman, the abbot withdrew into his pharaonic chapel, devoted to the gods of ancient Egypt. He took off his Christian habit and put on that of the High Priest of Amon.

He celebrated the awakening in peace of the creative power, and recited the words of transformation into light, devised at Heliopolis, city of the sun. These words of knowledge and of magic, containing the secrets of the afterlife, had been revealed for the first time inside the pyramid of King Unas, the last monarch of the fifth dynasty.* This fundamental text, the basis of Egyptian spirituality, had gone through various adaptations, through the *Sarcophagus Texts* and the famous *Book of the Dead*, whose real title was the *Book of Coming Forth by Day*.

Tutankhamun knew everything about these esoteric writings. He had even developed certain aspects of them, notably those devoted to the birth of light and the creation of life. And the papyri offered the key to the great mysteries that scientists, despite ever more developed technologies, would never succeed in solving.

Pacomas relived the young king's funeral ceremonies. Through

---

* Unas reigned from 2375 to 2345 BC. Before, the pyramids, notably those of Khufu, Kephren and Mykerinos on the Giza plateau, seemed dumb. But their geometric shapes are in themselves a language and a form of teaching.

the *ka*, the indestructible vital power passing from initiate to initiate, Pacomas had participated in the ritual and followed the long path from the embalming workshop to the house of eternity. A procession of ritual priests had transported the precious objects to the tomb, carefully hidden so looters would not find them and thus endure through the centuries.

Tutankhamun had fully accomplished his work and guided Howard Carter to the house of gold, where a new sun had risen over a world in perdition. As the excavator's task was not entirely complete, it fell to his son, Mark Wilder, to write the last page of the adventure.

But the professor and his allies stood in his way, resolved to destroy him if he came too close to the goal.

So Pacomas must work even harder and provide Mark with the strength necessary to accomplish his mission. Would he manage to find Adamson? Would he return safe and sound to Egypt? Would he and could he use the information he obtained?

The High Priest placed his destiny and that of Mark Wilder in the hands of Amon, the hidden god whose real name was not known either by humans or by gods. He turned the unjust individual into a dried-out tree, destined to become wood for the fire; but he turned the just person into a tree that blossomed in the temple garden.

And Pacomas saw altars decked with flowers, smelled the perfume filling the shrine, heard the song of the priestesses celebrating the victory of light over darkness. How sweet life was in the shade of the palms, in the evening after a long day of toil, when the north wind refreshed hearts!

The time of serenity had given way to the time of battle.

64

Mark tenderly kissed Ateya, who had fallen asleep the moment her head touched the pillow, and went back to his apartment to pack his suitcases. Leaving the woman he loved filled him with anguish. Far from her, he would be fragile, half-blind.

'Don't switch the light on,' advised John's voice.

'How did you get in?'

'With a key. My technical department works well, and I hate leaving signs of my presence.'

'I'm tired, John. I want to sleep and I have no intention of helping you.'

'Sorry, my friend, but it's vital. During your stay in Luxor, the situation has deteriorated, and America no longer sees it clearly. Farouk and his corrupt court have settled in Alexandria to enjoy the Mediterranean breezes, far from the blistering heat of Cairo. The king no longer listens to anyone but his chauffeur, his valet and his butler. Even Antonio Pulli's warnings have no effect. Believing he has the situation in hand, fat Farouk is convinced that the people and the army adore him. All the same, he ordered the arrest of the officers who dared plot against him, but the investigation came to nothing. Revolutionaries among the military? Surely not! Only patriots, faithful to His Majesty. The disinformation practised by Nasser's agents is working wonderfully well. And he remains in a protective shadow. What is the right solution for a radiant future? Appoint good old General

Naguib Minister of War. Between banquets, swimming and sexy
frolics, Farouk thinks and searches for the ideal Prime Minister
who can maintain order without being too heavy-handed. All
this is just show! I need to know what Nasser is *really* plotting.
And you can find it out, thanks to confidences from Mahmoud.'

'I tell you again, John, I'm tired.'

'This is urgent and vital, Mark. Our country's strategy depends
on this information. Sleep for a few hours and get on the trail
first thing tomorrow morning.'

Ateya was more beautiful than ever.

When she opened her eyes, Mark stroked her face for a long
time. She smiled at him, and they made love.

As they lay there, their bodies entwined, they savoured the
love they had decided to build, day after day.

'John was waiting in my apartment,' revealed Mark.

'What did he want?'

'He demands that I get back in touch with Mahmoud to find
out the revolutionaries' real intentions.'

'Are you going to give in again?'

'John talks to me about the higher interests of the USA, but
all I can think about is Egypt. If I could avert more riots and
many deaths, wouldn't I be useful then?'

'Don't forget Tutankhamun's papyri.'

'Don't worry. I'm obsessed by them. After meeting Mahmoud
– and I'll get that over with as quickly as possible – I'm leaving
for England.'

'And you'll come back . . .'

Judging by the way Mark displayed his love for her, Ateya
could have no doubts about that.

Mark was right. Mahmoud's network was tailing him with just
as much vigilance and perseverance as John's. Scarcely had he
left the apartment building when a shoeshine boy came up to
him.

'Three mandarins for one dollar, boss.'

'I'll follow you.'

The black Peugeot was parked about a hundred metres away. The American got in the back.

'Did you enjoy your stay in Luxor?' Mahmoud asked.

'The place is unforgettable. If destiny allows me, I'll go back and stroll around.'

'Did you gather any interesting clues?'

'Possibly. The solution may be hiding in England.'

'Ah . . . So you are going to leave Egypt?'

'Only because I have to. And before that I have to reassure John. The CIA feels that it is blind and deaf. It considers Farouk irresponsible, incapable of appreciating the gravity of the situation, but it doesn't know the real intentions of Lieutenant-Colonel Nasser and General Naguib. John has instructed me to find out in order to direct American policy.'

'I have just attended a secret meeting with all the Free Officers who are concerned about independence. The kernel consists of fifteen men in charge of three hundred active sympathizers. Their objectives remain the same: to drive out the British, put an end to colonialism, take control of the Suez Canal, end feudalism, give politics priority over economics, satisfy the needs of the people, establish a democracy recognized by all and form an army to protect the nation. But this process must take place gently, and without spilling one drop of blood. Nasser was deeply shaken by the assassination attempt that went so badly wrong. He now rejects all terrorist operations and believes only in the power of ideas.'

'To the point of persuading Farouk?'

'If the Americans force him to take General Naguib as principal minister, all will be well. That decent man detests violence and will be able to defend the cause of Egypt as well as that of the king.'

'So there's no devastating revolution in sight? You are sure?'

'Certain.'

After telephoning John to reassure him and give him information indicating what course of action to take, Mark phoned Dusty Malone.

'So, are you coming back?'

'Just be patient a little longer.'

'Still in love, then?'

'You'll have to get used to it, Dusty.'

'You, married! I can't get over it.'

'You're the only person who can organize a ceremony worthy of the name. How's business?'

'We're managing, but you're a lot more indispensable than you think.'

'No catastrophes on the horizon?'

'No, but some are bound to happen!'

'I have to go to England, Dusty, and you need to prepare the ground for me.'

'Good God, what are you up to now?'

'I want to trace a British soldier, Richard Adamson. Howard Carter entrusted him with the task of guarding Tutankhamun's tomb. I'm certain he's still alive and that he holds vital information.'

'You don't know any more?'

'Unfortunately not. And I won't mention rumours; they might falsify your research.'

'What if this guy has retired to Australia, Papua New Guinea or the Fiji Islands?'

'You'll find him.'

'Hell, Mark! Do you think I have nothing else to do?'

'It's urgent and it's a priority. I'm taking the London plane first thing tomorrow. In my opinion, Adamson's living out his days in England.'

'You're becoming impossible, Mark!'

'Haven't I always been?'

65

In London, downpours were interspersed with light rain; this June was turning out to be rather unpleasant. Mark had spent the last three days at the British Museum, where he scrutinized every piece in the Egyptian collection. Morning and evening, he made long telephone calls to Ateya, who was showing European tourists around Cairo's Coptic churches.

Despite his efforts, Dusty had not managed to track down Richard Adamson. But the lawyer's right-hand man was not the sort to give up. On the contrary, difficulty spurred him on.

And his fourth call was distinctly more positive.

'Your Richard Adamson does indeed exist,' he announced brightly. 'He worked in Portsmouth, in an establishment linked with the Admiralty, settled there and married Lillian Kate Penfold there on 24 October 1924. To date, she's given him four children. During the Second World War he was a voluntary reservist in the Royal Air Force. A quiet man, with an uneventful career and family. I'm beginning to wonder if you've not been sold a useless tip.'

'You obtained his address, of course?'

'Of course. And I've even fixed up a meeting for you with him. I told him you were an insurance agent, bringing him some excellent news.'

'I'm not an insurance agent, Mr Adamson, I'm a lawyer. I practise in New York, and I'm trying to put together all the small details of my father Howard Carter's extraordinary exploits.'

'Carter . . . ? You don't mean . . . ?'

'Yes, the Egyptologist who discovered the tomb of Tutankhamun, which you guarded so vigilantly.'

Richard Adamson sank into an armchair and closed his eyes.* Suddenly, he left the cosy comfort of his home, filled with leather armchairs, woollen carpets and coffee tables, and found himself once more in the Valley of the Kings.

'Tutankhamun . . . There's only one person I have told about the unforgettable nights I spent in his tomb, right beside him, and that's my wife. No one can imagine what I experienced. My camp bed was between the wall of the funerary chamber and the sarcophagus, and I had never imagined I might be a pharaoh's bodyguard! At the start I slept a long way from his mummy. The further on the excavations progressed, the closer I got. I was in the presence not of a dead man but of a living one who was watching human beings. According to Howard Carter, Tutankhamun survived in the spirit of the gods, and I felt that truth. I didn't sleep much, for a thousand questions were going round and round in my head. I couldn't answer them, but I knew that something fabulous was happening to me. I attempted to grasp it all, to remember it all, to savour it all. A part of me is still in the Valley of the Kings; a part of my soul seeped into the sand and the stone. How could I forget the moment when I awoke, facing two statues of the royal *ka*, with black skin and golden aprons? According to Carter, they kept the pharaoh's spirit intact and protected his tomb from malevolent forces. And I asked myself: "What exactly am I doing on earth?" Would those two statues answer me by bowing their heads? Would they move?'

'Some people have accused Howard Carter of stealing items,' Mark reminded him.

---

* For Richard Adamson's memories, see E. Edgar, *A Journey between Souls*, Lafayette, 1997.

'Liars! My boss was the most honest of men. His triumph aroused jealousy among many second-rate people who sought constantly to destroy him, but he held fast. Today, those imbeciles are forgotten, and he remains the most celebrated of all archaeologists.'

'Why did you insist that your name didn't feature anywhere, not even in Carter's personal notes?'

Adamson hesitated before answering. 'Do you believe in the supernatural, Mr Wilder?'

'It's present everywhere in Egypt, is it not?'

'At the time of the discovery, there was much talk of Tutankhamun's curse. And that rumour didn't make me laugh. I watched and took note. And what's more, I brought back a few souvenirs.'

'Would you mind showing them to me?'

'This is my secret; nobody has seen these documents . . . One day they will belong to history.'

Richard Adamson went to fetch a suitcase, which he opened cautiously.

Mark's heart beat faster.

What if the guardian of the tomb had kept Tutankhamun's papyri in his house?

There were photographs, notes relating the stages in the discovery of the tomb and personal impressions, and a list of individuals struck down by the curse. Adamson had specified the age of death and the official cause. There were around forty victims, including Lord Carnarvon, Arthur C. Mace, Weigall, Georges Benedite and Lord Westbury.

'I was very close to the royal mummy for many nights, yet I didn't touch it. Why did Tutankhamun spare me, if not because he accepted my presence? Basically, thanks to Carter, he was reborn!'

There was no sign of any papyrus in the suitcase.

'My boss didn't believe in that curse,' recalled Adamson. 'But I preferred to be cautious. In any event, today I'm a happy man, with a wonderful wife and fine children.'

'Did Howard Carter entrust you with any precious documents?'

The former soldier looked astonished. 'I don't understand . . .'

'I'm thinking of papyri found in the tomb.'

'I was only a guard, not a scientist! That story about papyri caused trouble, as I recall. Carter had hoped to find some among the treasure, but he was disappointed. Or at least he was officially.'

'And . . . unofficially?'

'Apparently he really did find some papyri, but he believed that their content was too explosive to be divulged. That's why he felt it necessary to protect them from common curiosity, until a favourable moment arrived.'

'Who might he have entrusted with such documents?'

'Howard Carter was solitary and secret, suspicious of everyone, and had very few close friends. Only one man, in my opinion, would have been worthy of receiving the papyri and capable of hiding them.'

Mark contained his impatience.

'He was a mysterious individual and I don't know his name,' Adamson went on. 'Carter respected him and held him in high esteem, on account of his reputation.'

'Was he an Egyptologist?'

'No, a monk. A Coptic abbot from Cairo. I don't know any more.'

66

In the plane taking him back to Cairo, Mark read at least a dozen newspapers. None of them mentioned the political situation in Egypt. To all outward appearances, Farouk was holding on firmly to the reins of power, and the Free Officers were not thinking of fomenting a revolution with unforeseeable consequences. Once again, the fat monarch was cleverly using persuasion, cunning and corruption to keep himself on the throne.

Mark was still in shock after Adamson's revelations. So it was Abbot Pacomas who possessed the Tutankhamun papyri! But why had he sent him off to search for a treasure he had possessed for so long? Why had he gone to such lengths to hide the truth from him?

Completely lost, Mark could not wait to hold Ateya in his arms and give her the incredible results of his stay in Portsmouth. She, too, was being manipulated by this devilish abbot with incomprehensible goals.

She was waiting for him at the airport, dressed in a yellow blouse and a navy-blue skirt.

Taking no notice of onlookers' stares, they embraced for a long time.

'Do you have . . . the papyri?'

'No, Ateya. And I have some extremely curious news for you.'

'Mark, Abbot Pacomas has disappeared.'

'Disappeared . . . or run away?'

'Why do you use that word?'

'Because Richard Adamson told me that Howard Carter had entrusted the Tutankhamun papyri to Pacomas.'

The young woman looked stunned. 'Impossible! Does he have proof?'

'No; it's his opinion.'

'And he gave it in those exact words?'

'No. He talked about a Coptic abbot in Cairo with an excellent reputation.'

'It's not Pacomas, Mark! There are other holy men in our community.'

Once again, the American's certainties were shattered. 'Pacomas has disappeared . . . Are you sure?'

'Unfortunately I am! Only yesterday he told me that he was under threat and gave me an emergency procedure to follow in the event of misfortune. We must go immediately to the Hanging Church to contact a priest who can give us information.'

A strong wind was raising clouds of sand and dust. This was an exceptional phenomenon at this time of year, slowing down traffic, irritating the eyes and throat. Early in the afternoon it was so dark that drivers had to switch on their lights. The inhabitants of Cairo were on edge, and lamenting several people who had been seriously injured by building materials falling from roofs.

Inside the Hanging Church, a burly, bearded priest was baptizing a boy by immersion, seven days after his birth. Around the font, filled with holy water, stood seven candles. On each was an envelope containing a Christian name. The priest was waiting until the seventh and last candle went out, and the child would be given the sanctified name.

As the flame guttered, the priest looked at Ateya. 'Unfold the paper and reveal to us God's choice.'

'Cyril,' replied the young woman.

Ateya refrained from reading what was written underneath, in Coptic:

Pacomas has been arrested by Farouk's police. Go and see Abbot Shenuda in the city of the dead and ask him for the living stone.

'I know this man Shenuda well,' said Ateya, driving through a red light. 'He is older than Pacomas and has often worked with him on ancient Coptic texts.'

'Did he meet Howard Carter?'

'That is very likely, since Shenuda shared his time between Luxor and Cairo. He has always been close to Farouk and instructed him how to behave towards the Copts.'

'Could he have had Pacomas arrested?'

'That's unthinkable!'

'You're too much of an optimist, my love. Experience has shown me that human nature is capable of worse. If Shenuda felt that Pacomas was a hindrance, he has got rid of him.'

'In other words, he has found the manuscripts and decided to eliminate his adversaries! In that case we are throwing ourselves into the lion's mouth.'

'We must keep an open mind, Ateya. Abbot Shenuda may be an ally who can help us to save Pacomas.'

'I warn you, the city of the dead is not a pleasant place, and foreigners are not welcome there.'

'I shall rely on your charm to pacify the spectres.'

'Don't joke, Mark. Unable to find a proper home, many families have taken up residence in former Muslim cemeteries. A complete town has developed, with its own laws.'

'Why has Abbot Shenuda decided to live there?'

'He strives to help the poorest people, whether Copts or Muslims. The presence of a man of God relieves tensions and gives people hope of a better future.'

Ateya drove with remarkable dexterity and was able to manoeuvre the car through the heavy traffic, especially at crossroads. The use of the horn was vital, as were the art of overtaking and of zigzagging. There was only one rule: not to allow oneself to be browbeaten and always to take the initiative.

Seen from a distance, Bassatine, the city of the dead, looked like a vast medieval necropolis, where caliphs, emirs, sultans and princesses lay. Gilded domes, mosques in marble tiled with gold and minarets had once offered wondrous homage to the powerful people of that distant time.

But the living had decided that the dead were having things too easy and that their vast tombs would provide homes, which in many cases were more comfortable than those in the capital's deprived areas. The authorities had not made any move to stop them, and whole families had given themselves ownership rights without feeling they were insulting the dead. Marble tiles and gold strips disappeared one by one, and the ancient monuments were soon reduced to poor cubes of masonry denuded of all attraction.

The city of the dead had its own economy, its own leaders, its own guards and its own police. Order prevailed, and no one thought to disturb it.

Ateya parked her car near one of the entrances.

No sooner had she and Mark set foot in the city of the dead than a stocky man armed with a club barred their way. 'You don't live here. Turn around and go home.'

'We have come to see Abbot Shenuda.'

'Ah . . . You're too late.'

'What do you mean?'

'He passed away last night.'

'Was it an accident?' asked the young woman anxiously.

'No, just extreme old age.'

'Did he leave any message?'

'He was expecting a visit from a foreigner.'

'I'm American and my name is Mark Wilder.'

The guard nodded. 'That's the right name. But you'll have to leave anyway.'

'Why?'

'Because the funeral arrangements are going badly. Two clans are in dispute, both of them claiming the abbot's possessions. They would both rather destroy everything than see the others win and take them. The affair is turning violent; don't get mixed up in it.'

'Abbot Shenuda wished to bequeath the living stone to me, and I must honour his memory. To betray it would be unforgivable.'

'Well, I warned you, foreigner. Come on, then. Follow me.'

67

The guard guided Mark and Ateya through a labyrinth of narrow alleyways bordered by tombs. Suddenly they detected a strong smell of incense. In front of a caliph's tomb, which had become Abbot Shenuda's residence, was a pool filled with turbid water, in which a silver cross floated.

Two groups of ten men stood on either side of a coffin wrapped in a white sheet. The first was led by a blind priest, who was chanting ancient laments in a low voice while his assistants read passages from the Gospel of Saint Mark. At the head of the second group was a giant with an incredibly broad chest and a slender face, elongated like a jackal's.

Ateya thought she would die of fear.

'The Salawa . . . It's the Salawa!'

At the foot of the coffin, women laid baskets filled with round loaves. This was the soloist's salary, and his magical incantations would ensure that the deceased had a peaceful afterlife.

'Eat one of these loaves in honour of our abbot,' begged the eldest woman.

She handed it to the blind priest, who ate it.

'Give this food to the hungry,' he ordered. 'Shenuda helped the poor throughout his life, and his death will not prevent him from helping them now.'

'Those loaves belong to us,' declared a thin, hairy man who was standing to the left of the Salawa. 'No one is going to steal them from us. We demand the abbot's house and all his possessions.'

'Do not utter words filled with venom, my son. Let us celebrate the dead man's goodness and venerate his memory.'

'Your soothing words are those of a thief! The abbot bequeathed all he possessed to our clan, not yours.'

'Are we about to unleash a horrible battle instead of quietly meditating?'

'Be off with you, and no violence will sully this funeral!'

'My brother, your heart is in the grip of unjust hatred. Drive away this destructive fury, and replace it with the love of your fellow man.'

'The person responsible for our confrontation is not you, but the foreigner Shenuda wanted to inherit what is rightfully ours. And that foreigner dares to defy us.'

The Salawa's right arm stretched out towards Mark, and all eyes converged on the American.

'He is the embodiment of evil,' declared the thin man. 'We must destroy him so that the holy man's soul may rest in peace.'

Ateya felt her blood freeze.

Mark had fallen into the trap set by the Salawa. Once it had chosen its victim, he had no chance of escape. And the miracle of Luxor would not happen twice.

Remembering Pacomas's teachings, the young woman stepped forward. 'The soul of a saint becomes a bird, which flies up into the sky, and only the righteous may gaze on it. This stranger, the late abbot's heir, is one of them. If you attack him, you will be damned!'

Whispers ran around the Salawa's clan. One of his supporters fled. Even the thin man could not stop himself trembling.

The man with the face of a jackal took a step towards Mark. Rooted to the spot, Ateya could not speak a word.

Conscious of the infernal power he was about to confront, Mark held up Pacomas's talisman.

The Salawa froze.

For a few moments Ateya hoped that the papyrus would be sufficient to stop it.

But the monster started walking forward again, its eyes flaming.

The sign of the folded fabric, symbolizing a human being's cohesion, was erased. Next to vanish was the floral garland, the sign of flourishing. And then the Osiran pillar disappeared: the embodiment of stability.

One by one the Salawa destroyed the magical defences.

The prayer to Isis, protector of the infant Horus whom Set sought to kill, could not resist the monster.

All that was left was the looped cross, the *ankh*, emblem of life.

One more step and the Salawa would strangle Mark with its enormous hands.

Refusing to yield, he slapped the papyrus on to the Salawa's face.

Darting forward like a snake, Ateya bit it on the neck, in the place where the energy rising from the vertebral column radiated into the brain.

The *ankh* sign became blurred but was still legible.

The Salawa put its hands around its own throat and let out a shout of such violence that the throng scattered like frightened sparrows.

A pestilential smoke came from the monster's eyes. It shrivelled up until nothing was left of its massive body but a heap of ashes.

'You have delivered us,' said the guard thankfully. 'The holy man's dwelling belongs to you.'

In a state of shock, exhausted, ignoring the fear of those who had witnessed this insane drama, Ateya and Mark entered the tomb where Abbot Shenuda had spent his last few hours.

To their great amazement they found themselves in a vast room made up of ancient blocks of stone, some of them adorned with hieroglyphs. One of them bore the name of Ramses II.

'Many come from the pyramids,' explained their guide. 'The holy man liked to pray here for the poor.'

'Where is the living stone?' asked Mark.

'At the very back.'

There was an inscription on the stone, which the American copied out carefully. 'Did the abbot explain its meaning?'

'No,' replied the guard. 'Apparently it was a coded text, which he showed to a French priest.'

'Cryptography . . . Thank you, friend. I bequeath this dwelling to you.'

Ateya and Mark ran from the city of the dead. They could scarcely believe that they had succeeded in driving the Salawa back into its dark world but were convinced that they now possessed a vital piece of information. Perhaps this inscription would lead them to Tutankhamun's papyri.

One expert was sure to be able to decipher them: Canon Drioton.

Ateya drove faster than usual, refusing to give way to anyone.

'We want to see the canon,' said Mark. 'It's very urgent.'

'Impossible,' replied the servant who took care of Drioton's house. 'He is on holiday in France.'

Dejected, Ateya and Mark got back into their car.

'Drioton, Farouk's Egyptologist . . . The king is at the centre of the game, isn't he?' pondered the American.

'Pacomas could read this inscription,' declared Ateya. 'We must find him and free him.'

'You're right; that's our absolute priority. And I know who can help us.'

68

After winning a game of chess, Nasser lit up a Craven A. He smoked a packet of cigarettes a day and drank the odd glass of whisky from time to time, without feeling that he was betraying his faith. A lover of table tennis, and a great admirer of the famous Egyptian singer Um Kalsum, whose Thursday-evening concerts could last six hours, the 'postman's son', as some nicknamed him, also enjoyed classical music.

On this particular evening he was listening to a recording of *Scheherazade*, by Rimsky-Korsakov, a Russian composer whose Eastern inspiration charmed him.

When the record finished playing, Lieutenant-Colonel Nasser declared sharply: 'I have made my decision. We shall take action at the start of August. The officers will have been paid, and they will feel ready to fight for freedom.'

A seller of flat-cakes led Mark to Mahmoud's car.

'I needed to see you urgently.'

'Same here,' replied the American. 'Abbot Pacomas has vanished.'

'The Free Officers aren't responsible. It must be a dirty trick by Farouk's police.'

'I want to know where the abbot is.'

'That won't be easy; other priorities are demanding my attention. Nasser has decided to take action.'

'Action . . . ? What sort of action?'

'He's going to seize power in early August.'

'I thought he wanted to find common ground with Farouk!'

'The situation has got much worse,' lamented Mahmoud, deeply saddened. 'The king stubbornly refuses to appoint General Naguib as a minister, and he persists in wanting to dissolve the Officers' Club, despite his Prime Minister's opinion to the contrary. The members will be transferred into garrisons a long way from Cairo, Naguib included. In this way Farouk intends to break the backs of any conspirators. It's a veritable declaration of war against the army officers!'

'Will the Free Officers be arrested?'

'No. The organization remains out of reach, thanks to Nasser's system of keeping cells separate, and to his sense of secrecy.'

'Why does he feel ready to emerge from the shadows?'

'Because events demand it. The king is about to appoint his henchman, General Sirri Amer, as Minister of War. That butcher will surely succeed in unearthing the revolutionaries and will strike without mercy. So Nasser wants to act quickly. Farouk is still unaware of the danger. He has changed Prime Ministers once again, and his press attaché,* who organizes his nocturnal pleasures, answered an anxious journalist: "Dear fellow, we are the ones who provoke revolutions, when we consider them necessary. And it does not cost us a great deal." We are in a time of complete madness, Mr Wilder! But Nasser knows where he wants to go. Warn the CIA. Otherwise rivers of blood will flow through the streets of the capital.'

John lit his cigar. With one eye he was watching a tennis match between two pretty English girls who still thought that Cairo would remain a piece of the West.

'Did you meet Mahmoud?'

'He fears the worst,' said Mark.

---

* Karim Tabet.

'He's right. The Prime Minister cannot convince Farouk to be more flexible in his position regarding General Naguib. That fat despot thinks he still holds all the cards.'

'Isn't that what you think?'

'It's not what the American government thinks.'

'Is the CIA going to abandon Farouk?'

'Because of you, Mark. You revealed Nasser's central role to us, and we took account of that decisive information. Farouk is now nothing more than a puppet, incapable of weighing up the situation and acting effectively. Around him are courtiers, speculators, flatterers and liars. He played, and he's lost. Tomorrow it's Nasser who will lead the country. He will use General Naguib as a man of straw and get rid of the poor fellow when he decides to appear centre stage and take full powers.'

'What if he turns away from the United States and chooses other alliances?'

'We'll do what's necessary.'

'Don't you fear thousands of deaths?'

'That's the fate of all revolutions. America herself paid the price of blood in order to acquire her independence.'

'Can you imagine Mahmoud's disappointment and distress?'

'He's just a pawn on the chessboard. The stakes go far beyond him.'

'How can you be so cynical, John?'

'If you want to become a first-rank politician, you'll have to forget feelings and conscience. All that matters is the goal you have to attain.'

'Is the choice of Nasser a final one?'

'America wants a strong regime and a business partner. Farouk is so corrupt that he's becoming dishonest and ineffective. When is Nasser planning to act?'

'Early August.'

'Try to find out more.'

'I have another priority,' replied Mark. 'Abbot Pacomas has

been arrested by Farouk's police, and you have to help me free him.'

'Sorry, my friend, but my network must maintain complete discretion.'

'I've done a lot for you, John.'

'In my profession, reciprocity doesn't exist. I don't give a damn about your abbot. On the eve of a coup d'état that will alter the future of the Near East, I have other preoccupations.'

'Then don't count on me to help you.'

'Mahmoud is out of the race, and events are going to move fast. You should leave Egypt as quickly as possible, Mark. From now on, only bad things are going to happen to you.'

The lawyer got to his feet and looked the secret agent up and down. 'You regard me as a sponge you can throw away after you've finished with it, but you're sorely mistaken. For a second and last time, I ask you: will you help me to free Pacomas?'

'Security obliges me to say no. Out of the question.'

'I shall remember this, John.'

'History will make you forget everything.'

'You're forgetting the importance of Tutankhamun's papyri. Only Abbot Pacomas can help me to find them. And the future of the region, even our whole world, depends on what they contain.'

'I don't have time to wait, Mark, and I have to adapt to circumstances. Listen to my advice, and don't linger in Cairo. Your role here is at an end. Think of your career and go back to New York. An individual of your stature shouldn't get bogged down in a sentimental liaison which is doomed to failure. Senator Wilder will have no difficulty in finding a wealthy wife who belongs to the best society.'

A shout of joy echoed around the court.

With the aid of a decisive smash, the younger Englishwoman had just won the tennis match. John applauded.

69

'Neither John nor Mahmoud will help me,' Mark admitted to Ateya. 'They don't give a damn about what happens to Abbot Pacomas, and their only interest is in how the political situation develops. Farouk seems finished.'

'He could react with extreme violence . . . And I must tell you the whole truth.'

He took her in his arms. 'What have you hidden from me?'

'I am Pacomas's only daughter. My mother died when I was born. She was thirty-eight years old, and he was fifty. He surrounded me with such affection that I managed to overcome the absence and the pain. Leaving me free to act as I chose, he taught me everything.'

'As regards us . . . Have you spoken to him?'

'Of course. He knows that we love each other and approves of your marriage plan wholeheartedly.'

'*Our* plan!'

Ateya smiled. 'Our plan.'

'We must free your father! But how are we going to find out where he's being held?'

'I may have the solution. Pacomas is not only a Coptic abbot but also the last representative of the line of the priests of Amon, which has survived to this day, despite the successive occupations of Egypt. And I am the only person who knows the pharaonic chapel where he officiates each day. There, I hope to obtain an answer.'

Ateya went to Pacomas's house.

The police were not watching it.

At the back of the library was a wall covered in pious pictures. By pressing on the Virgin's face, Ateya made it pivot.

Mark walked down three granite steps and found himself in an ancient shrine full of relief carvings describing pharaonic rites. Stunned, he felt himself suddenly transported into a distant past where these symbols were full of power.

Ateya meditated before an offertory table dating from the age of the great pyramids. 'We must purify ourselves with fire and water,' she announced. 'Then we shall attempt to enter into contact with my father.'

Playing the role of a priestess, Ateya burned three small balls of incense, the *sonter*, 'that which makes divine'. The smoke perfumed the chapel and opened the couple's eyes to the invisible.

Then the priestess took a vase containing water from the *Nun*, the celestial energy where all forms of life are born. She poured the contents on to Mark's shoulders and on to her own. Thus they would hear the great word passing across worlds and space.

Ateya read out the last ritual her father had celebrated, devoted to the peaceful awakening of divine power. She invoked the protection of Horus the Ancient, the immense falcon whose wings spread as wide as the universe, and asked him to give her access to the spirit of his faithful servant, Pacomas.

The face of the priest of Amon appeared on the surface of the offertory table. Around it were the walls of a prison, bars, a corridor, a street and some buildings.

And then the image disappeared.

'I know that place,' declared the young woman.

At midnight on 20 July 1952 the principal leaders of the secret movement of Free Officers (with the exception of Sadat, who was on a mission in Sinai) met Nasser and General Naguib, who bore worrying news.

Despite numerous interventions, King Farouk would not move an inch. He was on the point of appointing the fearsome Sirri Amer as Minister of War, in order to control the situation tightly and eliminate all his adversaries, using force if necessary.

Thanks to the precautions taken by Nasser, the regime's police did not suspect the existence of this meeting.

'This time,' said the lieutenant-colonel, 'we are in danger. If we remain passive, we will be exterminated. The operation planned for the start of August would be too late. That is why we shall act immediately. No one will hinder us: the discredited government is residing in Alexandria; foreign politicians and diplomats have returned home for their holidays. In short, the way is open.'

'What is your plan?' asked one of the conspirators.

'The army corps we control will assemble at the cavalry command post. Then we will order the tanks to take possession of key locations in Cairo, while other troops seize the army's headquarters.'

A long silence followed these declarations. Everyone was aware that he was taking part in a historical moment, taking the right decision that would change the country's destiny.

No one objected.

'Absolute secrecy,' he demanded. 'Our success will depend on it. Let us prepare the coordination of our various attacks, not allowing anything to filter out about our intentions. One careless word, and we shall fail.'

Mahmoud was on the point of nausea.

The inevitable civil war would produce massacres on a terrifying scale. Who would be the victor: General Sirri Amer or Lieutenant-Colonel Nasser? Who would mount his throne on mountains of corpses and a devastated capital?

If the Americans did not kill Nasser, they would allow Egypt to run headlong into the abyss. No one could make him submit.

Farouk, on the contrary, would become a puppet in the hands of the CIA puppet-masters.

Mahmoud must alert Mark Wilder as quickly as possible.

Nasser laid a hand on his shoulder. 'You shall play a decisive role, my friend. Your men will serve as liaison agents throughout the hours to come.'

'You can rely on me.'

'Courage, Mahmoud. We shall triumph.'

The Free Officers dispersed.

Nasser walked past two police officers, who paid him not the slightest attention. Up to that moment, not one of his supporters had betrayed him. He felt so confident that the anguish of these past weeks disappeared.

And he strode forward like a conqueror.

Terrified by such self-assurance, Mahmoud was distraught. If he disobeyed orders, Nasser would swiftly notice. It was now impossible to escape the inexorable onward march of destiny. Had the Americans decided to support Farouk or abandon him? The postman's son had no idea how risky his bet was!

Man threw the dice, but was it not God who dictated how they fell?

70

Mark and John met on a felucca. Tea and pastries were served.

'What do you have to tell me that's so urgent?' asked the secret agent.

'I know the location of the prison where Abbot Pacomas is being held. You're the only person who can intervene and free him.'

'Don't have the time, my friend.'

'I have a coded text that Pacomas must decipher which will lead us to the Tutankhamun papyri.'

'Sorry, Mark. I have other preoccupations. Soon Cairo will doubtless be a bloodbath. America must extricate herself.'

'I'm not asking you, John. I'm ordering you.'

The spy started. 'Sorry?'

'Farouk probably possesses the final key, which I need; Pacomas will confirm that to me. In addition, he is the father of Ateya, the woman I love. If you refuse to intervene, I'll reveal your true role to the embassy and the press. And if you kill me, Ateya will do it instead – and after her all the Copts in Cairo.'

John was as white as a sheet. 'You wouldn't do something that crazy!'

'You don't leave me any choice.'

'Do you know who I really am, Mark? During the war against Israel, in 1948, Nasser had several contacts with an enemy captain. It would be excessive to talk of friendship, but the two men talked a great deal. The Egyptian was fascinated by the way the Jewish people had won their independence. I knew Captain Yeruham Cohen very well, and his information was useful to me in directing the policies of my two countries.'

'You mean . . .'

'I am Jewish and American,* and I have a network of twelve Israeli agents who have infiltrated the important machinery of the state and even the army. These men risk their lives every second. Do you want to be responsible for their deaths, following terrible torture?'

Mark pushed away his cup of tea. 'You win, John. I'll get by on my own.'

'You win, too. I shall deal with Pacomas, but I'll need two or three days so things can go smoothly. And I may need you at some point, to communicate a message to Nasser. Now you know why I can't meet him in person. He must never suspect that I'm in Cairo.'

Mark got to his feet. 'I assume it's pointless to tell you the location of Pacomas's prison? You know it, of course?'

'Correct.'

On the morning of 22 July 1952 it was hot and sunny in Alexandria. On the five-kilometre-long seafront, people were hurriedly crowding the terraces of cafés prior to lunching in fashionable restaurants. And in the evening, after a restorative siesta and a swim, during which elegant women could show off their one-piece swimsuits, they would enjoy themselves in nightclubs worthy of the European capitals.

The city founded by Alexander the Great was still cosmopolitan, welcoming all races and all cultures, a fact that irritated the fundamentalist Muslims who promised themselves

---

* John bore the code name 'Darling'. He was never identified and, when his network was dismantled on 1 October 1954, he still could not be found.

that they would curb it as soon as possible. For the time being, the beaches were full; Turks, Armenians, Italians, Greeks, Jews and other nationals made up a peaceful community whose chosen language was French.

Ordinarily, on 15 May the court moved to the Montazah Palace, where it resided for five months, far from the blistering heat of Cairo. The royal residence, beside the Mediterranean, benefited from sumptuous gardens criss-crossed by paths leading to arbours, an orchard, a farm, a dairy and the officials' accommodation. Of course, His Majesty had his own private beach.

Crowned with turrets and pinnacles, the Montazah Palace comprised three storeys. The ground floor housed the reception rooms, dining room, Farouk's office and billiard room; the private apartments of the monarch and his wife graced the first floor.

That morning Farouk was in a thoughtful mood.

At 5 p.m. he would greet the members of his new government at his other palace in Alexandria, Ras el-Tine. And he would announce his principal decision: the choice of Minister of War, whose task was to save the regime by protecting royalty against sedition.

In the face of incessant criticism of the appointment of the violent Sirri Amer, Farouk had changed tack. Once again he would surprise everyone and prove that he was still the sole master.

Particularly pleased with himself and his business sense, the fat man ate a hearty lunch, enjoyed a long siesta and was then driven to the palace of Ras el-Tine, which had been built by his illustrious predecessor, the Albanian Mehemet-Ali, a great destroyer of ancient monuments, lover of modernism and unsubtle tyrant.

The fifteen ministers making up Farouk's government were waiting impatiently. So many rumours, so much ill feeling and anxiety . . . Was the cosy nook of Alexandria nothing but an illusion? It was up to the king to prove his authority by taking the right measures. Since he possessed all the powers, it was up to him to use them correctly.

The discreet Antonio Pulli hoped that the monarch would follow his advice. Already, he had abandoned the trial of force with the army. All he had to do now was call on General Naguib in order to ease tensions, obtain public approval and set off again with a clean sheet. Farouk had made enough mistakes to derive useful lessons from them and choose the path of compromise.

The fifteen smartly attired figures lined up.

When the king's brother-in-law* appeared, the Prime Minister could not conceal his astonishment. 'Majesty, I do not understand . . . What is he doing among us?'

'Gentlemen, this is our new Minister of War. Let us set to work.'

The government withdrew.

Like the ministers, Antonio Pulli was appalled. Farouk seemed to have lost his mind in appointing an incompetent to this key post. His brother-in-law was no more than that and exercised no influence over the army.

Pulli looked at his watch: 5.15 p.m.

A serious time.

---

* Colonel Cherine.

71

Ateya and Mark had just made love when the telephone rang.

For the first time since the lawyer had known him, John's voice was shaking a little. 'Farouk has deceived those around him,' he revealed. 'He's ordered the arrest of all the senior officers suspected of being hostile to him, beginning with General Naguib. Those loyal to Nasser will be caught up in the turmoil. You must warn him immediately.'

'How am I to contact him?'

'I'm sending you a driver, who will take you to his house. Tell him that the United States will not disapprove of his actions.'

'I don't occupy any official post, John.'

'And that's why I'm entrusting you with this mission. If Nasser fails, our country will not be implicated.'

'Don't forget about Abbot Pacomas.'

'I've just bought the loyalty of the prison governor. Have a little patience, and your priest will be legally free. With Nasser, you're risking your skin. Try to be convincing.'

Mark hid nothing from Ateya.

The young woman pressed herself tightly to him. 'Don't go, Mark. It's too dangerous.'

'I've made a sort of pact. If I don't help John, your father risks the worst.'

They kissed as if they might never see each other again.

A white car was waiting for the American outside the building in Zamalek. The driver did not speak a word and drove fast.

Mark recognized the district and the house in Manchiet el-Bakri.

As he exited the vehicle, two men approached and stood on either side of him.

'I want to see Nasser,' he said firmly. 'I have vital information for him.'

Taking the American by the arms, the two vigilantes frogmarched him towards the leader's house.

At the entrance, they searched him, then the lieutenant-colonel appeared. 'Mr Wilder! What brings you here?'

'Farouk has demanded a round-up. His chief of staff has summoned those loyal to the king at 10 p.m. They will decide to arrest the principal opponents and proclaim the king's omnipotence.'

Nasser stared fixedly at his guest. 'Then I shall act sooner than planned,' he announced. 'Wait a moment for me.'

The postman's son donned his uniform, gave his brother all the cash he possessed, kissed his wife on the cheek and took the American by the shoulders. 'Come with me, Mr Wilder,' he said.

'One detail: the CIA will not move. And America will not oppose your initiatives.'

'Let's verify that on the ground, shall we?'

At 7.10 p.m. Nasser and Mark climbed into a Morris. The lieutenant-colonel wished to warn his main supporters that operation 'seizure of power' had been brought forward.

'If we control the whole of the army,' said Nasser, 'we shall succeed. That is what the United States wants, is it not?'

Mark nodded.

Suddenly they encountered a roadblock. Soldiers aimed their rifles at the Morris, which halted.

'I have given the order to arrest officers of the rank of colonel and above,' revealed Nasser. 'These fine fellows are carrying it out.'

The revolution risked failing because its leader had been

blocked by his own supporters! His uniform did indeed mark him out as suspect.

The American sprang from the car. 'We're going to the HQ,' he declared. 'The United States supports you and will drive out the British.'

A subaltern approached and recognized Nasser.

Immediately he let out a shout of joy, and the Morris set off again, to the accompaniment of cheering.

'You know how to keep your cool, Mr Wilder.'

'Doesn't my job as a lawyer consist of finding the right arguments?'

It was 11.15 p.m.

In accordance with Nasser's instructions, a regiment favourable to the revolution had just imprisoned the generals loyal to Farouk and charged with bringing down the conspirators. Unfortunately for them, they did not play chess as well as the postman's son, and he was one step ahead of them.

The HQ was in the hands of the insurgents. Attempting to resist, two sentries had been killed.

On this decisive night, these were the only two deaths to lament. Everywhere else, there were no other battles. The soldiers were rallying en masse to the Free Officers and were thus regaining their lost honour.

Dumbstruck, Mark observed an almost bloodless putsch, minutely prepared. The tanks occupied strategic points in the capital, and Sadat, a specialist in communications, quickly seized the radio. Now that the republic had a voice, it could soon speak to the people.

'You have succeeded, Colonel.'

'A vital step,' he agreed, 'but only a step. We control Cairo, and the army obeys us, but Farouk is still head of state, and his reaction is liable to be brutal.'

'The United States won't support him. My country doesn't want a civil war.'

'What will the attitude of the British be? They occupy Egypt and will not abandon the Suez Canal.'

'There will be diplomatic pressures in order to avert a bloodbath. Taken unawares, the British will not have time to organize an effective counter-measure.'

'I am indeed relying on that. Whatever the case, their fate is sealed. For many years I have been determined to drive them out of Egypt, and I will succeed.'

'If you bring down Farouk, what will you do with him?'

For Mark, the answer to this question was vital. If the king died brutally, Tutankhamun's papyri would remain inaccessible.

'In my experience,' said Nasser, 'blood begets blood. Some of my companions will demand the execution of the tyrant, but I will not. I shall try to find a better solution. In the meantime, one of my entourage will first contact the American naval attaché, then the British chargé d'affaires. He will inform them that General Naguib has been appointed commander-in-chief of the army and that the Free Officers control the capital. They will appoint a new Prime Minister and force the king to ratify this decision. If the USA and Britain refrain from intervening, there will be no disorder and no foreigners will have to suffer under the new power. Now, Mr Wilder, go home and switch your radio on.'

72

A little before 7 a.m. Sadat read a communiqué over the radio, a communiqué signed by Mohamed Naguib, commander-in-chief of the army. He announced to the Egyptian people that the country was finally emerging from the darkest period in its history. After so many years of corruption, the army had been purged and was led by honest patriots who deserved the trust of everyone. General Naguib would not tolerate any violence, and any troublemakers would be regarded as traitors and severely punished accordingly. The army and the police would ensure that the law was respected, and foreigners had nothing to fear. Calm reigned everywhere.

Mark and Ateya stood on the balcony of Ateya's apartment, gazing at Cairo. Mark held Ateya tenderly against him.

'Nasser has won. The British will bend, and the Americans will abandon Farouk.'

'They will hang him,' predicted Ateya.

At the foot of the building, a car stopped.

Out of it stepped John . . . and Abbot Pacomas!

Ateya rushed down the stairs.

Mark hurriedly made some coffee, which they were all in need of. The old man bore the signs of his detention, but he refused to talk about those painful hours.

'I shall never forget what you have done,' said Ateya to John.

'We were lucky. They're emptying the prisons, which were full of Farouk's opponents, and filling them up with his supporters. That's how it goes with revolutions. The Free Officers' worst enemy, General Sirri Amer, is on the run.* He could not find sufficient men for a counter-attack. Good old General Naguib is merely a puppet in the hands of Nasser, who now controls all the armed forces. As for the new Prime Minister appointed by the revolutionaries, the experienced Maher, he is seventy years old and detests the British. He will be a mere pawn on Nasser's chessboard.'

'Ah, yes, the British . . . How are they reacting?' Mark asked anxiously.

'They've been knocked for six. Their diplomats and secret service agents didn't see anything coming.'

'It seems to me that you misinformed them rather well.'

'Our British cousins are mad with rage but forced to bow to the fait accompli, particularly since the United States is not hiding its satisfaction. Neither opinion nor journalists have yet realized the sheer scale of these events. That will give Nasser time to deal with the Farouk case.'

'Is he determined to fight?'

'He doesn't understand any of it either and persists in believing that the army will remain loyal to him. Antonio Pulli, on the other hand, has no illusions. He has just had contact with the American ambassador† and is begging him to save Farouk. Although no American warships are near Alexandria, which suits us well, the diplomat has promised that the king's life will be saved. He went to the palace in person to serve as negotiator between His Majesty and the revolutionaries. From now on, Nasser is master of the game . . . It's up to him to decide. In the coming days, many CIA agents and "advisers" will arrive in Egypt to help the country to emerge from colonial oppression without sinking into a Communist hell. The New World is bringing help to the oldest of civilizations.'

---

* He was arrested while attempting to enter Libya.
† Jefferson Caffery.

'I must speak to Farouk,' said Mark.

'Stay here, with Ateya, and wait until the crisis is resolved. And above all don't attempt to go to Alexandria.'

'You've finished your mission, John. But I must still accomplish mine.'

'Those famous papyri ... Forget them, get married and be happy. Don't end up like that poor guy Mahmoud, who killed himself at dawn on the day of Nasser's triumph. Officially, he could no longer bear the pain of an incurable illness. Up to now, you've come out of it well; don't push your luck. You're a good guy, my friend. Doubtless we'll never see each other again.'

'Give me the necessary authorization to get to the royal palace in Alexandria.'

'This is madness, Mark. No one knows what's going to happen down there.'

'You owe me this.'

'As you wish. In an hour you'll have a car and a driver.'

Detesting congratulations, John slipped away.

Abbot Pacomas was beginning to regain his strength. His daughter Ateya held his hands.

Mark showed him the hieroglyphic inscription he had copied out in the tomb where the dead Shenuda had lived.

'"Seek the perfect god in whom one glories",' Pacomas deciphered. 'This is a text by Tutankhamun. Unfortunately it gives us no indication of the papyri's hiding place.'

Mark was deeply disappointed. This time he had expected to take a decisive step forward. But the treasure was still out of reach.

'You escaped from the Salawa,' Ateya reminded him, 'and that was a veritable miracle! Don't insult God, my love, and accept this defeat. Is that not your opinion, Father?'

'My daughter is right,' nodded Pacomas. 'To persevere would be futile.'

'Surely not! I have the feeling I'm close to my goal. Since

Farouk is going to lose his throne and perhaps his life, why would he continue to lie? Thanks to Pulli, I shall know the truth.'

'The risk is too great!' protested Ateya.

'How long would you love a coward, who couldn't keep his word? I made a solemn promise to your father, and I shall see my journey through to the end. When I've found Tutankhamun's papyri, we'll get married and you can choose which country you would like to live in. If Nasser's Egypt becomes inhospitable, America will welcome you, and your father.'

Abbot Pacomas gave an approving nod, and his daughter could not come up with any argument worthy of persuading Mark to give up.

The CIA driver had the necessary authorizations to get through any roadblocks between Cairo and Alexandria. As Nasser hoped, the country was not a bloodbath. Everyone could see, particularly because of the presence of numerous tanks, that the Free Officers ruled the capital.

But what would become of Farouk? Would the skilful conjurer of yesteryear be able to hypnotize his adversaries and regain the upper hand? Moreover, experts in Egyptian politics were predicting the failure of the Free Officers' movement, because of a lack of substantial leaders. Only Naguib, originally from Sudan, was fairly well known because of his courage during the war in Palestine. But neither he nor his obscure companions possessed the least experience in government, and their adventure was bound to end in disaster. After a few somersaults, Farouk would rid himself of these troublemakers. Wafd, the old nationalist party, would take over again and the soldiers would get back into line.

Everywhere, people gathered around their radios, hoping for detailed news that would put an end to the rumours. In the blistering heat, the streets of Cairo were almost empty. They were passing through a strange world, suspended between fear and hope.

As for Mark, he thought only of the brief journey between the capital and Alexandria. Would the gods remove all obstacles for him?

73

It was 25 July 1952, and Alexandria was calm.

Anyone would have thought that the revolution had not happened, and that King Farouk's court was spending its usual tranquil holiday beside the sea.

Thanks to his accreditations, Mark passed easily through two checkpoints and, late in the evening, was greeted at the Montazah Palace by Antonio Pulli.

Farouk's right-hand man had aged ten years.

'Have you come from Cairo, Mr Wilder?'

'Indeed.'

'Do the revolutionaries really control the city?'

'Without any doubt.'

'What about the population?'

'They are favourable to the revolutionaries. They promise independence and the end of privileges and corruption.'

'How disappointed they are going to be! Human beings must live on nothing but illusions. Why did you wish to see me, Mr Wilder?'

'I'm still searching for the Tutankhamun papyri and I'm certain that they are in the possession of Farouk.'

'Because of the gravity of the situation, I have sent a number of His Majesty's treasures out of Egypt. The revolutionaries would have burned them. When ambitious men greedy for power take control, they always begin by destroying things. These people will not feel the same respect for pharaonic culture as does King Farouk. They will drive out foreigners, and Canon Drioton will never again see his beloved antiquities. This is the end of a world which has been over-criticized, Mr Wilder. And the one that is coming into being will be much worse. You, the Americans, will soon repent having abandoned Farouk.'

'Have Tutankhamun's papyri left Egypt?'

Antonio Pulli hesitated before answering. 'When he met Carter, Farouk made him a promise. From time to time, the king has kept his word.'

'In other words, you know where they are hidden.'

'Indeed not, Mr Wilder. Because of the curse, I advised His Majesty against taking too close an interest in these documents. He was without doubt wrong not to listen to me.'

'Have you seen the papyri?'

'Never.'

'Do you know what they contain?'

'Rumour has it that they reveal the secrets of eternal life, prove that pharaoh is the model that inspired Christ, give the exact circumstances of the Exodus and predict the future of the Near East for centuries to come. Our contemporaries could not accept so much knowledge and wisdom. All they want are passions, beliefs and politics. Leave Tutankhamun's papyri where they are. Howard Carter was right to conceal them.'

'And what if they have a positive effect on the future?'

'My master, King Farouk, no longer has much of a one. And I fear I shall have even less.'

'Tell me the whole truth, Mr Pulli.'

'That is all I know.'

'The king may be living out his last hours. Allow me to see him and question him.'

'In these tragic hours, His Majesty is overwhelmed with work. Nevertheless, I shall attempt to meet your request, but do not hope for a positive response.'

'Beg him to give me the information he possesses regarding these papyri.'

'Why should he agree to do so?'

'Doesn't he wish to prove his generosity?'

'A servant will take you to your room.'

'What are your plans, Mr Pulli?'

'To enable His Majesty to emerge from this disaster alive.'

'And what about yourself?'

'The revolutionaries will not allow me to go abroad. In the eyes of the Americans, I am nothing now. And tomorrow my best friends will say that they do not know me.'

'I shall speak to Nasser. He's not a bloodthirsty man.'

'Do not trouble yourself, Mr Wilder. The leader of the revolutionaries must make an example, as people say. Am I not the best example of all?'

Although the Montazah Palace had entered a sort of lethargy, the staff were still doing their jobs. Farouk still reigned, after all.

Mark was provided with a sumptuous dinner, and one of the security officers ordered him not to leave his room, which was worthy of a head of state.

At 2 a.m. someone knocked at his door.

Mark awoke with a start.

It was the driver who had brought him from Cairo to Alexandria. 'Get dressed quickly. We're leaving.'

'What's happening?'

'The sound of boots. It seems this palace isn't very safe any more.'

'Where are you taking me?'

'To Farouk's second palace in Alexandria, Ras el-Tine. The new Prime Minister and the delegates of the US ambassador are already there. So you are bound to be safe.'

'Is the king there?'

'With his family and his advisers.'

Mark must obtain an audience, however brief. He had only one question to ask the monarch and needed to be sufficiently persuasive to obtain an answer.

The Montazah Palace was in its death throes.

No one knew who gave the orders any more. No one knew how many breakfasts to prepare, sheets to wash or services to render to a royal court that was falling apart. Nevertheless, appearances must be kept up, in the hope that the future owners would appreciate luxury and protocol.

'Do you have any specific information?' the lawyer asked his driver as they sped along the road.

'In Cairo, the line has hardened. Certain officers are demanding the immediate execution of Farouk, whereas others want to put him on trial first. In any event, it looks bad. Troops are said to be heading for Alexandria.'

'Isn't the CIA thinking of evacuating the king?'

'Out of the question. That would be an insult to the country's new masters, who want to settle their scores with him. We're not moving, just observing.'

At Ras el-Tine Palace, the anguish was perceptible.

Antonio Pulli was handing out orders to staff and thanking those faithful servants of Farouk who refused to leave.

'Mr Wilder . . . It would be wise to leave.'

'Will the king agree to see me, even for a minute?'

'Wait, I beg of you. But I cannot promise you anything.'

Mark had suffered so many disappointments that he ought to have yielded to scepticism. However, he felt that this course of action was decisive. Farouk, and he alone, possessed the key to the mystery. One word from him, and the way to Tutankhamun's papyri would be open.

But would he utter that word?

Servants bustled about, serving him coffee and pastries on solid-silver plates. The night was warm, the air delicious.

Several times, Mark saw Antonio Pulli running about in all directions.

A little after 7 a.m. on the morning of 26 July 1952, the sound of engines alerted the palace guard.

The lawyer rushed to the window.

A column of tanks were taking up positions around Ras el-Tine. Nasser had decided to launch his final assault.

74

The moment the first shots were exchanged between the king's guards and the revolutionaries, the monarch's order was issued: there was to be no fighting, the palace doors were to be locked and resistance was to be passive. No one could say that he had caused the deaths of any of the soldiers in his own army.

Although he was now a prisoner, Mark had only one thought in his head: to speak to Farouk.

Terror gripped Ras el-Tine. Clearly Nasser had decided to crush the despot's residence in a hail of shells. His corpse, and those of his entourage, would be found amid the ruins.

Fearing that he would be assassinated by the last few people loyal to him, who would thus exonerate themselves in the victors' eyes, Farouk had gone to ground in his office. He no longer spoke to anyone except Antonio Pulli, whom he asked to call the American ambassador, to beg him to prevent a massacre and to guarantee that he would be allowed to live.

The tanks remained in position but did not fire.

At 9 a.m. Prime Minister Maher handed Farouk a letter signed by General Naguib. The new commander-in-chief of the Egyptian army, once deceived and scorned, reproached the monarch for his bad management, his violations of the constitution, his contempt for the will of the people, and the presence in the government of traitors and dishonest men, making scandalous fortunes. He ordered His Majesty to abdicate in favour of the

Crown Prince, his son Fouad, and to leave Egypt that same day, Saturday 26 July, before 6 p.m. If he rejected this ultimatum, Farouk would be solely responsible for the consequences of his decision.

Stooped and hollow-cheeked, Pulli sat down opposite Mark. They were served tea and pastries.

'His Majesty attempted one final manoeuvre,' he revealed. 'He asked legal experts to study the validity of the document signed by General Naguib.'

'What was the result?'

'The ultimatum has the force of law. The king is obliged to bow to it.'

'What does he ask for in exchange?'

'The chance to leave Egypt aboard his yacht, the *Mahroussa*, with all his possessions . . . and myself.'

'What was Naguib's reaction?'

'The yacht he accepted, but he rejected the rest. The king's possessions must remain in Egypt . . . and so must I.'

'That's condemning you to death!'

'Let's not see things too blackly, Mr Wilder. Since Nasser does not want to see blood flow, perhaps he will be content to send me to prison for a few years.* As His Majesty refused to leave without me, I advised him to give up that demand. "I am staying," I told him, "and I won't be following you." My attitude astonished him, and I could feel his deep sadness. We both had difficulty in holding back our tears. The world we had hoped to build on firm foundations is crumbling before our eyes, and we shall not even have the comfort of friendship. His Majesty will sign his abdication at 10.30 a.m.'

'Will he see me?'

'We shall talk about that again later.'

Around noon, Pulli reappeared.

Terrified, his hands shaking, Farouk had taken three attempts

---

* Pulli was not executed and became the owner of a small shop.

to write his own name correctly. All-powerful a few hours earlier, all that remained was for him to pack his bags and leave once and for all a country he had thought would be subject to him for ever.

His son Fouad, only a few months old, succeeded him. This masquerade deceived no one. Nasser would push the child and General Naguib aside before imposing himself as absolute master of Egypt.

Hearing the rumours, a crowd gathered outside Ras el-Tine Palace. Inside, there was turmoil. Staff were preparing for the king's departure, knowing for certain that he would never return.

Mark was growing impatient.

If the terms of the ultimatum were respected, Farouk would leave his palace without speaking to him.

Around 5.30 p.m. the American Ambassador, accompanied by Prime Minister Maher, entered the drawing room where Farouk stood, in the white uniform of an admiral of the fleet. Next to him stood the royal family.

Delighted by the peaceful turn of events, General Naguib had not opposed this diplomatic gesture. America was hailing the departure of the former head of state and the inauguration of a new power. Everything went off calmly, between people who had decided to give up trying to kill each other.

To everyone's surprise, Farouk was taking only two suits and six shirts. Taking in her arms little six-month-old Fouad, the queen used a discreet exit to get to the port.

Servants transported the trunks to the yacht, while the royal flag above the palace was lowered.

Twenty-one gunshots rang out.

At the moment when Farouk was preparing to climb the gangplank, a Jeep halted next to him. Out of it climbed General Naguib.

Everyone watching the monarch's downfall thought that the victor had altered the rules of the game and that this day was suddenly taking a dramatic turn.

But Naguib wished merely to conjure up a personal memory, one of the outstanding episodes of his career.

'In 1942, Majesty, I presented you with my resignation in order to protest against the humiliation to which the British had subjected you. I was then a faithful subject of the Crown. You refused that resignation, and I remained in the army.'

'Take care of it, General.'

'Have no fear, it is at last in good hands. The air force and the navy will salute you when you leave territorial waters, Majesty. Now Egypt shall be reborn.'

With difficulty, Farouk climbed the steps to exile.

As for Naguib, he was cheered by a celebratory crowd. He headed for Ras el-Tine Palace, now the property of the Free Officers and of the Egyptian people, who would soon be allowed access to these residences filled with riches.

A sixteen-year reign was erased.

At the entrance to the gardens, Antonio Pulli approached Mark. 'It is all finished. His Majesty will never see his country and his people again.'

The American was in low spirits. Tutankhamun's papyri remained out of reach.

'Farouk did not have time to receive you, Mr Wilder, as I am sure you will understand. But he listened attentively to your request and ordered me to pass on this message to you: "Tell him to study Breasted's testimony, and he will know."'

75

The CIA driver took Mark back to Cairo.

Tanks were stationed outside official buildings and embassies, and the army was guarding the bridges, but there were no riots or movements of crowds. Thanks to the radio, the population knew that Farouk had abdicated and left Egypt. No confrontation; no victims. The streets were once again filled with passers-by, and the shops with customers.

According to one newspaper published in French, the king's departure resembled a miracle worthy of Lourdes. General Naguib had become a national hero, a sort of saint who had driven out injustice and corruption.

A few overexcited people knocked down the gates of the Ezbekeya garden. From now on, the poor would not have to pay one piastre to enter this green space, which had formerly been reserved for the rich. Acacia, palm and mulberry trees would be cut down to make way for apartment blocks to house the disadvantaged.

People no longer spoke of 'royalty' but of 'the homeland'. And the Council of Regency, granting power to a child of six months who did not even reside in Egypt, would swiftly be replaced by a strong government whose true leader would be known only by a privileged few: the postman's son, Lieutenant-Colonel Nasser. An officer had just asked him to arrest singer Um Kalsum, as she was too close to Farouk. The head of the revolutionaries gave a stinging reply: 'I did not order you to destroy the pyramids!'

However, in cafés and around the family dining table, people wondered: would the new Egypt be a Communist satellite? Would foreigners be expelled? Would the army impose a dictatorship?

The euphoria that had accompanied Farouk's departure was succeeded by anxiety.

Mark forgot his preoccupations to embrace Ateya.

'I was so afraid I would never see you again,' she admitted. 'Some people were talking about bloody battles, the assassination of Farouk and the massacre of his entourage. And my father . . .'

'Your father?'

'He is dying, Mark. Although he denies it, detention and torture took away the last of his strength. Since you left, he no longer gets out of bed and has refused all food.'

'Have you called a doctor?'

'Of course, and he has left me no hope. Abbot Pacomas has only hours left.'

'Perhaps I can offer him one last cause for happiness.'

'The Tutankhamun papyri . . .'

'Farouk gave me a clue. Only your father can appreciate its value.'

When Mark entered Pacomas's room, the last High Priest of Amon opened his eyes. He was barely breathing.

'I was waiting for you, Mark. You have succeeded, haven't you?'

'Farouk knew the truth regarding the papyri. Before leaving Egypt, he revealed that Breasted's testimony would enable me to understand.'

James Henry Breasted, an American archaeologist who, under Carter's direction, had taken part in the excavation of Tutankhamun's tomb.

'I remember that stern man,' murmured Abbot Pacomas, whose

breathing seemed increasingly short. 'He was no ordinary scholar and no narrow-minded Egyptologist. On the contrary, he admired the spirituality of ancient Egypt. And when he worked inside the tomb, he heard the voices of the ancestors in the form of strange rustlings, which were attributed to alterations in the air inside the tomb. Breasted experienced an intense feeling of death and of the wear and tear of time. "The life of all the marvels that surround me is limited," he lamented; "in a few generations, the objects which are not made of stone, metal or ceramics will disappear."'

Although moving, the American archaeologist's feelings did not provide the smallest clue.

'Why did Farouk say that Breasted's testimony was vital?' Mark asked.

Abbot Pacomas took a deep breath. 'I remember . . . Yes, I remember! Breasted talked of Tutankhamun as a generous sovereign ruling at the time when Moses had not yet been born, and he was interested in the seals and inscriptions which were so difficult to decipher. And suddenly he saw one of the large, black-skinned statues which guarded the pharaoh's tomb wink an eye. It was alive and it was looking at him. Terrified, he felt like running away. Overcoming his terror, he plucked up the courage to approach. Then Tutankhamun passed on his final secret to him. Next, an acceptable explanation had to be given. Weren't the statue's eyebrows made up of a pigment that had flaked off and flashed as it did so?'

Abbot Pacomas overcame his exhaustion. He must bequeath every small memory to Howard Carter's son, enabling him to see his Quest through to the end.

'These two large individuals* are made of red wood covered in gold. They embody the *ka* of Tutankhamun, a spiritual giant whose task was to pass on the knowledge of the great mysteries to future generations. Symbols of those "of just voice", they

---

* 1.92 metres, including the base.

were honoured by a bouquet of eternity, evoking their perpetual blossoming, and watched over the journey between the antechamber and the chamber of resurrection, which was accessible only to the being of light.'

Pacomas propped himself up on his elbows. 'The text found at the home of Abbot Shenuda – "Search for the perfect god, in whom one glories" – is inscribed on one of the statues, charged with guiding the royal soul into the other world.'

'That means . . .'

'That means that Tutankhamun's papyri are hidden inside one of the statues, or perhaps both.'

Ateya squeezed Mark's hand.

Now they knew.

'You have travelled a long road,' said Pacomas. 'Now the truth is within your grasp.'

'You taught me everything, Father.'

'Your true father was Howard Carter. I am merely the intermediary between you and the world beyond. As I leave this earth, I have no right to tell you what to do. You know who you really are, Mark. That treasure is worth all the others.'

'Are you urging me to give up, when I'm so close to my goal?'

'Have you not discovered happiness? The time to risk your life is past.'

'You entrusted me with a mission, and I gave you my word.'

'I free you from it, Mark.'

'There's no better way to make me keep it. And I shall not disappoint you. First thing tomorrow, I shall go to the Cairo Museum and persuade the curator to extract the papyri from those statues.'

'I should like to gaze on the sunset,' said the abbot.

Ateya and Mark helped him to get up and sit in an armchair. The rays of an orange sun bathed the old man's face.

'How beautiful this country is . . . As long as the annual flood comes at its appointed time, as long as the sun and the moon rise in their places, the hope of a righteous life will spur us on. What matters the first death, the death of the body? We must avoid the second, that of the soul, for it condemns the foolish to annihilation. I bequeath to you the inheritance of several thousand years, Mark. With my daughter, form a couple which will resist all forms of destruction. Above all, do not forget that you are going to encounter evil and that it will tell you to extinguish the light. Do not have the vanity to confront it; escape through the window of the heavens. If not, the darkness will swallow you up.'

Pacomas laid his arms across his chest, in the ritual posture of Osiris.

Ateya laid her hands on the back of her father's neck, in the sign of protection. And the spirit of the last High Priest of Amon took flight towards the very first light.

'It's up to you to take his place,' Mark told Ateya.

'I shall carry out the rites, but only Tutankhamun's papyri can ensure that the wisdom is passed on, without which our world will be nothing but a rudderless boat, prey to every storm.'

'They will reappear, I promise you.'

'Most of all, promise me that you will come back.'

'Trust me, Ateya.'

76

It was late afternoon, and the Cairo Museum was closed. There were no extra police officers to guard its treasures, for the capital remained surprisingly calm. Farouk's abdication had entirely satisfied a population who hoped for reforms to combat misery and poverty.

Mark entered an office where the official was dozing.

'I must examine the treasure of Tutankhamun. It's urgent. Please be kind enough to take me there.'

'I'm sorry, that's impossible.'

'Then I'll come back with some soldiers,' announced Mark. 'Neither General Naguib nor Lieutenant-Colonel Nasser, who honours me with his friendship, will appreciate your attitude. Doubtless you are close to Canon Drioton, Farouk's Egyptologist?'

The official got to his feet. 'Not at all! May I know your name?'

'Mark Wilder.'

'One moment, please.'

Tea was brought, and the wait began.

It lasted only ten minutes.

'Follow me, Mr Wilder,' said the official.

Silent and deserted, the Cairo Museum was a disturbing place. The works of art, torn from their original sites, seemed to reproach predators and a society of curious people who were incapable of perceiving their real meaning.

The Last Secret

The American gazed at the two large statues housing Tutankhamun's *ka*, his creative power.*

Left foot forward, their feet clad in gilded sandals, they walked forward without fear along the paths of the world beyond. Carrying long canes, symbolic of power and authority, they marked their steps as they walked through the gates of eternity. Their wigs embodied the ability of the royal thoughts to cross the cosmos, beyond human limits. And the inscriptions identified Tutankhamun with the 'Horus of the twofold realm of light'. As for the club, 'the shining one',† it enabled the monarch to light up the darkness.

One detail interested Mark: were these two statues made up of several wooden panels? His careful examination proved that this was true. So they could be taken apart and had indeed served as reliquaries, housing Tutankhamun's final secret.

'Wondrous objects,' said the professor's soft voice. 'Why are you so intent on examining every nook and cranny of them?'

'Do you really not know?'

'Come into my office, Mr Wilder. We can discuss things away from indiscreet ears.'

The room was enormous and furnished in the style of Louis XV. It was lit by a single window looking out on to a street which had temporarily been closed off to traffic. The office lamp was lit.

On a low table were coffee, tea and pastries.

'The sofa is very inviting,' ventured the professor.

'I prefer to remain standing.'

'As you wish.'

Mark approached the half-open window. If he jumped out into nothingness, he'd be liable to break all his bones.

Why didn't he kill this averagely sized man? Dressed in

---

* Only one of the two statues explicitly mentions the *ka*.
† *Hedj.*

white, imperturbably calm, the scholar seemed anything but terrifying.

But Mark knew he must go beyond appearances, remembering Abbot Pacomas's warnings. He remembered what Dusty Malone had said, at the end of a complex case: doesn't the devil's supreme skill consist of making you forget him?

'We are living through dramatic times,' said the professor. 'Fortunately, violence has been averted. Let us hope that the future of Egypt will be radiant. When are you returning to New York, my friend?'

'Not before I find Tutankhamun's papyri.'

The professor smiled thinly. 'Still that chimera . . . Surprising, in a man of your quality and importance.'

'The road was long, very long. And I could have succumbed to the Salawa's attacks.'

'A legend designed to scare credulous souls! Egypt is still full of superstitions.'

'Of course, you knew that Tutankhamun's two large black statues contain the papyri. Carter knew that, too.'

'A pretty novelette, which no scientific man will believe, Mr Wilder. It has been established, once and for all, that the tomb of Tutankhamun did not contain any papyri.'

'But the two statues do.'

Elbows resting on his desk, the professor linked his fingers. 'Who will you tell this tale?'

'Not to the Egyptologists who report to you, but to the press, who will lead an enquiry and inform the public. It will take time, and the new Egyptian authorities will have to be convinced, but in the end the statues will be taken apart, without breaking them, and the papyri will be brought to light.'

'Assuming you are right, what are you hoping for?'

'Won't the whole world be excited about such a revelation?'

'Science must remain the property of scholars, Mr Wilder. The public at large would not be able to appreciate its complexity and depth.'

'Don't the Middle East and many other countries want to know the truth about the Exodus? Doesn't every human being want to discover the secret of immortality? And these are only two of the themes dealt with by the sages who wrote those papyri.'

'How can you be so sure?'

'Am I wrong, Professor?'

The scholar picked up a fountain pen and took off the top. 'Let us say that these documents exist and that their content is of some importance. Why disturb current beliefs by bringing up ancient beliefs from an era long forgotten? It is common sense not to ruin the established order and to let history take its course.'

'That's not a very scientific attitude, it seems to me.'

'Sometimes it is better not to exhume certain finds. The churches and various governments have given us many examples. Tutankhamun must rest in peace.'

'I have no intention of giving up,' declared Mark.

'The son of Howard Carter is as stubborn as his father! Didn't your protector, Abbot Pacomas, advise caution? If you forget these papyri, you can lead a brilliant existence, beside your wife Ateya. Is it not too adventurous to sacrifice such a future in the cause of such old documents?'

'Does our future not depend on values that were built up by civilizations like that of pharaonic Egypt?'

'You have no need of money, you do not covet a university post, you do not suffer from any exploitable vices ... It is difficult to buy you, Mr Wilder.'

'Impossible.'

'What goal do you really pursue?'

'The lawyer would answer "truth". I have always loved it and cannot bear any attempt to snuff it out.'

'Truth ... Our age is not interested in it. It prefers spectacles and lies.'

'I'm aware of your ability to do harm, Professor, and of the obstacles I'm coming up against. But, like me, you know that it is bound to happen: sooner or later, the papyri will be removed from their hiding place.'

The professor scrawled some strange figures on a sheet of paper. 'Nothing could make you change your mind, Mr Wilder?'

'No.'

The look in the professor's eyes hardened.

At that moment the American realized that the professor had decided to kill him.

The atmosphere in the room changed; the objects themselves became hostile. The professor was not alone. Around him were many destructive forces, which he manipulated as he wished. And their effectiveness exceeded that of any conventional weapon.

Facing this demon, even the bravest of warriors could not win. According to Abbot Pacomas's prediction, the only solution was to run away. So Mark approached the window.

'I have a solution to propose. As a lawyer, I prefer conciliation to confrontations and court cases. You can become the archaeologist who discovered the location of the papyri and acquire worldwide celebrity. Provided they are published and translated, I will gladly remove myself from the picture and leave you all the glory.'

A very long silence followed this suggestion. 'I greatly appreciate this attempt at negotiation, Mr Wilder. Unfortunately, it neglects one vital detail: I am the professor, and it is I who decides what human beings are to know. On the subject of the Tutankhamun papyri, my decision is final and irrevocable: they will remain inaccessible.'

'Answer me one question: did you remove the papyri from the statues, decipher the texts and replace them in their original hiding place?'

The professor smiled, thinking of the file containing the secret of Tutankhamun, for ever locked away with a seal of red wax that no one could ever break.

'I am a professional, and you are an amateur.'

The rays of the setting sun filled the office.

'Congratulations, dear friend. You discovered the truth, but you have lost. Only the scientific community is right, and its decision has been made: Tutankhamun's papyri do not exist. That is why your mouth must be closed for ever. It is a fine sunset, isn't it? I prefer the dusk. The light must be extinguished.'

EPILOGUE

According to friends in Cairo who lived near the apartment block where Ateya and Mark lived, the young woman left her apartment the day after the burial of her father, whose tomb became a place of pilgrimage for a few initiates.

No one ever saw her again in Cairo.

Mark Wilder did not return to New York, and, despite all his efforts, Dusty Malone could not track him down. In 1955 the Egyptian police informed him that they had abandoned their investigation, although they had in fact never begun one.

However, the guard at Tutankhamun's tomb swore to me that Mark and Ateya were living, under false names in a distant village, where foreigners were not welcome. There, they were living a happy, peaceful and secret existence.

The professor adapted extremely well to the regimes of Nasser and those who followed him. As far as I can tell, the papyri are still inside one of the two great guardian statues, or perhaps both. Why refuse to take them out and learn their message?

That is Tutankhamun's final secret.

Cairo, April 2007

POCKET
BOOKS

CHRISTIAN JACQ

The Queen of Freedom Trilogy

In this superb value three-in-one edition, Christian Jacq tells the enthralling true story of the Ancient Egyptian warrior-heroine Queen Ahhotep.

17th century BC. An army of barbarians has swept through Egypt, destroying everything in its path. Known as the Hyksos, the 'leaders from foreign lands', the invaders have reduced the land of the pharaohs to slavery.

Only one woman resists. Fierce, beautiful and courageous, the daughter of the last pharaoh refuses to accept defeat. Not far from Thebes, the only city which retains its independence, she establishes a secret military base, training the soldiers who will one day set her country free.

Heading an increasingly powerful army, Ahhotep prepares the Egyptians for the final, fateful confrontation. After a hundred years of occupation and thousands of violent deaths, at last the Egyptian empire looks set to rise again from the ashes - all thanks to the courage and determination of a woman.

ISBN 978-1-84739-367-8
PRICE £9.99

POCKET
BOOKS

CHRISTIAN JACQ

The Judge of Egypt Trilogy

**In this fantastic value three-in-one edition, Christian Jacq
combines historical fact with a potent imagination to
create a compelling murder mystery.**

Summoned to investigate the mysterious deaths of five
guards standing watch over the great tomb of Kheops, a
young novice judge finds himself embroiled in a hotbed of
greed and corruption. For Judge Pazair's refusal to sign a
document he doesn't understand has led him to uncover a
monstrous plot to assassinate the pharaoh, Ramses the Great.

With the aid of Neferet, the woman he loves, and the former
scribe, Suti, Pazair sets out to solve a series of brutal
murders, expose the conspirators and thwart a brazen attempt
to overthrow the State. But can he stay alive in the
process . . . ?

'Jacq weaves together an intelligent murder mystery and
injects life into every page of this truly authentic tale' *Good
Book Guide*

ISBN 978-1-84739-366-1
PRICE £9.99

**POCKET
BOOKS**

This book and other **Pocket Books** titles are available from your local bookshop or can be ordered direct from the publisher.

978-1-84739-367-8   **The Queen of Freedom Trilogy**   **£9.99**
(includes *The Empire of Darkness*,
The War of Crowns and *The Flaming Sword*)

978-1-84739-366-1   **The Judge of Egypt**   **£9.99**
(includes *Beneath the Pyramid*,
Secrets of the Desert and *Shadow of the Sphinx*)

Free post and packing within the UK

Overseas customers please add £2 per paperback
Telephone Simon & Schuster Cash Sales at Bookpost
on 01624 677237 with your credit or debit card number
or send a cheque payable to
Simon & Schuster Cash Sales to
PO Box 29, Douglas Isle of Man, IM99 1BQ
Fax: 01624 670923
E-mail: bookshop@enterprise.net
www.bookpost.co.uk

Please allow 14 days for delivery.

Prices and availability are subject to change
without notice.